The War of
Don Emmanuel's
Nether Parts

The War of DonEmmanuel's Nether Parts

A · NOVEL

Louis de Bernières

William Morrow and Company, Inc./ New York

It is the policy of William Morrow and Company, Inc., and its imprints and affiliates, recognizing the importance of preserving what has been written, to print the books we publish on acid-free paper, and we exert our best efforts to that end.

Library of Congress Cataloging-in-Publication Data

De Bernières, Louis.
    The war of Don Emmanuel's nether parts / by Louis de Bernières.
        p.   cm.
    ISBN 0-688-11129-7
    I. Title.
    PR6054.E132W3   1991
    823'.914—dc20   91-14016
                                                                                    CIP

Printed in the United States of America

First U.S. Edition

1   2   3   4   5   6   7   8   9   10

BOOK DESIGN BY LINEY LI

To the incorrigible and legendary
Don Benjamin of Poponte,
who entrusted me with
several children and three horses

Author's Note

In creating an imaginary Latin American country, I have jumbled up and adapted incidents from many different countries at different times in their history. I have borrowed words and phrases from Brazilian Portuguese and its regional variants, Latin American Spanish and its regional variants, and from many Indian languages and their dialects. In some of these latter there is, as far as I know, no standardized spelling. Since there is general anarchy in the use of accents, I have decided to dispense with them altogether.

I am indebted to many sources for my research, but I wish to acknowledge in particular my debt to Richard Gott's *Rural Guerrillas in Latin America* (Pelican, 1973), and John Simpson and Jana Bennett's *The Disappeared* (Robson Books, 1985). The political information in these books was invaluable.

I owe special thanks to Helen Wright, whose conscientious checking of the manuscript enabled me to eliminate a great many errors.

Contents

The War of
Don Emmanuel's
Nether Parts

1

Capitan Rodrigo Figueras's Finest Hour

It had been an auspicious week for Capitan Rodrigo José Figueras. On Monday he had with his platoon stopped a truck loaded with marijuana on the road from Chiriguaná to Valledupar and made the peasant park it near a bridge. According to the usual procedure, he had confiscated the truck and its contents from the driver, whereupon the driver, as was usual, offered to "pay the fine" instead, which meant buying the consignment back. He handed over to the Capitan one of several bundles which he carried for this purpose, one for each roadblock. The Capitan then shot the driver through the head and liberated entirely the truck, its contents, and many thousands of pesos. The lieutenant began to write a brief report on the driver—"shot while resisting arrest"—and sealed it in an envelope with the man's identity card. Meanwhile, the Capitan took the truck and the Jeep to the farm with the airstrip and sold the marijuana to the gringo with the airplane for many more thousands. Then he sold the truck for next to nothing to a white farmer who could arrange the documents, and then he drove in the Jeep back to his platoon's encampment by the river. Liberally he handed out a few thousand pesos each to the men and at his own expense sent the corporal to the village to buy a case of *aguardiente* and *ron cana* with orders to return also with a selection of whores from twelve to forty in several shapes and sizes so that all tastes could be catered for; consequently, the village men had to go without for a week. The Capitan was thirty-five, with a wife and five children who lived in some style in Santa Marta in his absence. His hairy belly spread his shirt apart at the buttons, he was thick-lipped and leering-eyed, and his hair lay flat across his head by the weight of its own grease. He had been trained in Panama by the United States Army, at its own expense, and he painted a little white mark on the door of his Jeep for every whore there had been.

Misael woke with the dawn, as he always did, and threw dried corn stems on the embers to get them going again so that he could have strong coffee with his *bocadillos* for breakfast before he left with his machete for the day's work. He was tall and grizzled, dark-eyed and cheerful, his body sculpted by the muscle of a life's labor into a Greek ideal. It was the same with all the mestizo and mulatto peasants, for their bodies were all perfect in shape, strength, and endurance; but their old age was not protracted, and hardship was a high price for beauty.

He checked his little boy, who had been terribly disfigured when he had sat in the fire as an infant, and decided not to wake him or his wife. Chinks of light began to filter through his brush house, and he took a friendly kick at the chicken that stalked ridiculously through the door-less door. It clucked indignantly and then ignored him, pecking furiously and futilely at a cockroach, while Misael checked his shoes for scorpions and spiders and ensured that no coral snake was in the brush roof. Satisfied that all was in order, he took his machete and went down to the river to whet it on one of the stones before he slashed down the bananas, cleared the cornfield, and gelded the mule. All this he had to accomplish before it got too hot to work.

He spit on the ground and cursed at the vultures lining the trees as he walked to the hacienda. Then he crossed himself, and for good measure muttered a *secreto* against evil that his mother had taught him in a language that he did not know.

Profesor Luis looked at the children on the floor in front of him. The oldest was fourteen and the youngest was four, and he taught all of them everything he knew and a lot of things he had not even realized that he knew until he taught them. He came from a good family in Medellín that he truly hated and from whom he had run away when he was seventeen. Now he was engaged to Farides, who cooked for the French couple, Françoise and Antoine Le Moing, at their *estancia,* and what he was not paid in pesos he was paid in gratitude and affection by the children and their families, who knew that education was the only way up. Every girl in the surrounding countryside wanted to marry him and have clever children. Whenever the weary priest came, every two years or so, to marry those who had already cohabited for years and to conduct funerals for those long-rotted since his last visit, he would visit Profesor Luis also, and they would talk about Camilo Torres, Oscar Romero, José Martí, and the oligarchy, and then the priest would go on his mule to the next stop in his vast parish, ignoring the contraceptives sold at the liquor and machete store and remaining polite to the *brujos,* the magicians who could cure cattle and raise spirits.

Profesor Luis observed the vultures in the trees and instructed the oldest boy to shoot one, and also an iguana, because today it was biology. There was a sharp report and a hideous cacophony, and the boy returned, barely able to carry the repellent creature; then he went to find an iguana. The profesor pointed out the parasites in the bird's feathers, and they talked about parasites in general. He disemboweled the bird and carefully explained that this was the liver, you must not drink too much or yours will swell and you will die. These are the kidneys, drink clean water. These are the lungs, do not smoke. He showed them how if you press up on the talons, they close automatically. He took two sticks, cut off the wings, plucked the tail feathers, and they made a glider so he could explain the principles of flight.

Then the boy returned with a large green lizard, and with the aid of an old car battery and two copper wires they traced in the animal's twitches the pathways of nerves and drew the pathways in a big diagram in the dust outside.

At the end of the day Profesor Luis threw the remains of the vulture to the vultures and roasted the iguana on a spit over the embers. It was cheap and better than chicken. Farides came to the door of his hut and said, "*Querido,* you must know that it is very bad luck to kill a vulture."

✳ ✳ ✳

Consuelo the whore was not looking forward to Friday night. She was a little nauseated from the alcohol, and her insides felt like ground glass, because she had had to satisfy all the men who normally went to the other whores who had gone in the Jeep. She thought of Friday night and said, "*Mierda*." She could not take Friday night off because she was a good whore, conscious of public service, and besides, it was the night when you earned the most, except for public holidays. She thought of how all the campesinos would be paid by the gringo farmers and come in on their mules. How they would become drunk and there would be the usual fights with machetes and someone would lose an arm. How the two rows of *puterías* up both sides of one street would be filled with lines of men getting drunker as they waited, and she would have to get drunk, too, so that she did not mind getting very sore indeed. What the hell; she was the only person in the whole village, apart from the other whores and Don Emmanuel's employees, who had been able to afford a concrete floor. A whore at twelve, plenty of children, a concrete floor at twenty. It's a good life, and no man tells you what to do unless it's fair exchange.

The little three-year-old who belonged to Dolores the whore needed milk. She breast-fed him, because there was no food at the moment, and the *niño* liked it, and anyway, all the whores breast-fed each other's children. It was a huge contented family with a thousand generous fathers, and every Thursday Don Emmanuel took you in a Land Rover to the clinic in Chiriguaná to check your blood so that you never made anyone ill.

Consuelo looked indifferently at the vultures and went inside to straighten out the frizzes in her hair. She accepted uncritically that the more Spanish you looked, and the less like a Negro, the more the men would pay.

Hectoro's mother was an Arahuacax Indian from the Sierra Nevada; but he looked like a conquistador, and consequently, he had three wives who lived in separate mud-block houses four miles apart on the exact angles of an equilateral triangle so they would never meet and fight because they were jealous.

Hectoro was an intelligent and intolerant man who looked on life very simply. A man needs women—he had three—he needs shelter—he had three—he needs money—he was foreman on the gringo's hacienda—he needs status—he had his own mule, a revolver in a holster, leather *bombachos*, he could rope a steer with infallible precision, and he could hold alcohol in his wiry frame like no other man. The doctor had told him he was to die of liver failure because of the drink, and truly his skin had become yellowed; but he was proud and fiery-tongued, and he had threatened to shoot the doctor, who had then changed his diagnosis to something less disagreeable.

Hectoro was so proud that he seldom spoke to anyone; indeed, he openly despised everybody, especially the gringos for whom he worked. They respected him and put him in charge of everything, and they turned a blind eye when he nearly murdered a rustler by shooting him in the groin. "By God," he said, "I turned the son of a whore into a woman and found a job for him in the whorehouse. Let no man say I am not generous." Even those who hated him laughed and bought him drinks and looked at him with the awe one has of a man who stalks death and would not mind dying, as long as it was over something important like a woman, or a mule, or an insult. On his left hand, his rein hand, he wore a black glove; in his mouth smoldered always a *puro*, a cool local cigar, and his eyes squinted against the sun, against the smoke, against danger, against the vultures. He rode over to see if a steer had died.

At fifty years old Pedro the hunter was an unusually old man. He lived alone in the scrubland by a pool of clear water with his ten carefully trained mongrel hunting dogs. He was strong and lithe and could stalk tirelessly for days without sleep or lapse of concentration. He walked so fast that a horse was entirely unnecessary, and everyone knows that horses will eat only good grass.

Pedro could trap any creature whatsoever. He could noose a caiman and let it grow huge in his pool, feeding it offal, until he could sell the skin for a few pesos so that some woman could buy an alligator handbag in New York for one thousand dollars. He could trap a boa constrictor with a forked stick and keep it until someone wanted one for magic. He could extract the venom of the coral snake for use in tiny doses as an aphrodisiac or in heavy doses for murder. He knew how to stand in the river with a lantern and spear fish more delicate than trout and twice the size, and he knew how to mutter *secretos* in a cow's ear so that its ulcers would disappear.

Today he both mourned and celebrated. For two weeks he had marked the spoor of the *tigre*, the jaguar that had become a rogue and killed two donkeys without eating them. For five hundred pesos the gringo had hired him to bring back the skin, and he and his dogs had gone with his wired Spanish musket. The dogs cornered the jaguar beneath an escarpment, and Pedro had shot it clean through the eye so the skin was unspoiled. He skinned it and sold the skin to the gringo for five hundred pesos. It was a huge cat, and it had fought bravely. Pedro celebrated his success and mourned for the beautiful rare cat and for the two hunting dogs it had killed.

In the hacienda the gringo swigged back a glass of Glenfiddich and turned to his tight-lipped, unhappy wife.

"I should get a fortune for that on the black market."

"You shouldn't have done it," she said.

It was early on Friday evening when Capitan Rodrigo José Figueras and several Jeeps turned up with the whores and the men of the platoon, the men to swagger and bully and the whores to fulfill the regular trade. No one liked the soldiers, and some men said they would not go to a whore who had had a soldier in her. "They are worse than gringos, because they try to be gringos when they are not. I spit on them."

As the day cooled and the alcohol warmed, the tension lessened, and hundreds of peasants arrived on muleback to get away from their women, their labor, their poverty, in order to forget and to live it up a little. The soldiers nearly stopped being soldiers, and even Figueras nearly forgot that he had been to the United States and had never really loved anyone.

But round about midnight, when Consuelo was already fully worn out and her concrete floor covered with cigarette ends and spittle, Capitan Rodrigo Figueras began to be bored and decided to go home to his tent by the river. He sent the lieutenant and the corporal to gather up the men, who cursed as they were dragged from the whorehouses and separated from their bottles. Formed up in a straggle in the dusty street, the Capitan made sure there were twenty-five men and ordered them to their Jeeps.

Leaning against the leading Jeep, Profesor Luis, twenty-two years old and the gentlest man in the world, was tenderly kissing Farides, seventeen, and the loveliest girl in the whole district.

Figueras forced himself between them and thrust his stubbled face into that of Luis.

"So"—and the spittle spattered Luis's shirt—"so, you son of a peasant bitch, you think you can grope your whore up against government property. I suppose you think you can spy on my Jeep."

"Don't be ridiculous," said Luis, his eyes flickering. "I meant no harm, and she is not a whore. She is a virgin, and she is my fiancée."

"Would you marry her"—and the Capitan coughed and spit and had to step back for balance—"if she were not a virgin and had been whored by twenty-five men?"

The soldiers looked at one another and smiled nervously, not sure whether to be horrified or delighted.

Profesor Luis wanted to shrink away, but he said, "I would defend her to the death. I shall go to the police."

Figueras turned to the corporal. "Show him who are the police."

Profesor Luis crumpled as the rifle butt crunched into the back of his neck. Farides threw herself down on her hands and knees and wailed. The Capitan leaned forward and jerked her upright by the hair. "Tell us," he said, "that you are a little whore, and we will not feel obliged to turn you into one."

A whore is a whore and has a whore's honor. Farides was a virgin, and hers was a virgin's honor. They are both honor, but they are separate and must not be confused. Her eyes bulged and rolled as the Capitan began to rotate his hand on her breast. She felt an urgent need to vomit, and her knees shook, but she said, "I am not a whore. I am the fiancée of Don Luis the profesor."

"Take the little whore to the schoolhouse and prepare her," ordered the Capitan. They dragged her off, shrieking and writhing, and began to tear away her clothes. They slung her across the desk and pinned her down while she wept and pleaded and the Capitan finished his cigarette and thought of a new paint mark on his Jeep.

He was about to crush the stub beneath his foot when in the doorway appeared Pedro with his Spanish musket, Hectoro with his revolver, and Consuelo the whore with a machete.

"Capitan," said Hectoro, emphasizing every word, "if you do not release the girl and leave this village immediately, your body will be fed to the caiman in Pedro's pool and your men will be able to report that one stinking son of a diseased sow has ceased to serve himself and the *yanquis* and the pretense of a government!"

Sweat trickled down the temples of Capitan Rodrigo José Figueras, and a dark patch spread down the armpits and the back of his military shirt. He glared at Hectoro defiantly, but his lower lip quivered. "*¡Vamos!*" he said to his men, and they filed out, almost apologetically. Farides turned on her side and whimpered until Consuelo the whore came in and covered her with a blanket and whispered words of comfort to her.

The Jeeps roared away into the night, scattering the chickens and raising a plume of dust. A shocked and indignant knot of people gathered in the street, and Farides emerged trembling, wrapped in her blanket. Shyly she kissed Hectoro and Pedro on the cheek and then knelt down and cupped Profesor Luis's head while somebody fetched some water.

One mile down the road Capitan Rodrigo Figueras ordered his driver to stop and took something from a box on the back of the Jeep. As he had been trained by the gringos in Panama, he slunk swiftly and noiselessly back along the track. He circled the huts through a cornfield and came out between two of the dwellings just next to the knot of people. He drew a pin from the grenade and lobbed it, spinning, into the crowd before he ducked away.

Three days later the national radio issued a broadcast: "Three days ago a unit of government troops near Asunción in César surprised a group of Communist insurgents and killed five of them, wounding twenty in a brief engagement. No troops were killed, and Capitan Rodrigo Figueras has been promoted to comandante and recommended for decoration. General Carlo María Fuerte, military commander in the area, said in an interview this morning that he and all units under him were deeply committed to, and would continue, the fight against the Cuba-led Communist conspiracy to terrorize the free people of this country and subvert their liberties."

It was on that same night that Federico, the fourteen-year-old who had shot the vulture for Profesor Luis, got out of his hammock at two o'clock in the morning, stole his father's rifle and two boxes of shells, and disappeared somewhere in the foothills that are neither quite in one country nor in its neighbor.

2

In Which Doña Constanza Evans Resolves to Save the Swimming Pool from Drought

Doña Constanza Evans, having risen from her silken sheets at ten o'clock when the air conditioning had finally lost the daily battle against the heat and humidity of the equatorial morning, took a cool shower in water from her own purification plant and toweled herself dry before the mirror. She possessed the gift of all spoiled women, that of being able to follow several inconsequential trains of thought simultaneously and to believe them all to be of incalculable importance. Thus she inspected her forty-year-old body according to the habit she had followed since puberty and thought about the recent exploits of the army in the village, in which her groom had been killed by a fragment of grenade. She thought also of the problem of the swimming pool, which lost half its water, turned green with algae, and became full of grateful frogs during every dry season.

I do not know how I am expected to exercise in such a pool, she thought as she raised a plump but unprepossessing breast in order to dry beneath it. *It is long since I saw my navel unconcealed by this terrible fat; it is the price of children, and little good they do you at birth or after.* As she dabbed at her face, she paused suddenly. *Next time I am in the Estados Unidos*

I will make inquiries of operations so that I may be as young as I please. I had no idea Juanito was a Communist. I wonder if my two children caused my passage to expand; perhaps that is why Hugh no longer demands his rights of me at night. Still, if the army says he was a Communist, then he was a Communist and he should have been killed as he was. No doubt Hugh has taken a woman—probably a campesina whore, they are all sluts. The army, after all, is trained by the yanquis, *and so no doubt they know their job. I swear the skin of my thighs is becoming coarser. I should take a campesino lover, for preference a big shiny black Negro with muscles, or a mestizo, and see how Hugh likes that! Really the pool is an abomination; one could die of cholera like Tchaikovsky. Juanito would have been a fine lover if you saw him petting the horses. A man who has a way with animals has a way with a woman, so they say. Perhaps it was Beethoven.* She parted her legs and dried herself there with more application than she had intended. *By the Virgin, I must be more careful with myself or I shall be burned away! I must find a new groom. Truly life is one hurdle after another, for it appears we are not born to happiness in this world. I wonder if it was typhus. I hear that there is such a thing as spontaneous combustion. It would be fortunate if there were a man or a maid with a bucket of water nearby. They say the fragment went through Juanito's temple and destroyed his brain inside his head.* She put a dainty foot on the mahogany chair to dry between the toes, looked up through the window (consisting, in fact, of fine antimosquito mesh, for even the Evanses were not stupid enough to have glass windows in such a climate), and admired the hundred or so pedigree horses of different varieties that grazed in the field. She was trying to spot her finest palomino when it occurred to her that she could divert the Mula. *I will dig a channel toward the purification plant from the river, and I will install some kind of gate to lower into the water so that it flows down the channel when it is required to do so. Moreover, I will not tell Hugh, or he will invent some reason to prevent it. I will pretend that it is a present to him for his birthday, and in this way, when I go to New York, I will not have to spend my allowance on a gift.*

Doña Constanza pouted alluringly to herself in the mirror and thought suddenly of Juanito. A twinge of sadness and regret passed simultaneously behind her eyes and through her heart. But then she drew herself up and breathed deeply inward, and the traces of the sixteen-year-old she once had been vanished from her face as the mantle of cold dignity settled itself about her. When she had dressed, she emerged for breakfast every inch the Spanish aristocrat.

There were in that country, as in all those troubled countries, only four social groups to speak of. At the bottom of the social scale were the fourteen million Negroes who were directly descended from thirteen hundred slaves imported by the conquistadores to build the giant fortress of Nueva Sevilla after they had discovered that Indians made very inadequate slaves. The Indians would not give up their gods and preferred to starve themselves to death rather than submit to indignity. The Negroes, on the other hand, being from different parts of West Africa, had no common language, so it was a simple matter to confuse them and to brutalize them into being enlightened by Christianity. It is, after all, a consolation for present hell when one is promised future heaven, and their irrepressible humor and stoicism, along with their magnificent physiques and stature, enabled them to labor prodigiously under the whip and the brand. When the fortress was complete, and its dungeons well stocked with English pirates with royal patents from Queen Elizabeth, the slaves were released to fend for themselves. From these humble beginnings they emerged eventually as campesinos, the indispensable providers of nourishment for the entire nation. Consequently, they were the poorest of all people and the most despised, even by themselves. Those who took to the *favelas*, the barrios, and the innumerable shantytowns were driven by poverty and disease to theft, extortion, prostitution, violence, and drink and were therefore even more comprehensively reviled than the peasants, their brothers.

Existing in a world almost wholly unrelated to that of all other classes were the Indians. One half of them, the Incas, lived almost exclusively at altitudes greater than seven thousand feet. At all such altitudes they reckoned, accurately, that almost no one would bother to come and look for them. Thus they lived peacefully in their carefully built grass huts, tending their terraces, chewing coca leaves, worshiping Pachacamac, and coming back to the plains solely in order to sell *mochilas* (their very practical and beautifully decorated carrying bags with a shoulder strap) and potatoes. If you were to see a particularly fine mule, it would always have with it a particularly fine Indian dressed in a white tunic, with a white domed hat set upright on a shining black head of hair. It was not so much their Mongolian features that impressed everyone, although these were both beautiful and impressive, but their sandals made from car tires and the phenomenal muscularity of their calves. Most of them carried muskets in perfect working order, which had been taken from the Spaniards centuries before, and on account of this, and because it was commonly said that all Indians had syphilis, everyone left them alone. The government was dimly aware that they were a species of national monument and appointed officers to ensure their protection and preservation, who, fortunately, did nothing to earn their salaries. Thus the noble people lived on undisturbed, except by the not infrequent crashes of army helicopters, the inoffensive and almost unnoticeable visits of diffident anthropologists from Oxford and Cambridge, and the straggling parties of mountaineers with peeling noses and diarrhea who also came for the most part, and perhaps curiously enough, from Britain. It should surprise no one if in two thousand years there are still Acahuatecs and Arahuacax sucking coca pounded with snail shells from their pestles at altitudes greater than seven thousand feet in the Sierra Nevada de Santa Margarita, for they are a people who have learned by their own blood the wondrous disadvantages of an eventful history.

The other half of the Indian population occupied the jungle regions below the foothills, and although the one population graduated into the other, they were quite different in appearance and way of life.

Slightly above the Negroes but not wholly so was the class of mestizos and mulattoes. These people of different racial mix were perhaps physically the most surprising of all the peoples in that land for while they all possessed the broadish nose and frizzy hair of the Negro, sometimes the hair was blond or ginger, and sometimes the eyes were blue, or green, or amber. Their skins were pale yellow, and most faces would have one or two dark brown beauty spots. Perhaps some of them were sallow-complexioned thanks to the many preparations one could buy for whitening the skin, for in lands where power is not in the hands of the majority, the masses invariably adopt the snobberies and prejudices of the rulers, as if to say, "Look, I am not one of the oppressed; I, too, am superior." From the mestizo class was being born an embryonic petite bourgeoisie that lived in the suburbs of the bigger towns and bought television sets that received only the confused flickerings of the transmitters in the capital. The signal, having been bounced from peak to peak over hundreds of miles so that all the wavelengths were canceled out by interfering with themselves, arrived at sets powered by anything between one hundred and three hundred volts, depending upon the vagaries of the public generating system or their own generators. One could walk down the streets of Valledupar at night and see through the windows mestizo families peering intently at the bright square of leaping and buzzing lines and spots as though they were interpreting runes or the flight of birds. When by some freak of atmospheric conditions a picture appeared or a line of speech was discernible, there would follow a minute of animated discussion and comment from the family and the mother and the oldest sister would come in from the kitchen, and then they would return, leaving the family to gaze hypnotized once more by the scrambled and undecipherable traces of old cowboy films, *The Flintstones,* the usual nonsense from the United States, and advertisements for skin whitener.

The pallid mulattas provided the country's most industrious and most popular prostitutes, for from a white's point of view they were sufficiently black for them to be exotic and for congress with them to be naughty without being too shocking. From a black's point of view they were sufficiently white for them to be exotic and for congress with them to be something of an honor. To mestizo men, mulatta women were, of course, absolutely ordinary, so they frequented the black brothels, which were sufficiently exotic and naughty for such visits to be satisfactory. White prostitutes did not exist, but if they had, they would have been immensely popular, tired, and rich, and no doubt many blacks and mesitzos would have been trampled to death in the rush every Saturday night.

To say that there were no white whores is, on reflection, a little misleading, for I have yet to come to the Spanish aristocracy, which constituted the oligarchy, whose daughters were out for nothing but to marry the richest men they could find in order that they could live the idlest and most fatuous lives possible. These virtuous ladies, of course, gave their doting husbands as little congress as possible for their money, thus driving them into the arms of those women who were somewhat less chaste, virtuous, and untouchable. It would be impossible to describe what manifold and formidable maladies the ladies of the rich could feign. They pined away for the most part in exquisitely refined boredom alleviated only by the careful and repeated perusal of risqué and romantic novels which they paid their maids to buy for them from shops with fat, sweaty, and balding proprietors who put on literary airs. Thus these ladies lived life at one remove from everything that makes the world interesting and exciting and sought each other's company as if by gravitational force in order to create rumors and spread scandals, which nearly always ended unfortunately, since unsuspecting husbands found themselves dragged in to defend family honor over slights and fabrications upon which lawyers grew rich and which could even lead to assassinations by highly paid professionals known as *jaguncos*.

The oligarchy was a large network of immensely rich landowners, descended from the conquistadores, who had been illiterate robber bar- barians who had destroyed entire civilizations in the name of Jesus, the Virgin, the Catholic kings, and gold. In this way they ensured a per- petual sinecure in paradise for their immortal souls, and perpetual admiration from generations of schoolchildren who were taught in his- tory lessons of their magnificent and daring exploits against the pagan savages whose phenomenal towns and monuments one can still see today (in ruins).

The oligarchy was, of course, all related to one another by marriage and by self-interest, now more than ever after *La Violencia*. During this period, which lasted ten years, two factions of the oligarchy had con- ducted an unprecedentedly bloody campaign of violence against each other in which perhaps three hundred thousand souls perished at the hands of *jaguncos* and guerrillas, both of whom accrued so much money that it amounted to a redistribution of wealth that was almost significant.

The oligarchy was divided into Liberals and Conservatives, who were united in their terror of communism after the success of the Cuban Revolution, especially since many of them had had interests in the brothels and casinos of Havana; others had had interests in pharmaceu- tical companies that manufactured drugs to cure the diseases spread by the former, and some in supplying guns to be used by gangs struggling for control of the latter. However, the Liberals and Conservatives differed over how to combat the spread of such appalling beliefs as "equality," "fair pay," and "democracy." The Conservatives believed in coming down hard on them; this involved being curt with your campesi- nos, keeping them illiterate, and paying them a fixed wage of 150 pesos a week. The Liberals, on the other hand, believed in being jolly with your campesinos, teaching them to read bits of paper with instructions on them, and paying them a fixed wage of 150 pesos a week. In this way they hoped that the peasants would become too contented to bother to be Communists. The whole situation became infinitely confused by the Conservatives' habit of describing the Liberals as "Communists."

Eventually, in a historic feat of compromise, democracy was restored by the abolition of elections, and the two parties agreed to rule alternately for four-year periods, thus postponing *La Violencia* indefinitely.

As peace settled once again, the oligarchy returned to its old pursuits of appointing its eldest sons to high office in the state, its second sons to high office in the church, and the rest of its sons to high office in the armed forces. Meanwhile, some of the peasants almost became Communists without even having heard the word.

Doña Constanza Evans, with whom our digression began and with whom it now finishes, was a Conservative, being a direct descendant, like all aristocrats, of a particularly brutal and successful barbarian. Her husband, Don Hugh Evans, was in fact the descendant of a nineteenth-century Welsh speculator and was still officially a British citizen. Consequently his two sons went to Harrow, where they became fairly muscly in the legs and extremely Anglophile, apparently under the illusion that Harrovians were representative of the English as a whole. Naturally they felt very much at home among such civilized people.

Doña Constanza sent for her foreman to instruct him to dig a canal and sent a message to Profesor Luis which read, "Did Tchaikovsky or Beethoven die of cholera or typhus?"

3

In Which Federico's
Romantic Gesture Takes On
Wider Implications

When Federico crept away from his father's adobe house with the rifle and the two boxes of shells, it cannot be said that it was with any clear idea in his head of what he was going to do or how he was to do it. All that there actually was in his head was a kind of astonished outrage and a relentless determination to do something spectacular by way of vengeance. He had frequently witnessed bloodshed in his short life, but what he had just witnessed in the village was of a different kidney from machete fights over a woman or an insult, or the gruesome amputations of snakebitten limbs, or even the incomprehensible agony of his mother when giving birth to Francesca, which he had watched from the corner of the hut with a sense of desperate awe. The difference was that all the violence and pain he had seen hitherto had seemed to have a point to it, and while it was regrettable, it had never been spurious and had therefore not been shocking. The carnage accompanying Capitan Rodrigo Figueras's little exploit, and the subsequent hysteria, triggered into life that sense of moral anger and disgust that hitherto Federico had only experienced the glimmer of when Profesor Luis blamed him for something he had not done. Secondly, the campesino has a most rigid sense of honor, which is the most precious and prized possession of those who have next to nothing and which is the one public and personal voice that must at all times be obeyed without question, even beyond common

sense and death. It is honor that will cause a man to spend thirty years
not talking to his favorite brother or his son because of an affront or to
starve for a year in order to pay a debt or keep a promise. It is honor
that will spur men to the most futile, heroic, and stupid extremes out of
bravado and machismo, and it is as though they have never heard that
the days of Tirant lo Blanc and Don Quixote are long dead. This kind
of honor is an exclusively male preserve, for the women of these lands
have a code of honor that is infinitely tempered by compassion, humor,
and common wisdom, which has nothing to do with those irrational,
dogmatic absolutes of the male that provoke him either to astonishingly
fine feats of valor or the most depressingly fatuous feats of unfathomable
insanity. Sometimes these are inextricably mixed up together, and one
would not know whether to weep with despair or to weep with admiration. Capitan Figueras, for example, probably had thrown his grenade out of injured honor, for he had been comprehensively dishonored
and humiliated by a hunter with a musket, a man who looked like a
conquistador with a revolver, and a whore with a machete.

Federico, on the other hand, had lost his uncle Juanito, he had seen
his teacher beaten to the ground with a rifle by a repulsive fat officer, his
cousin Farides nearly violated, and his own dog so badly mutilated that
his father, Sergio, had been obliged to shoot it between the eyes with the
very rifle he was now carrying away like a kidnapped baby. Federico
therefore had a most personal reason for wishing death upon the capitan,
who was in the army, which was in the employ of the state. It is surely
true that ultimately all campesino revolutionaries are motivated in the
first place not by ideals or economic theories but by a deeply felt sense
of offended dignity. But even if this were not generally the case, it was
certainly true of Federico, who would only learn to hate the whole
army, the state, and the United States, which propped them up long
after he took to the hills in order to live wild and ruminate over his
plans for retribution and the satisfaction he would feel in exacting it.

At this point he was still a one-boy revolution with a large part of
him consisting of a mush of romantic impossibilities. It had not occurred to him that he could not kill every officer in the army just to
ensure that he got Figueras, nor had he thought he would miss the
cheerful, anarchic poverty of village life, the bright eyes of Francesca,
or the corralling of the *ceibu* steers at market time. He thought of

himself as a heroic avenging angel of death, not as a wandering boy with a rifle that would bruise his shoulder every time he fired it, with nothing else but a *mochila* filled with *bocadillas* wrapped in palm leaves, three avocado pears, and two boxes of shells.

By the time that dawn launched the red sun rapidly above the mountains, Federico was in a humbler frame of mind than he had been at two o'clock that morning. He had walked several miles, it is true, past the hacienda of the gringo with the airplane, and he was already near the jungle before the foothills of the cordillera where the ground is half in patches of lush verdancy and half in stony waste, sprouting with the lunar columns built by termites; but he had been startled by every whistle and rustle of every creature that crossed his footsteps. He started and sweated with fear each time he came face to face with the enormous silhouette of a steer or a rock, and he imagined that every glimmer of moonlight on his path was a coral snake rearing to strike. In addition, the sling of the rifle was already wearing a sore on his shoulder, and the magazine constantly thumped the same spot above his kidneys as he stumbled through the darkness. The Lee-Enfield also seemed to be growing heavier; but he clung to it doggedly, and when there was sufficient light, he sat on a rock and caressed its stock in much the same mood of tenderness and exaltation as that he had dreamed he would feel when first caressing a woman.

He set the rifle aside and reached into his *mochila* for the *bocadillas*, whose sweetness and savor of guavas stroked away like a mother's hand the recent terrors of the night. He carefully wrapped the remainder of the slab in the palm leaf and looked around for a spot where the sun would not fall for a few hours. He fell asleep among the stones in the shade of the rock, where he dreamed of his mutilated dog and the coarse hairs of the belly of Capitan Figueras where they bulged through the buttons of his shirt.

When he awoke at midday, it was for two reasons: first, because the sun had moved over the rock and was so hot that he dreamed he was being turned to ashes and, secondly, because a young kid was chewing the leg of his trousers. When he opened his eyes and looked into those of the goat, his immediate thought was that the devil had come for him, for there is in the yellow iris and rectangular slot of a pupil in the eye of the goat something that is horrifyingly alien and impersonal. The kid skittered away a couple of yards, and Federico gazed at it a few seconds before deciding to shoot it for meat. With trembling excitement, but also guilt, he stood up, slid the bolt back and firmly forward, and raised the rifle to his shoulder. The crash of the .303 sent him stumbling back with the agony of what felt like a broken collarbone, and he thrashed in the air to regain his balance. When he had done so, he was strangely relieved to find that he had missed the goat completely, even from such close range, and that it was looking at him with a kind of comic surprise from behind a citrus tree. He was wondering whether his shoulder could stand another attempt and was cocking the gun once more when a voice behind him said ironically, *"Buena' día', Señor."*

He turned around suddenly and pointed the gun from the hip in a panicky parody of that move so well documented in cowboy films, to come face-to-face with a very tall campesino of dark complexion who was smoking a *puro* and holding a long staff in his hand. He spit, looked about coolly, and said, "I suppose you like to shoot other people's goats for no reason."

Federico returned his gaze ashamedly and said, "I did not know it was your goat, Señor."

"All goats belong to someone."

"Yes, Señor, I am very sorry, Señor."

The campesino tapped the end of the rifle with his staff. "Perhaps you should point that somewhere else. I am larger than the goat and not so easy to miss."

Federico lowered the gun and began to walk away backward, wondering if he should do so with dignity or break into a run, but the peasant said, "I think you should give me the gun. It will be compensation for shooting at the goat."

"The gun is not mine to give," replied the boy, astonished and confused. "It is my father's, and I did not shoot the goat."

"Ah," said the peasant. "The priest says that the evil intention is as bad as the evil deed itself. You should therefore give me the gun."

"But it is my father's!"

"You are your father's responsibility. To save me going all the way to see him, I will take the gun directly. I see it is a very enviable gun, and I will have it." And he strode forward to take hold of the barrel.

Federico felt panic rise from his stomach to his throat, and suddenly a torrent of salty sweat poured down his forehead into his eyes and blinded him.

"No!" he shouted, and pulled the rifle. The peasant hit him across the side of the head with the palm of his hand and took advantage of the boy's discomfiture to pull hard at his end of the barrel.

What he had not known, and had not even thought of in his eager attempt to steal the weapon from the boy, was that the boy's forefinger had already taken up first pressure on the trigger; there was another resounding crash as he wrenched the weapon toward him, and the bullet passed clean through his sternum and shattered two vertebrae on its way out of his back. An expression of wonder passed over the man's face as he toppled backward and began to die, while Federico, paralyzed with shock, fell forward on his knees and vomited violently before he started to weep and rock backward and forward with his hands over his face, whimpering as his mutilated dog had done.

When Federico dared look up from his weeping, he saw that a dark stain had spread across the shirt of the peasant, that his eyes had clouded and glazed, and that blood was trickling gently from the corners of his mouth. The body already looked as though there were nobody at home, and the *puro* lay smoking in the stones as though nothing very important had happened. Federico knew without looking that the man was completely dead and that he was responsible. He sat numbly against the rock and, in a strange but appropriate gesture of respect, smoked the rest of the dead man's cigar down to the stub, just as the dead man would have done. Federico was not to stop shaking and retching for two days. After this he merely shook; this was his second encounter with pointless death in as many days.

Federico began to pile stones around the body, but he could not bear to see the man's upturned eyes every time he approached, nor could he bear to see the flies that had already gathered to lay their eggs, or the ants that had appeared from nowhere and were crawling in a black unanimous stream up the man's cheek, into his eyes, and into his open mouth.

There was a guttural croak behind him, and he turned, violently frightened, to see a repulsive hook-beaked, bald-headed, moth-eaten turkey vulture on the ground, its wings stretched and beating slowly. It was looking at him with one eye. He bent down and picked up a rock to hurl at the bird, which croaked once more and skipped backward impatiently. There was a flurry of wings, and two more birds arrived to see if the corpse was really dead. One of them tentatively pecked at an upturned eye and plucked it out, at which point Federico gathered up the rifle and ran stumbling away, unaware that Pedro the hunter and Aurelio the Indian had been watching him for the last ten minutes from the cover they had sought while tracking a small deer.

It was purely by chance that Doña Constanza was inspecting her tack in the stables when Pedro was outside confiding in Sergio that his son had killed a man. That night, full of that indignant public spirit which all Conservatives manifest over matters of law and order, she wrote to the nearest chief of police two hundred miles away in Cúcuta. Not wishing to be disturbed by having to do his job, this official sent it to the capital, where three months later it was filed and forgotten, to molder ominously for years like a forgotten land mine.

So it was that Federico's personal revolution, like all wars and revolutions, began with the death of an innocent, who in this case had four children to provide for and had always wanted to own a gun.

4

In Which
Sergio Grapples with the
Problem of the Canal

In the last few days events had conspired to disrupt Sergio's life quite
severely. First, his twin brother, Juanito, had been murdered by the
army, but the following night he had appeared in a dream and reassured
Sergio that everything was all right. He had also confirmed that when
his body was well rotted, Sergio could disinter his head and hire it out
for magic at a good profit, for everyone knew that the skull of a twin was
by far the most potent channel of communication with the angels. The
loss of his beloved brother, therefore, was a grief that could be borne
with some degree of equanimity.

Secondly, Federico had disappeared with the rifle, Sergio's most
treasured possession, and moreover, he had, according to the hunter,
killed a man with it. Sergio knew in his heart that his son had gone off
on some necessary business that was to do with becoming a man, as he
himself had done at roughly the same age when he had gone to look for
emeralds in the cordillera, but he was angry about his Lee-Enfield even
though in fact, he had never used it but always kept it against the day
when violence would erupt in the countryside as his twin's intuition told
him it surely would. He was also anxious that the relatives of the dead
man would find out who had killed him and arrive one night with
blazing torches to exact vengeance in the name of honor.

Thirdly, Doña Constanza's bizarre plan had placed him in a truly invidious position, as had rapidly become apparent in the bar of the brothel when he had divulged it to the company. They had all babbled excitedly at once, but it was Hectoro who had expressed the problem most concisely.

"The fact is," he said, looking around from face to face, "that the Mula supplies all of us and our fields, and such a canal would reduce our crops to dust in the dry season and ourselves to skeletons. It is only in any case a puddle of piss in the dry season and that's without any of it being drawn off by Doña Constanza."

"The face also is," replied Sergio, "that Doña Constanza owns the land where the Mula runs, she employs nearly all of us, she has the legal right to do what she wants, and it will be we who have to dig the canal for her stupid swimming pool."

"Doña Constanza has the best land hereabouts," said Misael, "and yet on it she keeps only horses that do no work. I know where she can put her legal rights, and that is a place where Don Hugh seldom goes for fear of his health."

Misael grinned, his white teeth gleaming in the lamplight. He crossed his eyes and made a lewd corkscrewing motion upward with his index finger, so that even Hectoro laughed.

"Surely," said Josef, screwing up his eyes against the ghostly blue cigar smoke that was curling and twisting about the room before accelerating upward out of the door, "a canal would not hold the water, or even a trench, for the earth is so dry it would suck away the water faster than Hectoro drinks *aguardiente*."

"Then we should tell Doña Constanza to make a pipeline with a windmill pump of the kind that Profesor Luis knows how to make, and that would do it," replied Hectoro. "And I will not have my honor insulted, Josef, or I will feed your *cojones* to the pigs."

"My wife has already bitten them off," exclaimed Josef. "But to return to the matter which is more important than your honor, or even my testicles, I think you are right, Hectoro. I think Sergio should suggest a pipe; though it is still a waste of water, it is less stupid than a canal."

Dolores and Consuelo had been listening to this male discourse and whispering to each other from their position behind the bar, and at last Dolores let out a long, throaty chuckle and said in her rum-and-cigars voice, "Ah, you men, the trouble with you is that you approach every problem directly."

"And the trouble with women is that they should hold their tongues when men talk of serious matters, but they never do," rejoined Hectoro.

"Nor should they," said Consuelo. "You men should listen to Dolores, who has more sense than all of you, especially as she has learned to read and therefore knows about the world."

"Yes," said Dolores, "but this is just common sense. The Mula, you ought to know, runs through the land of Don Emmanuel after it has been past the pueblo, and he needs the water as we do. Go to see him, and he will stop Doña Constanza for his sake and for ours. It is obvious."

There was a long silence, during which Hectoro finished his drink before announcing, "*Compañeros*, it is great grief to me when women are in the right."

"Dolores," said Misael, his eyes twinkling with mischief, "that is an idea so intelligent that in future I will let you fuck me for nothing."

"That is very kind," retorted Dolores, "but for you it is still five pesos!"

"Then warn me when you have been with him," said Josef, "for I should not like any of mine to get mixed with his!"

Don Emmanuel was an anomaly. His father had been an eminent progressive educationalist in England, who had decided that his son should attend his own establishment, and consequently, Emmanuel had grown up half naked and unusually blunt. He had also known, through his father, the immensely cerebral and unhappy philosopher Bertrand Russell, and so he collected all of Russell's works out of sentiment. He never read them, and if you were to have opened one, you would have found it neatly bored in a thousand different directions by termites, so that reading them would be double the intellectual exercise that that very clear philosopher had intended; indeed, they had become so full of obscurity that one would have had the impression of reading surrealist verse or perhaps an American disciple of Wittgenstein.

Don Emmanuel had attended Cambridge in order to study botany and had joined the Conservative, the Labor, the Liberal, and the Communist parties all at once "to get a balanced view." In his second

year he had arrived in the tropics with an assortment of gangly, earnest, and bespectacled botanists, lepidopterists, anthropologists, and
zoologists in order to study the flora and fauna of the Sierra Nevada
de Santa Margarita. However, he was not at the assembly point at the
appointed time of departure and, indeed, never arrived at it. After a
long, futile, and exasperated search, which consisted of horrendous
treks through unmapped territory with the assistance of an army helicopter, whose pilot was in fact just admiring the view, the party left
disconsolately, believing that Emmanuel must be dead at the hands of
brigands.

In fact, he was living with the Acahuatecs, with whom he stayed for
a year, after which he went to live with the Arahuacax, thus qualifying
himself as the only white man who was able to act as a guide when
mountaineers came from Britain to get peeling noses and diarrhea.

After this he came down to the plains and found the tiny pueblo
where he now lived, a place so insignificant that you still cannot find it
on the map, even though it now has concrete floors thanks to the trade
in marijuana and cocaine, which has indeed almost saved the country
from the economic ruin that is always imminent.

When he arrived, dressed like an Indian, the first thing he did was
go to the brothel, where neither his strange appearance, his outlandish
Indian dialect, nor his lack of funds prevented him from trying out each
of the whores in turn.

Having thus established his credibility, he spent several days wandering about the countryside until he came to a spot by the Mula that
inspired him with a vision of a flourishing *estancia*. He immediately
built himself a grass hut, Indian style, thatched it with palm, and, to the
wonder of the locals, began to live like Diogenes and labor like Sisy-
phus, except with better results. By the time that the events described in
this narrative began to unfold he owned a cool white hacienda, which he
had built himself, he had made a waterfall in the Mula to drive a
generator, he had a tractor, more thousands of hectares than he could
possibly count, thousands of steers that he would weep over when they
went to market, and relations with the peasants as good as his relations
with other rich whites were bad. This was because he had learned his
Spanish in the brothel and the fields; therefore, his conversation was
enlivened with an astoundingly rich and varied lexicon of truly graphic

expletives, and moreover, he spoke it as though he had no front teeth, for the simple reason that the people from whom he had learned had, for the most part, no such front teeth themselves. Whenever he visited the capital, a sort of collective shiver of horror would run up the spine of sophisticated society as he became more and more of a virtuoso enfant terrible, more especially as he was publicly proud of being officially dead and of having got away from his mother, who was so possessive that she moved to the United States in order to be close to his body, sublimely unaware that South America was a lot farther away than a simple glance at a globe would seem to indicate and that her son was alive and fucking.

Don Emmanuel had become a local legend both on account of his delight in healthy dissolution, his choice of peasants as his natural friends, and his prodigious social concern. He had built the village school and employed Profesor Luis to teach not only knowledge but wisdom to the raggedy children; he paid a quarter more than any other *padrón* in the whole department, and he adopted a method of making breezeblocks in a wooden lattice so that he could build a little house for each of his employees. It was in his Land Rover that the whores went every Thursday for their checkups, he arbitrated in domestic disputes, he never failed to labor alongside his men, and many local women were able to testify that even the purest-bred Negros were not more lusty or more satisfying than he was. The only thing that they thought unacceptable about him was that he always refused to smoke, a quirk that was considered antisocial in a land where everyone of peasant stock, man, woman, and child, always had a large cigar stuck in their mouth, where only effeminate oligarchs smoked cigarettes, and where pipes were smoked only by French engineers and English alpinists. These cigars are, like their coffee, easily the most sublime in the world, but of both commodities they keep the best for themselves, exporting only the dross for the world's connoisseurs to praise. To smoke one of those cigars outdoors of an evening in a hammock while drinking half a quart of thick black coffee is to condemn oneself unknowingly to a lifetime of nostalgia.

When Sergio and his friends arrived to tell Don Emmanuel of Doña Constanza's calamitous plan, they found him stark naked in the Mula, washing his clothes and singing a very rude ditty at the top of his voice to the tune of the national anthem, a melody so turgid and unmemorable that even oligarchs sometimes fail to recognize it and stand to attention.

When he beheld the four men approaching him, he stood up and waded out toward them, shouting greetings and friendly insults. Sergio, who did not know him very well, was astonished when Don Emmanuel stopped, raised a leg like a dog, farted, and told him, "Replace your hat, *cabrón,* or I will piss in it. If there is one thing I cannot tolerate, it is respect."

Sergio hastily replaced his sombrero, and Misael remarked, "Don Emmanuel, your *paloma* grows more huge and battle-torn by the day. It is said you borrow it from your donkey."

"On the contrary, my burro borrows it from me," replied Don Emmanuel. "I swear by the Virgin these women of yours have *chuchas* such as to stretch any man by suction. When I die, I shall need two coffins."

"Leave it to me in your will," said Josef, "and I'll dry it in the sun for a bullwhip."

"Indeed, you will do no such thing, for I believe you would use it on your wife!"

"His wife would no doubt use it on herself," exclaimed Misael.

"Then she will by God's grace leave me alone," said Josef.

After many more such inoffensive pleasantries, in which Hectoro was too proud and too dignified to participate, he informed Don Emmanuel of Doña Constanza's project and was told, "I'll stop it, or by God, I swear I will only pleasure pigs for the rest of my life. Before you go, you must witness my new method of taming goats."

They followed him to the caracolee tree, where a large yellow-eyed and hostile billy goat was absentmindedly mowing the grass in a circle. Don Emmanuel went down on his knees and shook his head at the animal, which lowered its own and feinted with its horns. "Whooba!" yelled Don Emmanuel, and butted it hard between the eyes. He then clasped it around the neck and kissed it lovingly on the nose. "There," he said proudly.

"He is not at all like a gringo," commented Sergio as they walked back to the pueblo.

"That is because he is not a gringo," replied Hectoro. "He is an Ingles."

"England must be a fine country then," said Misael. "I would go to it if anyone knew where it was."

"Don Emmanuel knows," said Josef.

"Not anymore," said Hectoro, so enigmatically that the others did not dare ask him what he meant.

5

Remedios
and the *Pistacos*

The Indians of the Andes believe in the existence of angels of death who have white skin and who cut people into little pieces. Nobody knows precisely why they believe in these *pistacos,* but it is commonly assumed that it is a legacy of the civilizing influence of the Spanish conquistadores and the enlightened activities of the Inquisition. It is still dangerous for the white man to go into some parts of the cordillera, not just because of the *ladrones,* the robbers, but because of cases of mistaken identity where public-spirited *cholos* think that they are bravely destroying *pistacos* to the greater benefit of humankind.

Remedios, when she was a little child with a round belly—earning her the nickname Barrigona—and two little black braids and big, round eyes, was already a materialist. She did not believe in God, or spirits, or *pistacos.* When she grew older, she still did not believe in God or spirits, but she knew for certain that the *pistacos* were real and that their existence was not a superstition, for she had seen them with her own eyes.

She did not believe in the spirits of the earth, the rocks, the waters, the forests, and the valleys, to whom one offered a little piece of whatever one was eating, saying, "Take, eat, so that you do not eat me." She did not believe that if you fell over running, you had to wrap yourself hastily in your skirt so that you did not fall pregnant to the earth spirit.

Nor when she fell over, did she believe that you had to place a little earth in your mouth so that you ate the spirit before it could eat you. Nor did she believe that the spirits could melt you down to use for tallow. But she did come to believe in *pistacos*.

Remedios's mother was a Bracamoros Indian whom her father had met when he was a migrant worker on a hydroelectric project in the *montaña* and who blackened her teeth for greater beauty. Remedios, defying all laws of heredity and probability, accepted neither her mother's animism nor her father's ardent Catholicism and believed only in what she could see, hear, smell, taste, or touch. Her parents' constant disagreements about her metaphysical upbringing ensured that she was simply a humanist who read small children's books concealed in a breviary whenever she was forced to go to church.

When the violence started, Remedios was four years old and mainly interested in cakes, playing in the gutter, and poking at dog excrement with sticks. When the violence reached the little town of La Cuenca, she was seven years old, still interested in cakes but even more interested in climbing trees.

The violence was the first spasm in a civil war that has never truly ended because no one ever understood why it had begun. It is possible to trace its origins in the manner of a historian, but not without becoming confused.

In 1946 a Conservative government came to power after a thirty-year rule by the Liberals. In the next year the charismatic leader of the Liberals, Ignacio Menéndez, made a famous speech indicting the government of fifty-six acts of violence in eleven provinces. In the year after that he made an even more famous speech, known as the *"Oración,"* in which he appealed for peace.

It is hard to understand why the Liberals and the Conservatives were such bitter rivals and why they expended so much hatred on each other since both parties consisted of oligarchs and had exactly the same politics. But be that as it may, the terrible spark that blew the powder keg occurred during a Pan-American Conference when Mr. Marshall, Mr. Harriman, and General Ridgway had arrived to announce that they were worried about revolution but could not spare any money, and Fidel Castro was also in the city to attend a student anti-imperialist congress. Señor Menéndez was walking through a crowd, genially shaking hands and receiving the good wishes of supporters, when someone stepped up and shot him. A man selling tickets for one of the plague of lotteries that are a national institution rushed up to grapple with the assassin, his tickets flying off in the wind. Another man ran out of a restaurant with a chair and smashed it over the assassin's head, and then the crowd kicked him to death, so that afterward no one was able to tell who the man was, he was so disfigured. Almost immediately mobs began to sack the city. They incendiarised the United States Embassy, public buildings, the Capitol (where the conference was taking place), and looted the shops. Secretary of State Marshall and the British ambassador blamed the Communists, but that does not explain why the Communists were as surprised and confused as everyone else and totally unprepared. The leader of the Communist party spent the two days of the rioting under a desk at the offices of a Liberal newspaper and displayed the Communists' traditional reluctance to become involved in revolutions, preferring to plot ones that never happen. The hypothesis of Secretary of State Marshall also does not explain why the rioting ended as soon as the Conservatives agreed to accept some Liberals into the cabinet.

Then there began the violence, and the Liberals refused to participate in the next election, for reasons that will be forever opaque, so that the Conservatives were elected unopposed.

The violence grew apace. *Guerrillero* bands of peasant Liberals and Conservatives reduced the countryside to a desert of desolation, and the Communists, not wishing to be left out or to appear nonconformist, dabbled in violence now and then as though to get in practice for the eventual revolution. During the next election the Communists, greatly reduced in number owing to the rise of Menéndezismo, still managed to split the Liberal party by telling their own members to vote for a dissident right-wing Liberal who had once been a Communist. Because of the split, the Conservatives were reelected on 40 percent of the vote. Then the Communists, having denounced the Liberals as fascists, swung around and supported them.

If we attempt to simplify our way through the extraordinary complexities of the civil war that followed, we arrive at something like the following account.

Liberals and Conservatives massacred each other. The Communists expounded theories, made speeches and published pamphlets, and then decided to organize the peasants, including women and children, into "battalions." Communist peasants declared an independent republic in Viola, which was so successful that it became rich and prosperous, so the Communist party denounced it for "bourgeoisification." The Liberals and Conservatives continued to massacre each other. The Liberals were hoping to force a military coup, and the Conservatives hoped to keep the president in power. The Communists tried to unite the left wing, a project which has never been found to be possible in any country of the world at any time with the single exception of Cuba. They did, however, succeed in extracting a statement of anti-imperialist and antilatifundist intent from the otherwise futile meetings.

A new independent republic of Menéndeziana was founded in the north of the country, and to it there flocked Liberals, Conservatives, Catholics, Protestants, Communists, Jehovah's Witnesses, all looking for a little peace. They were all allowed in and left in peace, provided they called themselves Conservative Communists, Catholic Communists, and so on. The new republic was so successful and became so prosperous that the Communists condemned it. It became so independent that its president once wrote to the real president protesting against border violations and threatening to break off diplomatic relations.

Then General Panela, known as El Azúcar, deposed the Conservatives in a coup and declared an amnesty for all guerrillas. The Liberals and Conservatives laid down their arms, and the Communists, grasping the opportunity to be in the limelight at last, decided to become seriously involved in guerrilla warfare but did very little.

Panela could not prevent the general violence from continuing, however, because the relatives of those killed in the violence began to take revenge, and a plague of blood feuds arose. Additionally, the Liberals and Conservatives began to suspect Panela of being left-wing and formed a coalition supported by the Roman Catholic Church to get rid of him. The former enemies to the death announced a perpetual coalition government, in which the presidency and all official posts were alternated between Conservatives and Liberals every four years. They organized a rigged plebiscite to ratify the arrangement and won it by two and a half million votes. In this way the oligarchy finally arrived at the perfect formula for democracy within the oligarchy. Together the new democratic government turned on the former allies of the Liberals, the Communists, and continued the civil war ad infinitum, concentrating especially on breaking up the (by now) nine independent republics. The Communists beat a tactical retreat into the mountains, to continue their "armed propaganda" from a point of safety. In fact, the Communist party renounced revolutionary violence on the ground that "the historical conditions are not yet fulfilled" and went back to making involved speeches, publishing pamphlets, and plotting revolutions that will never happen—or if they did, certainly not under its leadership, which does not exist except nominally. This means that the Communists still fighting in the hills are non-Communist Communists.

All this is history, but it does not do justice to the reality of the times in terms of the demonic wind of brutality and inhumanity that scoured the bodies and souls of innocent and guilty alike. It was as if some demented Qliphothic force had escaped from the gates of hell to ravage every last morsel of decency out of its last hiding place. The Four Horsemen of the Apocalypse ceded precedence to the Beast, the Mega Therion, which visited such inconceivable havoc upon the lives of the people that when it was finished, *La Violencia* had claimed over two hundred thousand of them. It is hard not to believe with hindsight that an infectious morbidity of the soul had contaminated the whole nation with an insanity of bloodlust thinly disguised as ideology and moral stance. There was a spreading sickness of ethical depravity that blew apart the eternal calm of the countryside and covered everything with a sticky slime of obscenity, viciousness, barbarity, and pointless cataclysm.

The first thing that the band of *guerrilleros* (no one knew whether they were Conservative or Liberal) did when they marched into La Cuenca was mass-rape all the little girls in the primary school. This had become commonplace, but it was the first and, to date, the last time that Remedios ever had congress with a man.

Torn and bleeding, the little Remedios lurched her way home

clutching on to walls and fences, her eyes filled with tears, her face smeared, her clothes torn, and her brain whirling with incomprehension. When she arrived home, the door was ajar, and there was a terrible screaming coming from inside. She stood on an empty paint-pot and watched through the window as her parents were skillfully murdered.

During *La Violencia* human intelligence reached new heights of ingenuity and sophistication. Brand-new methods of scalping, beheading, disemboweling, and quartering were improvised and perfected by empirical experimentation and assiduous practice. A complex technical vocabulary grew up around this new science: the *corte de corbata, corte de mica, corte de franela,* etc.

Remedios watched catatonically as her papa was subjected to *picar para tamal,* a technique involving slow death by having one's body cut into minute pieces in such a manner and pattern that one did not die until perfectly shredded.

Her mama, who had been forced to watch all of this and who had been the one screaming, was the next to suffer. The *guerrilleros* ripped from her womb the fetus that was to have been another brother for Remedios and replaced it with a cockerel. Then they set about the complex operation of *bocachiquiar,* a kind of exaggerated acupuncture which involved covering the body with thousands of tiny holes so that the victim seeped very slowly to death.

Remedios tried to take care of her brother, Alfredo, and they became orphans of the gutter, living off banana skins, licking sweet wrappers, chewing discarded bones left by the dogs, and stealing fruit from the few *chingonas* and *tiendas* that were still operating and that nowadays mostly stocked only the cheapest alcohol.

Remedios was taken in by the Sisters of the Montfortian Mission, and Alfredo by the Brothers of the Divine Will, and from then on she hardly ever saw him, as the two missions were rivals in a dispute over a rich bequest from a pious *latifundista*'s widow.

Remedios was at the convent until the age of sixteen, during which time her loathing of religion reached such heights that the nuns unwittingly exacerbated it by having her exorcised. She emerged from having her head shaken and squeezed by the sweating and chanting priest convinced that she had to spend her life fighting in the cause of sanity.

She left the convent having imbibed only the nuns' fanaticism and their morbid frigidity.

Upon leaving, she discovered that she also hated the Liberal-Conservative coalition, which was now called the National Front. She did not know who had killed her parents or which way her parents used to vote, so she divided her hatred of the two parties impartially and blamed them equally. It was this that caused her to choose the only remaining alternative, the Communists. The Communists had two major attractions for Remedios: One was a utopian vision of the future, and the other was a very clear idea of who the enemy was—everyone who was not in the party and who must therefore be a part of the gigantic conspiracy to oppress the masses.

Remedios worked very hard to persuade the masses to become class-conscious and to organize but became disillusioned when she realized that they preferred to be disorganized, did not consider themselves to be part of the masses ("My grandfather was a Capitan"), and continued to vote Liberal and Conservative, if they voted at all, which 80 percent did not.

Remedios tried to reach the 80 percent of the nonaligned, but every new organization formed to align them eventually turned into its own party, which would not align with any of the others, especially the Communists, who immodestly believed that being nonaligned meant being aligned with themselves.

The proliferation of squabbles and pompous pronunciamentos of the luminaries of the left forced Remedios to realize that there was never any hope of success by democratic means, as a vote for one faction of the divided left was a vote lost in the fight against the National Front coalition. At the age of twenty-two she traveled to the Independent Republic of the 26th of September, and joined its armed force of guerrillas, disappearing into the hills with one of its factions when the national army invaded in order to liberate the republic and to bring it back into the fold.

Remedios was by now a strong character. She radiated firmness of purpose, unshakableness of vision, moral and physical courage, and a tender sadness that made all her *compañeros* love her. She was well built and shapely, with black hair tied back in a ponytail, and she had a kind of beauty that was half Indian and half Hispanic, even though her father had been a Negro. "Somewhere there's a bit of conquistador in your blood," her mother used to say. "I hope it never comes out in your character."

Remedios, for all her generous heart and gifts of nature, had never been in love, and no one had ever been in love with her. She was without sexuality; but all the poor people of the earth were her family, and she had seen the *pistacos* with her own eyes of a child.

6
The General
Plans His Leave

He was called Carlo after his Italian grandfather, and he was the finest possible kind of soldier—that is to say, he was not at all interested in swaggering about intimidating people, in social climbing, in glamorous warmongering, or in genuine Scotch whiskey. He was, on the contrary, a sensitive and intelligent man of broad education and many interests; that is why the military authorities treated him with enough suspicion to send him to César and also why the civil authorities were so obstructive when he got there. A man of integrity in high office was a rara avis that could very easily disrupt the smooth operation of corruption and incompetence even more than a man of arbitrary megalomania or extreme violence. He caused enormous resentment on his second day of office by jailing the police chief for the rape of a mestiza woman and doubling the sentence when the guilty man courteously and discreetly offered him a large bribe according to time-honored custom and practice. Everyone thought he was mad or, even worse, a Communist when he publicly denounced the city police chief. The police force spontaneously went out on strike. Nobody noticed the difference, and the strike was in any case rapidly ended when the lepidopterological general threatened a thorough investigation into the record of every single policeman in the department.

General Carlo María Fuerte had to his credit an anthology of respectable verse on patriotic themes and the most complete work on the nation's butterflies that had ever been compiled. Since his country was the world's foremost producer of those cardboard books with pictures that can be moved by pulling tags, his book incorporated a life-size representation of the calicos butterfly that looked like an owl. It could be made to flap its wings and move its antennae. It was a great mortification to him that this splendid and compendious work had been bought by practically every important library in the world but that not a single copy had sold in his own country. He attributed this to lack of patriotism, not realizing that comparatively few people could read, that even if they could, they could not have afforded the book, and if they could both read and afford it, then they were the kind of people who would have got their servants to squash any butterfly that came near them. He was now compiling a work on the nation's hummingbirds, meticulously illustrated in oils done with the help of his own photographs, and was unaware that he had discovered three species hitherto undocumented. Like his butterfly project, his *Picaflores de la Cordillera y la Sierra Nevada* was motivated by patriotism.

There are two types of patriotism, although sometimes the two are mingled in one breast. The first kind one might call nationalism; nationalists believe that all other countries are inferior in every respect and that one would do them a favor by dominating them. Other countries are always in the wrong, they are less free, less civilized, are less glorious in battle, are perfidious, prone to falling for insane and alien ideologies which no reasonable person could believe, are irreligious and abnormal. Such patriots are the most common variety, and their patriotism is the most contemptible thing on earth.

The second type of patriot is best described by returning to the example of General Fuerte. General Fuerte did not believe in "my country, right or wrong"; on the contrary, he loved his land despite the faults that he could so clearly see and that he labored to correct. It was his frequently stated opinion that anyone who supported his country when it was obviously in the wrong, or who failed to see its faults, was the worst kind of traitor. Whereas the first kind of patriot really glories in his own irrationality and not in his country, General Carlo María Fuerte loved his country as a son loves his mother or a brother his sister.

He loved the Amazonas, with its impenetrable cascades of the lushest green vegetation, its enormous trees, its poisonous yellow frogs and giant snakes, its *tigres*, its crazy-faced monkeys, its aborigines who still went naked and hunted with blowpipes and poisoned darts. He loved the Caribbean Sea with its lugubrious fish and its million shades of aqua blue, its shimmering white and yellow sands. He loved the ancient Spanish towns upon its coast, the huge semiwild pigs that dug themselves hollows and slept all day beneath the palms, the fishermen's wives who stared out to sea at dusk, watching for their returning husbands and fearing sharks on their behalf. He loved the Pacific coast, which rose almost immediately into spectacular mountains, and he shared the national grief with every earthquake and tidal wave that beat this shore into desolation and terror at times of the full moon, just as he shared the national pride in his countrymen's abilities to fight back to normal thereafter, when even thieves did no looting and hardened rapists helped distressed women find their children in the cataclysm of mud and debris.

Unlike almost all his countrymen, the general even loved the savanna, whose heat in the dry season would bleach the bones of the living and split the red rocks into shards with a report like that of a howitzer, and whose humidity in the wet season would drive people to sit all day up to their necks in rivers like Japanese monkeys in order to cool the body of sweat and evade the mosquitoes, whose relentless envenomed probings could turn so easily into ulcers. The general walked about these deserts of reptiles and heroic desiccated grasses, peering up into the stumps of trees hollowed by lightning in order to see the swarms of inverted vampire bats, which at night settled on the necks and rumps of horses and mules and spread rabies more effectively than dogs. He would beat against the walls of the trees with his military cane and guess by the light of a match how many of the twittering and squeaking creatures there must be whirling and wheeling in that unnatural darkness, dropping excrement of pure blood.

He loved, too, the moon so large and resplendent that one can see all the seas and pockmarks without the aid of an instrument. In Europe he had been so contemptuous of their moon's insignificance and lack of splendor that that, above anything else, had made him long to return home, where one sees as clearly but more magically by night as by day. In Europe he had pitied the thunder and lightning, for at home the thunder cracks as though from inside one's own head like the gun of a tank and reverberates inside it until the plates of the skull seem to shiver apart at the seams. At home the lightning is brighter than the flame of magnesium and freezes the world into tableaux like a randomly set stroboscope; it fells huge trees before one's very eyes and splits apart to dance at the tips of mountains.

And it was the mountains that General Fuerte loved the most, for as one proceeds through the altitudes, the climate and the life change through three distinct stages. For the first seven thousand feet it is the Garden of Eden, a luxuriance of orchids, hummingbirds, and tiny streams of delicious water that run by miracle alongside every path. Above this height for three or four thousand feet is a world of rock and water draped like hanging gardens with alien lunar plants in shades of brown and red and yellow with a habit so curious and enchanted as to be found in books of legend and romance. Above this is the Venusian world of ice, of sudden reckless mists of palpable water, of lichen and trickling springs, of fragmenting shale and glistening white peaks, where human realities become remote and ridiculous, where the sky is actually below you and inside you, where breathing is an accomplishment in itself, and where condors, inconceivably ponderous and gigantic, wheel on the upcurrents like lords of a different and fantastic universe. It is here that the Incas trap them; they know that a condor needs more space to take off than to land, and so they place a carcass in a small corral and wait. The feathers they use for robes, and of the hollow thigh bones they make that eerie flute the *quena*. The Incas rightly kill anyone who shoots a condor for "sport" or curiosity or vainglory, and they leave the corpse for the condors and the lesser vultures.

Unlike nearly all patriots, the general also loved the people. It filled him with awe to see the sculpted bodies of the campesinos with their Greek muscles and the veins etched in relief beneath their black skins like maps of rivers. He felt a mysterious and mystical pride in the unapproachable Incas and their ruined civilization and always reflected that once, after all, his countrymen had fought indefatigably and undauntedly with Simón Bolívar to unite the countries of the northwest, including Panama, and to throw out the Spanish with all their corrupting hubris and incomprehensible cruelty. He longed, like a man born out of time, for the return of such a fiery and magnificent spirit in the people, who were now as venial as their ancestors had been indomitable.

The general also loved the army, which to him was like a wife—that is to say, he was frequently at odds with it; he found it tiresome and sometimes boring. He was often obliged to attend to details that he thought were unimportant, and he was often tempted to leave. However, it gave him order, stability, direction, and purpose; he liked to have to stick to regulations because it saved him from having to agonize over decisions, and like most of the finest officers, he conceived of the army not as a means to war but as an instrument of stability and peace. He had never contemplated participating in a coup and had seen battle only once, in a futile and piffling little war over a patch of territory that was no use to anyone, and so he had as far as possible avoided putting his men in danger and never wished to do so again. When he thought of the army, he thought of it, indeed, as a man thinks of a fine wife of many years, not with passion but with swelling pride and affection that warm the heart and prove that contentment is more to be desired than happiness.

So much for what the general loved. What he loathed was communism, which to him was a word so broad and hazy of definition that one might describe it as South African. That is, to him a Communist was anyone who wished to rock the boat so much that people fell out of it or got splashed. To a peace-loving and contented man, who loved his country and found life to be unfailingly interesting, random assassinations and economic sabotage seemed both brutal and stupid. "Why," he would ask, "if they are for the people, do they blow up bridges and railways built for the benefit of the people? Why do they slaughter their *patrones* so that all the *fincas* go to ruin through mismanagement? Why do they not work for change from within, rather than try to impose it from without, by violence?"

The problem, of course, was twofold. One was that like even the guerrillas themselves, the general knew next to nothing of what the theory of communism was. It did not worry him that the ideology was atheist, for example, because he had no sympathy for the church himself, and it did not worry the guerrillas either, who still prayed to the angels before battle and asked spirits for advice on tactics. It did not worry him that the guerrillas wanted land reform because he thought that would be a good thing. What worried and angered him was that his soldiers were being shot at by ruffians with foreign weapons and bushy beards, who spoke only in slogans.

He also knew that Communism was the opposite of the American system, and it was the American system that he wanted for his country: good highways; a good diet; a car for everyone; new hospitals; political stability. He had been to the United States and found the people decent, honorable, and hospitable, and he therefore dismissed as irritatingly crass propaganda all the stories he had heard about CIA shenanigans, about the way that for every two pesos lent three pesos went out as interest, about U.S. corporations sucking out the resources of the country. It did not seem to him at all credible.

What he did believe, however, was what he read in the newspapers, what he heard from high-ranking officers, government ministers, and his acquaintances among the U.S. military about what slavery the Communists wished to impose upon the free world. And why should he not believe this? No one had ever given him any reasons to believe otherwise, and this leads us to the second half of our twofold problem.

This was, that being a general removed him as a matter of course from the front line—that is, he had no reason not to believe in the literal truth of reports sent in by people such as Capitan Rodrigo Figueras. As far as he was concerned, there was no evidence that such men were not strictly honorable and competent, and even if there was any evidence, he always had to consider the possibility that it was Communist propaganda. He had been told that the Communists frequently murdered the peasants in order to blame it on the military. Additionally, coming as he did from a respectable family in Cúcuta, he had seen the poverty and humiliation of others with his own eyes but never with his heart, as he had never experienced them himself. Consequently, he had no clear idea of the very personal reasons that guerrillas came up with for taking up arms.

Neither, as it happens, did the few Cuban agitators and military experts who had slipped into the country to infiltrate the labor movement and the bands of guerrillas. They came over with their heads full of ideals and theories about armed propaganda, the dictatorship of the proletariat, jungle tactics, and the opiate of the masses, only to be baffled, amazed, and disgusted by the guerrillas' superstitions, unclarity of purpose, habit of going home for harvests and fiestas, inability (or rather, refusal) to organize, lack of interest in theory of any kind, and their odd reasons for fighting (the *padrón* would not lend me fifty pesos, the *padrón* shot my dog, in Venezuela they are paid better, I want to be able to go to France and they will not give me a passport because I have no birth certificate, which means I have not yet been born and I want the right to be born). Most often, however, the guerrillas were fighting because some were too rich and everyone else too poor, and because they had become victims in some way of the army's random hooliganism. It was enough for them to know what they were fighting against; they did not need advice about what they were fighting for or how to set about it.

General Carlo María Fuerte did at least know what he was fighting for, but today he was planning his leave, a very easy matter for him since he was in charge of all dispensations in the area. He was going to take a donkey, his military pack full of provisions, his service revolver for protection, his binoculars, and his camera, to look for humming-birds in the Sierra. In his pocket, to put himself in the right mood, was a copy of Hudson's *Idle Days in Patagonia*.

7

Don Emmanuel's Ineffective Diplomacy and Its Consequences

Don Emmanuel may have been the obvious and logical choice as emissary to Doña Constanza, but he was a long way from being the best. This was because ever since someone had told him in an "old-boy-just-a-word-in-your-ear" manner that his Spanish was unacceptably vulgar, especially in his choice of adverbs, adjectives, and common nouns, he had adopted a style of speech when talking to influential and respectable people that consisted partly of his customarily outrageous bluntness and partly of that elaborate courtesy which one finds in medieval romances. The not entirely unintended effect was that of extreme sarcasm, and his reputation as an outstanding boor was thereby greatly enhanced, more especially as he never tried to abandon or modify his peasant's accent.

His customary mode of conveyance was an unfortunate bay horse with a white blaze on its forehead that had earned it the unromantic name of Careta. The beast was unfortunate first in that although Don Emmanuel was a fit and strong man, he had a very large belly as tight as a drum, which contributed an unreasonable quantum of extra pounds to the horse's load. Secondly, the horse was a *pasero*, which in this case does not mean a ferryman but a horse that has been carefully trained not to trot but to move at a steady, undulating lope. This was the one pace at which Don Emmanuel never rode it, so it had not only a sagging back but also the depressed, irritated, and frustrated air of a natural artist whom financial straits have reduced to taking a job as a bank clerk. The horse always breathed in hard when its master tightened its *cinturón* and would stop in the middle of the river in order to exhale so that the girth would loosen and Don Emmanuel would fall off sideways. Don Emmanuel was very proud of his horse on account of this trick and always quoted it as irrefutable proof that a horse can have a sense of humor. However, he took to waiting for the horse to breathe out before tightening the *cinturón,* and Careta became probably the only horse in the world to have discovered for itself some of the techniques of hatha-yoga.

Don Emmanuel rode his dispirited *pasero* through the only street of the pueblo, raising little plumes of dust that were caught up and whirled away by the dancing dust devils, and wishing "*¡Buena' día'!*" in the customary nasal drawl to everyone he saw. He passed the three brothels with concrete floors, the little shop that sold machetes, alcohol, contraceptives, and the huge avocados that little boys stole from his own trees; he passed a small field of corn and Profesor Luis's creaking little windmill that generated electricity and turned left up the track to Doña Constanza's hacienda, all the while thinking of things he could say to irritate her.

Doña Constanza looked out her window, where she had been reading a copy of *Vogue* that was already three years old, and witnessed his arrival with a fascinated mixture of dread and excitement. She watched him tie his horse to the lemon tree, his torso bare and his trousers hanging from halfway down his buttocks, and challenged herself to remain cool and dignified in the face of this impending trial of her patience.

Her maid, an unprepossessing and clumsy mulatta who affected oligarchic manners, ushered him into Doña Constanza's room and waited to be dismissed.

"Doña Constanza," said Don Emmanuel, "it is a sign of the exquisite times in which we live that a lady's maid may be as lovely as her mistress!"

The maid flushed with pleasure, and her mistress flinched visibly. "Don Emmanuel, you are as charming as ever. Now, as I am very busy, as you see, perhaps you would tell me the purpose of your visit?"

Don Emmanuel made a show of scrutinizing the degree of her industriousness and bowed, removing his straw sombrero with a flourish. "Madame will forgive me for not perceiving her busyness. It is a sign of the highest breeding to be able to be busy while appearing idle to the uninformed observer."

Her mouth tightened and her eyes flashed before she regained her composure. "Señor is full of signs today. Now what is the purpose of your visit?"

"It has come to my ears, dear lady, that you intend to divert with a canal the very river which waters my land and that of the campesinos in order to replenish your *piscina*. I must say, as I know you appreciate frankness, that I and the local people will be fucked, buggered, and immersed in guano of the finest Ecuadorean provenance before we permit such a thing to occur."

"The permission," she rallied, her temper rising almost immediately beyond control, "is not yours or theirs to grant. I will do as I wish with the water on my land."

"I appeal," said Don Emmanuel, "to your highly developed social conscience and to your concern for my nether parts."

"Your nether parts?" she repeated with astonishment.

"Indeed, señora. In the dry season the Mula is the only water where I may rinse the dingleberries from my nether parts."

"Dingleberries!" she exclaimed with mounting outrage.

"Dingleberries," he said, assuming a professorial air, "are the little balls of fluff that appear in one's underwear and sometimes entwine themselves in one's pubic hair. Frequently they are of a gray color and woolly texture."

Doña Constanza oscillated between amazement and fury before remarking icily, "Indeed, I should bear in mind your nether parts, as you call them, for I hear they often are found in the most unsavory places."

"Indeed," said Don Emmanuel, "it is often most unsavory between one's legs, which is their usual location, as a lady of your wide experience will doubtless know, and this is why I appeal to you—"

But Doña Constanza was already leaving, and Don Emmanuel was already aware that he had allowed himself to fail in his mission out of perversity. He rode home with a heavy heart.

So it was that under Don Emmanuel's and Hectoro's secret supervision Sergio and his men began to dig a canal, for Doña Constanza had absolutely refused to consider any of the more sensible and less disastrous alternatives, her one purpose now being to annoy Don Emmanuel.

They started to pretend to dig a very shallow canal from the swimming pool end with the intention of routing it the longest possible way. For three months Doña Constanza watched the peasants, their muscles gleaming with perspiration, slaving with enormous energy and achieving almost no progress with their picks and spades. When she saw that the canal was both too shallow and heading in the wrong direction, she issued instructions to dig it deeper and to take the most direct route to the Mula. Sergio told her that the Mula was lower at that point and that "We cannot make the water flow uphill."

"Kindly do as I ask," was all she said.

So the canal was started again and dug about four inches deeper at a prodigiously slow rate of progress. When it was half complete, the rainy season began, the Mula flooded over its usual floodplain, work ceased, and when the water had receded and the mosquitoes had disappeared, the canal was full of silt, small stones, and tree trunks. Not only this, but the Mula had diverted itself into its other bed six hundred feet farther over, as it often did. In between the two beds was a huge outcrop of solid pink rock.

Doña Constanza was undeterred, but the campesinos were elated that she would continue to pay them at above the standard rate to work at a project that had no prospects of completion before the end of the world. When a further six months of toil had elapsed, it became clear that Sergio had fortuitously been in the right and the dry bed of the Mula was indeed too low even if it had carried any water. Doña Constanza instructed Sergio to dig the canal deeper and reasoned that next year the Mula might change course back into its previous bed. Profesor Luis arrived with poles and pieces of string and calculated that at the swimming pool end, the canal would have to be sixteen feet deep, and at about the same time Sergio and his men discovered that beneath the depth of four feet there were massive boulders of the same indestructible pink rock as the outcrop between the beds, at which point Doña Constanza had a brain wave.

The bulldozer took one month to arrive from Asunción, two hundred miles away. It was not just that the machine was slow, which it was, or that the roads were appalling, which they were; it was simply that the driver was easily bribed into doing all sorts of lucrative little odd jobs along the way, especially since he reveled in the people's admiration for the awesomeness of the feats that his beloved machine could perform with magical ease. He gave free demonstrations to interested knots of people who never tired of seeing trees pulled over to no purpose and huge fearsome bulls dragged along by a rope around the horns despite their having their hooves firmly planted against the soil and all their muscles straining. Halfway to the pueblo he had to turn back to Asunción to fetch more diesel.

When the bulldozer finally arrived, it immediately began to make triumphantly easy work of the canal, so much so that Don Emmanuel became alarmed and took to leaving bottles of *aguardiente* near the machine every evening. He also told Sergio to tell everyone in the village to be very generous every time the driver came into it after dark. The driver took on a haggard and bilious mien, work began later and finished sooner, and Doña Constanza threatened the man with imprisonment, which was hardly an idle threat, since all magistrates without exception would find someone guilty of something in return for a gratuity. Doing one's civic duty was therefore both an honorable and profitable burden, and posts were eagerly sought and sedulously canvassed for with the aid of bank notes, usually in the form of U.S. dollars.

When the driver returned to his former diligence and the pink boulders began to be piled up in the river to redivert it, Hectoro began an heroic campaign of covert sabotage. Don Emmanuel ordered Pantagruelian quantities of *ron cana* and *aguardiente* from the little shop, and Hectoro ensured that it found its way into the fuel tanks of the bulldozer along with small quantities of sugar dissolved in water.

On the first morning the bulldozer started perfectly on the unsullied fuel that was left in the lines. After a minute or two, however, the engine raced, then backfired several times, releasing puffs of pure white smoke into the air from the exhaust, and then became marvelously erratic. There were periods of preignition, periods of spectacular explosions like gunfire, and periods of total stoppage, which found the perplexed and frustrated driver tinkering for hours with the fuel pump, which he believed to be faulty, bleeding fuel lines, which he believed to be full of air, and, his mouth stinging with diesel, kicking the massive tracks and shouting with rage until, his face buried in his hands, he would sit with his back to the machine, a picture of pure dejection. Eventually he threw back his head, looked at the sky as if for aid and inspiration, rose slowly to his feet, and climbed into his cab, where he sat grim-faced before turning the key. The machine fired, operated briefly, backfired, raced, and cut out, whereupon the whole pantomime began anew, watched by audiences of washerwomen with baskets of laundry on their heads and cigars in their mouths who would say "Whooba!" softly at every explosion and "Ay, ay, ay!" every time the machine stopped. Having watched the driver tinkering and cursing for a while, they turned as though unanimously and walked off in a line, to pound their washing on the largest flat stones in the river, singing rhythmic songs of forgotten meaning that are probably still sung in West Africa.

Needless to say, work progressed with wondrous slowness and infinite pains. When the canal seemed to be roughly right to the naked eye, the driver took the first opportunity to jerk his explosive way back to Asunción, where his much-abused machine slowly recovered its health with transfusions of unadulterated diesel and where the driver slowly recovered his erstwhile good humor, taking once more to pulling over trees and dragging bulls. However, like a man who has once found himself impotent, he never quite regained his faith in himself and his powers.

There were unexpected and terrible consequences of this lighthearted but essential sabotage. It was not that it had not succeeded, because it did—the river was not diverted, and the canal was still dry—nor was it that the driver was psychologically somewhat battered.

What had happened was that word had spread around the area that there were many explosions coming from near the pueblo that sounded like gunshots and bombs and shells. Farther away there arose rumors that there actually were gunshots, bombs, and shells going off in the pueblo, and by the time these stories reached Valledupar they had been elaborated into graphic accounts of skirmishes and even pitched battles between "the Cubans" and the beleaguered peasants, who at this very moment were being tortured, raped, and pillaged without pity. General Fuerte being on leave, searching for hummingbirds, Brigadier Hernando Montes Sosa sent a company of men by truck, armed to the teeth and twitching with nervous fear, to defend their country and their democracy.

Thus it was that Comandante Rodrigo Figueras found himself once more at the scene of his humiliation, but with three times the number of men and different insignia on his epauletes. The first thing anyone knew about it was when Doña Constanza answered the door to be confronted by an unpleasant, lecherous-looking, surly character with greasy hair, a revolver, and a large number of soldiers at his back.

"Where are the Communists?" he demanded.

8

Aurelio
Is Disinherited

Don Hernández Almagro Méndez, descendant of conquistadores and owner of inconceivably vast tracts of land exhausted and enfeebled by overgrazing and familial irresponsibility, found himself inclined to acquire a little more land. The barren scrub where now there grew only a few eucalyptus had once been virgin jungle smelling of spices, draped with orchids and lianas, glittering with metallic morpho butterflies, reverberating to the cough of the jaguar, creeping with giant mugale spiders, and echoing after sunset to the eerie crowing of the nighthawk.

Then the Méndez family had arrived and enslaved the Indians, who were set to work under the lash and the sword to destroy their former homes by fire until the whole forest was consumed by an inferno whose orange glow could be seen in the sky after dark far away in the sierra. It is inconceivable how many creatures perished in the conflagration; afterward there lay among the charred stumps of the trees the calcined remains of tapirs, of armadillos, of capybaras, of garapu stags, of three species of anteaters, of leguan lizards, of peccaries, of sloths, of capuchin monkeys, of coati raccoons, and of frogs that could call with a sound exactly like a child weeping.

No sooner had the great pall of white ash descended on the land than the captive Indians were set to cultivate it. Many died of diseases, of malnutrition, of cruelty; the remainder died by hunger strike or escaped the packs of dogs and the horsemen to take their chances with the hostile clans of headhunters in what jungle was left beyond the *encomienda*. To replace the Indians, the Méndez family brought in Negroes from West Africa who were more easily resigned to servitude.

The land was worked for bananas, tobacco, cotton, and cattle, but it failed completely in a few years as the fragile soil was swept into the rivers by the torrential inundations of the seasons of rains. Deep gullies grew apace in the fields as the waters carved them out in horrifying flash floods, which swept away cattle and houses alike and eventually reduced the former Eden to bare rock and infertile packed earth which supported only scrub grass and a few herds.

In places the jungle began to reclaim the land; it crept slowly and unsurely, unable to re-create in centuries that which it had lost in a few days, but sending out tendrils and feelers, creating tongues of verdure where once more there were bromelias, piassaba palms, and situlis with their exquisite crimson flowers. The Mendezes left the farm alone, for they had gone to live in perpetuity in the capital, leaving the management to *enganchadores*, who hired *jornaleros* and *macheteros* to work hard but without commitment to grow what little could be grown and to keep count of the cattle.

The *enganchadores* adopted the usual method for not paying the workers; they would sell them the basics of life—food, tools, leather, horses, fake medicines made of seawater and chicken blood—and ensure that the campesinos always owed more than they earned. Enormous debts that were never to be paid off were inherited by sons and passed on in turn to their children, and there was an agreement among all *latifundistas* that they would never employ a peon who still owed money to his *padrón*. In this way generations of the same families passed their protected but impoverished lives on the Vida Tranquila Hacienda.

Centuries later Don Hernández, who had been speculating on government bonds with great success, decided that it was time to put his money into minerals, and gold in particular, with a little coffee cultivation as a backup. He knew that in the highlands beyond and above the Vida Tranquila he could grow the very finest arabica beans for the connoisseur market in Europe and North America, and he also knew that beyond and above that there were a great many Inca mines which, if reopened, might yield a viable amount of ore. To examine these old workings, he hired a French engineer, who came back with favorable reports but who said that the mountains were still populated by Aymara Indians who were likely to be hostile to any industrial activity.

Don Hernández decided to go ahead in any case, and his work force first went into action to erect fences way up into the hills and clear them for the coffee planting. This part of the plan went perfectly smoothly, but it was not quite so simple to fence off the mountains above; one cannot drive stakes into solid rock in neat lines over peaks and chasms, even if one does have a property deal signed by a government official. Eventually Don Hernández was obliged to reconcile himself to having piles of stone erected at intervals around the periphery of his property and to allowing free passage to travelers. But he was possessed of the fixed idea that he had to get rid of the Indians, whom he regarded as lower than the animals and far more dangerous.

He sent bands of ruffians on forays to burn the Indian settlements and to hound the *cholos* off the land, even though they were officially protected by the Indian Protection Agency and even though he had not a shred of legal justification for evicting them. Having moved their villages two or three times, the Aymaras naturally began to defend themselves, and very soon there was irregular warfare taking place all over that part of the sierra which put an end to several centuries of peace. Don Hernández's bands of thugs were showing every sign of losing this war when he struck on the idea of laying mines bought on the sly from the quartermaster at the Corazón Military Depot and spraying the Aymaras and their crops with concentrated pesticides and herbicides from a crop-dusting airplane.

When the people found themselves not only living in a plantless wilderness but also coughing up blood, becoming covered with blisters, going blind, and being blown up by the "sudden-death-by-thunder," they moved away at last, and some of them, Aurelio included, wandered far away forever.

Aurelio, although only a boy of fourteen, traveled southward among the upper slopes of the foothills, staying in many *pueblitos*, working a little here and there. Often he was cold and hungry, shared caves with wild bulls, and risked his life following the goat trails around the vertiginous sides of mountains. He knew neither where he was going nor what he intended to do, until one day he climbed high on an eastern slope and looked out over the jungle below.

As far as the horizon in all directions the rolling verdant forest stretched, unbroken. He had heard from his people that only Indians lived there, and others could not survive. He had heard that the jungle Indians are bad people, who kill without quarter, who collect people's hands and heads, and who speak strange tongues. He had heard of the poisonous snakes and plants, of the white and black rivers teeming with vicious fish, of the enormous floods in the rainy season that made it necessary to build homes on platforms, and of the fevers that burned a man's body so terribly that his soul would flee to avoid being burned up with it.

But from where he stood the forest appeared enticing and secure. It seemed a place of indescribable peace, richness, and anonymity, where death, when it came, would not come by airplane or by bombs hidden in paths. And it did not matter to him if he became lost, for he did not know where he was going.

He followed a stream down through the chasms, the *quebradas,* the ravines, the valleys, until at last he came within sight of the forest itself. It began gently enough, with a steady increase in the density of vege-tation and the astonishing activities of the hummingbirds, those tiny creatures that jungle Indians call "living sunbeams." He saw a flock of the jeweled little birds darting among some blue passionflowers beneath a magnificent aguache palm, when a hawk descended in circles, seeking prey. The hummingbirds fled, with the exception of one, which uttered a tiny, shrill squeak and threw itself into the attack. Had it been able to cope with such a minute enemy that could fly in any direction at light-ning speed, the great hawk would have been able to kill it outright with one peck of its beak, one contraction of its talons, or one beat of its wings. But the hummingbird annoyed it so much by flitting about its head and jabbing at its eyes that the hawk suddenly soared upward and left. The little speck of a victor settled itself on a twig and emitted a belligerent squeak of triumph, to be joined once more by its friends coming out of hiding. Aurelio always remembered this incident, and always the memory would make him smile.

Aurelio soon found that there was no way through the forest. He was obstructed at every step by giant lianas that twisted high into the trees, by swaths of fleshy orchids, by plants that oozed white poison, by plants whose stench caused migraines, by insula ants, whose bites made him ill for five days, by scolopendras, whose bites nearly killed him and made him ill for weeks, by branches whose touch raised blisters on his hands, by impassable tauampas swamps, by thick clumps of *cana brava* bamboo, by sapoeira, by razor-sharp fucum palm that cut deep gashes in his flesh, which became infected, by swarms of stinging mutuca flies, by the cuts of piassavua; by the whole forest and everything in it. That is, he discovered for himself what all jungle dwellers know: that it is best to follow the waterways, where the dangers are almost as terrible but where progress is more rapid.

By the time that he discovered this, he was already ill with fevers and with hunger, for he had not yet learned to cover himself with annatto and urucú to keep off insects, his skin was not thick like a jungle Indian's, and he had exploded for himself the myth that in the forest food practically presses itself into one's mouth. He did not know yet that anything eaten by toucans, macaws, and capuchin monkeys could also be eaten by humans, he had no weapons for the hunt, made fire only with great difficulty, but he caught fish and shrimps in the same way as his people had in the mountains, not yet having acquired the methods of the jungle.

Having given up the attempt to hack his way into the dense foliage, he journeyed along the stream, skirting around the falls, rapids, and cataracts, wading along the bed when it was not possible to jump the rocks or follow the banks. Then one day, when the stream was joined by two others and broadened out into a river, he noticed caimans on the banks, and he trod on an arraia. The sting of the ray, so valuable as an arrowhead but so vicious in the flesh, made him fall backward in the water and crawl to a sandbank, where he sat clutching his foot, rocking with pain, and sweating with stoically suppressed terror as the caimans watched him from the fringes of the banks. When he looked into the eyes of these animals, especially when they glowed at night, he appreciated why the Indians of the forest believed them to be the origin of fire.

Aurelio decided to make himself a raft to see him safely down the waters. The jungle hung so thickly now that in places there was a deep gloom; where the sun broke through the foliage the light was so incandescent that it hurt to pass through it, and one could come up in blisters even beneath one's clothes.

It was in cutting himself a raft and binding it with lianas that

Aurelio took his first real step in the long process of metamorphosis from sierra Indian to jungle Indian. He discovered that some woods are too hard to cut and others too heavy to float, and he discovered that some creepers are good for binding and others merely break as soon as they are twisted. In drifting with the current, he found that he needed a pole to prevent the craft from becoming stuck in the many fallen trees that lay across the water, to push himself away from the bank or from shoals which grounded him, and to push away the hanging creepers as he passed through them. He found, too, that the raft tended to revolve on the water as it drifted, so he cut himself a paddle to make it more controllable.

Aurelio was unnaturally lucky. The rapids he had to negotiate were mild, there were none of the usual whirlpools such as once sunk the steamer *Ucayali* on the Amazon when the captain was drunk, and there were no falls which he did not see in advance and circumvent with a portage. He bathed in waters full of piranha fish, which were not hungry because the dry season had not yet caused overcrowding, and when he urinated while swimming, no barbed sheatfish entered his urethra, so he did not suffer the fate of many a European explorer who has had to have his penis cut open to remove the fish. He was fortunate, too, that there were no rains to turn the rivers suddenly into cataracts and the jungle into a chain of giant lakes, and that no chushupi, rat snake or pit viper dropped from among the overhanging drapes of orchids, and that the anaconda that watched him pass had already swallowed a peccary.

In other ways Aurelio was not lucky. He was emaciated with hunger and recurring fevers, his body was covered with sores caused by jiggers, his flesh was crawling with the writhing grubs of the warble fly, and he was suffering from jungle madness. A relentless loneliness and self-doubt had overwhelmed him. There was nothing there at all for him to love or to like. He was stifled by the humidity, which made him perspire so copiously that a wave of his arm would send an arc of sweaty droplets flying. He was stifled by the arcane forms of life, the blinding colors that possessed the surreality of nightmares, the hideous lust for death, the brutality and loathing of all the grotesque creatures that ravenously consumed one another without thought or pity. He was oppressed and horrified by the merciless buzzing of mosquitoes, the calls of the trumpeter birds, the shrieks of the black-faced howler monkeys with their hideous goitered necks, the sound of trains mysteriously created by ducks in flight, the prehistoric grunts of caimans, the strange greetings of tapirs, sounding exactly like "Hi!," the irritating cracking of fingers made by the ageronia butterflies, the ringing of bells made by some mysterious fish beneath his raft, the outraged idiotic squawks of hundreds of different kinds of parrots, the coughs of the forest fox, the chatting of the ani birds, the demonic laughter of otters, the unearthly beautiful song of the white-eared puff-birds, the unnerving nocturnal hilarity of the laughing hawk, the "Koro! Koro!" of the cayenne ibis, the piping of guans, the jaguar calls of the tiger heron, the rattles of the cocoi heron, and, worst of all, the demented scrapings of armies of gigantic crickets.

Aurelio, overwhelmed by the horrifying plenitude of nature at her most sybaritic and dionysiac, was troubled by tormenting dreams in his hammock at night. By day he gibbered to himself and gesticulated as though addressing an audience. He started at every noise, like a nervous dog, and scratched furiously at his bites until they ulcerated and suppurated. He forgot to steer his raft and drifted, revolving on the current, his sanity and Inca stoicism inexorably draining away as his imagination filled with apparitions, monsters, and nostalgia for the cold, clean sierra.

He was awakened out of his verdantly foliated stupor by the sight one day of a man struggling with a huge *sucuri* snake with coils as thick as a man's thigh. The water snake had come up behind the fishing Indian, sunk its fangs into his shoulder, and wrapped him in coil after coil in order to crush his ribs and to drown him.

Aurelio had never seen such a snake in his life, and at first he thought it was a part of his tropical dream. He stood up on his raft and poled it to the scene of the unequal struggle. The Indian, a pocket Hercules of a man, was trying to slash at the snake with a bamboo knife but was on the point of losing consciousness. Aurelio leaped from his raft, which drifted away downstream, and threw himself on the serpent. He cut gaping gashes in it with his machete and was thrown down more than once by its lashing tail. Suddenly the animal released the Indian from its jaws and made as if to clamp Aurelio by the neck. The latter slashed its head, and the creature immediately went into violent death throes that were as lethal as its tactics in life. Aurelio strove to unwind its quivering and contracting body, and when the thrashing reptile had floated away to feed the fishes, he and the victim of the attack struggled to the bank and collapsed side by side.

Aurelio spent the first day of his ten years with the Navantes unconscious. The reasons he was not killed immediately by them were that he had saved the life of the subchief, Dianari, and that the people were curious to know who this ulcered apparition with the braid in his hair actually was.

The *paje* of the clan took ayahuasca and yague to learn from the spirits whether or not they would give up Aurelio's soul, and he bartered and parleyed with them for a long time before they consented. Then he blew smoke over Aurelio's body, scoured the parasites out of it with the teeth of the traira fish, and rubbed it all over with healing mud and bark and copaiba oil.

The *paje* was normally the most feared and therefore the most short-lived of all members of a clan, but this one was moved uncommonly by the spirit of compassion and had once lain motionless for two weeks while a nest of mice hatched in his hair. When Aurelio recovered, he was eventually to become a pupil to the *paje*.

Back in the Sierra, Don Hernández Almagro Méndez lost half his fortune in mines that were long ago exhausted, and an anomalous frost ruined his coffee plantation.

9
The Tribulations
of Federico

Life is nothing if not a random motion of coincidences and quirks of chance; it never goes as planned or as foretold; frequently one gains happiness from being obliged to follow an unchosen path or misery from following a chosen one. How often can one refrain from wondering what portentous events may not have arisen from some trivial circumstances that thereby has acquired a significance far beyond itself?

It was coincidence that a young man of fifteen, burned dark by the sun and his eyes flashing with a zeal born of hatred, was standing watch on the easternmost crag of the mountain when an athletic and middle-aged man of distinguished bearing, dressed like a peasant, passed below with a donkey. He carried a pair of binoculars, a camera, and a service revolver which was stuck in his belt. It was this weapon which attracted Federico's interest, because guerrillas are always short of weapons and have a habit of collecting them as others collect stamps or seashells.

Federico was much changed in the year of his absence. It was not just that he was taller, more arrogant, and more articulate; it was that he had come through immense difficulty and hardship and become at last a man in his own eyes.

It had been terrible in the beginning, after he had run away from the corpse, shaking with fear, horror, and nausea, and yet too proud to go home and also too ashamed. The worst thing was that he had not known what to eat, how to obtain it, or how to cook it when he had no matches, no pans, and had always eaten what his mother produced by apparent miracle, without thought to how she had turned raw matter into good food. He had remembered that you could eat corn, and for a day or two he stole it from the fields of the *minifundistas* which were scattered among the foothills, and ate it raw. Then he remembered that you could eat the roots of the yucca, which grew wild everywhere; but these were not good raw, so instead he ate mangoes, avocados, and guavas, which filled his belly but did not satisfy his hunger for meat.

It had not been very difficult to steal and kill a chicken, and it was not hard to pluck it; but he had no knife to disembowel it, so he walked for hours with it among the rocks until he found a piece of quartz sharp enough to pierce the yielding flesh of the belly. But he could not make a fire. He struck rocks together over dead leaves and dry grass; once or twice there were sparks, but there was never a fire. He rubbed wood together as Pedro did but did not know the right woods to use. That night he slept with the chicken beside him in his *mochila,* and in the morning the *mochila* was several yards away and the chicken gone. He wept with frustration and fury, cursing the wild beast that was so immoral as to steal his stolen chicken. Painstakingly he dammed off a little patch of a stream and hit a fat comelón on the head with a stick; it is a fish more delicate and succulent than trout, but not without fire. He abandoned it to the enciso ants when it began to stink. He lived off fruit until he stole a box of wax matches and a machete from the *barraca* of some unfortunate mountain peasant and discovered that the only way to cope without utensils was to roast on a spit or to bake in the cinders. He grew to understand later why the most prized possessions of the *guerrillero,* besides a weapon, are a magnifying glass, for focusing the rays of the sun, and a cooking pot.

The second to worst thing was solitude, for he was not of an age when it is eagerly sought and welcomed. It is true that there were times when he felt an extraordinary euphoria, when he was overwhelmed by the joyfulness of liberty as he cavorted in rock pools, being tweaked at by those strange little fish that love to eat the scabs off mosquito bites. He often felt entirely at one with himself and the world, living wild almost without purpose in an Eden of clear water, darting humming-birds, luminous vegetation, and a sky of startling angularity. But he knew he was already half crazy for want of friendship when a sob came to his throat one day at the sight of a large, friendly-faced cavy. His heart had reached out to the creature. He became possessed of a tyrannical grief.

Tears are wept best in company, so he bled them inwardly, missing with all his soul the life and the people he had left, and so it was that his already wild existence gradually became increasingly disordered. He stopped bothering to wash properly every day, fed himself only by starts, and talked loudly to himself whenever he did anything that required concentration, as though he could not have performed it without an explanation. The trouble was that he had been avoiding other people needlessly, thinking that they would be suspicious of him, as though his crime and his plans were written across his face and as though anyone would really have cared if they had been.

This phase of his existence came to an abrupt end when he rounded a curve of the path and came face-to-face with an old man pulling a donkey laden with bananas. It was to late to duck into the undergrowth.

"¡*Buena' día'!*" exclaimed the old man, grinning through his lack of teeth. "A fine day for hunting!" He was nodding his head vigorously toward the Lee-Enfield, and his voice had in it a warm and friendly crackle, like dried leaves.

Without taking time for thought Federico raised his right hand and replied, "*Saludes, señor,*" as he passed by. He turned and watched the old man disappear down the stony path clucking at his donkey and exclaiming "Ay, burro!" every time it felt disposed to stop. Federico realized at once that from now on he could walk unremarked and unmolested as a hunter, and he laughed at himself for behaving so fearfully hitherto. That night he set a trap as Pedro did, and in the morning he found he had a small brocket. He did not shoot it because bullets are precious and rare, but he knocked it senseless with a rock and cut its throat with his stolen machete.

Later that morning he entered a *pueblito* with the deer across his shoulders and swapped it for a fine knife, a chicken, several pounds of dried fish, matches, and a pair of Indian sandals with soles made of tire rubber. He stayed long enough to partake of a little of his deer, which was roasted that evening, and to take a small portion of its liver, the seat of its spirit, into the wood. Here he wrapped it in a dried banana leaf, and burned it at the base of a giant brazil nut tree in order to honor the angels that watched over his fortune. He gave thanks to them and also muttered a *secreto* which would bind them absolutely to guide his footsteps for at least one cycle of the moon. Back in the *pueblito* he knew that his prayer was answered when he was warned that not much farther up the sierra were *guerrilleros* who would probably steal his gun.

He met them three days later when he was rudely awakened in the middle of the night by a sharp kick in the ribs. He sat up with surprise and saw that he was encircled by four silhouettes, each of which featured the unmistakable shadow of a rifle.

"And who are you, *compañero?*" said one of the silhouettes, in a voice that sounded as though spoken through broken teeth.

Federico began to tremble with both fear and excitement, but mostly the former. "I am Federico," he said, in a voice as clear and bold as he could manage. "And if you are the *guerrilleros,* I have come to join you."

A flashlight clicked and shone unexpectedly in his face, so that he put up a hand to block its light from his eyes. One of the men stepped forward, grasped his hand, twisted it in a movement of the deftest violence, and wrenched his arm up behind his back. Federico blanched with pain and blinked against the terrible light of the flash. He realized that there was a knife against his throat, and the thought came to him that these were not *guerrilleros* but the army.

"And if we are the *guerrilleros, compañero,* why should you want to join us?" said the same voice, mockingly.

"There is no need for cruelty," said another voice, softer than the last. "Can't you see he is very young? Now tell us, little one, why you want to join us."

"The army," said Federico, too terrified to speak a full sentence.

"The army?" said the softer voice, puzzled. "What about it?"

"You killed Uncle Juanito and the others, and you tried to rape Farides, and you killed my dog. Are you going to kill me, too?" Federico fought to choke back the tears of desperation and horror.

The silhouettes began to laugh. "Let him go now, Franco," said the softer voice, and he was abruptly released from the agonizing half nelson.

"We are not the army," said the voice, "and I am sorry about your uncle and the dog. You are too young to be with us, but we have taken your rifle to help us in the struggle. I will give you a receipt, and you will be recompensed after the victory."

The flashlight shone on a notepad, and the man scribbled for a moment before tearing out the sheet of paper. He stepped forward and pushed it into the chest pocket of Federico's shirt. As he did so, Federico lurched upward, his fists flailing, screaming, "No! No! No!" It was too much; he could not allow his father's gun to be stolen. He hardly felt the blow on the back of his neck that knocked him unconscious on the forest floor.

When he awoke, it was daylight and a man was crouching over him offering him coffee. "How is your neck, *pobrecito?*" said the man.

"It hurts," said Federico, reaching behind him to feel the bruise that made it too painful to move his head.

"Our Franco is not known for gentleness," said the man. "But we decided in any case to keep you with us for a little time. We think it was brave what you did, and so we carried you here to see our leader, who will make a final decision. Drink this coffee and you will feel better."

"Where is my rifle?" said Federico.

"It's right next to you!" called the man as he walked away, and Federico looked down and saw that it was. He put the battered tin mug to his lips and startled himself with the scalding of the liquid. He thought he would let it cool, so he put it down and looked around him.

He was in a small village consisting of huts made of brush but in a dilapidated state, apparently long abandoned by the Indians. They were arranged roughly in a circle around a central area in which chickens and goats wandered freely, and he saw that there were some more huts on either side of the path that led into and away from the tiny settlement. He himself was lying facing the largest hut, which had a curious arrangement of brushwood and sticks on the top, splayed out in the manner of the sun's rays. He knew, somehow automatically, that it had once been a temple.

In the doorways of the huts and in the shade of the trees were groups of people in khaki fatigues. This was not exactly a uniform, because every guerrilla had added or taken away to suit his own fancy. One or two dressed simply in the manner of peasants, and some wore ponchos in the manner of Indians. Nearly everyone had a *mochila*, and all of them carried weapons. Some of them were industriously engaged in dismantling, cleaning, and reassembling their guns; others were fast asleep with their sombreros over their eyes. Three men and a woman were playing at dice, and two men nearby were ardently discussing conquests of the nonmilitary variety. Altogether there must have been about thirty people, of whom about ten were, if you looked carefully, quite plainly women. Federico found this disquieting because he had not expected it.

He was just finishing the coffee when its provider returned. "Come, señorito," he said. "It is time to see our leader."

Federico got up groggily, and the sun hit him like a falling wall when he stepped out of the shade, causing his head to throb. He crossed the little patch of earth that passed for a plaza, and where he kicked up the dust, the chickens dived in straight afterward in the hope of newly revealed grubs. He was led into the temple hut, where the sudden cool darkness deprived him momentarily of sight. During the period of adjustment his companion vanished, and when he could see again, he found himself standing in front of a woman seated behind a crude wooden table. She looked as though she were about twenty-seven years old and was dressed entirely in khaki.

"¿Vale?" she said. "Well?"

"I have come to see your leader," said Federico. "But I see he is not here." He looked about the room. "Am I to wait for him here?"

"No need," said the woman, the corners of her mouth twisting ironically. "He is already in this very room. Perhaps you should look harder."

Federico looked around again, saw nothing, and began to feel a kind of astonished confusion. "I'm sorry," he said, "but—"

"Your leader is a woman," she said. "If your sense of machismo is offended, you may leave at once, but without your rifle, and with your testicles in your mouth."

Deep shame came down upon the young boy, and he hung his head bitterly. "I am very sorry, señora," he said. "I just did not expect—"

"Shut your mouth before you say anything stupid!" she exclaimed. "I am not 'Señora,' I am *compañera* and my name is Remedios. Now tell me why you are here."

Federico recounted his story falteringly, and when he had finished, Remedios shook her head.

"It is not enough to want revenge. I don't want to fight alongside barbarians; it is barbarians against whom we fight."

"Why else should I fight?" asked Federico, genuinely puzzled. "I want justice."

"They are not the same thing!" she exclaimed. "I want you to remember what Guevara said, that all true revolutionaries are motivated by the profoundest feelings of love."

"I don't understand!" he said agitatedly.

"Now look," she replied. "I suspect you of being ignorant and inexperienced, but you are young enough to learn. I also know that you are brave and persistent, which is good. Therefore, I will provisionally accept you, and you will be taught everything in both theory and practice that you need to know, and I warn you that you will be fully extended both physically and mentally. Sometimes it will be torture. Good-bye for now. García!"

The man who had brought him the coffee reentered and led him out. On the way back to the shade the man said, "I suppose you are wondering why our leader is a woman."

Federico made a noise in his throat that was intended to be non-committal.

"It is because," García said, "she does not practice brutalities. We elected her when we realized that she had more brains and more balls than all of us put together."

10

Comandante Figueras
Disrupts a Fiesta

Doña Constanza was caught for a moment between Hispanic pride and a natural inclination to panic; it was not often she was confronted by a group of sweaty-looking uniformed ruffians asking strange questions. Tossing her head and looking at them disdainfully, she found her dignity and said, "What Communists?"

"What Communists!" echoed Figueras. "If you don't know where they are, you must be one of them." He lowered his rifle and pointed it at Doña Constanza's stomach.

She snorted and replied even more haughtily, "I am a Conservative and proud of it, and next time I see President Veracruz, I shall personally inform him of your disgusting manners and violent temperament. Kindly don't point that weapon at me."

The comandante was torn between fear and the temptation to ridicule. His instinct was to slap her down and humiliate her, but his common sense told him that someone who was so obviously rich and well bred probably really did know the president. Doña Constanza glanced at his shoulder and said, "Your number is FN3530076. I have already memorized it."

Figueras and Doña Constanza stared each other down, she with absolute contempt and he with a growing conviction that he had already lost. Then one of his soldiers, a tubby and bleary-eyed man with a sadistic face, piped up with "Let's kill the rich bitch, Comandante."

Figueras, profoundly grateful for the excuse to break his gaze away from Doña Constanza's, whirled around and slapped the astonished soldier across the face. "How dare you suggest such a disgraceful thing?" he roared. "You dishonor the national army! You will be court-martialed unless you apologize at once!" He brought the butt of his carbine down on the man's foot, and the soldier hopped up and down, clutching it.

"I am sorry, Comandante," he said in an aggrieved and sulky voice. "It's what we usually do."

"Infamy!" bellowed Figueras with a wild glare in his eyes, which had more than a tinge of desperation in them. He turned to Doña Constanza, bowing and clicking his heels. "I apologize profusely, se-ñora," he said, and a little bead of perspiration ran down his temple and disappeared down into his collar. "However, I must ask you again, where are the Communists?"

"There aren't any," she said. "The army came in and killed a lot of people some time ago, including Juanito, who was my stableman. They were supposed to be Communists, but I have my doubts. What do Communists look like?"

Figueras wondered for a second if she was trying to be funny or was genuinely stupid. "Señora, we have received reports of gun battles and explosions in this vicinity."

"Then the reports are mistaken," she replied. "There have been no such things."

"Nonetheless, we are obliged to investigate. May we please set up our camp on your property? I assure you there will be no damage."

"Indeed, there will not," she replied tartly, "or the governor will hear of it—I also know General Fuerte. You may use the field nearest the pueblo, and I will be obliged if you do not disturb the horses. They are most valuable."

"Perhaps," said the lieutenant as they walked away, "she is in league with the Communists."

"She is an oligarch, and oligarchs are not Communists."

"Camilo Torres was an oligarch," said the lieutenant.

"Camilo Torres was a priest," replied Figueras.

"Then perhaps she is afraid?"

"Somehow I doubt it," said Figueras, with feeling. "Lieutenant, take four armed men and question the people in the pueblo. You must return by dusk and report to me directly."

The lieutenant saluted with his usual lazy wave of the hand and departed shortly afterward with a corporal and three nervous conscripts, all of whom had bayonets fixed and twitching trigger fingers. They were startled twice by vultures, once by a steer, and once by a scarecrow in the cornfield, which was holding a branch fashioned into the shape of a gun, so that by the time they reached the village, in which nothing was happening at all, they all were in urgent need of refreshment. The lieutenant ordered them to search house to house and to ask questions; he himself went to the bar at the farther end and drank two Inca-Colas and an Aguila. His men searched principally in the brothels and satisfied themselves that there were no terrorists even in the orifices of the whores, reporting back to the lieutenant that when they asked if there were any armed ruffians in the district, they invariably received the reply "*Ustedes solo*" or "Only yourselves." They also reported that that very evening there began a two-day fiesta, a thing irresistible to any trueborn patriot. This convinced them that there could not possibly be any guerrillas in the area, and it also convinced Figueras when they reported it back to him, so that he immediately ordered himself and all his men to attend it, for the sake of "enhancing public relations."

The fiesta had been invented twenty years before by villagers anxious to commemorate the foundation of the community. As nobody knew when this had been, a *brujo* had been consulted who, by means of sacred herbs steeped in *ron cana* in the trepanned skull of a murderer, drunk by a clairvoyant mulatta, had established the exact date and the fact that it had taken place in the afternoon. The pueblo was 321 years old.

Toward five o'clock in the evening there began a steady influx of campesinos from the surrounding countryside, all of them bearing machetes in leather-tasseled scabbards at their side. This was by no means a signal of hostile intent, for it is unknown for any peasant not to have a machete at his side at all times. Those on horse- or muleback have shorter ones than those on foot; these former are often chromed and made of softer (and more easily sharpened) steel than the heavy-duty machete of the peasant on foot, which is never chromed. The machete is the indispensable all-purpose tool; machetes are sharpened assiduously on special boulders in the rivers until they are sharp enough both to shave with and to chop down trees. They are used to slaughter animals by decapitation, which is very quick and humane, and to clear ground of unwanted growth by a skimming motion flowing from the wrist. They are excellent for work among the sugarcanes and also in the banana plantations, where, once the fruit is ripe, you cut down the stems of the plants completely, since bananas are not grown on trees, as most gringos seem to believe, but are, in fact, a giant species of grass. Machetes, when they are old and worn out or broken, are ground down on the stones to make all manner of knives.

Machetes are made mostly in Colombia, and these days the handles are, regrettably, made of Bakelite, while the elaborate Indian patterns in bright colors that are conspicuous on the scabbards are, on close inspection, revealed to be made of plastic stitched on with thin string. Foreigners are sometimes surprised to find that their souvenir machete bears the stamp of a company called Collins.

A further use of machetes was for fishing. The fiesta about to begin was largely a fish fiesta on account of the fact that the founder of the village was one Esteban the fisherman. So it was that this evening the festivities began with a solemn procession down to the Mula River, which was mercifully still in an undammed state. Leading the procession of 150 people was Pedro, carrying his Spanish musket and surrounded by his dogs. Pedro was naturally the leader because of his age, his mastery of sorcery, and his fearlessness; tonight at midnight he would drink ayahuasca in front of the whole crowd, and in his trance he would meet with Esteban the fisherman, who would divulge to him all that must be done in the following year.

Behind Pedro came two virgins, certified as such by a committee of women, bearing straw effigies of the Blessed Virgin, which would be cast in the river before fishing began. Behind these were Hectoro with the black glove still on his rein hand, his revolver at his side, and his leather *bombachos* creaking on his legs as he walked. Today he felt awkward at being on foot, as he never left his mule or his horse except to eat or sleep or fornicate and had even trained his men to make concrete and mortar in real gaucho style, by riding their horses backward and forward over the mix. No man, however, could be mounted on this procession, not even Hectoro, and so he walked, feeling foolish and vulnerable.

Beside Hectoro came Josef, who as ever was thinking about the ignominy of not having a proper funeral, and behind these two were Profesor Luis, Consuelo, Farides, and all the occupants of the pueblo and its countryside, including the children, who chanted a repetitive song in order to charm the fish. Everybody, including all children above the age of ten, smoked a large *puro* cigar so that the air would be fragrant enough to repel evil spirits and thick enough to materialize the good ones.

The procession passed the hacienda of Don Emmanuel, who was preparing an alcoholic *guarapo* made of pineapple skins, in order to treat the processors on their way home, and crossed the field to the Mula, which had this year swapped to its southern course during the rains. Here Pedro turned and raised his arms, and a silence fell on the crowd. To his right the sun began its sudden descent behind the hills, until its reddening rays struck the snow of the mountains opposite and the sky glowed and vibrated in the 360-degree sunset that strikes religion into the hearts even of animals and birds, which fall into a hush broken only by the riple of water.

Pedro threw back his head and his arms and, as though encircling all the holiness of the universe, began the long ululating chant. Against the stillness of the falling night the pagan enchantment of his voice stirred the crowd so that chills of fire ran from their loins to their spines, and each felt a glow of invisible light dance above their head. Many stood as though paralyzed, with tears streaming silently down their cheeks, and others sank reverently to the earth, brought down on their knees by the incomprehensible and the numinous. Against the rapidly gathering darkness the figure of Pedro the hunter began to grow. At first it seemed he was larger by a hand's width, but then he seemed to be as tall as a horse. Soon he appeared as tall as a tree, and the people knew that he had assumed the form of a god. Summoned up from the stomach, the seat of emotion, Pedro's voice issued forth from his throat, now echoing as a cavern echoes. Nobody understood the words in that forgotten language. People did not understand it, but they apprehended it; they apprehended the language of the ancient gods of Africa.

When Pedro stopped, a final chill of fire ran back down the spines of the people and returned to their loins. There was a stillness, a relief, and a sense of privilege and humility.. Pedro was once more a silver-haired black hunter, now leaning on his musket and smiling benignly. "*Vamos, pescadores,*" he said.

The straw virgins were cast into the water, the people lit their lanterns and torches, drew their machetes from their scabbards, and waded carefully into the river, for although it was only knee-deep, its current was extremely strong. The fish, confused, disoriented, and attracted by the lights, swam up near the surface and wriggled blindly among the fishers. Each man and woman struck one fish, for that was all that was permissible, and then they waded out to wait for the others. It is no easy matter to catch fish in this manner, for one has to allow for the displacement of light when shining through water, and more important, the broad blade of a machete is easily sent off course when slicing through water, so that it is alarmingly easy to wound one's own feet and legs by mistake. This is no small thing when the blow is fierce and the blade razor-sharp; it is easy to remove a foot or sever a muscle with the suddenness of thought.

As soon as one's fish was brought to the bank, one's luck was set for the following year, the degree depending upon whether one had caught a gamitana, a zungaro, a chitari, or a comelón; in this way everyone had some luck, but some had more than others, an attitude which is both optimistic and realistic at the same time. When all the people had a fish, the crowd proceeded back to the village, drinking Don Emmanuel's *guarapo* on the way; Don Emmanuel himself joined the procession, his red beard glinting in the torchlight and his crude remarks causing squeals of delight among the older women. For the rest there was a mood of nervousness, for by that time everybody knew that the army was once more in the area and that there would be soldiers at the fiesta.

The soldiers were already in the village when its inhabitants arrived. Comandante Figueras wore his cap low over his eyes in his anxiety not to be recognized, and as the people drew into the single street, he brought his two columns of men sharply to attention. The procession stopped, and there was an uneasy murmur. Figueras stepped forward and saluted the crowd, a gesture that would have struck them all as wildly comical if it had not also seemed so odd.

"Citizens!" he exclaimed in a voice that was as full of fervor as he could feign. "Do not be alarmed! We are on our way to another place, and we join you in your celebrations before we leave, hoping to bear with us your good wishes!"

He turned about, snapped his heels together, and bawled, "Present arms!" The men presented arms and in one slightly ragged movement brought the weapons to their shoulders, stepped forward with one foot, and pointed the barrels to the sky. "Fire!" he yelled, and a crowd of vultures hastily left the tree nearby. "Fire!" he yelled twice more, and the metallic clash of the shots receded into the night. Figueras turned once more to the perplexed and astonished crowd, and called out, "¡Vamos!"

In English, Don Emmanuel muttered to himself, "Twenty-one-bum salute," and Josef tapped Hectoro on the shoulder. "There will be trouble tonight."

"Good," said Hectoro.

The fiesta proceeded at first better than might be expected; Profesor Luis had rigged his little windmill generator to a record player, so that people could dance. Every time the breeze changed the music went faster or slower, but nobody minded because it's not difficult to dance faster or slower after all.

A dancing area had been cordoned off in the street, and very soon so much dust had been kicked up by the dancers that it was impossible to see anything. In those days before rock music had got as far as the village everybody was crazy about Bambuco and Vallenato, two types of dance music characterized by a fascinating complexity of syncopation and by the use of the tiple, a ten-stringed instrument that looks like a small guitar and is played rather like a mandolin or a bazouki. At that time the popular dance was El Pollo Del Vallenato which was intended to be an imitation of the chicken. The people would scratch in the dust with one foot in imitation of looking for bugs, they would strut with the ludicrous solemnity of cockerels, they would make darting movements of the head in imitation of pecking, and they would flap their arms. At the end of the record they would let loose a startling cacophony of clucks and squawks and then break into delighted laughter before peeling away to fetch another bottle of Aguila.

On account of the night and the fact that everyone was disinhibited by alcohol and made expansive by marijuana, nobody had recognized

Figueras, who was soon lying flat on his face outside Consuelo's whore-house, whose small staff had been augmented by a busload of excep-tionally young whores from Chiriguaná. It was a cause for much pride if one had a little whore in the family, because of the excellent income, and so many girls began at twelve; however, girls who were not whores were expected to remain virgins until sixteen, and marriage. Any de-tected lapse of this code was dealt with by bullets. It must be said, nevertheless, that on this night the whoring was intense and arduous, and many girls came out to dance rather than get wearier and sorer.

It was drawing near to midnight, and the revelry had reached such a pitch that nobody really knew what was going on anymore, when a late-arriving vaquero decided to make a grand entrance in the style of the ancient cowboy films that were the staple fare of urban cinemas. He galloped into the village, whooping and firing his revolver into the air.

The effect on the reeling soldiers was dramatic and instantaneous. They all reached the same conclusion at the same time: They had been set up for a Communist ambush. Mayhem ensued as they dropped to the ground or dodged behind buildings, firing wildly into the crowd, which dispersed as though by magic, leaving behind a horse whinnying in stricken pain, two dead infants, three dead adults, and several more wounded, who lay moaning and quivering in the dust without hope of rescue.

The gun battle that ensued lasted until each man had used up all his ammunition, which took about an hour and a half. Not knowing where the Communists were, the soldiers fired at the places where they could see the flashes of shots—which is to say, they shot at one another. This was done in a haze of intoxication and bowel-wrenching panic, and so only four were slaughtered and ten wounded. The hideous finale of this melancholy episode occurred when a soldier lobbed a grenade behind a partition and a corporal emerged from behind it, staggering and clutch-ing at his stomach. He lurched to the center of the street, stood mo-tionless for a second, and began to howl a long unearthly howl of terror and supplication. He raised his arms to heaven, and in that one move-ment his entrails burst from his stomach and slithered grotesquely to the earth. Whimpering and weeping, he fell to the ground among them.

The soldiers, stunned into sobriety by horror, began to call out to one another and then very cautiously began to emerge. They gathered around the body of their corporal and looked at it and at one another in silence, looking away and shrugging their shoulders with gestures of "I am not guilty; all this has nothing to do with me" whenever another caught their eye.

Figueras awoke from his stupor outside Consuelo's whorehouse and sat up groggily, rubbing his eyes. He rose unsteadily to his feet and urinated for a very long time against the wall of the building. He belched with sonorous satisfaction and turned around. For a second he could not believe his eyes as he stared with stupid incomprehension at the carnage around him; "*Mierda maricón*" was all he could think of to say.

He swayed as he walked over to his men, looked down at the corpse, and crossed himself. "Let's go back to camp," he said, his face ashen white.

The soldiers left the village in a clumsy attempt at furtiveness, and the villagers slowly began to appear from the houses. They stood in the street exactly as the soldiers had done, in bewilderment and amazement. Profesor Luis turned off the record player, which all this time had been repeating and repeating again the merry strains of "El Pollo del Vallenato," and Pedro spoke up clearly. "They must be repaid for this!" Hectoro took his revolver from his belt and strode off. Ten shots were heard as he dispatched the wounded soldiery.

When Figueras and his men left in the truck and the Jeep the next day, they passed the bodies of some of the soldiers hanging in the trees, already half stripped by the vultures. Beneath the bodies the dogs fought for the bits that fell off. Figueras did not stop. Nor did he stop until he reached Valledupar, a town in which he later heard the news that he was to be awarded another decoration for his heroic resistance to a vastly superior guerrilla force. He was also to receive command of an enlarged force of men who were to destroy the Communists once and for all, by whatever means.

11

Aurelio's Education Among the Navantes

The Navantes were proud that white people were scared of them and called their river the River of the Dead. They dropped hints that it had been they who had killed Colonel Fawcett, his son, and Raleigh Rimell, and they possessed a carbine said to have belonged to Winton, whom they had purportedly poisoned with adulterated *chicha* and set adrift in a canoe. They were hospitable to white people on condition that they never tried to leave; if they did, they were clubbed to death with *bordanas*. They called a knife a couteau, a word they had learned from a French explorer and pronounced in the finest Parisian accent, and they knew a song called "Cuddle Up a Little Closer, Baby Mine" that they had learned by heart from a diamond and gold prospecting party of *yanquis*, Peruvians, and Brazilians that had befriended them with gifts of salt and displays of Roman candles, but that had managed to escape in 1935, in the time when Maharon was chief. The song, a little altered by the folk process, was still sung at initiations of subchiefs and at weddings.

The Navantes, like the jungle Indians in general, are the most widely traveled people in the world even though they never leave the forest or the *cerrado*. They accomplish their cosmopolitan itineraries with the aid of ayahuasca potions, which give them unlimited powers of telepathy (hence the alternative name of *telepatina*), and the ability to leave their bodies and arrive at their destination without crossing the intervening space. They were particularly fond of going to New York, where there were millions of boxes that moved by themselves and huge termite mounds where people lived like ants in vast colonies. It was those travelings through the noosphere that persuaded them that they never wanted to leave the jungle, where life was very easy, as there was no routine whatsoever and one never did anything at all unless one felt like it.

They lived in very large *chozas* which contained upwards of thirty people each and also the animals that they took to bed with them for warmth at night. The husbands' hammocks were above their wives', which were above their children's, and after dark they would block the low entrances to the hut and kept logs smoldering so that a homely atmosphere of impenetrable smoke was created. There was also a communal hut used for some parts of ceremonies and for councils, and the huts were always laid out in the shape of the crescent moon, which they believed to be made of *oropéndola* feathers. When the time came to leave a village because the soil was exhausted, they sometimes left their household possessions behind in order not to have to carry them; otherwise the women carried them because they were considered to be the owners.

The Navantes had no jobs and did no work beyond cultivating bananas, corn, wheat, and groundnuts. The rest of the time they amused themselves. The young women made elaborate hammocks, while the old women made *chicha* by chewing cassava and spitting it into a bowl in order to ferment it. The men spent most of their days hunting and fishing. In his time with them Aurelio came to realize that in fact, food very nearly does press itself in one's mouth in the jungle after all. Virtually every animal, including the haruzam toad, was edible; there were forty-seven varieties of edible nuts, including the wonderful *castanas*; and they had several ingenious methods of fishing. One of these necessitated standing like a stork in the water with bow and arrow (the latter being nearly six feet long). Another method was to erect a barrier across the river like a wickerwork hurdle. Some would wait on one side of the hurdle in their pirogue canoes while the others would thrash the water and drive the panicking fish to leap over it into the canoes. Another method was to beat the water with ushchachera branches, so that the poisoned fish simply floated to the surface to be harvested. The variety of fish was enormous. Piranha was very tasty but full of irritating bones. The *bufeo* was considered a friend and killed only when one wanted the skin of the female genitals to make an aphrodisiac talisman. The pirarucu was the largest freshwater fish in the world and took a very long time for even a whole village to eat. Crampfish was not eaten for fear of paralysis, candirus were nearly six feet long and made a good feast, characins had tubes in their upper jaws for the fangs of the lower to nest in, and their teeth or those of the traira were excellent for the extraction of thorns and general surgery. The mailed catfish was delicious when grilled on palm leaves, but the electric eel was to be studiously avoided; when a good catch was made, the returning fisherman would whoop with joy as he approached the *aldea* so that everyone could run out to admire it. To keep it fresh, it would be buried in wet sand.

When it came to hunting animals, the Navantes very rarely used the cerebetana blowpipe with darts tipped with curare. Instead, they were very skilled archers. They had a method of holding a sheaf of arrows in the left hand that gripped the bow so that one could keep up a rapid fire. Arrows were very difficult to make, and this was probably the only reason that they expended so much effort in becoming expert. The arrival of missionaries was always greeted with enthusiasm because after they had been killed or driven out, one could extract the nails from their cabins to use as arrowheads, these being much better than bones. The Navantes hunted for four reasons: for food, to get rid of dangerous predators, for tools, and for adornment. The capybara, a kind of mentally retarded guinea pig and the largest rodent in the world, provided teeth that made perfect chisels, and the Indians hunted birds with blunt arrows. They did this to pull out the prettiest feathers to make acangatara headdresses. When the stunned birds felt better, they were either set free or kept in captivity to become dejected featherfarms. Sooner or later they would die of incomprehension.

The Navantes were particularly fond of eating parrots; ciapu (banana soup); bushmaster snakes; turtles' eggs dug out of praias; curassows, both tufted and razor-billed; wild honey; an obnoxious greasy soup called piquia, which they gave to unwanted visitors; and monkeys of all descriptions, which they shot with four-pronged arrows and which looked alarmingly like children when skinned and were full of intestinal parasites.

They regarded animals as equals, neither inferior nor superior, and always kept large numbers of unlikely pets. Some animals they would not eat at all, such as the sun bittern, which ate lice, or the *urutaú* bird, which was the special guardian of maidens, or squirrels, which they associated with sleep. They showed no repugnance at eating vast numbers of leaf-cutting ants, wasp grubs, and locusts, which, when toasted, tasted pleasantly of aniseed.

Hunting for ants was one of the few times when a woman would remove her *uluri*. This was a little triangle of bark with sides a bit more than an inch long, attached to a plaited thread worn around the waist. From the lower apex of the triangle ran another plaited thread that passed snugly between the outer labia and was attached above the buttocks at the back. The purpose of the *uluri* was to draw attention to the genitals, since the triangle acted like a little signpost toward them. They were considered the mark of the postpubertal woman, and she was indecently undressed without one. Women always had a spare triangle, just in case. Both men and women also wore necklaces made of about a thousand tiny circles of snail shells. The women would take six months to make these, by grinding the shells on stones until they were very small and thin. Each circle would be drilled in the center with a tooth or a piece of hardwood and then strung on wild cotton. Boys usually wore one of these necklaces around the waist, and men usually wore nothing at all except perhaps a necklace of jaguar claws or bark ringlets around their ankles. They used to spend hours delousing and deticking each other, just like the occitan Cathars of medieval times, according to pecking order, lice and ticks being the sole parasites that resisted removal during their frequent daily baths. The only sense in which they were ever clothed was when they were plastered from head to foot in the pigments they employed for celebrations. Piquia oil (as used in the soup) was mixed with annatto to make yellows and reds, white was made of wood ash, and genipap was excellent for blues and blacks. These dyes made their naturally light skins tobacco brown and also helped keep away the hordes of stinging insects, such as buffalo gnats, and the sandflies that caused lechmaniosis leprosy. In their anxiety to be as unclothed as possible, the people would conscientiously depilate their whole bodies, excepting their heads, with their fingers dipped in wood ash, giving rise to the popular myth that Amazonian Indians are naturally hairless.

Aurelio, despite his braid, assimilated very quickly into the life of the tribe. He learned the art of living a perfectly simple life without having to do too much work; he learned how to be busy without being industrious and to take a childish joy in simple things, such as *toke-toke*, the word for sexual frolics.

Aurelio acquired the art of happiness; the Navante idea of heaven was that it was exactly the same as earth, except that one would meet there those who had gone before and also the tribal ancestor Mavutsi-nin. Aurelio learned from the *paje* the full art of medicine and the methods of contacting and negotiating with the spirits. He learned all the myths and their most powerful esoteric meanings. He learned the names of all the stars and constellations, including the gaps between them, his personal one being the "tapir," which lies just by the Southern Cross. He learned their language and hence discovered a new way of thinking. The Navantes had no words for classes of things, so they were not prone to making generalizations. They collected in immense detail the names of specific things, however, which meant that their language tended to evolve with such startling rapidity that it was necessary to go and stay with other villages of the tribe to keep up with developments. An English anthropologist once described their language as primitive and barely usable, having once questioned a girl who had been expelled from the tribe as mentally defective. In fact, their vocabulary was easily larger than Shakespeare's and definitely larger than the hasty anthropologist's.

Aurelio learned of all those aspects of social life that make a people distinctive and became popular with the children by making them toys in the traditional style. For example, their rattles were made of a cicada fastened to a stick, which vibrates indignantly when shaken. He fastened balls of cotton to mutucana horseflies so that the children could watch them fly short distances, become exhausted, and then catch them again. He made them little bows and arrows, and especially the kinds of arrow that are tipped with hollow nutshells that ring in flight.

Aurelio learned the art of wrestling, which had become quite sophisticated since the captive *yanqui* had taught them jujitsu and which, just like judo, finished when one contestant was pinned to the ground. He picked up the art of chest patting, which was done as a greeting and varied according to perceptions of social status. He found out how to make animal calls to communicate in the forest and also to lure prey. He was taught how to make knives and arrowheads out of teeth, mussel shells and split bamboo, he played music in the huts on panpipes, bark trumpets, and the goo. No woman was ever allowed to see the musicians play in case she should think it effeminate, and any woman who did see was obliged to allow the offended musician to prove his virility. If the woman was a little girl, the musician would have to wait until she reached puberty before he could retrieve his pride.

Aurelio was married twice through the mating dance and learned what it was to have to feed a mother-in-law, to whom one was not allowed to speak except through one's wife. Both his wives, before they died, produced children, so that he learned to undergo the couvade. He took to his hammock for four days at each birth, groaning with the pain of the delivery, to be tended by his anxious spouse, who had given birth squatting over a hole in the ground. In this way the men took away the pain of birth and took it on themselves.

Twice he made the marriage vows:

> "I will nourish this woman as I do myself.
> "I will take the same care of her as I do of myself.
> "I will give her the use of my virility."

He never had to beat his wives for infidelity, as required by law, and his wives were never raped, so he did not have to beat any rapists, who were forbidden to resist, or use the rapist's wife in the same way. Crime was, in fact, unknown, except against other tribes, when it was common to attempt to abduct their women, especially the ones who were good potters. The women accepted this as normal and settled down happily wherever they were, some of them having belonged at one time or another to several different tribes.

The women had their own rites to which the men were not a party. When a husband died, the wife cut her hair off, and no one could ask her hand in marriage until it was regrown. This permitted a decent period of grieving, and since the hair took about nine months to grow, it incidentally prevented any confusions about paternity. The women also believed that the period of transition during puberty was very dangerous, and there should be no shocks, surprises, undue elation, or disappointments during that time. Accordingly they sat on palm shoots in a hut, behind a screen, with their hair over their faces for six months, not talking to anyone and only going out at night for a walk with their mothers. They would emerge from this chrysalis state as full-grown women who were entitled to wear the *uluri* and get married. The boys, less privileged, were allowed only three months to become men and were never allowed into the special corral for menstruating women, which was like a social club for which musicianship was the counterpart for men.

How and why Aurelio lost his wives and his children and how and why he had to leave the Navantes are part of another story that waits to be told, as is his meeting with Carmen in Chiriguaná and his marriage; but in the details given here are found the reasons why Aurelio, an Aymara Indian of the sierra, became so expert a jungle dweller—a thing that always puzzled Pedro—and why, since this is the only way one can proceed in the jungle, he always walked in single file for the rest of his life.

12

Federico Is Taught to Be a Guerrilla and General Fuerte Is Captured

García was assigned to be Federico's instructor and special minder; to Federico's surprise he turned out to be one of those revolutionary priests who dispute every teaching and every command of the church and yet remain through and through a priest and a Catholic, at the same time as being a Marxist and a revolutionary.

García had come from a middle-class family in Medellín, a pleasant town on the side of a mountain from which Profesor Luis also came. At the age of nineteen he had fallen in love with a young woman of better family who had been sent to live in Costa Rica with relatives in order to put an end to the socially unacceptable relationship. In San José she had married a stupendously wealthy Uruguayan, and García, heartbroken, took instead to the arms of the Holy Mother Church. As a seminarian he was solitary, serious, and studious, but he sometimes alarmed his superiors by expressing heterodox opinions. He was therefore sent far into the countryside to a little town where such things did not make any difference, and there he set about his duties conscientiously.

It often happens that certain women of the bourgeoisie conceive a hysterical and irrational passion for their parish priest, even going as far as to prostrate themselves before him, offering him the use of their charms. When this first happened to Father García, he tried to be gentle and understanding, and he told the woman firmly but sympathetically that such a thing was impossible. But she continued to pester him and to follow him so persistently that soon the whole town was scandalized by the quite unfounded rumor that the priest was an adulterer. One day, in a rage of frustration, he told the woman in no uncertain terms to leave him alone. She took his rebukes more personally than Christianly, and in her wounded pride she haughtily vowed revenge: She wrote to the bishop that the priest had attempted to rape her on frequent occasions, especially in the confessional box and upon the altar.

The bishop's investigators arrived secretly and soon found themselves listening in bars and whorehouses to all kinds of salacious gossip about Father García, along with numerous ribald jokes featuring Father García as protagonist. At his trial before the ecclesiastical court Father García protested his innocence in vain and was defrocked by the bishop for fornication.

The sentence weighed heavily on Father García's mind, for he was only too aware that in falsely condemning an innocent man, the bishop had committed a mortal sin. Night upon night he was tormented by vile dreams in which the bishop writhed hideously amid the flames and tortures of hell.

One morning after fervent prayer García decided to save the bishop's soul by destroying his own innocence and committing the very crime for which he had been condemned. In the brothel the girl crossed herself before she made love to him, and García gave her absolution afterward. It would not be far from the truth to say that García acquired a taste for fornication thereafter; he quite possibly believed that by committing the sin as often as possible he made doubly sure of saving the bishop's soul.

García continued his ministry on his own and unsanctioned by the church by becoming mendicant. He wandered from pueblo to pueblo, comforting the sick and the dying, begging alms, preaching the Gospel, and blessing the unions that substituted for marriage. Daily he grew more angry, bewildered, and depressed by the poverty, ignorance, and suffering of the campesinos, and when he was finally abducted by the guerrillas on suspicion of being a spy, he found himself at last among his true brothers.

They had taken him when one of their number had observed him entering and leaving three brothels in a row. Reasoning that he could not possibly be a priest, must therefore be in disguise, and must therefore be a spy, Franco had marched him off at the business end of his Kalashnikov.

The camp at that time was run by the second leader; the first leader had organized an extortion campaign throughout the countryside in order to raise funds for the revolution. When a very large sum had been amassed, he had absconded with it to Spain. The second leader was to do exactly the same thing a year later, but at the time of which we speak he was unpleasantly present and knocked Father García about with his boots and his rifle butt until the priest was spitting blood and almost unable to cross himself. He was tied to a tree and left for the night, but in the morning he proved he was a priest by reciting the service for the burial of the dead all the way through, after which he absolved the second leader of any blame for the previous night's violence. This left the guerrillas with a dilemma: Most of them did not want to kill a priest, however lecherous, and on the other hand, it seemed unwise to let him go because he might inform. The second leader wanted to cut his tongue out so that he could not talk, cut his hands off so that he could not write, pull his eyes out so that he would not recognize them again, and then let him go. "These are small things to lose for your country," he told Father García solemnly.

"There is no need," replied García. "With your permission, I will stay and fight alongside you."

"We would shoot you at the first sign of betrayal," said the second leader, considerably taken aback.

"At the first sign of betrayal I will shoot myself," replied García.

"¡Tiene cojones!" exclaimed the guerrillas, chuckling.

García was a small, lithe man, with quick movements and the lugubrious face of a hare. Very soon he was bearded and burned brown like all the others and had the same crow's-feet about the eyes from squinting into the distance against the sun. However, he never discarded his ragged ecclesiastical dress even though it somewhat hampered his movements and made him very hot indeed. In time his gentleness, his heroic deeds, his wise counsel, and his active concern for his comrades endeared him to the whole band, and even the genuinely atheist Marxists among them grew to respect him, especially because he could quote pieces of the Gospel that sounded just like Engels.

It was García who took the fledgling Federico under his wing and taught him how to use a gun, how to trap animals, which berries were poisonous, which plants were medicinal, always fought beside him in skirmishes, and always tended the cuts that Federico liked to think of as "wounds." He it was also who heard Federico's confessions and absolved him of the death of the tall campesino whose goat he had tried to shoot.

He was with Federico when the latter spotted General Carlo María Fuerte from the top of the crag.

"Let us take his gun," whispered Federico.

García considered for a moment, tugging the end of his beard.

"I think," said García, "that if he has a revolver rather than a rifle, he must be something a bit different. No one sane uses a revolver for hunting. I think we had better take him and his gun and show them both to Remedios. I also think that it is suspicious that he has binoculars; peons do not habitually carry them, in my experience."

Federico restrained himself from showing that he was impressed by García's reasoning; replying with the air of an equal, he nodded and said, "In addition, García, his burro is too healthy to be campesino. That, too, is suspicious."

García smiled to himself and indicated to Federico with a stabbing motion of his finger that he was to go down first. Adeptly and silently they slithered and skipped down the mountainside and stationed themselves in the scrub at either side of the steep path, just on the blind side of a bend.

General Carlo María Fuerte came around the corner, whistling a sentimental tune from Juárez to find himself face-to-face with two heavily armed men, one of them obviously little more than a boy. He was so surprised that all he could do was say, "¿*Bandidos?*" in a strangled tone of voice.

The boy leveled a rather long and old-looking weapon and said proudly, "No, señor; *guerrilleros.*"

"Ah," said the general, even more taken aback.

"May I inquire who you are?" said García, "and what you are doing here?" García prodded the binoculars and the camera with the end of his submachine gun, clicked his gun, and added, "May I also ask the function of this apparatus?"

The general decided to tell part of the truth, as his instincts told him that he might pay a heavy price for lies. "I am a researcher into butterflies and hummingbirds. At present I am researching humming-birds, and my name is Fuerte."

"Ah, hummingbirds," said García. "Are you familiar with a wonderful piece by Sagreras called '*Imitación al Vuelo del Picaflor*'?"

"Indeed," said Fuerte. "I heard it in Buenos Aires once. I know it by the shorter title of '*El Colibrí*.'"

"It is a pleasure to meet a cultivated man," exclaimed García. "We shall continue our discussion while you come to meet our leader. Please do not oblige me to use force."

Federico jabbed his Lee-Enfield into the small of the general's back, and they set off up the path with no events other than the frequent refusals and whimsical obstinacies of the general's burro, which Federico was leading by its halter.

By the time they reached the deserted Indian village which served as their camp, García and the general had discussed the Venezuelan waltzes of Antonio Lauro, agreed that the Paraguayan guitarist Agustín Barrios must have been very eccentric and blessed with huge hands, had deplored the music of the Argentine Ginastera, praised that of the Mexican Chávez and also that of the Brazilian Villa-Lobos. When they arrived, García was singing "Mis Dolencias" to the general to demonstrate a real case of "*saudade*," and the general was listening to him with surprise, having only just noticed that his frayed and filthy garments were those of a priest.

As they entered the camp, a crowd of guerrillas appeared as if from nowhere to witness the event, some of them not breaking off their conversations; the general heard them as through a thick plate of glass, wondering if this was all really happening to him.

In a moment he was standing before Remedios, who listened attentively to García's story. "Search him," she ordered.

García turned to the general. "With your permission?"

The general nodded assent.

Unfortunately for him, the general had not had the presence of mind to attempt to dispose of his *cedula* and his military identification card, and García very quickly found them in his shirt pocket.

"*¡Madre de Dios!*" exclaimed Remedios. "We have here not only a general but the military governor of César! I don't believe this! We must instantly hold a council. Federico!"

Federico ran out into the sunlight, straight into the pack of people who had been attempting to listen. "Council! Council!" he shouted, waving his arms, and more ragged warriors emerged from the huts and hurried to sit down in a ring in front of Remedios's hut, eagerly asking one another what was going on.

Inside the hut García reproached the general. "You lied. You said you were a lepidopterist and a hummingbird expert. To lie is a sin before God and very stupid before men with guns."

The general looked at him with amusement. "I told no lies. My book on the nation's butterflies is in my baggage if you care to look. You may read it if it pleases you."

"Thank you," said García, "and may I also read *Idle Days in Patagonia?*"

"Of course," replied the general, "but try not to crack the spine."

"This climate and the insects will destroy your books before I do," responded García.

"That's very true," said the general. "I have had holes drilled straight through my books by termites, and in the rainy season I dare not open them since the humidity unglues them entirely."

García laughed. "In more peaceful times, General, we should invent books indestructible in the tropics."

"In more peaceful times we should also teach the people to read them, but I fear that too much money is spent feeding the army that defends us from you."

"I do not feel," said García, "that when released from active service, your soldiers would necessarily become teachers. When they come across teachers in the pueblos, they customarily kill them, unless they are women, in which case they rape them first."

García and the general looked at each other in silence for several seconds, until the general said, "If that was true, my friend, I would have them court-martialed. However, I do not believe it."

García laughed ironically and slapped a mosquito off his arm. "General, I think you will stay with us for a little while—that is, if we don't shoot you—and you will soon find out for yourself what the army does. Since you are in charge of it in César, I am very surprised that you do not know already, especially as it is you who orders it to do what it does."

"Padre," said Fuerte, very seriously, "I have never ordered indiscriminate crime. You insult me to suggest otherwise."

"Then the left hand knoweth not what the right hand is doing," said García.

"I think the left wing knoweth not what it is doing either," replied Fuerte. "But in any case, Padre, may I ask you one thing?"

García nodded.

"I would ask of you that if I am to die, you would first take my confession and afterward bury me decently."

"I doubt it will come to that," said García, "but naturally I would do as you wish in the event."

"Thank you, Padre. Now may I ask what you are doing fighting? You, a man of God?"

"I want to do some good in the world. And why on earth are you in the army, a cultivated man who likes butterflies and the music of Chávez?"

At that moment Federico walked in agitatedly. "Bring him out, García. He is to be tried by the council as an enemy of the people and of civilization."

The general smiled wryly. "Let's go then, Padre. And the answer to your question is the same as your answer to mine."

The ornithological general stepped out of the cool darkness of the old grass hut into sunshine that burst on him like a star shell.

He shielded his eyes against the heat and found himself standing in a seated semicircle of about thirty ruffianly warriors, some of whom examined him with idle interest and others of whom stared at him with a hatred and malice that seemed to crash into him with an intensity even more stunning and surprising than the tropical sun of the mountains. He turned and caught García's eye, "Also, be good to my burra. Her name is María."

13

The Only Way
to Turn a Campesino
into a Gunman

Campesinos do not become guerrillas for the same reasons as middle-class intellectuals from towns. In the case of the latter, the theoretical conviction comes first and is nourished by the long hours of involved conversation is cafés and student union refectories. Then some of the intellectuals disappear into the countryside, as Hugo Blanco did in Peru, and attempt to organize and politicize the peasantry and the miners in the mountains. Or else, like the poet Javier Heraud or Che Guevara, they throw their lives away in the jungle or the mountains by staging heroic *focos* which never win any territory permanently and which are always crushed because the peasants and defectors give away their positions to the army.

Campesinos often speak no Spanish, have no education at all, and live in places where they have been cut off from the rest of the world all their lives. They have no interest in ideas signified by long words and rarely become guerrillas because they accept things being the way they are and cannot leave their *minifundios* for fear of losing a crop or their steers.

A sizable proportion of them, however, work in feudal conditions on giant *encomiendas* that can take a week or more to cross on horseback. In Bolivia and Peru there have been land reforms, but these have seldom been implemented by local authorities far out in the interior, and they have always been bogged down in a morass of bureaucracy and sharp dealing.

Some of the *encomiendas* are run by enlightened and benign *padrones* who build houses, open schools and clinics, and pay for local policemen; such a one was Don Emmanuel.

The Carillo brothers were of the other species, however. The Carillos paid their thousands of workers nothing at all but obliged them to work six days a week in return for allowing a *minifundio* to each family, of which three fifths of the produce had to go to the Carillos.

As if these by no means uncommon conditions of slavery were not enough, the Carillos had a permanent gang of thugs hired to keep the peons in line and did not readily permit local authorities access to their land. The Carillos freely exercised the jus primae noctis and raped and brutalized when and where the whim came upon them.

One day the two brothers raped a young woman, wife of Pedro Arevalo, and then murdered her and left her body in the coca plantation. To forestall Arevalo's complaints, they denounced him to the police for theft and then returned with the police to arrest him. On the way they stopped for a few drinks and became so incapacitated that they sent a young boy called Paulo to fetch him. He arrived on his burro, and there ensued a violent altercation in which Pedro Arevalo denounced the Carillo brothers for the rape and murder of his wife, and the Carillo brothers accused him of larceny and of bearing false witness.

The police, who, besides being drunk, had no great fondness for the Carillos, returned to their post, having sorted out nothing at all, and Pedro and the Carillos returned to their respective homes.

Pedro Arevalo had two younger brothers, Gonzago and Tomás, who worked beside him on the banana plantation and on his *minifundio*. They heard talk in the village that the Carillos' *jaguncos* were coming to get Pedro the next evening, so in the morning Tomás and Gonzago, with a small band of campesinos, went to the police post to explain that they needed arms to protect Pedro against the Carillos. The three policemen listened sympathetically but said that they could not just hand out weapons. The sergeant was just about to propose that he and his two men should return with the peasants to protect Pedro Arevalo, when Tomás, impatient and hotheaded as ever, drew his revolver and threat-

ened to shoot if arms were not handed out immediately. Gonzago leaped
on his brother, and in the ensuring scuffle the sergeant was accidentally
shot in the head. The campesinos then had to tie up the other two
policemen to prevent them from arresting Tomás for manslaughter.
They took four rifles and some ammunition from the armory and returned in a band to Pedro Arevalo's *barraca,* only to find that they were
too late. Pedro was hanging from a caracolee tree, and his hut was in
flames.

Outraged, the band marched on the hacienda and took up positions
in the trees around it. When Alberto Carillo appeared in the doorway,
his gross form presented too easy a target to miss, and a volley of shots
sent him sinking to his knees before he fell sprawling down the wooden
steps. *Jagunco* faces immediately appeared in the windows, saw the
invasion of campesinos, were shot at, and disappeared.

There began a long siege of the hacienda. Gonzago cut with his
machete the thick black plastic piping that fed water from the water
tower and also hacked through the power cable from the generator,
giving himself a severe electric shock, which knocked him off his feet
but which had the desired effect of cutting off the air conditioning.

As the day grew older and the sun reached its zenith, the heat inside
the concrete building became unbearably suffocating. A man who came
to a window for some fresh air was shot dead in mid-breath. The
campesinos waited, snatching brief periods of siesta in the shade of the
trees, and the men inside the hacienda became more and more desperate.
They drank all the beer that was in the fridge, undid their buttons,
mopped their faces with their shirts, and tried to shake the stinging
sweat from their eyes. Unable to bear the heat and the fear anymore, one
man slipped out the back door and tried to run for it. The peasants
waited for him to overrun them and then hacked him to death with their
machetes so that his screams could be clearly heard in the hacienda.
Then they strung the body up on a tree where it could be seen.

The peons watched the house all through the night, firing on two
jaguncos as they tried to creep away under cover of darkness. Only one
of them was killed; the other lay under a window, keening and implor-
ing the Virgin to help, until he died shortly after dawn from the bullet
in his bowels.

At the time of these events Gonzago was nineteen years old and

Tomás was eighteen. Their brother Pedro was twenty-two when he died, and his wife was seventeen. The three brothers had lost their mother when they were very young; she had died giving birth to a little girl who would have been their sister, and the boys were looked after by their father and a network of aunts. There was no school for them to go to, but they were taught to read by an aunt who herself had been taught by nuns from a convent which the Carillo brothers had "bought" to convert into warehouses. Their father had died when Pedro was fifteen in an accident involving the felling of timber in the southern forest of the *encomienda*, and since then they had worked for the Carillos and also on their *minifundio*, cultivating manioc for making *chicha*, and corn, pigs, lemons, and chickens.

Their clothes were always ragged and crudely patched, but the boys were renowned for their pranks, their good looks, and their ability to break in horses. It was reckoned that an Arevalo boy could subdue a wild stallion in half the time that it took anyone else, so much of their time was spent taming horses and mules for local people, or the Carillos, usually being paid in chickens or cuts of meat.

Pedro was a stocky man with powerful shoulders and a droll way with words. He knew many jokes, mostly involving animals, and although he knew only one melody, he was able to extemporize new verses to it indefinitely, many of them either bawdy or sacrilegious. He had won the heart of Rosalita mainly by making her laugh but also by reciting love poems to her that he made up on the spot.

Gonzago and Tomás looked so much alike that Gonzago grew a Zapata mustache so that people could distinguish them. They were both slightly built, with striking dark eyes and eyebrows that met in the middle. Both had disarmingly charming grins that one usually describes as "boyish," and both of them had thick black hair that proved that there was a little Indian in their ancestry. Gonzago was particularly proud of his one gold tooth, which sparkled when he smiled and which had been painfully installed by an itinerant *cholo* dentist. The boys had a distinctive Mexican look about them that contrasted with the mestizo appearance of most of their neighbors and made them favorites with the local girls, who taught them the art of wanton glances when they were still very young. They were, however, a little different in temperament, as Tomás was quick-tempered and volatile, while Gonzago was easygoing and an avoider of argument. Tomás liked chewing coca, and Gonzago preferred to smoke marijuana, which grew freely in the countryside, and that, perhaps, points most assuredly to the differences in their personalities.

Neither of them, however, would ever have dreamed that they would one day be part of a lynching party that would ring the hacienda of the most powerful landowners in the province. The hacienda occupied several hectares of its own grounds. It was a long, low one-story building that enclosed a rectangular courtyard in which there were fountains, peacocks, and reproductions of classical statuary. In addition, there was a separate stable block and, nearby, a large swimming pool in the kind of abstract shape popular in the United States, where the Carillos spent at least a quarter of every year, mostly in Florida and California. In a long field near the house was a hangar with their two-engine executive airplane in it and a huge Cadillac that was virtually useless on the rough local terrain, especially in the rainy season.

As morning broke, the remaining Carillo brother, Peralta, and the ten remaining *jaguncos* decided to attempt to shoot their way out and make a dash for the airplane. The eastern horizon was just beginning to break up into yellow and orange streaks when a door burst open and the eleven sprinted toward the hangar.

Caught unawares, the campesinos were slow to respond. Gonzago shouted, started firing at the running men, and soon all of them were firing as rapidly as they could. They dropped six of the *jaguncos*, and Peralta Carillo, who on account of grossness equal only to his brother's was lagging behind, was hit in the leg and toppled headlong. He was the only one who knew how to fly the airplane, so the remaining four men leaped into the Cadillac. One of these men was the Carillos' chauffeur, and he was able to produce the keys and start the engine. He brought the car, bouncing wildly on its springs, across the field, onto the lawn, and to the head of the drive. One of the peons put a blast from his shotgun through the windshield, and the car careered off the drive and juddered into a tree. The campesinos rushed the car, dragged out the stunned thugs, and beat them to death with their rifle butts without even uttering a curse.

This done, they stood for a minute, looking with some little horror at what they had done, and then walked back to the hacienda. There was an ill-judged whimper from the prostrate Peralta Carillo. If he had not cried out, there might have been a chance for him to escape, but as it was, he soon found himself being dragged across the lawns to the trees, alternately screaming threats and pleading for his life.

The campesinos let down the *jagunco* they had hanged and hauled up Peralta in his place. The fat and doomed feudal lord, his face turning blue and frothing at the mouth, struggled and flailed wildly on the rope, his eyes rolling and his tongue protruding. He tried to reach above his head to grasp the rope and release its tightening grip a little, but one of the old peasants slashed deftly across his bulging stomach with a machete, and his distended entrails heaved, quivering, to the ground. The campesinos stood, their hands and knees shaking, and watched their former master die like a bullock on a meat hook.

They went into the hacienda and emptied it entirely of its contents, which they left on the lawns for whoever might claim them. One by one they looted the expensively appointed rooms and smashed anything they considered useless. Then they set fire to the buildings and stood outside, watching the flames licking the air, sending up sparks high into the sky. They stayed there until the evening, when the roof had fallen in and there was nothing left but charred timbers and the gutted concrete walls. They left the peacocks to fend for themselves as best they could and dispersed to their homes in silence, leaving the bodies to the vultures and flies. The next morning the population of the nearest village arrived to squabble over the spoils and spit on the bodies of the Carillos.

The two police officers unfortunately knew exactly who Tomás and Gonzago were, as Tomás had broken in a mare for one of them a year before. When a passing campesino untied them the next day, they went straight to the Arevalo *barraca* and found it burned down, with the body of Pedro hanging from the tree. They waited for Tomás and Gonzago to return, and while they did so, they unstrung the body of Pedro and laid it on the ground so that they could keep the vultures and the ants away.

The two brothers came down the track and stopped dead when they saw the two policemen. "Ola," said Gonzago warily.

"*Salud*," replied the older of the two officers, whose name was Fulgencio Vechada. "I see you have come to give us our weapons back."

Tomás gestured to the body of his brother and the burned hut. "Now you see why we needed them and why you should have given them to us. Look!"

Fulgencio sighed. "I am very sorry about all this," he said. He removed his cap and scratched his head. "Listen, I have to arrest you for the manslaughter of the sergeant, for taking the weapons, and for tying us up without our permission."

"We have killed the Carillos and their pet monkeys as well," said Gonzago. "You can arrest us for that, too."

"Both of them? All of them?" asked Fulgencio. "On your own?"

"Of course," said Tomás. "We alone."

"Naturally I will have to arrest you for that, too, when my investigations have proved that you were responsible." Fulgencio smiled and shook their hands. "Good-bye, Tomasito, good-bye, Gonzago, and buena suerte, eh? My investigations will take three days, so you had better leave as soon as possible, OK?"

"Thank you, Fulgencio," said Gonzago, unlashing his flashing grin. "I suppose you want these guns as well, no?"

"Keep them," said Fulgencio with a dismissive wave of his hand. "As I said, my investigations will take three days, and we have plenty of them."

The four men buried the body of Pedro next to that of Rosalita, and then the policemen gave the two brothers a lift in the Jeep to the highway, fifty miles away. They embraced, and then the brothers took trucks all the way to the temporary Independent Republic of the 26th of September, where they fell in with Remedios's faction of the People's Vanguard and continued the struggle they had commenced far away at home, becoming guerrillas for the only reasons that campesinos ever become guerrillas: personal ones.

The peasants of the Hacienda Carillo divided up the huge *encomienda* among themselves, or to be more accurate, they continued to farm their own *minifundios* and treated the *encomienda* as common land, introducing fish into the swimming pool. Months later the paramilitary police arrived to keep them off it, but they did not care because they no longer had to give any of their produce away and were much richer for less work, despite knowing nothing about the forces of the market. They never grew the right quantities of anything at the right time, but they were happy subsisting as they were, trading locally.

No one would buy the Carillo ranch for fear of suffering the same fate, and eventually the police left, leaving it to revert to scrub and jungle, to be used as common land, and to be the only place in the country where there was a colony of wild peacocks.

14
Parlanchina
Goes to Her Wedding

Aurelio had a severe toothache, so he stuck his knife into the ground and prayed to the angels, knowing that in this way he would be cured by sunset.

Like most Indians, he was short and strong. His face was flat and his beard wispy, and he still dressed like his ancestors, with the distinctive *trenza*, the long queue that makes Aymaras look like displaced Chinamen. In a gourd he pounded coca leaves mixed up with snail shells, so that most of the time he was energetic and happy from the effects of sucking the pestle, which bulged in his cheek like a lollipop.

Aurelio had become a prodigious breeder of dogs; he had heard once that the Maya Indians of Mexico had had dogs that did not bark, and he had made it his life's obsession to re-create this species for himself. Aymara is famous for being the most logical language in the world, with a syntax and grammar to fill with joy the heart of the most arid computer. But the logic of his language had failed to make Aurelio himself a rational man. Perhaps he wished to breed barkless dogs out of a sense of solidarity with that long-vanished civilization or perhaps it was because he knew somehow that all men need an obsession to bring meaning and purpose to their lives, and, for this, one obsession is as good as another.

Aurelio's acquaintances all knew that he would pay good money for a quiet dog, even though he was not a rich man, and some people with no principles even trained their dogs not to bark so that he would buy them for breeding. This deceit, once he had become wise to it, caused Aurelio to grow skeptical about the general trustworthiness of humankind. Even to his wife he would say, "I trust my dogs more than you, even though I love you more."

Carmen, Aurelio's wife, was a small Negress with tight curls of ginger hair that indicated a little miscegenation somewhere in her ancestry. She had a raucous laugh and easy manner and smoked huge *puro* cigars whose soggy tips she clenched between her teeth. She was a happy woman, living in the clearing in the jungle with Aurelio and his dogs, gathering *castana* nuts from beneath the huge trees, tapping a little latex from the rubber trees, and growing a little corn in the impoverished earth. She had, despite enthusiastic efforts, managed to conceive no children by Aurelio, and they had taken in a little urchin girl that Aurelio had found huddled in a doorway on one of his dog-buying excursions to Valladolid.

At first the little girl had spoken not at all, and the couple had wondered if she was dumb. "Everything is the wrong way around," said Aurelio. "All my dogs give voice, and my child is silent." But it turned out that the trouble was that the child, who was about four years old, had simply never learned to talk for lack of opportunity and occasion. By the time that she was a vivacious and funny girl of twelve with budding breasts and coquettish eyes, she spoke in positive torrents, and the couple nicknamed her Parlanchina, a name that translates roughly as "Babbler."

But it had not been easy to bring Parlanchina out of her animal state. She communicated at first in hoarse grunts of a very hostile nature, and she frequently bit Aurelio on the hand when he tried to come near her. Worse than this, she preferred generally to go on all fours and associate with the dogs rather than with the loving couple. She refused to wash or let her clothes be changed, and she stank horribly. Aurelio knew that it was time for drastic action when she actually bit one of the dogs on the ear while competing for kitchen leavings, and on the same day he discovered that in her excrement was a writhing mass of parasites. "It is time," he said to his wife, "to be a little cruel in order to make her human."

Carmen agreed. She went out into the jungle and gathered bitter barks and herbs. These she steeped in *aguardiente* in order to make a tincture, and the couple managed to force this down the child's throat after a long and bitter struggle which left Parlanchina bruised and more hostile than ever and the couple extensively scratched and bitten. Carmen was satisfied, however, upon inspecting the child's next dollop of feces, that the parasites were expelled and dead.

Then the couple decided to educate the child with a system of rewards and punishments. The punishment side of the project was easy because animals have in common with humans a general dislike of pain. The rewards were more difficult to find because Parlanchina had the same tastes as the dogs, and Carmen and Aurelio did not think it right to reward her with bones and kitchen slops since these were precisely what they wished to wean her away from. Eventually they found to their delight that Parlanchina was crazy about nuts and guavas, and some part of the day was always therefore devoted to gathering them.

At first Aurelio thought that there was no point in trying to speak with Parlanchina, "because she does not understand and does not answer," so he tried to communicate with her in grunts and gestures.

"I think," said Carmen one day, "that we should give up all this grunting business. I find it tiresome and tiring. Perhaps we should continue to point and wave our arms about, but I think that if we do not speak to her, she will not learn to speak. I think we should speak all the time without stopping."

So Carmen and Aurelio spoke without stopping. They pointed to things and named them; eventually Parlanchina learned to follow the line of their pointing instead of staring at the tip of a pointed finger with a puzzled expression. Then she learned to point as well. Carmen and Aurelio spoke all the time. They spoke about everything, they spoke about nothing, and they spoke about how fed up they were with speaking.

One day Parlanchina pointed to a guava on the table and smiled her very first smile. "Gwubba," she said, distinctly and with precision. The couple threw themselves upon her with delight, and from that point there was no looking back.

For a week the little girl tried out "gwubba" in different intonations and emphases until she became bored with it. Then she began to acquire vocabulary at a steady and breathtaking pace. Soon she found ways of making elementary sentences that missed inessential words and began to refer to herself: "Me want dog," "Me go pee-pee."

Exhilarated, Carmen and Aurelio continued to speak all the time, and Parlanchina began to speak to herself as she did things. "She's thinking out loud," reported Carmen. "It proves she can think," replied Aurelio. Then she started to speak overgrammatically, making no allowances for the idiosyncrasies and oddities of language. "I wented and seed the sheeps," she would say, and Aurelio would say, "Did you? I went and saw the sheep, too," correcting her by example. Carmen and Aurelio carried on speaking all the time, and by the time she was seven Parlanchina believed this was normal and began to turn into the inveterate chatterbox that she remained until the day of her death.

In other respects, too, she learned well. She learned to eat with a knife, and delicately with her fingers, licking them without slurping, as civilized people do, and she stopped putting her food on the floor and diving into it headfirst. She stopped growling as she ate, she learned to eat slowly rather than bolt the food voraciously, and she learned to belch roundly, like a respectable Indian.

Parlanchina was taught by Carmen to excrete in the jungle, away from the house, and she was taught to wash and perform all the necessary tasks of life. Additionally, she became playful and affectionate and would sit on Aurelio's knee, trying to tease his real name out of him. She would kiss him on the cheek, whisper nonsensical little nothings in his ear, and say "Papacito, come on, tell me your real name."

"Donkey face," said Aurelio.

"Oh, Papacito, what is it? You can tell me." And she would laugh prettily and wheedle a little more.

"It's Melon Bum."

"Oh, no, Papacito, it isn't. Tell me. I will cry."

"No, you will not, and I will not tell you either. If I tell anyone, they will have power over me, and you have enough power over me already."

"Oh, Papa, am I good? Do I not do as you say?"

"Not always," replied Aurelio.

"Ooh, you big liar. Anyway, why do you have a real name?"

"I have told you hundreds of times, little one."

"I know, but I like to hear it. It is so scary. Tell me again."

"Well," said Aurelio, putting on his storytelling voice, "at the entrance to the afterworld there is a monster, a big, ugly, fierce monster with teeth like machetes. If you cannot tell him your real name, he will not let you into the afterworld. Instead"—Aurelio made gnashing and swallowing noises, and patted his stomach—"the monster eats you up, and your spirit remains forever in his stomach, where it is dark and stinking, and your spirit howls forever with horror and despair."

Parlanchina shuddered and shook her long black hair. "Papacito, when will you tell me my real name?"

"I will tell you when you grow to womanhood, little one. The monster lets all children pass. I will tell you when your little breasts swell and the blood flows from you according to the cycle of the moon."

"When will that be, Papacito? When?"

"Soon enough, little one."

Parlanchina never grew completely out of her wildness. She took to the jungle as naturally as a *tigre*, and as fearlessly. From her parents she learned to name all animals, all fish, and all plants, and she learned all their properties and uses for food and medicine.

On her own initiative she learned to track the animals, discovered their habits, and found how it was to be that animal. She learned to imitate their voices and dupe them into panic or into approaching her. She made a pet of an ocelot kitten that grew big and handsome and terrified the dogs, even though he was smaller than they were. The cat stepped prettily after his pretty mistress and slept on top of her in her hammock, sticking his claws in her every time she moved. "He believes that one's mattress should stay still," she said.

Parlanchina grew taller than her parents. At the age of twelve her long, smooth legs seemed so long that they appeared to reach her armpits. Her black, straight hair she parted in the middle and wore down to her waist, so that it flowed about her as she moved with grace, silence, and precision through the jungle about her home. She found a way of tossing her hair back with a flick of the head and then looking at you sideways with her huge brown eyes. Gently she would smile, as if she knew a wicked secret, and when she smiled, the tip of her nose moved just a little downward. Her voluptuous skin was somewhere between olive and black, and it had already some of the softness and glow of a teenager. Like a teenager, too, she would have periods of dreaming, her chin on her hand as she gazed into the distance, as though she were gazing into the future.

"That girl is so lovely that I am afraid for her," confided Aurelio one day to his wife. "She reminds me of a faun."

"Why are you afraid?" asked Carmen, surprised.

"I am afraid that one of the gods will fall in love with her and take her away from us. I have a terrible fear."

"I think it is more likely," enjoined Carmen, "that a young man will take her away, and that is how it should be."

Aurelio ran his fingers through his wife's copper curls. "Do you think she could make a man happy? Wild and beautiful as she is?"

"I think," said Carmen, after a little thought, "that she would make a man so happy that if he did not die of it, he would certainly go mad."

"A son-in-law and some little ones would make me very happy," said Aurelio sadly. "I shall make an offering to Santa Barbara and also to the gods that it may come to pass."

"Aurelio," said Carmen, kissing him on the cheek and embracing him maternally, "remember that fear causes to happen the very things it fears. That is why fear should be unknown to us."

In fact, Parlanchina discovered men before they ever discovered her. Rememdios's group passed along a jungle path five miles away quite regularly en route from the foothills to the sierra, and army patrols also occasionally passed by. Parlanchina was fascinated, and she tracked them as silently and efficiently as she would track any other animal. She observed their demeanor: how the *guerrilleros* were always laughing and joking and making a lot of noise and how the soldiers always crept along, sweating and suffering beneath the weight of their clinging uniforms and bulging backpacks. She saw how their eyes bulged with nervousness and how their mouths gaped with fear like beached fish. She saw how they started every time their feet cracked a twig, and she began to play games with them. From the cover of the trees, with her ocelot crouched beside her, she would suddenly let out a coughing growl like a *tigre*, screech like a parrot, or whoop like a howler monkey. Giggling with delight, she related to both her parents how the soldiers had leapt with fright, had fallen flat on their stomachs, and had fired shots wildly into the vegetation. They would shake their heads and admonish her, but she would not stop because she was always hoping to see Federico. Federico was the secret cause of her daytime reveries, and she followed him whenever he passed, to gaze on his fine, slim body and his handsome face. She found herself imagining what it would be like to stroke his flat belly and his long legs, and when she saw him, her heart would leap in her breast, and something would catch at the back of her throat. When she did not see Federico, tormenting the soldiers was a little consolation. But no one ever saw her; the soldiers never knew that they owed some of their torture to her, and Federico never knew that the most lovely and most voluble girl in César was in love with him.

One day Parlanchina came home and said to her father with surprise and amusement, "Papacito, the soldiers are hiding dishes on the path. Why do you think they are doing that?"

Aurelio took his knife out of the ground, thinking wearily that he would have to put up with his toothache. He would have to go see what she was talking about, and he would not go anywhere without his knife, even if it was bad luck to break a spell. He and Parlanchina walked through the trees and then crept to within a few yards of the soldiers and observed them. They were indeed hiding dishes, dishes that looked like two plates stuck together and that they were handling so carefully that at first Aurelio thought that they must be sacred objects. But then something clicked in his memory, something his father had told him, back in Bolivia, when he was a child and long before he had come all this way by river and on foot. He remembered that when the whites had wanted to drive the Indians off their land, they had hidden things on the paths that made a terrible noise and threw people's limbs into the trees. He waited until the soldiers slunk away and said to Parlanchina, "Little one, those things are called sudden-death-by-thunder. If you tread on one, it tears your body with metal and flame. It seems they want to drive us away, as my people were driven away. We must destroy those things, but we cannot touch them."

"How will we destroy them, Papacito?"

"I am going back to get my rifle. I will destroy metal with metal and fire with fire, from the safety of the trees. Little one, you must stay here, and you must stop any man and any animal from going on the path, and you must not go on the path or you will die a terrible death.

When I return, I will discover the dishes, and I will shoot them from far away. Do you understand, little one?"

"Of course, I do, Papacito. Return quickly."

Aurelio slipped away, and Parlanchina settled her long limbs down by a tree to watch the path. Nothing stirred. Aurelio seemed to be taking a long time. It was very boring. She began to doze in the dappled sunlight. She was dreaming about Federico. How fine he was!

Then she woke with a start. Something was wrong. Then she realized what it was. Her little ocelot had grown bored as well and had stolen away. She saw his spotted tail waving in the undergrowth as he strolled toward the path. She sprang up, horrified. "¡Gato!" she called. "¡Gato! Come here, venga! ¡Venga!" The cat turned his head mischievously and broke into a trot. He often played this game. It was very amusing. "¡Gato!" shrieked Parlanchina. Three hundred yards away Aurelio heard her and broke into a desperate run, snagging himself on thorns and cursing as he went crashing through the undergrowth.

Parlanchina stood for a moment in indecision, a terrible fear rising in her belly, and then she ran after the cat.

Aurelio heard the explosion. He ran as fast as his dread and his sinking heart would allow, and he burst through the greenery and fell on his knees beside his beautiful child. His eyes were not prepared to see this; nothing in his whole life had prepared him for this.

Beside the shredded body of her beloved cat she lay. Through eyes blurred with grief and through heart leaden with horror he saw her in a welter of blood. He saw her long legs shattered and twisted and stripped and blackened even in the gore. He saw her soft belly torn open and its contents still pulsing.

But her face, her beautiful face, her face of an earthbound angel! It was untouched; it was perfect. He bent over, sobbing, and kissed her lightly on the lips. He felt a soft breath from her mouth, and he jerked up, hope glimmering forlornly in his breaking heart. She opened her eyes, her huge, glowing eyes, and she looked at him with the look of one who says farewell to an old love.

"You will marry a god, little one," said Aurelio, tears streaming down his cheeks in spite of his upbringing. But he would not blink while she still looked into his eyes; he would blink when she could not look anymore.

Her lips quivered, and she moved her head a little to see a little better into her father's eyes. A huge tear rolled out of the corner of her eye and trickled down toward her ear. It hung briefly like a raindrop and fell to earth. Softly, pleadingly, as though about to caress him, she murmured, "Papacito."

Aurelio bent down, and in her ear he whispered to her her real name. When he moved upright, Parlanchina was lying with her eyes wide open, astounded at her own death.

Aurelio lifted her broken body in his old arms and carried her home, his anger battling with his sorrow, his soul rebelling against the futility that is the delight of the gods, and blood soaking into his clothes. He laid the body before his threshold and called Carmen. She came out bearing a bowl of bananas, but when she saw the corpse, she bent down and carefully placed them on the ground. She and Aurelio stood silently looking at each other over the body of their exquisite child. Aurelio gestured limply toward Parlanchina. "It is our little Gwubba," he said.

Aurelio dug two holes two yards apart and two yards deep, and then he created a tunnel between them. In the tunnel he laid a bed of brush. Upon that he laid out her hammock, and the child he laid there to rest. In her arms he wrapped her beloved cat.

He filled in the grave, and with the soil that was left he made a mound. In the mound he stuck straight twigs, and Carmen wove among them a potent symbol.

"It is a terrible thing to die a virgin," said Carmen as she lay one night in her husband's arms.

"She died because of the love in her heart," said Aurelio. "And there will be lives lost because of it. I have sworn it, and the gods and the angels and Santa Barbara will hold me to it. I have finished with dogs."

Carmen clutched him tighter. "Would you make other fathers weep? Go carefully," she whispered, and stroked his head. She had learned that men possessed a kind of obstinate stupidity that made them at once beastlike and godlike. She would not fight against it. Some things you cannot fight. You can only pick up the pieces, afterward.

"Tomorrow," said Aurelio, "I will go and tell the *guerrilleros* where the soldiers have hidden the sudden-death-by-thunder."

15

General Carlo María Fuerte Is Tried for Crimes Against Civilization

Against the pressure of Franco and some others to shoot the general straight away, Remedios insisted on a properly conducted trial. Remedios appointed Father García to defend the general and appointed Franco to prosecute him. The verdict was to be delivered by a vote of the entire camp, and Remedios herself was to pass sentence in the event of the verdict's being guilty.

The general, still dressed in his peasant clothes, looking old and weary, was brought out into the clearing. The *guerrilleros* lounged about on the grass, some of them unashamedly dozing, and Remedios had her table brought out from her hut. She seated herself before it, cleared her throat portentously, and rapped the table with the butt of her revolver. "The court will come to order," she said. "The court is in session. Franco, you will speak first."

Franco arose, spit, and said, "The son of a whore commands the army in this area, and every one of us knows what that means. I shouldn't need to tell you what has been happening around here, and it appears that the only one who pretends not to know is the commander. The army committed a massacre in Federico's village, for example, just because they stopped the soldiers from raping a young girl, and, talking of rape—" he turned furiously on the general—"your soldiers even hold down the little boys and girls and sodomize them!" The general winced.

"In this department, to my certain knowledge," continued Franco, "the army has ransacked fifteen villages, one of them twice. They have murdered teachers, doctors, and priests. I also know that they run profiteering rackets with marijuana and cocaine; we all know this. They steal as they please, when they please, and they commit regular brutalities so often and so cruelly that ordinary peasants like us, and intellectuals like Remedios, and even priests like García are forced to fly from their homes and take up arms." He pointed his finger furiously at the general. "And this is the man who is responsible for all this! Is it not obvious that he should die?"

The general was visibly agitated. García spoke: "I think the general would like to say something."

With quiet dignity the general said, "I know nothing of all this. I have always taken this kind of talk as idle propaganda, and I still think so. I would like to hear from you all these stories, however, and if I am released, I will undertake honorably to repair these wrongs, if they exist, and bring to justice those who committed them. I reformed the police force in Valledupar, and I would do the same with my soldiers. Let me say, I have always acted on the information I have received. It is not my fault if I received misleading information. You cannot blame me for that. It would break my heart if I were obliged to begin to have to believe that the army, which is my life and which I love, could have done these things."

"But it is not just the army!" interrupted Franco, still furious. "You are governor of all César. You want us to believe that you are honorable and decent, but look around you! I will tell you things that every peasant knows! There is no justice unless you are rich, for nothing can be done in law without bribing judges and magistrates, and before them, the police, if you can find them. All over this department officials will do nothing without bribes, and even then they are idle and evasive! Everywhere you look there is poverty! Why? Because local officials divert all public funds into their own pockets! It is a national scandal that lies heavily upon us with a weight of shame. Dishonesty is a way of life here, and you, General, are presiding over it! What can your decency and honor be worth before all this? What can your life be worth?"

"My life is worth nothing," replied the general. "I have toiled all

my life for the motherland, and with God's help I shall die toiling for
it!"

"You shall die because you have done nothing for it, strutting about
in your fancy uniform, going to your dinner parties, writing books on
butterflies while your people perish! You disgust me!" Franco spoke
with such scorn that when he had finished, there was a long moment of
silence.

"Come now, Franco," said García gently, "do you seriously expect
the general to put right immediately four hundred years of custom? You
know as I do, Franco, that this country was conquered by barbarians,
greedy illiterates who destroyed ancient civilizations. Today we are
governed by the families of those who descended from them; only they
are not illiterate any more. In this country it has always been as you
describe, a Christian country where God never shows His face, a country where He is ashamed to walk among us! All this is not the fault of
the general. And who are you, Franco, to talk of justice? There is no
justice even in this court! All of you want to see the general shot, and
you will all say 'guilty' when the time comes, even if you know in your
hearts that he is a deluded innocent! Is that justice? In civilized countries
one is tried by one's equals. Which of us is equal to the general? He is
a man of culture and honor, as all of us can see. According to the
constitution of this country, which I admit is observed least frequently
by the government, the general should be tried by a military court. Is
this a military court? He should be tried by his equals. Are we generals?
No, we are not."

"Remedios is our general, and we are all soldiers," replied Franco.
"And the constitution means nothing, as we all know. I am talking not
about what justice is in the lawbooks, which no one reads. I am talking
about the justice of the heart, which we can all read.

"And also, I want to say something else which is important to us.
This dog, Fuerte, is a member of the government, appointed to direct
the affairs of this department, without even being elected! Our government is the puppet of a foreign power. . . . After all, where does the
money come from? Who regulates the trade? We know who it is who
does these things! Listen to my reasons. Our government works for
foreigners, Fuerte works for the government, and therefore, Fuerte
works for foreigners. He works not for us, not for his motherland, but

for the gringos. And what is the name of a military man who works for foreigners? It is 'traitor.' And what is the penalty for traitors? It is death!"

Many of the guerrillas were pleased with this speech. "Bravo!" called one of them.

"To death," called another.

General Fuerte signaled to Remedios that he wished to speak, and she nodded. Wearily he spoke.

"You are mistaken. I have never worked for the Americans. It is the Americans who work for us. They give us money, more money than you can imagine, and they help us build roads and bridges and hospitals that we could not otherwise build. I have been to America, many times, and I find people who are rich, generous, friendly, hospitable, decent, and honest. The Americans are not our enemies; they are our friends. Powerful friends. This country would not run at all without their help."

Remedios spoke. "I, too, have been to America, when I was a student. I saw things in the poor parts of American cities that make the *favelas* look civilized."

"The judge is not supposed to give evidence or venture opinions," said García.

Remedios shot him a withering look. "I rule that my evidence is necessary and relevant."

Franco said, "But what is the price wed pay for this 'help'?" He spoke the word with the utmost sarcasm and spit afterward. "Sure, the *gringonchos* invest money, lots of it, but where are the profits? Where do they go? Do they go to the workers they employ? No, they do not. Do they stay in this country? No. So what happens? They take everything from us, and nothing is returned. They are leaving us naked. How else do they 'help'?" He spit again. "They train our soldiers to kill those of us who want things to be fair. I have heard this, that the gringos have a camp where they train our soldiers how to resist torture. Why do they do this? Do the *guerrilleros* torture soldiers? No. So what happens? In fact, our soldiers learn from the gringos how to be torturers because they are told by the gringos about the many varieties of it. And why do they give us so much brotherly 'help'? So we learn to depend on it, and then they can control us like a father controls a little boy. Our government and our oligarchy behave to the gringos like I used to to my mother when I wanted a piece of *panela*!" He put on a baby voice, whining and cute. "Mamacita, mamacita, gimme some *panela*, please, mamacita, I promise I'll be good!" The *guerrilleros* laughed, and General Fuerte smiled.

"There is a little truth in your words," he said, "but it is better for the gringo to pay a hundred pesos a day to a hundred workers in a mine they have opened than for one hundred men to earn nothing a day from a mine that has never been opened because no one thought of looking for one."

"Our government opens no mines because it sells all concessions abroad," rejoined Franco, "to get money. And why does it need money? Why does it have no money to open mines? Because all profits go abroad so that gringos can sit in the shade all day and grow huge backsides!" The men laughed; gringos were famous for their fat backsides.

"I want to speak," said one of them. Remedios nodded her permission.

"I have a cousin in Bolivia. He works in the mines, and he earns almost nothing, and he is dying from diseases of the lungs. He breathes like an old dog, and he is thirty years old. He is poor because if they put up the price of tin, everything will be made of plastic instead. The foreigners catch us in such traps, and we are poor forever."

Remedios rapped her table with the butt of her revolver. "This court has wandered far from the point, which is whether or not the general is guilty of crimes against civilization. It is growing very hot, and we have talked a long time. I think it is time we came to a conclusion before we melt into lard. Do you have anything more to say, Franco?"

Franco shook his head. "I am tired of speaking. I have said everything."

"And you, García, what do you say?"

"*Compañeros*," said García, "there are two questions. One is whether General Fuerte is responsible for what has happened in this department, and the other is whether it is his fault. He is the governor, and so he is responsible. But I do not think it is his fault. If he did not know what was happening, it cannot be his fault, and so he is innocent."

"It is his fault because he should have known!" blurted Franco angrily. "And how do we know that he did not know? We have only his word, which is worth nothing because he is afraid of death."

General Fuerte could not contain himself. "I? I afraid of death! Señora Remedios, I will with your permission take your gun and blow my own brains out and you will see that I have not feared to tell the truth because I fear death! Give me your gun!"

Remedios stood up slowly and hesitantly handed him the gun, butt first. The general took it and looked at it. He passed it from one hand to the other, as though weighing it.

"This is a military pistol," he said, looking up at Remedios. "I suppose the original owner is dead."

Remedios smiled. "No, he left it behind when he ran away."

The general smiled gently and looked around him, as if to say farewell to the world and all its pain and beauty. He glanced up at the sun. "It is a fine day to die," he said. "I am very glad it is not raining."

He raised the pistol and pointed it toward the roof of Remedios's hut. The men, as of one mind, raised their weapons and aimed them at him, all thinking that he was about to try to shoot his way out. The general smiled gently again, closed his eyes, and placed the gun against his temple. He stood there for a few seconds, and the men watched in horrified fascination as his finger slowly took up first pressure. Then his eyes opened suddenly, and he said, "Forgive me, I have forgotten to make confession. I wish to confess to Father García. I cannot die an unhallowed death."

Everyone was both relieved and annoyed. "García," snapped Remedios, "confess him, but be quick, before the sun kills all of us."

On his knees the general said, "Father, forgive me, for I have sinned. I have thought and done evil things—"

"Under the circumstances, I think you can spare the details," said García, and with his finger he made the sign of the cross upon the forehead of the general. "*Absolvo te.* Go, my child, and sin no more." He bent down and whispered in the general's ear, "Stay there."

He walked off purposefully toward his hut, and the general remained kneeling in the sun, his head bowed. A moment later García reappeared with a corn tortilla, a tin mug, and a bottle. He made the sign of the cross with his index finger and forefinger over the tortilla, muttered some words, and broke a little piece off. He placed it softly on the general's tongue. "The body of Christ, which is given for you. Eat this in remembrance of me." The general withdrew his tongue and swallowed the bread with difficulty. Some of the men crossed themselves.

García poured some cane rum from the bottle into the tin mug and blessed it with the sign of the cross. He tipped the mug against the general's lips and said, "The blood of Christ, which was shed for you. Drink this in remembrance of me." Again, some of the men crossed themselves. García placed his hand a little above the general's head, and the general distinctly felt a kind of healing warmth come from it. García prayed a moment and then looked down at the general. "Die in peace," he said.

"Thank you, Father." The general rose to his feet and placed them firmly apart. Once more he closed his eyes and slowly raised the weapon to his temple. Firmly he took up first pressure, and García signaled frantically to Remedios that she should stop him. She shook her head vehemently.

General Fuerte pulled the trigger, remembering his training all those years ago. "Squeeze, don't snatch! Squeeze, don't snatch!" He remembered the little corporal who had drilled them in weapons training. "This is the hammer; this is the chamber; this is the breechblock. The weapon must be kept scrupulously clean or it may jam or the barrel may burst and blow your balls off. I shall inspect your weapons every day, and if they are not as clean as a nun's underwear, I shall blow your balls off myself!"

The general's soul was already halfway out of his body when it jerked back again. Nothing had happened except for a click. He looked at the gun in puzzlement and flicked back the release catch. As the men burst out of their silence into wondering chatter, he opened the gun and looked into the revolving chamber.

He looked at Remedios reproachfully. "It is empty. You have put me through all this for nothing. Why did you do this?"

"I am not a barbarian, and I have no wish to see anyone blow his own head off." She smiled. "Also, I am not an idiot. I'm not the kind of fool who bangs a loaded revolver on the table with the barrel pointing straight at myself, nor would I hand it loaded to a prisoner. Kindly credit me with a little intelligence."

The general smiled wryly, and Remedios took the gun back from him and banged it on the table. "I want you all to go and sit in the shade somewhere and discuss whether the verdict is guilty or not guilty. You will come back here after siesta and tell the court your decision. Do not forget to appoint a foreman."

The men trooped off to the shade of a huge caracolee tree and fell into hot discussion. General Fuerte turned to García as the priest led him back to the hut that served as his very insecure prison. "That cane rum tasted foul. I nearly choked."

García smiled. "The taste of blood is not good either, my friend. Remember it was blood you drank."

"It was sweet to be about to die," replied the general. "I will always remember that."

When the court reconvened, the general was brought out again. "What is your decision?" demanded Remedios of the foreman, an extractor driver from Asunción.

"We decided sort of guilty and sort of not guilty," he said, grinning with embarrassment and scratching his head.

Remedios raised her eyes to heaven and tapped her fingers on the table. "That is not helpful," she enunciated slowly, emphasizing the "not."

"It is our decision," said the foreman, more bravely. "He *is* sort of guilty and also sort of not guilty, so that had to be our verdict. But we don't want you to shoot him. *Tiene cojones.* We don't want a man who is brave to die like a dog."

"In that case," announced Remedios, "I will pass sentence." She turned to look at the general, who had listened to the foreman with one eyebrow raised. "General Fuerte, you have been found 'sort of guilty' and also 'sort of not guilty.' For the 'sort of not guilty' I disallow a capital sentence. For the 'sort of guilty' I sentence you to be detained by us until I think what to do with you. The court is finished. We have to prepare for the return of Gloria, Tomás, Rafael, and Gonzago with another captive. The general will have company."

Remedios indicated to two men to return her desk and chair to her hut, and then she turned to the general and approached him. "What do you think of the verdict, General? It is not one you would hear in a 'real' court, is it?"

The general smiled and passed his hand above his eyes. "No," he said. "But maybe they are right. I realize that I have done nothing wrong. I have always done my best, with good conscience. If I am guilty, it is because I have not done enough."

"Know thyself," said Remedios, placing her hand on his shoulder.

The general laughed ironically. "I do not think I will ever have the opportunity to do enough anyway."

"I might ransom you," said Remedios.

16
Doña Constanza Receives an Unwelcome Surprise

At the same that General Fuerte was being tried for crimes against civilization, and at the same time that Commandante, or rather Colonel (as he was now) Figueras was setting out with a battalion of men from Valledupar, four *guerrilleros* from Remedios's group were descending from the mountains with a very special mission, and Doña Constanza was again reading her three-year-old copy of *Vogue*. For all these people the heat was stupendously oppressive, and all conversation was restricted to the repetition of a single phrase, *"Ay, el calor!"* The four *guerrilleros* hurried from the shade of one tree to the next and from one stream to another for a drink. The soldiers jolted along in the back of the trucks, their heads hanging miserably, their foreheads cascading with sweat. It ran down their arms and into the mechanisms of their M-16's; it ran prickling and tingling from their crotches down into their boots; it formed crosses on their backs which grew into soaking dark sodden patches on their shirts, which then dried into salt about the edges; it ran down from their hair into their eyes so that there was not one of them who did not squint against the stinging and shake his head and blink. When the trucks stopped for the men to urinate, the urine was the darkest yellow and pungent, and some found they had no water left in them with which to micturate.

In her hacienda Doña Constanza instructed her maid to bring her a huge jug of lemon juice sweetened with *panela* and cooled with ice. Then the maid was dismissed, and Doña Constanza removed her towel and lay suffering and naked beneath the slowly rotating fan. She put down the copy of *Vogue* because the sight of all those tight clothes made her feel all the more unbearably hot, and she, like all the nation, oligarch and peasant alike, lay stricken and hopeless in the state of necessary torpor that makes siesta the only refuge of the sane.

If the rest of the world does not always need a siesta, it does always need money, and Remedios's group was no exception. Indeed, the thing which is frequently most galling to good Communist guerrillas is that they have to trade with capitalists and become capitalists themselves in order to fund the revolution. More often than not, they are obliged to pay gunrunners in the hated *yanqui* dollar; contrary to popular myth, the USSR has given no direct aid since 1964, and the many groups that fund themselves by means of the drug trade are obliged to demand payment in dollars in order to buy the guns. In this case the revolutionaries at least have the satisfaction of knowing that the cocaine paid for in dollars goes straight to the hated United States and eats away at the lives of its citizens and its social fabric. Thus it becomes the victim of the strength of its own currency, and as Lenin said, often quoted by Remedios, "The capitalists will sell us the weapons with which we will destroy them."

Connected closely with this irony is another—namely, that in order to secure peace, justice, and a better distribution of wealth, revolutionaries must prosecute war, perpetrate injustices and immoralities, and appropriate cash and goods from those whose interests they may have at heart, the ordinary people who cannot afford it. Like most groups, that of Remedios issued receipts for all goods appropriated, to be redeemed after the victory. Most of the people could not read these receipts, and those who could did not know what to do with them. In some places that had been cleaned out of pesos these receipts became a substitute for currency, their value depending upon the amount of writing upon them, so that one could hear such remarks as "I paid fourteen words for this machete" or "One word for four mangoes." People being raided by guerrillas would beg their raiders to write their receipts in even greater detail; this caused, however, a kind of word inflation, and the guerrillas eventually ran out of the goodwill to write them. Nonetheless, the receipts of the various guerrilla groups, even though they were inter-changeable, never achieved a status equal to Pancho Villa's amazing feat in the Mexican Revolution of 1913—that is, entirely supplanting the federal currency.

There comes a time when the revolutionary conscience becomes troubled by revolutionary justice, and the revolutionaries try something that actually affects those against whom they struggle—the establish-ment and the oligarchy.

Thus it was that four of the People's Vanguard crashed through the door of Doña Constanza's hacienda as she lay stark naked and torpid beneath the fan. Doña Constanza sat bolt upright, emitting little shrieks, her hands flitting from one part of her body to another in an effort to cover herself.

The four guerrillas lowered their weapons and stood goggle-eyed and gaping before the spectacle. "*¡Madre de Dios!*" exclaimed Tomás.

Rafael giggled nervously and wanted to make a dirty remark with-out being able to think of one, and Gonzago, in an absurdly formal tone of voice, said, "Good afternoon," whereupon Rafael giggled again.

Gloria snorted with amusement, bent down, handed Doña Con-stanza her towel, and said, "*¡Callate!*" sharply to Rafael. "*¡Basta ya!*"

"*Perdone,*" said Rafael, still chortling, "but I find this very humor-ous."

"I do not!" exclaimed Doña Constanza.

"One day you will see the funny side of it." Gloria attempted to console her.

"I doubt it. Now get out of my house or I will call the police."

"How?" said Tomás, looking genuinely puzzled. "We went around the house twice looking for a telephone wire in order to cut it. You do not have a telephone. No one has a telephone around here."

"Perhaps she is telepathic with the police chief in Valledupar," commented Gonzago.

"He has no thoughts for anyone to read," said Rafael.

"Shut up, all of you!" ordered Gloria, and she turned to Doña Constanza. "You must get dressed in something very practical. We are taking you hostage against a ransom of half a million dollars. Behave and we will treat you with respect. Misbehave and we will shoot you. It is simple."

"But," replied Doña Constanza, her eyes wide with astonishment, "he would never pay it!"

"Does he not love you?" asked Tomás, genuinely concerned.

"Quiet, Tomás!" said Gloria. "He will have to pay it or he will be shot some other time." She took the receipt book from the breast pocket of her khaki shirt. "You will write a letter to your husband which we will dictate to you."

Doña Constanza, her lip and her hands trembling and her eyes brimming with tears, took down the following note:

> I have been taken hostage for half a million dollars by the People's Vanguard. If you do not pay, I will be shot and you will be shot at some other time, either before or after the victory. The money will be paid in cash and must be left beneath the arches of the bridge at Chiriguaná at 7:00 P.M. on Friday, March 15, in two weeks' time. You will be alone or both you and I will be shot. I will be released some days later. You can trust the People's Vanguard if they can trust you. Onward to victory! ¡Patria o muerte!
>
> CONSTANZA

Underneath, Gloria wrote, "Respected Sir, this is witnessed by Gloria de Escobal, and hereto I append my signature. Gloria de Escobal."

Gloria escorted Doña Constanza to her dressing room and ensured, against the latter's protests, that she dressed in the toughest and most practical clothes and shoes, took no more than two pairs of underwear and two shirts, and nothing else.

When they returned to the living room, Rafael, Tomás, and Gonzago were all poring over the three-year-old copy of *Vogue*.

"They are strange women," said Tomás.

"They are all skinny, and they have no hair on their legs or in their armpits!" remarked Gonzago.

"Why would anyone want a book of pictures of white women who are obviously ill?" demanded Rafael.

"I would like to take this with me," said Doña Constanza, reaching over to take it.

"You may," said Gloria. "Give it to her."

"Are you a doctor?" asked Rafael, and Doña Constanza looked at him contemptuously.

"No, I am cultivated."

"Like a field?" asked Tomás, puzzled. "How?"

Doña Constanza was instructed to summon her maid, who was plainly terrified and could barely understand what she was being told. Gloria handed her the receipt, and her eyes lit up. "Ah," she said, "you are appropriating the mistress and redeeming her after the revolution?"

"Not quite," said Gloria. "You must give this to Don Hugh Evans without fail, or both he and Doña Constanza, and probably you, will be shot. Do you understand?"

"Yes, madame," said the maid tearfully, and she curtsied out of force of habit. Rafael giggled.

"Come," said Gloria. "We have many miles to walk. It is cool now, and we should be back by dawn."

"Walk?" said Doña Constanza. "I cannot walk!"

"Why not?" demanded Gloria.

"I have never walked. I would die in five minutes."

"You have never walked?" said Gloria, astonished. "Well, you are going to have to." She prodded Doña Constanza in the back with her rifle, and the group filed out of the back door and passed beneath the bougainvillaea above the terrace. The maid watched them go past the swimming pool, full as ever with algae and contented frogs, and saw them disappear into the dusk in the direction of the foothills. Then she ran back inside.

Don Hugh Evans returned twelve days later from the capital. He was a very tall, dark-haired, and distinguished-looking man of sturdy and athletic build, having used his extensive leisure time playing rugby at the Welsh and Irish Club and playing tennis at the Club Hojas. As he drove through the village, scattering the chickens, he felt that the people were looking at him in an odd way, and he was still wondering why when he brought his Japanese Jeep to a halt outside the hacienda. Inside, he found the maid tearfully biting her lips and twisting her skirts as she anticipated the storm.

Don Hugh strode from room to room, looking for his wife, and then came back into the hall. "Where is your mistress?" he said. "Is she out riding?"

"No, sir," replied the maid, choking back her sobs. "The revolution came a week ago and took her away, sir."

"The revolution?" He took her by the shoulders, towering over her, and shook her. "For God's sake, you mean she has been kidnapped?"

"Yes, sir. It was a week ago, sir."

Don Hugh stepped back and put his palm to his forehead. He wiped away a trickle of sweat. "Well, why in God's name did you not tell me before, you stupid woman? Are you a complete cretin?"

The maid shrank back before his fury. "Only the mistress knew where you were, sir. We went to Chiriguaná with the receipt to use the telegraph, but the station was destroyed by the revolution months ago, sir."

"Christ in heaven!" shouted Don Hugh. "What receipt? Tell me what receipt?"

"The one they made Doña Constanza write to you, sir." The maid was by now sobbing bitterly and barely capable of speech.

"Well, where is it, woman? Show it to me!"

"Oh, but sir, I cannot. We spent it."

"You spent it? What do you mean you spent it, you disgusting mulatta bitch?" Don Hugh advanced upon her, his eyes darting fire and his hand raised to strike her.

"Please, sir," pleaded the cowering maid, "we could not contact you, so it was no use. We could not tell the police because the revolution said they would kill you and my mistress if we did. So we spent it."

"How in God's name can you spend a receipt, for Christ's sake?"

"It was one hundred and twenty-two words, sir. We bought a lot of things and had a fiesta in the village for three days, sir." Her eyes lit up at the memory for an instant, and she looked coyly up at Don Hugh. "Everyone got very happy, sir."

"Oh, did they?" he yelled. "And who has the receipt now? Tell me before I twist your head off!"

"Oh, sir, it is in the provisions shop in Chiriguaná. Please do not hurt me."

Don Hugh put one huge hand around her neck and suspended her four inches above the floor against the wall. "When I get back, you half-breed moron, I am going to tear you into fragments and feed you to the vultures!"

He dropped her and turned on his heel. Back in his Jeep, he set off with a screech of tires, and did not stop for man, chicken, or dog until he arrived outside Pedro's Grandiosa Tienda de Ultramarinos in Chiriguaná. He kicked out at the chickens as he went in and marched up to the proprietor, who, sensing great peril, nipped smartly around the back of the table.

"Can I help, sir?" he asked unctuously. "*¿Ron cana? ¿Aguardiente?* Avocados? *¿Anticonceptivos?*"

"I want the receipt now. Come on, the receipt!" demanded Don Hugh, snapping his fingers in the man's face. "The receipt, or you are a dead man!"

"The receipt?" said the shopkeeper, puzzled. "What receipt?"

"The one for one hundred and twenty-two words!" shouted Don Hugh. "Give it to me!"

"But it was spent in my shop, so it is mine," said the shopkeeper. "So you can't have it. And anyway, I have already spent it myself." He dodged Don Hugh's attempt to grab his collar. "I bought something substantial from the policeman."

"The policeman!" exclaimed Don Hugh in astonishment. He turned, and in his rage and frustration he kicked out at a stack of guavas, sending them careening across the floor and further startling the chickens. The dog, which had been dozing by the door, slunk out with its tail between its legs, whining.

"Where the fuck is the policeman?"

"He's gone away. He went to Valledupar, but he said he would be back in four days."

Don Hugh returned to his hacienda blind with fury, cursing the country that could have its policeman take four days' unofficial leave and for no good reason. When he arrived, he found that the maid had already disappeared forever. Not having one inkling how to cook, he dispatched Sergio under threat of dismissal to find a cook by that evening. Sergio set off about his mission good-naturedly and returned with Consuelo the whore. "Oh, my God!" was all that Don Hugh could say, and soon found out that Consuelo was overgenerous with pimiento sauce. His mouth and throat on fire, he threw her out of the hacienda and spent four days alternately drunk and apoplectic with rage and indignation before driving at horrendous speed back to Chiriguaná.

The policeman, a bloated, bleary-eyed pig of a man with cross-eyes and a scar across his nose, was milking a goat in his kitchen when Don Hugh arrived. Five minutes later Don Hugh emerged still shaking with fury and this time agog with disbelief. For 122 words, the policeman had bought the use of all the whores in the *putería* as often as he liked for six months.

When Don Hugh entered the brothel, which was easily the best-appointed building in the whole pueblo, he was instantly set upon by half a dozen gaily chattering girls of all different shapes and sizes, making salacious suggestions. Don Hugh bellowed and threw them off. Just after he did so, the madam appeared; she was a huge mulatta as tall as Don Hugh, and possibly half as heavy again. The sight of this formidable lady had a calming effect upon the desperate husband, and in a voice that was almost controlled he asked if he could have the receipt for 122 words.

"No, señor," she said, "it is mine, why should you have it?"

"Then let me read it. The life of my wife depends upon it!"

"Very well, señor, but if you try to steal it, Felicidad will shoot you."

From the corner of his eye he saw that an innocent-looking whore of about fifteen was very expertly aiming a revolver at him.

"I will not steal it. Just let me read it!" Don Hugh was pleading.

Slowly the gigantic mulatta lifted the hem of her taffeta skirt, and from the top of her bulging thigh she took the receipt. Don Hugh took it from her and read it. He sank slowly onto a chair and buried his head in his hands. It was already too late.

Dumb with disbelief, he stumbled back out into the sunshine able to think about only one thing. It was completely irrelevant, but it was all he could think of. He called back in on the policeman. "What was the substantial thing that the shopkeeper bought from you? I'd just like to know."

The policeman looked up from his milking. "It was my niece from Valledupar. The man's a pedophile; it is really disgusting."

Don Hugh passed the shop on the way back to his Jeep. There was a skinny little girl of twelve piling up cassava, and as he walked by, she caught his eye with a saucy, coquettish glance before she turned away.

My God, he thought, *truly this country of mine is a sink of abominations.*

He was already nearly home when he heard a huge explosion. He stopped the Jeep and looked back to see a monstrous cloud of dust and debris ascending into the sky over Chiriguaná. Unable to resist his curiosity, he turned the Jeep around and sped back.

17

A Letter Home

La Estancia

M<small>A CHÈRE</small> M<small>AMAN</small>,

I am writing to you with the heaviest of hearts, for it seems that if anything can go wrong, it assuredly will. Everything, in fact, is going so badly that I am thinking seriously of putting an end to my seemingly futile endeavors and coming home to France, where at least I know that a warm and loving family awaits me, though who knows what kind of job I can take there after fifteen years of farming in the tropics?

To begin with, *ma chère Maman*, Françoise is terribly ill. Her health was never good at the best of times, but the heat and humidity of this place has so enervated her and depleted her resources that every mosquito bite seems to turn into an ever larger and more intractable sore. Believe me, I have tried everything. First, I tried lemon juice because its acidity makes it antiseptic; it stings formidably, but I have always found it effective on my own cuts and tropical ulcers. Secondly, I tried the purple ointment that I use on the cattle; this stings even worse but is also useless. Then, and this shows the measure of my desperation, I brought in the local hunter, who is a *brujo*, a kind of witch doctor. His name is Pedro, very tall and grizzly, and he has a huge reputation locally for his powers. They say he is in communication with angels, and he knows spells that he calls *secretos*.

Now, Maman, I know what you are thinking, that this is plain diabolism and that as a good Christian and a Catholic I should heartily excoriate it, but truly this place can drive one to such extremes of helplessness and desperation that one's choices are taken away.

Anyway, Pedro came by and laid his hands on Françoise's neck and looked very hard into her eyes. He whispered something into her ear which she did not understand even though her Spanish is, as you know, quite fluent, and then he came to see me privately. He told me that there is a lot more wrong with her than ulcers. As if I did not know already!

At about the same time I found some antibiotic powder in a cupboard that was three years out of date and sprinkled it on her wounds. She was better in a week! Perhaps I will never know whether it was the powder or the secrets of Pedro that cured her, or perhaps it was both. In this country reason does not apply to anything.

It also does not apply to Françoise. You must know, Maman, that I am more convinced than when I last wrote to you that she has cancer. Her breasts are now more discolored, deformed, and grotesque than ever. I cannot describe the obscenity that now disfigures her once-beautiful form. I also believe that the cancer has spread to her kidneys, as she is beginning to urinate blood and she is permanently exhausted. She is as pale and insubstantial as a ghost in this country where everyone else is deep-roasted by the sun!

But there is nothing I can do! She believes only in "natural" medicines and in her faith healer back in Toulouse who cured her of migraines fifteen years ago. I have tried earnestly to persuade her to let me take her to a doctor in the capital or even to her faith healer in Toulouse, but she steadfastly refuses. Instead, she has written to him to heal her from a distance, since she says that that is perfectly feasible. The man has sent me a bill for ten thousand francs already! As you know, Maman, my farm brings me in the equivalent of twenty francs a day, which makes me a very rich man by local standards, but a pauper by the standards of France. The fact is that I cannot possibly pay the man, quite apart from the sheer difficulty of going hundreds of miles to a town where I can actually arrange an international money order.

The hunter told me that the only cure for cancer that he knows is to eat a freshly killed coral snake raw. Imagine! And you have to do it every week! These snakes are lethally venomous, and people kill them on sight, so they are not as common as they once were. Nevertheless, I offered rewards for live coral snakes, and I now have a couple of months' supply in a large wooden crate. We killed the first one, and Françoise did manage to eat it at great pain to her conscience, as she has now been a vegetarian for many years. She said it was not as vile as she had anticipated, and the cancer did seem to retreat. However, she has refused to eat any more snakes, as she says that she has to stick to her vegetarian principles, and to be honest, Maman, I think that really she wants to die.

After all, she only came out here to be with me on the rebound, so to speak, and we never found the kind of happiness we might have had the right to expect from a marriage. She misses not being able to do her pottery; I did build her a pottery recently; but we cannot find any clay, and we cannot possibly fuel a kiln either. She also finds the peasants unspeakably crude and venial. I got used to it long ago and adapted to it, and she does not like that either. Also, the humidity of the rainy season reduces her to abject misery. To make matters worse, a rift has come between us over matters of the body. I am so repelled, and she is so humiliated and ashamed, by her condition that all marital congress ceased long ago, at about the time of her last miscarriage.

I wish I could end this letter with some happier news, but I am afraid that there is yet more bad news to come.

I have been visited by the guerrillas of the People's Liberation Force. They arrived on Thursday night as we were all sitting out after dinner, and I have never seen a more ruffianly bunch. There were three of them in khaki with their shirts undone. They all had shaggy black beards and wild hair, and every one of them was draped with so much armament and ammunition that you would not think they could walk at all. They were surprisingly polite, but that does not make their demands any more reasonable.

They gave me one week to deliver a quarter of a million dollars in cash to them! I could not possibly explain to you how shocked and astonished I was! I was so amazed that despite shivering with fear, I could not help bursting out laughing; thus it was their turn to be surprised. I tried to explain to them that European origin does not automatically signify immense wealth, that I earned only a few pesos a day, and that my wife was too ill for me to leave her at all. When they saw her, they at least believed me on that score. In the end they agreed that I should supply them with food now and again. I know that this is absolutely wrong and that I should refuse to deal with them at all, but in fact, I have no choice. The police force here does not in any real sense exist; I had to bribe a magistrate to have a man who stole my donkey arrested, and it was sheer chance that the animal found its own way home over fifty miles. Nor can I go to the army for protection; it is grossly incompetent, and its presence would instantly ensure my death at the hands of the guerrillas. The army has already indulged in two minor massacres near here, and the local population would probably kill me if I invited it to come and protect us. Certainly they would not trade with me, and I would lose fifteen years' worth of trust and goodwill overnight. Also, I am considerably more afraid of the army than of the guerrillas, for the latter at least have some ideals and a lot more discipline. The guerrillas have a system of paper credits for everything they take and promise to redeem them "after the victory"; the good thing about this is that you can use the credits as currency around here, so that if I am only supplying food, I would actually make a decent profit, which would not be the case if I was giving them money.

However, Françoise and I are terrified that they might

decide to kidnap the children now that they know where we are. Recently they (a different group, I hear) kidnapped Constanza Evans for a ransom of half a million dollars, and her tenants celebrated for three days amid scenes of the most indescribable lewdness and exaggerated revelry. I know she was a bad land-lord, but it just goes to show that one cannot automatically count on the loyalty of one's work force.

Therefore, Françoise and I decided to send Jean, Pierre, and Marie to stay indefinitely with friends in the capital. At first they refused to go at all. They are real country children, and the thought of being away from their beloved horses, dogs, and cats and not being able to swim in the river or tease the alligators (I always tell them not to) caused a lot of tears and protests. I did my best to explain to them that they were in great danger, but that made them even more reluctant to go, in case anything happened to Françoise and me. Eventually Marie donned the mantle of eldest child and agreed to go, so then the other two also gave in, and I took them away last week. The train took two days, and the journey was just appalling. The tracks are so roughly laid that they have to import especially sprung seats to make traveling bearable. Consequently, you bounce up and down like some demented trampolinist, and ordinary behavior is impossible. At first the children thought it was hilarious and were acting like idiots, trying to bounce even higher; but then they all were sick more or less at once, and we could not find anyone to clear it up, so it just lay there and stank until some-body's dog came along and ate it, at which point I was sick as well. We lived on *arepas*, and I hope that they are not now as constipated as I am.

There was also, Maman, a dreadful accident on the train. You know how the girls here always ape American fashions? Well, there was a mulatta girl on the train in high heels, and I suspect she had had too many beers—we all had, in the effort to cool off—and she fell out of the side of the train. It seems that the train lurched just as she was passing from one carriage to the next, and she toppled over sideways on her heels. There is no concertina there to stop you from falling out, so out she fell. The train stopped and went backward, and they carried her into our carriage.

I do not, Maman, have the words to describe the horror of the scene. She had lost all the flesh down the left side of her body by ricocheting along the stones of the embankment, and we could clearly see all her bones. There was blood dripping from her body, but we could do nothing for her as there were no hospitals for hundreds of miles and no such thing as an ambulance or a telephone with which to summon one. She would not lose consciousness, and all she did was lie there crying silently for two hours until she died. When that happened, we were all thankful on her behalf, but there ensued at least another two hours' worth of weeping and hysterical wailing on the part of everyone in the carriage. You would think we had all known her for years, although all we knew was that she was called María. The children were very badly shaken, and they had no tears left with which to wish me farewell.

The farm now seems like a mortuary; when I got back, everything was silent and still, and I realized it was because the children were not here, shouting and fooling about and squabbling among themselves. I went into their room, and I sat on Pierre's bed and wept with the sorrow of it all.

Maman, I feel as empty as a cave and as desolate as a desert. When I first came to this country, I was brimming with optimism and energy, and I was determined to carve myself a good life after that fracas I caused in France. Back then at least this country had some semblance of democracy, before *La Violencia*, and there was a little culture to be found to remind me of home. One could actually go to the capital and hear a fine orchestra, or see a good play, or stroll down an avenue without getting mauled on all sides by begging lepers. There was some prosperity then, but now there is 200 percent inflation, and it appears that all money goes to pay interest on foreign debts. Nowadays the government just strips its assets, and everything goes to ruin. Honestly, Maman, you would not believe what a mess everything is, it makes me sick to the heart, you cannot buy the most elementary necessities, and even my plans to mechanize the farm have had to be shelved because although you can buy the machinery from the Casa Inglesa for preposterous sums, you simply cannot buy spare parts anywhere. The people here have developed an incredible ability to improvise with almost nothing, and the only way the peasants keep going is by cultivating cocaine and marijuana, which has made everyone dishonest. The prostitutes (forgive me for mentioning them) become younger and younger, and everyone lives in fear of assault and robbery.

And yet I still feel, *ma chère Maman,* how glorious this country is, and how romantic. Even the moon is four times the size of that of France, and the birds and butterflies are indescribably beautiful and joyously colored. The people, too, are brightly arrayed and seemingly always laughing and delighted. The soil is fertile, and we even have emeralds and oil; but it seems nothing ever comes of it. People here help each other out for nothing, and yet no official will ever more a finger without a bribe—isn't that a contradiction? They love all humanity, these people, but kill each other with not a moment's thought!

I think, all in all, that it will break my heart when I have to leave, as one day I will surely have to. I love it here, so much, and I have put fifteen years of toil and sweat into improving my portion of it. I have even managed to continue to love Françoise, who has never forgiven me for not being Jean-Michel and who has often made me unhappy. I detest the thought that I may have to leave her body in this soil. If she dies, Maman, as I know in my bones she will soon—no, don't click your tongue and reproach me for being morbid!—I am resolved to sell everything I have—but who would buy this land in what is becoming a war zone?—and return to France with the coffin. This country, which I have grown to love and even, God knows how, to respect, is causing me too much grief, and I cannot bear its cruelty much longer. When I die, Maman, I hope that although my body rest in France, my heart be buried here.

I do not know if you will get this letter. You cannot buy stamps here anymore, and so you have to give the letter and some money to buy stamps with to the train driver when the train passes through Chiriguaná. In these straitened times I do not know if I can rely on his honesty.

I give you many kisses and always remember you.

Your son,

ANTOINE

P.S. I have just heard an explosion. I wonder what it is?

18

The People's Liberation Force Confounds the People's Vanguard and the National Army in One Stroke

On Thursday, March 14, a very weary campesino, covered with pale dust and sweating prodigiously, arrived on his mule at the secret encampment of the People's Liberation Force, which was situated in a small valley accessible only through a narrow defile, which was heavily guarded at all times.

On either side of the valley rose sheer walls of rock; the guerrillas had, by observing the local wild goats, worked out how it was possible for them to leave the valley by ascent if necessary, in the complete confidence that any pursuers would not be able to follow them. In the event of any incursion by the army into the valley, the guerrillas planned to pick them off from above, having blown up the passage through the defile, for which purpose they had strategically placed two barrels of dynamite. This dynamite they had bought from the government Inspectorate of Mines by posing as gold prospectors. They had produced a document showing proof of ownership of the "find," drawn up by a guerrilla who had once been a lawyer, and had offered the official 5 percent of profits for life in return for plentiful supplies of free dynamite. Generally they used the dynamite for blowing holes in banks so that they could use the money for paying off the "5 percent of profits" to the official, but the remainder they used for the revolution.

The People's Liberation Force was mainly a demolition group, whereas, for example, the People's Vanguard was mainly an ambushing group, the People's Liberation Front dealt mostly with kidnapping, the Popular Action Front specialized in blackmail and extortion, and the Revolutionary Socialists in assassinating important people. The People's Liberation Force probably chose its particular specialty because it was one of the safest; there is, after all, very little danger in planting bombs and then retreating to a safe distance. It apparently never perceived that you cannot help alleviate the plight of the masses by destroying the infrastructure built up painfully slowly for their benefit on what little national wealth remained. But however paradoxical its behavior, what happened to the People's Liberation Force was simply according to a general rule that applies to all humankind. This rule is that people always think that if they are very expert at something, that thing must therefore be extremely important. The People's Liberation Force was expert with explosives and therefore thought that what it did was crucial.

Its little valley in the mountains was densely wooded and well watered, and the guerrillas lived a life of Arcadian simplicity and leisure, only venturing forth when one of them had a good idea about what to blow up next. The old campesino on the mule, who was their "eyes" in Valledupar, had arrived with an excellent idea, and he went with it straight to the commander of the group, who was known appropriately as El Golpe.

El Golpe had once been a Montonero guerrilla in Argentina but had left when General Videla's campaign of terror had got out of even Videla's control and anyone who even looked left-wing was "disappeared." El Golpe had seen for himself how futile it is to attempt, as a guerrilla, to confront a highly disciplined, numerous, ruthless, and fanatical enemy, and he had therefore come to this country to wage war on a more vulnerable enemy—one that was numerous, ruthless, fanatical, undisciplined, and incompetent. El Golpe was proud of the fact that he looked very like Ernesto Guevara, with his gentle eyes and black beard that would never grow as abundantly as Fidel's, and there was something about this similarity to Che that inspired in his men a warm respect and fierce devotion. Most of them tried to imitate his Italianate Argentinean accent and his fluid gait.

What the campesino told El Golpe was that a soldier in a bar had been heard saying that he and his battalion were going to Chiriguaná to suppress a local rebellion and were intending to encamp on the savanna on the northern side of the Mula. As the peasant said, "Chiriguaná is not far to go from here, and there must be something you can blow up." El Golpe immediately realized what that "something" was and went off to find two of his most expert demolishers.

He found them sitting side by side on the riverbank with their feet in the water, involved in an earnest conversation about aphrodisiacs. "I tell you," one of them was saying, "she gave me no rest for a month. . . ."

"In my case it was two months, and I came near to death."

"You two," interrupted El Golpe, coming up from behind and placing a hand on each of their shoulders. "I have a little job for you." And he explained carefully what it was. That evening they loaded a donkey with dynamite and set out through the defile.

"¡Buena suerte!" called the guard.

"We need no luck," replied one of the men. "This one's simple."

"Well, good luck anyway. If you find a willing girl, give her one for me!"

"No, my friend, I would not wish to infect her with one of your diseases."

"May she give you one of hers then!"

At about the same time Gonzago, Rafael, and Tomás were setting off with General Fuerte's burra, María, to collect Don Hugh's ransom money, which was due to be deposited the next day. The plan was that they should lie in wait in the scrub near the bridge in order to observe all movement for several hours both before and after Don Hugh left the money. In this way they could ensure that they were not going to walk into an ambush, and they would be able to see Don Hugh coming and going and make sure that he was unaccompanied.

They arrived just before dawn and selected a good spot in which to conceal themselves, with a clear view of the bridge and the road that crossed it.

The bridge was a simple ferroconcrete structure of the cheapest and most serviceable kind. It arched at either end and was supported by four concrete pillars, evenly spaced at intervals, which were set on piles sunk into the riverbed. It had been built in the first place by a United Nations team as part of a long-forgotten development aid project, and its original function had been to prevent the loss of vehicles incurred by foolhardy truck drivers attempting to ford the river during the floods brought on by the rainy season. Before the road from Valledupar to the capital was opened, the bridge had been on the main commercial arterial route from the seaports, and during the floods commerce had almost always come to a halt. But now it had fallen from its former glory, and its users were mainly local people on foot or on horseback; consequently, it was in a very poor state of repair. The tarmac had been squashed up sideways by vehicles passing over it during the midday heat and was badly broken up. The original designers had not catered for the stupendous humidity and heat of the region so that now, twenty-five neglected years after its construction, the concrete was soggy and flaky, and huge lumps of it had fallen off into the river below. Additionally, the fierce current of the Mula, which in full spate was capable of carrying large stones hurtling along with it, had largely eroded the arches and pillars. Any heavy vehicles that had passed that way in recent times usually chose to ford the river as in former times, rather than risk the bridge, and as in former times, the river now contained the rusty hulks of partly salvaged and pirated trucks.

Despite its ramshackle state, the bridge still appeared from the middle distance to be a dignified and imposing piece of architecture, and the locals were very proud of it since it was the only one in the whole area, and it was theirs. At either end of it was a notice which said, "You are now crossing Chiriguaná Bridge." Also on the notice were graffiti detailing the states of people's hearts ("Without Erendira There Is No Life"), political slogans ("Down with the Oligarchy"), and extraneous information and exhortations ("Juanito Fucks Donkeys," "Come to Consuelo's").

Tomás, Gonzago, and Rafael sorted out a system of watching the bridge by rotation, one hour on, two hours off. During their time off the men would smoke, doze, toss pebbles at lizards, and converse. By midday all three of them were feeling the effects of having been trekking all night. It was also the time when the whole country stops for siesta, even in wartime. This had nothing to do with the "natural indolence" imputed to Latinos by the rest of the world; it had to do with not being able to breathe, not being able to move without pouring with perspiration, not being able to see anything (because of the sweat in one's eyes and because of the shimmering heat hazes and mirages), and it had to do with not being able to touch anything outdoors for fear of being burned. The whole nation sank gratefully into torpor somewhere in the shade, and one had as little chance of being detected of misdeeds during siesta as one did under cover of darkness; even making love noisily during siesta scandalized neighbors, not because it was making love but because it was noisy and therefore antisocial when enervated people were trying to doze.

Tomás and Rafael slumbered in the shade, and Gonzago stared at the bridge for as long as his eyes could stand the glare of the wavering image. He closed his eyes and rested them on his arm until they stopped itching and hurting, and then he watched again. The sweat soaked his shirt and his trousers; a thirst rose in his throat as though he had half swallowed a porcupine. The intervals between resting his eyes and watching became gradually longer and longer, and then Gonzago, too, fell into a profound sleep, in which he dreamed guiltlessly that he was still watching the bridge.

All three of them had been obliviously asleep for two hours when they were brought back to wakefulness by what appeared to be the end of the world. First there was a rumbling that shook the earth and sent stones skittering about like demented cockroaches. Then there was a roar like the voice of God and a rush of air that sucked their breath out of them and drew their straw sombreros high into the air. Then there was a mighty wind as the air rushed back into the vacuum and returned them, flat on their backs, into the position from which, bewildered, they had half arisen. They could see an enormous cloud of dust and smoke billowing out above where the bridge had been, and it advanced on them like a sandstorm in a desert. They hastily tugged their shirttails over their mouths and noses, only to be thrown to the ground by a furious hail of debris that seemed to appear out of nowhere. Rocks, stones, lumps of steel and concrete, water, and mud descended on them at prodigious velocity and in enormous volume, until, half buried, grievously bruised, and wildly disorientated they rose groggily from the detritus to take stock.

"*Mierda,*" said Gonzago.

"*Madre de Dios,*" said Rafael.

"*Hijo de puta,*" said Tomás.

The land about them was laid to waste in a small but extravagant apocalypse; bushes were uprooted and leafless; the ground was littered with little pieces of bridge. Among the stones a fish flapped its tail forlornly as it gulped for air; Gonzago hit it on the head and slipped it into his *mochila*. "For later," he said.

"You two have a nosebleed," observed Tomás.

"So do you," replied Rafael, and then he squinted through the cloud of dust that had begun to settle around the area of the bridge. "My God, look at that!"

There was nothing left where the center span of the bridge had been. Steel rods projected from the broken spars, and the pillars leaned raggedly sideways, buckled and twisted. In the river was an overturned army truck, some distance from the bridge; it had clearly been vaulted all that distance by the explosion. From somewhere near the truck there came a pitiful and haunting wailing; it was a soldier staggering out of the water, carrying his amputated arm.

The three guerrillas saw with consternation amounting to panic that the whole area of the bridge was crawling with soldiers. They were in complete confusion and disarray, but they could clearly see and hear the fat figure of Colonel Figueras ordering his men to fan out and search the area. Just as the three were about to turn tail and flee, they saw a Jeep come tearing along the track, halting at the bridge only just in time. They saw a tall, dark-haired European get out and walk to the edge of the abyss and stand there in amazement surveying the chaos.

"That's Don Hugh!" exclaimed Rafael. "He must have brought the money."

"Well, we can't go and get from him," said Tomás.

"Let's go," said Rafael.

"Let me shoot a soldier first," pleaded Gonzago.

"If you can find your rifle in all this rubbish," replied Rafael. "Don't be stupid. Let's go before the bastards get us. God knows where the donkey is."

They were not in the best condition for walking, still concussed from the blast, still confused and disorientated, but the fear of being caught by the soldiers spurred them to hurry despite their uncooperative legs and feet.

When they staggered into the camp six hours later, they were a pitiful sight. They were colored all over a uniform shade of gray from the paste of watery dust that had descended on them. Their clothes hung off them in rags, and all three were limping. Only their eyes shone forth whitely through the muck and grime, and all of them were caked in dark blood from the cuts they had sustained. Tomás's forehead was oddly distorted by a huge bruise on one side. They lurched to the center of the clearing and fell flat on their faces. When Remedios came out to question them, they were sprawled out, fast asleep from shock and fatigue.

The camp was in uproar, agog to know what had befallen their three comrades, but Remedios ordered that the three men should be brought into the medical hut and cleaned up. Federico and Franco fetched water from the stream, and the men were undressed, washed, and reclothed without waking or even murmuring. Doña Constanza, aware that her fate depended upon what had happened to Tomás, Rafael, and Gonzago, went into the medical hut and tended them most solicitously, wiping their foreheads unnecessarily often with a wet cloth, and muttering little prayers for their health. She noticed with a sharp little pang how handsome Gonzago was and how innocent he appeared in repose. She wiped his forehead more often than the others.

When they awoke at midday the next day, Remedios questioned them rigorously despite their appalling headaches and the fact that their bruises made it impossible for them to get up or even lift an arm. When Remedios had finished, she summoned Doña Constanza. "It seems your husband arrived with the money but was unable to hand it over because the place where he was to deposit it was blown up. So we cannot shoot you yet. You have a remission."

"Yet?" queried Doña Constanza. "Can you not just send to my husband to arrange another place?"

"No," replied Remedios, gravely shaking her head. "It appears that we have a more immediate and pressing problem that takes priority. The army has invaded the area. We must concern ourselves with that."

Constanza looked puzzled. "I do not want to be pedantic, but an army cannot 'invade' its own country."

Remedios snorted. "Ours can. It frequently does."

"Oh," said Doña Constanza. "In that case may I have your permission to continue tending the wounded?"

"Certainly," said Remedios. "For once in your life you can do something useful."

With a light heart Doña Constanza returned to the medical hut and wiped Gonzago's forehead more often than the others'. He smiled painfully up at her. "Doña Constanza, there is a fine fish in my *mochila;* I would like you to have it, or it will grow rotten for nothing."

19

In Which Josef Contemplates Death and Plans Are Made

On a day when he had smoked too many *puros* and drunk too much cane rum, the evening found Josef lying in his hammock beneath the bougainvillaea while the crickets scraped and rattled in the scrubby hedgerows and a vast tropical moon rose high above the caracolee tree, where from time to time the howler monkeys whooped and cavorted like schoolboys on an unexpected holiday. In the distance he could discern the gruntings of the caimans, which lay somnolent in the green waters of the spring and whose eyes glowed red if ever he passed that way with a lantern. He had often thought of catching them and selling the skins so that women rich beyond his imagination in Paris or New York could have handbags, shoes, and purses of "alligator skin" that would cost several hundred times more than he would be paid for all the skins of all the caimans on the entire farm; but Josef was sentimental about the idle creatures and did not care for the rich ladies of New York and Paris any more than he cared for the army or the governor, and so he let them be and instead flattened the heads of vipers and coral snakes with his machete. It was a rule never to cut off their heads, for it was said that they would still bite and that the viper could still leap at you by flicking its jaws against the earth. In the village there was a man who had had his arm amputated with an ax because he had ignored this advice and because there were no doctors to administer antidotes and perform operations within 350 miles. Unlike most others, Josef conscientiously refrained from killing boas, on the ground that they ate rats, and he shot iguanas only for meat and not for wantonness. The remains he threw in the river for the pleasure of seeing the waters boil with the little fish competing for scraps and morsels. Sometimes he shuddered at the thought of being such scraps and morsels himself and vowed that when he died, he should be buried deep, in the proper place, and to this end he had already paid the priest, in installments, the price of his burial in a box, not in a sheet. Often he said, "I will never be eaten by wild pigs, ants, *tigres,* or fish!" and this became a joke among his friends, who shrugged their shoulders and said, "Who cares? When you are dead, you are dead," or, "At least as food you might die more usefully than you lived!"

On this day Josef was indeed thinking of death, but not of his own. He was thinking first of the death of the insects that fizzled and spit in the flame of the lamp, of the singed, fuzzy little aliens that each morning he swept off the table and off the stones or scraped out of the lamp with a grubby finger and a pursing of the lips. He was thinking of how like the death of human beings this was, for with every death of every creature a whole universe dies, too, yet strangely enough, no death really seemed to make much difference. *We all are insects,* he thought, *but because I am this very insect which I am, I am the center of everything,* and he rolled that phrase *de todo* about his mind until it appeared to mean so much that it was no longer intelligible.

He thought secondly, with sudden and startling clarity, *Perhaps we should shoot only the officers.* He decided that in the morning he would relay this thought to Hectoro, Pedro, and the others, who were preparing for the return of the army, now that people coming from Chiriguaná had reported that the whole area was swarming with soldiers. Everyone in the village realized that the army had returned with the intention of securing revenge for its previous humiliations, and everyone was in a state of nervous anticipation, wondering what to do and looking for solid leadership.

In fact, the division of leadership fell fairly naturally into place. Consuelo the whore emerged rapidly as leader of the women and organizer of the children, and Dolores the whore emerged as her lieutenant. They supervised the storing of supplies in strategic caches, tore up old clothing in anticipation of the need for bandages, practiced leaping from behind doorways, machete in hand, and squabbled with the men for being too proud and stupid to arm them properly with rifles. The women worked alongside the men to construct a rampart across the street topped with barbed wire stolen brazenly from Don Hugh's *finca*. They slashed and burned the fields immediately surrounding the village so that the army would have no cover for sneaking up, and they filled every available receptacle with water, both for drinking and for putting out fires.

Among the men, things were not quite as clear. Misael, Pedro the hunter, Hectoro, and Josef formed, as it were, a leadership cadre. Josef was fundamentally an ideas man; he submitted intelligent suggestions to the others, who usually decided to carry them out. Misael was expert in sorting out the minute details of what needed to be done. Hectoro was excellent at issuing orders charismatically and in such a manner that one could not refuse, and Pedro was the one who planned strategy and who would also emerge as the tactician when hostilities commenced. Professor Luis acted as general lieutenant and messenger boy for all of them, his not being the kind of decisive and wily intelligence required of a warrior. He was also useful for implementing some of Josef's ideas; for example, it was he who worked out how to electrify the barbed wire with power from the same little windmill that had once powered the record player, and he also worked out how to dam the Mula so that the army could not easily cross it.

Behind all of these men, functioning as a sort of éminence grise, was Don Emmanuel himself. He did not give any orders or make any decisions, and he did not directly involve himself in the preparations, except for turning a blind eye when his tractor was borrowed to help in constructing the rampart. All that he did was give his opinion.

When Josef suggested to the others that they should aim to kill only the officers, they all approved immediately.

"The soldiers are conscripts on National Service," said Josef, "and they do not want to fight anyway."

"They are campesinos like us," observed Misael. "They are our brothers, so we should not kill them."

"I agree," said Pedro. "No army can fight with no leaders. Without leaders they will not know what to do, and they will go away."

Only Hectoro had reservations. "Maybe you are right, but it will be hard to hold off from firing until one sees an officer. Also, nothing puts an unwilling soldier off fighting more than seeing his comrades killed all around him. I know this."

"I think we should ask Don Emmanuel," said Josef.

They found Don Emmanuel, stark naked as usual, sitting in the river cooling off after work. They stood on the bank, looking down at him, and put Josef's idea to the test.

Don Emmanuel said, "Ah," thoughtfully and stroked his immense red beard. Then he shook his head. "I think it may be a bad idea."

The four men were astonished. "Why?" asked Josef.

"Because," replied Don Emmanuel, "officers have the smallest balls. If you are to feed the vultures, do it with the largest testicles, out of charity."

The four looked at each other in even greater astonishment. Misael, realizing that Don Emmanuel was beginning the conversation with his usual pleasantries replied, "Then we should shoot you first, as your *cojones* are largest."

Don Emmanuel pretended to clutch his genitals protectively. "In that case, my friends, I will give you some more reasons. But first, what makes you believe that you can tell which ones are the officers?"

"It is obvious," said Josef. "They wear different uniforms. They are lighter green in color, and they have little soft hats with peaks. They are armed only with a pistol in a black holster, they have rather white faces, and they speak Spanish very badly. You see them taking charge of everything and giving orders, and they are always chewing."

"Chewing?" said Don Emmanuel. "I can assure you that the uniform of the officers is exactly the same as the soldiers', and they speak Spanish perfectly. These other people are not the officers."

"Who are they then?" asked Pedro. "Camp whores?"

"No," replied Don Emmanuel. "They are Rangers."

"Rangers?" said Hectoro and Misael simultaneously, an expression of puzzlement on their faces.

"Rangers are American military advisers. I am told that some of them are CIA, but I do not know anything about that. They are mostly Vietnam veterans who are expert in jungle warfare and counterinsurgency. They come here to tell our officers what to do and to look after American interests."

"That is even better," exclaimed Misael delightedly. "If we kill the Americanos, our officers will not know what to do, and they will go home with the soldiers!"

"It would be a mistake to kill Americans," said Don Emmanuel.

"But if we kill them, the Americans will go home!" said Hectoro.

"You do not know Americans," replied Don Emmanuel. "For one thing, they are quite happy to throw their men away in futile causes. Secondly, they always believe they are in the right and that God is personally fighting for them, so they never give up. If you kill one gringo, they will send two in his place, and if you kill them, they will send over a fleet of helicopters. In any case it is better for you if you do not kill them, for they do you a lot of good." Don Emmanuel smiled.

"And why is that?" asked Hectoro.

"It is simple," replied Don Emmanuel. "Although they are fanatics, they are mostly decent men. When they are present, our officers feel ashamed to commit atrocities. Of course, some of them are not decent at all, but a lot of them are. Secondly, they do not speak Spanish very well, no"—he corrected himself—"they speak some Spanish Spanish, but not true Castilian Spanish like you and me. They learn it in academies and when they come here, no one understands them and they do not understand anyone either, so their advice is always misconstrued." Don Emmanuel laughed. "It helps to keep our army in chaos, and that is good for you. Also, most of the soldiers do not like them because they are gringos, they are rich, and they think they know everything. But they do not know us, and they do not understand us, and all that happens when they stay here is that they get angry and frustrated."

"So if we do not shoot the gringos," said Josef, "we can still shoot the officers?"

"If you can tell who they are," replied Don Emmanuel, "but they have a reputation for leading from behind, and in any case, that, too, would be a mistake."

"And I suppose you will tell us why," interjected Hectoro, who was becoming impatient.

"Yes, Hectoro, that, too, is simple. They are the sons of the oligarchy, that's why. If you kill them alone, the oligarchy will mobilize every last centavo, every last soldier, every last policeman, and they will use the foulest and most desperate means against you. I advise you simply to wound them, in which case they will have to go home, they are heroes, and everyone is happy. Mama cries with joy over her returning son. If you kill him, she cries for revenge and threatens to withdraw her funds from the Conservative party unless drastic action is taken." Don Emmanuel laughed to himself. "Now may I make some suggestions?"

"Go on," said Pedro. "But do not make any more jokes about testicles. All this is very serious."

"I think," said Don Emmanuel, "that you should find ways of making them miserable. Poison the water in the places where they drink. I have a dead steer I would be glad to lend you if you would like to immerse it in the Mula. Also, I advise you to piss and shit in the Mula as much as possible, below the village, of course. Sell them meat and fruit with rat poison in it, just enough to make them vomit a lot. I think you should frighten them, too. Most soldiers are afraid of the dark. I am sure you can think of something. Also, I have done a little something for you myself. And I confess it has something to do with testicles." His eyes twinkled with amusement. The four men waited.

"It concerns a pretty little whore in Chiriguaná, called Felicidad."

"A very fine whore," said Hectoro.

"Indeed. I discovered from the doctor in Chiriguaná, at the clinic, that Felicidad has been to Barranquilla and has picked up a fine dose of the clap and also a little touch of syphilis. I have given her four thousand pesos to wait two weeks before she has the injections, on one condition."

"Upon what condition, Don Emmanuel? I hope you are not playing with us!" exclaimed Hectoro, who was still impatient and was shifting uncomfortably.

"Upon the condition that she enters the army camp all full of enthusiasm for the conquering heroes and sleeps with as many officers and gringo advisers as she can manage. I think that within a month most of the officers and gringos will have pretty little chancres on their *palomas,* and possibly in their mouths, and they will have pus dripping also from them. Within a month, when they urinate, they will feel as though they are pissing broken glass, and I think they will withdraw rapidly to Valledupar to attend the military hospital."

The four men began to laugh, and Don Emmanuel broke into a happy grin. "I thought you would be pleased."

As they walked back to the village, Hectoro said, "All the same, it will be difficult to resist the temptation to shoot a gringo."

"I think I will shoot just one, for the satisfaction," responded Misael.

"And I will shoot just one officer, in the legs," said Pedro.

"But," said Josef, "we still have one month at least of the army, even if Don Emmanuel's plan works. We have still got one month in which we will have to fight, and that is a very long time. I think we should take the fight to them so that they do not come to the village and destroy our homes and our fields. I think we should attack them first."

"I will go," said Pedro. "I am a hunter. I know many ways to kill and not to be seen, God forgive me for it. I will go to Chiriguaná."

Thoughtfully Hectoro said, "And I, too, will go to Chiriguaná. I must go to the doctor in any case."

Misael looked concerned. "You are ill, Hectoro?"

"Not yet, but I would like to be sure. I had a fine time last week, with Felicidad."

20

The Innocents

Aurelio arose just before dawn and put on his clothes. He stirred the embers of the previous night's fire and added to it a little dry grass. When that flared up, he added bark and twigs, and very soon the delicious smell of frying cassava was wafting out over the clearing and into the trees. In the woods the animals were stirring, and their calls reminded him with a pang of how Parlanchina had once delighted him with her impersonations. He stood in the doorway of the hut and looked out over to the mound where the girl lay in peace. "Good morning, my sweet one," he said, and he heard her chattering gaily and saw her striding toward him.

"*Bueno' día'*, Papacito," said Parlanchina, and she kissed him on the cheek before she disappeared, her long hair swaying. Before she went into the trees, she looked over her shoulder and smiled gently.

Aurelio always saw Parlanchina at this time of the morning, and usually they spoke a few words together. Once she had come to him when he stood by the river waiting to spear a fish; she touched him on the shoulder and whispered, "Tell me your real name."

Aurelio had turned to see her laughing at him, and he reached out to her. She touched his fingers to her cheeks and kissed them, and she had laughed again and said, "I know your real name now anyway. But to me you are always Papacito, and I will not say your name in case anyone hears."

"Parlanchina . . ." he had begun to say, but she had touched her finger to his lips and had faded away. It always filled him with the most exquisite sadness when she left him. He had wanted to ask her if the cat was still with her.

Carmen stirred in her hammock. "*Querido,* why are you doing my work? It is for me to make breakfast. You should not change the order of our lives; it brings bad luck."

Aurelio turned and walked over to her hammock. He looked into her sleepy eyes and laughed ironically. "The order of our lives is changed already."

"Have you spoken with Gwubba?" asked Carmen.

"We have spoken."

"Why do I not see her? Why does she not speak with me?"

"It is always so," said Aurelio. "A son appears to his mother and a daughter to her father. If we had had a son, he would have come to you and I would have seen nothing. And besides, I am an Indian. Spirits appear naturally to us. To your kind they must be summoned by spells, and the white man refuses to see them anyway."

Carmen reflected a moment. "I am sad that I do not see her. Aurelio?"

"Carmencita?"

"How do I find my real name if I have never known it?"

"You do not need one," replied Aurelio. "You are not an Indian. Your afterworld is not the same."

"And if I want to be with you?"

"Then," said Aurelio, "someone must tell you your real name. But I cannot; I do not know it."

"Gwubba was not an Indian," said Carmen, "and she had a real name."

"You will have yours if you want it," said Aurelio.

They squatted in the gentle light of the dawn and ate the cassava in silence. Then, without a word, Aurelio stood up and walked off to find the path where Parlanchina had met her brutal death. When he reached the path, she was waiting for him, tall and beautiful, and in her arms she bore the cat. She smiled at her father and put the cat down. It strolled away, its tail waving in the undergrowth. Fondly Aurelio watched it disappear. "Are you coming with me?" asked Aurelio.

"No, Papacito. I am staying to watch."

Aurelio stood on the path a second, gathering his energy and purpose for the long walk into the cordillera, and then he strode off, keeping a sharp eye open for any new mines with their telltale triple antennas. He tried mostly to keep to the side of the path.

Four hours later he walked with dignity into the center of the camp and sat down. The *guerrilleros* gathered around him, astonished by his effrontery, mesmerized by his exotic appearance, and curious about what he was doing. Aurelio was engaged in dropping coca leaves and snail shells into the neck of his gourd. With the skill of many years of habit he rapidly crushed and pounded them with deft movements of the pestle, and then he stuck the pestle into his mouth and looked up at the men and women who surrounded him, some pointing their weapons. "I would speak with the woman who is your leader."

The warriors looked at each other, surprised.

"How do you know our leader is a woman?" demanded Franco. "Are you a spy?"

"I do not know the word," replied Aurelio. "I have eyes."

"How did you know we are here?" asked Federico, who had always believed that the encampment was a secret to all the world.

"I live in the jungle below," said Aurelio. "I have always known. I have something important to tell the woman. I have something that all of you should know, if you would live."

Federico ran off to fetch Remedios, who came more out of curiosity than a sense of urgency. "Here is the woman," said Aurelio, and gravely he stood up and faced her. "I have news, if you would save your life."

Remedios sensed that it behooved her to listen with respect to this old man with the wispy beard and the outlandish costume of a foreign Indian. "Speak," she said, and put her hands on her hips as she listened.

"The soldiers have hidden sudden-death-by-thunder on the path you take through the jungle when you go to the savanna. You must make another path."

"Sudden-death-by-thunder?" asked Remedios. "What is that?"

"They are dishes," said Aurelio, "that are hidden in the ground. When the feet press upon them, the legs and the body are flayed and broken. You must make another path."

"He means mines," said García, shocked. "They have planted mines!"

"Mines," repeated Aurelio slowly. "Is that another name?"

Remedios nodded. "Sudden-death-by-thunder is a better name. We thank you for telling us. Why did you tell us?"

"My daughter liked you," said Aurelio. "She used to watch you. She was killed by the sudden-death-by-thunder. I did not wish the same for you. Also," added Aurelio, "I have planned death for the soldiers on that path, and you should walk another way."

"You have planned death?" asked Remedios.

"Yes," said Aurelio, "I have planned death."

"I see," Remedios said. "But if they come back, they will step on their own mines. They will not come back."

"They come back," said Aurelio, "to see whom they have killed. They mark by each dish with a secret mark, and they do not step on them. The animals do not die because my daughter watches over them, but you will die if you cannot see her."

"Your daughter?" said García. "I thought you said she was killed."

"She was killed," said Aurelio patiently. "Why do I have to say everything twice? Her spirit watches."

Gonzago and Tomás crossed themselves fervently.

"Old man," said Remedios, "will you be with us, if you hate the soldiers?"

"I have a life to live," said Aurelio, shaking his head, "but I will watch for you, and I will watch over you. My daughter and I will watch over you."

"Thank you, old man," said Remedios.

"My name is Aurelio," he said as he walked away, his dignity as solid and impressive as it had been when he arrived.

"That means," said Remedios, "that the army has an idea where we are."

"I do not think so," said Gloria de Escobal. "It would be just like them to put mines in any old place and just hope they get someone."

"Tomorrow," said Remedios, "we will think of moving camp. I think there is a risk."

"A pity," said García, "I like it here."

"You would not like it when the helicopters come in and carpet us with napalm," said Remedios. "I remember how my *compañeros* died in my former group." She shuddered. "Their screams as they ran burning I shall remember all my life. It sticks, and it cannot be shaken off. If you beat it with your hands, your hands burn also. It is the worst form of death. God help me, when I die, may I do so cleanly, by blood and not by fire."

"By God's grace," said Gloria, "you shall die in your bed, beloved of the nation, long after the victory."

Remedios smiled sadly. "It hurts to think what one has thrown away." She walked off slowly to her hut, and García watched her go.

"Blessings on you, Remedios," he said.

Aurelio arrived home just before sunset, as he had planned. He first went to the compound and opened the gate wide. The dogs gathered around, whining and barking in expectation of food. "My friends," he said, "I give you freedom to roam and live in peace, nobly. If you are hungry or sick or when it is time to die, I shall welcome you and I shall care for you. I shall listen for you in the forest. Beware of the path, and heed Parlanchina when she warns you away."

He turned and walked to the door of the hut, leaving open the gate. The dogs milled around, confused by the want of food, the open gate, and the change of routine. Then one of them, who was to be their first leader, picked up a scent in the air and was off across the clearing, nose to the ground. One by one the others followed, except for an old weary bitch, who plodded over to her master and placed her wet muzzle in his hand. "Ah," he said, "old friend, you may stay." She settled on the ground at his feet and fell asleep. From that time on the dogs came and went as they pleased, and Aurelio became their uncle rather than their father and mother.

When the dogs had gone, Aurelio fetched his machete and went out to cut several straight stakes. These he divided into three piles. He made two frameworks of one of the piles. On the pile of shorter stakes he fashioned sharp spikes, which he hardened in the fire. Then he did the same with the larger stakes. The smaller stakes he lashed to the two frameworks. He fashioned the springs from twisted hide and flexible wood, and then he set the release catch. He prodded it with a piece of wood, and the contraption sprang up as he had intended. Then he made another one. He took a spade and a machete and the pile of long stakes tied in a bundle on his back, and on the path he dug two deep pits. The stakes he set in the ground at the bottom, and then he cut twigs with the machete and laid them across the top of the pits. On top of these he scattered leaves from the forest floor. Beside each pit he left a secret mark, as the soldiers had done with the mines. Then he returned home and fetched the two contraptions. For these he scooped shallow pits, and again covered them with leaves. When he had finished, he sat down to rest and to suck coca from his pestle. Then, at the beginning of the series of traps, mines, and pits and also at the end, he urinated across the path. Every day he returned with a gourd of his urine collected in the previous twenty-four hours and sprinkled it in the same places. In this way he ensured that all animals, scenting humans, would avoid the dangers of that section of the path.

Remedios and her group moved out of the huts and went two valleys away to a place more inaccessible but nearer to Chiriguaná. There they built their own brush huts in the trees. They were careful to make no telltale clearings that could be seen from the air, and they became more professional about stealth and concealment. Only Aurelio, and perhaps Parlanchina, knew where they had gone.

After their hurried departure the Indians, who had never really deserted their village, moved straight back in to resume their ancient, unhurried, and peaceful life, remote from the people and the civilization they feared and despised. Once more little naked children ran in the clearing, and women, leaning against doorways, suckled babies at their breasts. Once more old men chewed coca in the shade, and young ones cultivated bananas and cassava on the terraces.

And then, as it had to, the day prophesied by Remedios arrived. The aerial photographs taken by a foreign spy plane in the upper atmosphere had clearly revealed activity, and the mountain rangers had observed the People's Vanguard through powerful binoculars from a neighboring peak.

Two weeks after the People's Vanguard had moved out and the Indians had moved back in, the Indians heard a rumbling and a rhythmic whirring in the distance. They had seen helicopters before—did not the army often crash them in the mountains? Were not those pilots human sacrifices that the white men made to their gods? The Indians came out of their huts and stood in the clearing to watch the helicopters pass.

The first gunship to appear over the roof of the trees was flying so low that they thought it was going to crash, and they started to run. Two rockets streaked from the tubes beside the fuselage, and simultaneously

machine gunners opened up from either side through the open doors.
The rockets exploded in a cataclysm of molten shards of metal, the
machine guns yammered and rattled, and the terrified and mutilated
people on the ground either lay twisted in their death throes or crawled
desperately, dragging their broken and bleeding limbs. No one made it
to safety. The women and children keened and screamed in their fearful
agonies, and the men, conscious even in the presence of an apocalypse
of their proud stoic tradition, bit back their anguish and moaned softly.
One of their number raised his bow to fire back in defiance, but he was
enveloped in flame, as were they all, as the napalm cluster from the
second gunship fell hungrily among them. They rose and fell and
thrashed, these burning people, their eyes melting in their sockets, their
bones calcining as their blood boiled among the obscenely ballooning
blisters. Some of them fought to wipe away the adhesive chemical of hell
and flailed and writhed or staggered drunkenly, convulsed with the
delirium of their incandescent excruciation.

This scene from the vilest imaginings of Satan was almost anticli-
maxed by the fléchettes of the third gunship. The steel darts whined and
whirred among the smoldering bodies and the few corpses that still
stirred. They were superfluous as they transfixed and tore apart the
blackened remains of the Indians.

The helicopters passed over once more and then passed back to land
farther up the valley. The soldiers pouring out of them fanned out and
advanced in V formation to the commands blown on the captain's whistle. No one fired on them from the rocks and the trees, and the airborne
troops began to relax.

When they charged upon the village over the last hundred yards,
they were screaming and firing. But something made them falter in the
last steps of their headlong rush. Gingerly they stepped among the
charred and tortured remains. The loathsome stench of burning flesh
mingled with the delicate scent of napalm. In the trees the parrots began
to screech against the silence. The men looked at the corpses and saw and
smelled a vision of the inferno of hell. One by one they staggered away
to double over, to vomit, and, when there was no more vomit or saliva,
to retch.

The capitan saw the bodies of little children and even recognized
the outline of charcoal of one or two women. He went and looked into

the huts and found the meager possessions of Indians but not the arms of terrorists. Outside, he walked numbly among the bodies, his handkerchief over his nose and mouth in a vain attempt to exclude the noisome fumes. He went and sat away from the village, on a rock, and his men wandered like zombies, demented with horror.

The lieutenant came and sat next to the capitan, and, his face contorted and pale, blurted out, "*Mierda*, Capitan, they were *cholos*. There were children and women. Even dogs."

The capitan did not reply. He bent forward and was sick between his feet. He buried his face in his hands and began to shake violently, uncontrollably.

"*Mierda*," said the lieutenant.

The capitan began to weep, and the tears flowed out between his fingers.

21

How Doña Constanza Falls in Love for the First Time and Loses Several Pounds

General Fuerte fell into a profound melancholy during his captivity, but it was not the loss of his freedom that tormented him. As a military man he had never really known freedom anyway, bound up as he was with regulations and duties. To some extent he was oppressed by boredom, and the time hung heavily with him. He was cloistered in the same hut as Doña Constanza, but even though they had known each other before the events here related, they found that they had little in common and were not affected by incarceration in the same way.

What tortured General Fuerte was that he no longer knew what to think. The *guerrilleros* generally seemed to like him, and they brought him fruit or nuts to eat, and would slap him on the back and say, "Don't worry, *cabrón!*" Fuerte also grew to like them, against his will. Father García, particularly, became close to him, and they passed long hours in earnest conversation, sometimes becoming heated and vehement. Fuerte became infected by García's glorious vision of the world to be. He listened to García lyrically describe his prognostications of an arcadia where they were no more countries and therefore no possibility of war, where there was a universal brotherhood of man sharing all things equally, and where the means of production was owned by the people and produced what was needed by the many rather than what was wanted for the frivolities of the few. García talked of the theology of liberation, in which it was a part of loving one's neighbor to fight for their freedom.

He talked also of the injustices suffered by the people and told the general long, horrific stories about cases he knew of brutality, greed, and oppression.

The general flinched inwardly when he heard all these things. He argued strongly with García that all utopias breed misery, that the people who win revolutions are the worst possible people for running countries afterward, that only a free market is flexible enough to supply the people's changing needs, that it was a blasphemy and an obscenity to kill in the name of God ("Your side does," replied García), and that there would be no need for repression by the state if it were not for left-wing subversion and terrorism. "There would be no need for it," replied García, "but it would still happen. It always has."

Both men appealed to experience, to the lessons of history, to the will of God, to reason, and neither man would give ground. But Fuerte was infected by García's visions of Eden, and like all infections, it prickled and irritated and itched, and the more he scratched it, the less it went away. Fuerte was a man philosophically at war with himself, and he became enmeshed and entangled in ifs and buts, in qualifications and exceptions, corollaries, definitions, oughts and shoulds and possibilities and rights and injustices. The two ideologies fought full-scale set piece battles in his mind, and he drew farther and farther away from that clarity of vision which he had carried with him all his life. He looked back at that vision with regret and nostalgia but also thought of it as a time of immaturity. Like all intelligent men who no longer know what to think, he sank into a depression so paralyzing that he became estranged from himself.

Doña Constanza was different. Nothing exciting or interesting had ever happened to her before, and she looked back at her life with a sense of wonder at so much time wasted in ennui and in being annoyed about little details. As a kidnap victim she felt like a protagonist of a wonderful melodrama enacted on a broad stage.

To begin with, she had been very fearful about being raped, or tortured, or starved, or treated like an animal, and she had existed for several days wide-eyed in a state of mortal terror. But she was fed, allowed to wash and to relieve herself, and Remedios and Gloria even called in to ask her if she wanted anything and showed her how to roll and fold pieces of cloth to use as sanitary towels. The *guerrilleros* turned out to be more conscientious servants than her mulatta maid at the hacienda, but she became inspired by the energy and enthusiasm of her captors and began to look around for something to do for herself.

She found Fuerte and García very boring, with their interminable political arguments, and so she sat outside the hut beside whoever was supposed to be guarding her. She watched the life of the camp. In the beginning, she found it very disgusting. The men spit copiously and relieved themselves brazenly in public against the trunks of trees; sometimes they waved their penises at her when they had finished, crossing their eyes and leering obscenely. She would look away disdainfully but could not help glancing back out of the corner of her eye. People washed themselves naked and unashamed in the river, but eventually she grew embarrassed about being the only one clothed and the only one dirty and stinking; she stripped her own clothes off and sidled coyly into the water. It was a very pleasant feeling. She found the variety of the men's bodies quite fascinating; she had never seen so many naked men, only, in fact, ever having seen her hulking husband in the nude before. Against her will she found herself comparing and taxonomizing their genitals. There were long, thin ones with a heavy glans, like a donkey's. There were short, fat ones that nestled like an acorn in a cup. There were delicately tapered ones. There were ones with drooping foreskins, and some with none at all. Testicles, she decided, were generally alike, except the larger ones tended not to hang so low. She found herself observing their slim, muscled bodies and became aware that some of them contained eyes that surreptitiously observed hers in return.

To begin with, she loathed the coarse conversation of the men and was horrified when she found that the women among the *guerrilleros*, while disapproving of the men's conversations, indulged in exactly the same kinds of discourse among themselves. She listened to exaggerated tales of prowess, hilarious tales of humiliations, sorrowful tales of betrayal and was one day amazed to find that she was laughing and smiling. She despised herself for a little while for letting her standards slip, but eventually she forgot to be ashamed.

The healthy diet, the fresh mountain air, the sight of naked bodies, and the ribald conversation all began to inflame Doña Constanza's imagination. Her dreams began to become scenes of entangled limbs and uninhibited bacchanalia. People copulated and cavorted in improbable positions with superhuman gusto; sometimes her imagination's eye panned across multitudes of heaving bodies, and sometimes it closed in and scrutinized in astonishingly vivid detail the minutiae of sexual delight. She awoke to find herself sweating, tingling, and moist and lay there intoxicated with the furious ecstasies of lust.

Doña Constanza began to lose the disfiguring roll of fat that childbirth and idleness had contributed to her body. As she grew more active, she became as lissome and lithe as she had been when she was younger, and as when she was younger, her eye began to rove among the young men around her.

Doña Constanza lost her fat ultimately because she told Gloria that she was bored with doing nothing. "I would like to work," she said when what she meant was "I want to go out and be with the men." Gloria told Remedios, and Remedios consented, warning her that she would be shot instantly the moment she tried to escape.

"Escape?" said Doña Constanza. "Where to? I don't know the way home, and I am not going to go down into the jungle or up into the mountains on my own! I want to stay here!"

"Do you?" said Remedios. "Are you beginning to believe the same as us?"

"Oh, no," said Constanza.

Remedios was puzzled but let her go to work anyway, after she had appointed someone to be personally responsible for guarding Doña Constanza. Remedios cast her mind over all the numbers of the band and made her choice. The chances of Doña Constanza's getting exactly the man she desired the most were exceedingly small; but the gods smiled on her, and she was overjoyed to find herself more or less permanently in the company of Gonzago.

Doña Constanza had never been so blithe in all her life, not since her children had departed for England to go to school. She whistled and sang as she worked, she laughed and made jokes, she did her share of the cooking and washing, and she even impressed the guerrillas one morning by proving that she could still do a handspring. They began to refer to her as *pájara* (songbird), and although she was ten years older than most of them, many of the men among the *guerrilleros* began to find her desirable.

Gonzago was twenty-five years old. He was not a tall man, but he was slim and quick. When he laughed, his white teeth and his one gold tooth seemed to sparkle, and his dark brown eyes seemed to go black. He had the face of a Mexican Romeo, but his hair was straight, black, and thick, like an Indian's. He had an air about him that Doña Constanza found impossible to resist.

This soon became very clear to Gonzago, even though Doña Constanza tried and failed not to be too obvious. If he had a mark on his face, Doña Constanza flirtatiously removed it with her finger. If he cut himself, she fussed about him, tending the wound as though it were mortal, and if he was very hot, she wiped his forehead as she had done upon his return without the ransom money. Doña Constanza began to leave her shirt buttons undone so that Gonzago got tantalizing glimpses of her plump little breasts, and indeed, he sometimes found it difficult to look into her eyes when talking to her because his eyes always seemed to be drawn downward. When the zip in her shorts sprang irreparably apart, she just carried on wearing them. The other *guerrilleros* began to wink at him and make lewd gestures with their fingers as he passed by at Doña Constanza's side, and they asked him questions like "When will the little *pájara* lay eggs?" One day Gonzago had even caught Remedios smiling at him knowingly, and he had smiled sheepishly back.

Gonzago was pleased about this, and Doña Constanza pleased him also. It was quite something for him to be thought to be having an affair with a Great Lady of the Oligarchy, and he also enjoyed her company. She was very merry and feminine, yet she worked harder than a man and was also very seductive. Gonzago found himself making love to her in his dreams in his hut, while she dreamed of making love to him in hers.

They particularly liked to go off foraging together because then there was no one else about. They would go off in search of guavas, papayas, lemons, yucca roots, mangoes, and avocados, working together but always feeling that spark of desire darting between them. She would look at him, and his heart would race; he would look at her, and she would tingle in her nipples; she would laugh, and his penis would jump, so that he had to turn away to hide the bulge in his trousers; he would laugh, and a churning lust would stir in her womb.

But Gonzago was very shy. He did not know how to bring it all to a head. What does one do with a Great Lady of the Oligarchy? And the longer they waited, the more their desire mushroomed into a mighty roaring inferno, waiting to blast away the doors of the furnace.

It was Doña Constanza who found a way. One day at siesta time they were driven by the sun to find the shade of a great tree. They sat side by side with their backs against the trunk, taking great swigs of water from their canteens and eating mangoes. Both of them were very soon dripping with sticky juice and laughing about the mess. Wantonly, while looking into his eyes, Doña Constanza lasciviously licked her fingers, and his mischievous penis sprang rather self-evidently into life. Doña Constanza looked at the growing hillock while pretending not to. "I think," she said, "I will have to take a little sleep. May I use your shoulder as a pillow?"

"By all means," said Gonzago.

She laid her head on his shoulder and pretended to sleep. Gonzago furtively opened her shirt a little to see her breast. Doña Constanza moved her right leg over her left and turned over, at the same time sliding down a little so that now her right leg was a little over his, and her head was nuzzling into his neck. Gonzago had to move because his tightening penis was painfully caught up in his underwear and was crying to be released. Doña Constanza moved her right hand innocently to a more comfortable position, which was, miraculously, inside his shirt over his left breast. Doña Constanza felt the nipple harden. Gonzago now not only had a penis weeping for liberation, but he also had pins and needles in his right arm where Doña Constanza was lying on it. He eased it from beneath her, exercised the fingers to bring back the blood, and began to tickle her neck and the lobe of her right ear. Doña Constanza breathed hotly on his neck and licked it under the pretense of moistening her lips. At the same time she very gently began to stroke his chest with her right hand, teasing the hairs with her fingers. Her hand began to wander farther afield and lightly brushed over his belly. His penis was now in a torment of imprisonment, and he caressed her ear and neck with furiously renewed subtlety. The sleeping Constanza moved her hand very deliberately and dropped it disingenuously onto his trousers.

As her grip tightened on his penis, he let out a cry, and as if by a signal prearranged they threw themselves upon each other with a fury unprecedented in the history of concupiscence. Gonzago thrust her breast into his mouth and ravished it with his tongue. Constanza, with one movement of her hand, sent the buttons of his trousers spinning away across the leaves and greedily gathered in her trembling fingers the tender fruit of her dreams. Gonzago gasped and knelt upright and astride her, kneading her breasts as she took his aching and ever-expanding penis in one hand and stroked his testicles with the other. Brutally Doña Constanza threw Gonzago over and pinned him down with her body. She kissed him furiously about the mouth and neck, her wet tongue darting and her lips throbbing. She began to rub her crotch on his thigh, and like the gentleman he was, Gonzago raised his knee a little to make it easier. Doña Constanza squealed wild little cries as she pivoted at the hips. Gonzago thrust his hand down her shorts and folded his fingers around her vulva, which was now pouring with such juice as to put any mango to shame. Her volley of squeals grew to new crescendos, and she masturbated herself against his fingers with such rapidity that her squeals became one long squeal and she trembled and shook as though in a fit. Wild-eyed and disheveled, she sprang to her feet and threw herself upon Gonzago's trousers. Grasping them at the waistband, she hauled with such force that Gonzago was dragged a full yard across the forest floor before Doña Constanza triumphantly threw them aside and danced upon one leg and then the other to rid herself of her own shorts. Still wearing her unbuttoned shirt, she bestrode Gonzago, and uttering a joyful yell, she wiggled into position and plunged him into her as deep as it was possible to go. Both of them exploded simultaneously, and Gonzago and Constanza shouted and bellowed and thrust and gyrated until suddenly Constanza collapsed forward onto his chest. She let out a long moan of ecstasy and slid off him sideways, painfully bending his penis at the root.

Gonzago was ashamed. "I did not mean to come so soon. I could not help it. No one has touched me for a long time."

"It does not matter . . . it does not matter . . . it does not matter . . ." said Constanza, trying to catch enough breath to finish her sentence. "I have already come three times."

They fell asleep in the shade of the tree, Doña Constanza with her head on his stomach and her hand grasping protectively those parts she had coveted for so long.

She awoke before he did. She opened her eyes to see that the one-eyed pink gentleman was looking back at her. Drowsily she began to play with it. She caressed it lightly, and it stirred a little. She slipped her hand around it and cupped his testicles, and the penis stirred a little more. Caught up in this novel form of experimentation, she tickled the hairs of his perineum. The penis began to lengthen and straighten. She moved her right hand to cup his testicles, and she maneuvered her left to massage his penis up and down. She touched its tip, and it sprang as if in response to electric shock, so she tried it once or twice again. The penis was now hard and strong, and its glistening end was right against the tip of her nose. She looked to check that he was still asleep and could not resist the temptation to try something she had only heard whispers about at school. Tentatively she flicked her tongue across the tip of it. It was not too bad. *It tastes of me,* she thought. She flattened her tongue and rolled it around the end of the penis as though she were savoring a lollipop. She found the texture had a vulnerable quality about it. She licked it all the way up the shaft, first on one side, then on the other, and then up the middle. She looked up to check he was still sleeping and nestled between his legs to lick his testicles, tickling right behind them with the tip of her tongue. When she uncrossed her eyes, she could see that the penis was visibly pulsing with his heartbeat. Against all her previous expectations and prejudices she realized that she was having a marvelous time. With one hand she caressed him, and she knelt over and took his penis fully in her mouth. At first she tried to see how deep it would go without choking her, and then she rolled her tongue deliciously around it as she moved her head up and down.

Gonzago awoke to find that the unbelievable dream he had been dreaming about having the most exquisite blow job of his life was actually true, and by that time Doña Constanza was too oblivious with enjoyment to worry about whether he was asleep or awake. They made love for a very long time two more times and then had the problem of trying to reconstitute their shredded clothes so as not to arouse suspicion when they went back with the fruit they had gathered.

Gonzago and Constanza made love where and when any opportunity arose and in every possible manner. Sometimes they made love at frenzied speed, nipping behind a rock and tearing their clothes off, and sometimes they made love slowly and languorously in the evening sunlight. They got used to having their backsides bitten by ants, and at night Gonzago stole into Constanza's hut. They made love all the more fervidly for the necessity of not waking the general, whose depression fortunately had turned him into a very heavy sleeper.

Their feverish passion fed itself until they both grew thin, wild-eyed, and pale. Doña Constanza, who by this time had acquired a colorful turn of phrase, one day announced breathlessly as they were lubriciously devouring each other with their ravenous genitalia, "Gonzito, I want to stay here with you forever fucking you like this until my feet turn green and my head drops off!"

"You will have to join us," said Gonzago, in between gasps and thrusts.

Remedios accepted Doña Constanza's application, and the latter became the only member of the band who had not a clue what she was fighting for. Who cares about such things when one has found one's niche in life?

22

In Which Colonel Rodrigo Figueras Forgets the First Two Principles of War and Imperils His Prospects

Hectoro and Pedro were waiting for nightfall. Hectoro was watching the dust devils whipping up the sand and skipping erratically along the track, and he was in a good mood because the doctor had said that his blood was clean. He would not have to worry about telling his three wives and not being able to savor a woman for three months. He scratched his face through his conquistador beard and pulled his straw sombrero lower over his eyes. Recently he had stopped drinking so much for lack of time, and his grateful liver was allowing his skin to return to a color less jaundiced.

Pedro was observing the soldiers with the cool and practiced eye of the professional hunter. He had not hunted men before except when tracking down rustlers for the gringos. But the situation was different because the soldiers were not on the move and they were all gathered together in one camp. Pedro smiled at the thought that maybe the officers had not wanted to move out because they wanted to stay near Felicidad. He had watched her creeping from one tent to another in the night and had listened to her furtive gigglings and whisperings.

Pedro and Hectoro had given the soldiers plenty of reasons for wanting to leave, however. The villagers had dumped the dead steer upstream from the camp and were diligently defecating and micturating in the same spot. Most of the camp now had severe fits of stomach cramp and diarrhea, and there had begun an epidemic of vomiting. The villagers had found it impossible to sell poisoned food to the military because they had brought their own provisions; but Misael had sold them *aguardiente* made of wood alcohol, and two soldiers had already gone blind.

On the first night of the two weeks since they had first begun to torment the invaders, Hectoro and Pedro had dug up one of the soldiers who had died in the previous raid and dressed the skeleton in khaki that had been taken from one of the bodies before it was buried. They nailed the rotting body to a makeshift cross and left it right in the middle of the camp, where it oozed slime and putrefaction so appallingly that even the vultures left it alone. They stole several weapons as they left. The scene in the camp at reveille kept the two men chuckling all day, for the soldiers had beheld the corpse with terror and stupefaction, and held their noses, and an argument had developed about how to dispose of it. An officer had forced two junior conscripts to remove it at gunpoint.

On the second night the guard had been doubled, but Pedro made a doll of a soldier and said *secretos* over it as he banged nails into its eyes and groin. He left it in the middle of the camp and returned to Hectoro. They waited for a guard to fall asleep, and Pedro strangled him. "I don't have the will for this," said Pedro, and so it was Hectoro who removed the man's eyes and genitals and stuffed them into the mouth of the corpse.

In the morning there was panic in the camp, and the men were gesticulating and saying to the officers, "We cannot fight magicians," and the officers were saying, "There is no such thing as magic. Don't be superstitious. We are dealing with terrorists."

Hectoro and Pedro watched that night as four soldiers stealthily deserted. They caught one of them, and Pedro forced him to swallow a mixture that would make him insane for two weeks. They propelled him back into the camp and watched as he stumbled around, babbling about ghosts and spirits and falling over tents. The camp came to life, and there was a deal of running about and argumentation.

For the next two nights Pedro and Hectoro did nothing, but they watched as six more men deserted. No one in the camp, however, knew whether the soldiers had deserted or been spirited away by the forces of darkness, and there was no one there who was not nervous or febrile.

On the sixth night Hectoro and Pedro went to the large pool on Don Emmanuel's *finca* and noosed a caiman. It was a huge animal, and it struggled and lashed furiously with its tail until Pedro jammed a stick between its jaws and blindfolded it. He stunned it with a sharp blow between the eyes, and the two men carried it back to the camp. They waited for two men from the same tent to desert and for a guard to fall asleep, and then they carried the caiman and a dead rat to the tent. They put the dead rat in the mouth of one of the sleeping bags and they zipped the caiman into the other, drawing the string tight so that it could not crawl out. In the morning the tent was shaking and bulging as the caiman tried to escape, and they heard a soldier, white-faced, run about screaming, "Suárez has turned into an alligator! Suárez is an alligator!"

Figueras halted at the foot of the writhing sleeping bag and stepped back sharply when he found that there really was a very furious monster in it. At that point the imprisoned beast broke the drawstring and crawled angrily and rapidly out of the camp. The men ran to safety and watched it disappear toward the Mula. Figueras ordered a young private to enter the tent and search it. The young man, obviously still in his teens, crossed himself and gingerly opened the tent flaps. Seeing nothing, he felt emboldened and crawled in. He reversed out rapidly and stood bolt upright. His lip quivering, he reported to Figueras, "Sir, the other one has turned into a rat. He is dead, sir."

For the next week Hectoro and Pedro did nothing at all. They were very busy during the day, working with Sergio and Professor Luis, looking in dark corners, collecting. They knew that terror thrives on suspense, and they knew that the soldiers were already both ill and terrified and were still deserting in the night.

Hectoro and Pedro carried the three sacks to the camp, and Hectoro was watching the dust devils and scratching his beard and feeling good that his blood was clean. Night came down, and the camp fell asleep, except for the guards, who huddled together for solidarity when they should have been posted evenly around the perimeter. Pedro had stupefied all the beasts with special smoke and *secretos*.

They flitted between the tents, and Hectoro put large tarantulas in the boots that were laid out neatly outside the flaps of the tents. They were not poisonous, but nearly everyone thought that they were. Pedro moved around invisibly, gently placing coral snakes inside every tent. Coral snakes, if feeling themselves endangered, are swift to attack, and their venom is lethal within a day. These sleepy snakes would not feel endangered until morning, and in the meantime, they coiled up and happily slept among the sleeping men.

Hectoro and Pedro released the bagful of vipers half in the latrine tent and half in the provisions tent.

The whole village laughed unrelentingly about the results of this maneuver, even though Hectoro and Pedro were too doubled up with hilarity to relate it coherently. People would look at each other and for no apparent reason burst spluttering into hurricanes of laughter. If they were drinking coffee at the time, they sprayed each other with it, and if they were eating, they splattered each other with food. Dolores nearly choked to death on a morsel of banana and was saved only by Josef's punching her so hard under the ribs that the food was blown out of her windpipe.

The army moved out the same day, defeated by forces they never understood and never saw. They made camp thirty miles away, passed a peaceful night, and stayed there thankfully until one morning when Figueras came groggily out of his tent and stumbled to the latrine. He fumbled with his buttons and got out his penis. As his eyes focused on it and he tried to relax enough to urinate, he saw that near the end of it there was a small red crater seeping with glistening fluid. His heart sank, and he refocused his eyes just to make sure. *"Mierda,"* he said. He tried to pass water but found he was blocked. He squeezed his anal sphincter to try to force it out, and a blob of yellow pus fell out and splattered on the zinc. He bent down and inspected it. He sighed and pulled himself upright. *"Qué puta,"* he muttered. Again he tried to relax, and the urine began to trickle out. The expression on his face changed from stunned surprise through agony to despair. He had to piss, but his urethra was on fire. It burned him to piss, and it burned him not to piss. He decided not to piss and deferred the pain for another half hour until he was vanquished by the pressure of his aching bladder. That day and on the days that followed he and his officers and the gringo adviser found out what it was like to piss broken glass.

Figueras sent a party of soldiers to arrest Felicidad.

"On what charge?" asked the corporal.

Figueras could not think of any crime. He scratched his head and squinted against the sun. Eventually he spoke more truly than he knew. "Arrest her on a charge of sabotage."

But Felicidad was not to be found. She had taken her injections in Chiriguaná and gone to rest at Don Emmanuel's. Don Emmanuel gave her the second half of her two thousand pesos.

"Now I am very rich," she said happily.

"Very rich?" echoed Don Emmanuel.

"Yes," she said. "You do not think I let them have it for nothing, do you?"

"You little devil!" exclaimed Don Emmanuel.

"Not at all," she said, pouting indignantly. "I earned it. I am a very fine whore."

"So says Hectoro," replied Don Emmanuel, "but as yet I do not know the truth of it."

She laughed and rubbed her thumb and forefinger together in the sign for money. "In three months' time, when my blood is pure, I will give you a little taste of my guava. And"—she leaned forward conspiratorially—"if it is very good, I may not charge you."

Don Emmanuel placed a kiss on her forehead and went out to brand some steers.

Felicidad was feted in every house in the village by turn, even though no one knew exactly how effective her sabotage had been. Pedro and Hectoro also received treatment fit for heroes; neither of them was accustomed to such outbursts of demonstrativeness toward them, and they found it hard to come to terms with. After all, Pedro had always been a solitary hunter, and Hectoro had always been proud and aloof; they tried to be inconspicuous.

Things turned out differently for Figueras. An officers' council at the camp revealed urgent military reasons for returning to Valledupar. They cited the general sickness of the men, even though they were recovering now that they no longer drank from the Mula. "In any case I need to consult with my superiors," said Figueras loftily, "and I cannot do it here as they are beyond reach of the radio."

The sexually transmitted diseases department of Valledupar Military Hospital was open on Tuesdays and Thursdays, officers from 9:00 A.M. to 11:00 A.M., and other ranks from 3:00 P.M. to 6:00 P.M., thus allowing plenty of time for siesta. On Tuesday morning the officers' council that had found urgent military reasons for leaving Chiriguaná found itself reconvened in its entirety in the anteroom of the clinic. The officers looked at one another, crimson with embarrassment. There was a long silence until Colonel Figueras strode in. He took stock of the assembly and stood, his legs apart and his hands on his hips, nodding his head. "Felicidad?" he asked. Every one of them nodded gloomily. "The hot little bitch said I was the only one," said Figueras.

"She said that to me, too," said the lieutenant, who looked as though he were about to cry. The rest of them nodded with resignation.

Then Figueras chuckled. "All the same, my friends, it was worth it, and I would do the same again. Yes, by God!" The rest of the men smiled, and most of them agreed. Figueras looked at a *graffito* on the wall which said, "No one below the rank of brigadier is allowed to claim that he got it from a lavatory seat."

The brigadier was not pleased with Colonel Figueras. Figueras stood carpeted before his superior while the latter sifted through a sheaf of reports, including Figueras's.

"Your report is illiterate," he said, looking up at Figueras over the top of his half-moon spectacles.

"Thank you, sir."

The brigadier sighed heavily. "However, your rapid promotion hitherto has been owed to conspicuous bravery and success in the field and not to literary flair."

The brigadier sifted through the reports again, frowning and clicking his tongue. "Colonel," he said, "I read of a demolished bridge, of skeletons, diarrhea, vomiting, insanity, black magic, snakes, dead rats, spiders, alligators. I read of two soldiers going blind inexplicably and one guard being mutilated. I read of weapons and ammunition disappearing. I read of the loss of forty men of your battalion. Forty men!" The brigadier waved his hands in despair. "And how were they lost? Was it in battle? Out on patrol? No! Thirteen of them were lost on account of snakebites, four in the exploding bridge, and the rest you list as *desaparecidos!* How did they disappear, Colonel?"

Figueras was sweating heavily, and his eyes were glazed. "I believe they were picked off by the enemy," he said.

"Right in the middle of the camp? None of the disappeared are listed as being on guard duty; I could understand their being picked off if they were guards! But no, you have put 'disappeared while sleeping'!" The brigadier stood up and turned his back on Figueras, frowning out of the window. Then he turned and banged his fist on the table. "They deserted, Figueras! And I have a simple explanation! One, your guards were not doing their duty. Two—"

"All the men were terrified," said Figueras lamely. "They believed we were fighting against evil spirits."

"Don't interrupt a superior officer! Two, they were demoralized and frightened." The brigadier paused and said wearily, "Did they tell you at officer training school about the nine principles of war?"

"Yes, sir."

"What are the first two?"

Figueras searched his memory in vain and made a wild guess. " 'Fight' and 'Don't retreat.' "

The brigadier sighed wearily. "The first, Figueras, is to select and maintain an aim. The second is that morale should at all times be maintained."

"Ah, yes," said Figueras, "I remember now."

"You remember too late. If your men deserted, it was because morale collapsed. Let me tell you, Colonel, that the best way to maintain morale is by adhering rigidly to the first principle and keeping your men busy at achieving it." The brigadier paused again and shuffled the papers. "What was your aim, Colonel?"

"To annihilate the Communists, sir."

"And did you do anything about annihilating the Communists? There is no record of any patrols, either for security or for reconnaissance. There is no record of a single shot being fired, even accidentally. There is no record here, Figueras, of anyone even seeing a terrorist. You did not do anything at all, did you, except go camping in the country for a month?"

Figueras stared down at the tip of his boots. "We did not know where the Communists were, sir."

The brigadier frowned. "I have several points to make. One is that you failed to liaise in any way with the Air Force Internal Security

Group, or with the Army Air Survey, or with the Jungle Rangers, or with the Mountain Rangers, so it is not surprising that you met no Communists. Secondly, when I read of your troubles with 'black magic,' I conclude that you were being terrorized not by *guerrilleros* but by peasants; alligators in sleeping bags are not a part of classical rural guerrilla tactics, and neither are coral snakes and vipers! Thirdly, there are no accounts in your report of your usual decisive heroism against the terrorists. You have been promoted twice and been awarded the Andean Condor Medal for Gallantry twice, one silver and one gold. I am tempted to conclude that in your report this time you could not include accounts of heroism because you knew that our military adviser, Major Kandinski, would also be submitting a report, and that yours would have to tally with his!"

Figueras continued to stare miserably at his boots and continued to sweat copiously.

"However," continued the brigadier, "against my better judgment I have decided for the time being to give your previous reports the benefit of the doubt. I am not going to investigate them yet." The brigadier emphasized the "yet." "And do you know why?"

"No, sir."

"Because, Colonel, I have found another reason for your inactivity during your camping holiday." He flicked through the pile of reports and drew one out. "This is from the chief medical officer. Are you aware that homosexuality is, in the armed forces, cause for instant dishonorable discharge? I see from his report that you and your officers are already suffering from a variety of dishonorable discharges."

"Homosexuality?" echoed Figueras.

"Yes, Colonel, homosexuality! And before you protest that medical details are supposed to be confidential, let me read you section sixty-six, subsection five, clause ten, paragraph three of the Manual of Military Regulations, ratified by Parliament under the Armed Forces Act of 1933." The brigadier picked up the book and turned to the page he had dog-eared. " 'The competent military medical authorities are obliged to report to commanding officers all details of a usually confidential nature, when, in the opinion of the medical authorities, military efficiency and discipline may be adversely affected by failing to report the same.' " The brigadier put the book down and picked up the medical report. "It says here that all the officers of your battalion are suffering from the same two sexually transmitted diseases; one is common gonorrhea, and the other is syphilis of the strain common around Barranquilla. The simple explanation for this, Colonel, is that you and your officers had congress with each other."

"Yes, sir, that's true," said Figueras, who thought that "congress" was a kind of parliament.

The brigadier was astounded. "Then you admit that your holiday camp was for the purpose of homosexual orgies?"

"Oh, no, sir. We had military councils and briefings every day, Sir. Sir, I didn't know you could catch the clap by talking to each other." Figueras hung his head miserably.

The brigadier exploded with exasperation. "Colonel Figueras! You fail to understand me! I am saying that you and your officers and, it seems, Major Kandinski spent your holiday sodomizing each other, and that is why you all have the same diseases!"

Colonel Figueras was shocked and horrified. He lost his fear and shame and cried vehemently, "I am not a *maricón!* Any man who calls me a *maricón* should not be afraid of death!"

The brigadier smiled for the first time at this outburst. "Then what, Colonel, is the explanation?"

"Felicidad," said Figueras, spitting out the word.

"Felicidad? Colonel, 'happiness' does not give you the clap, as you call it."

"No, sir, Felicidad was the girl's name, the little whore! She seduced every one of us and told each one of us we were the only one. We were fooled, sir."

The brigadier nodded and put his hands on the desk, leaning forward. "It seems, then, Colonel, that you and your companions were the victims of a nymphomaniac with a predilection for officers."

The brigadier returned to the window and watched the soldiers drilling below. Figueras apprehensively watched the back of his head. Without turning around, he said, "Colonel Figueras, my first instinct was to relegate you to the ranks for gross incompetence. However, I have had to take into account your past honorable record and the scandal to the reputation of the army if you were court-martialed. So"—the brigadier turned on his heel and looked Figueras hard in the eye—"I am giving you one last chance. You will be passed fit for combat duty in three months. I advise you to take your military duties seriously and to find yourself in the front line of the fighting. I am putting all this on your record, and I will not remove it until I am assured that all this bungling was an exceptional case. You are dismissed."

Figueras saluted and said, "Thank you, sir." He marched out as smartly as his figure would allow and leaned back against the wall in the corridor.

Figueras was still mopping his face with his handkerchief when the brigadier returned to his desk to resume working on an intractable problem. Where was the military governor?

23

The Unofficial Monarchy of the Catholic Kings

Freemasons throughout the world are inclined to say "Our society is not a secret society; it is a society of secrets" and when they are not meeting for the purposes of their arcane rituals, they raise money for charities and worthy causes. Each lodge builds up its own distinctive character during the years of its existence, and often it attracts a membership that comes mostly from within one profession.

There was one lodge in the capital with links with the Vatican Bank whose members were drawn solely from within the upper echelons of the armed forces and that raised money solely for causes like Catholic Action Against Communist Subversion and the Society for the Christianization of Education.

Normally the branches of the military were jealous and possessive of their own prerogatives and regarded one another as rivals for power. The navy, indeed, had become so worried about being removed from the center of power that it had transferred its training establishments and headquarters from Puerto del Inca on the coast to the capital (hundreds of miles inland) so that generations of seamen were trained to defend the territorial waters on dry land. The lodge was the pivot of interservice cooperation because Admiral Fleta, General Ramírez, and Air Chief Marshal Sanchis were all members of it, and often after the rituals and initiations they sat in the plush lounge rooms and discussed the state of the country and how something must be done.

The three men were ardent Catholics, strong believers in the Motherland, the Family, and Law and Order, but all around them they saw atheism and Marxism, divorces, fornicating, banner-waving libertarian students, striking workers ruining the economy, and a civilian government that did not dare take strong action for fear of foreign opinion. It need not be said that all three of them favored a military junta run on the principle of "one third each," as there had been in Argentina, but they were also realists. It seemed quite possible that if the Democrats won the election in the United States, the flow of dollars would cease in the event of a coup. But they also knew that whatever the monetary policies of the government were, the president would always give them all they wanted because he feared a military coup more than anything else in the world. Even so, they decided that the operation code-named Los Reyes Católicos should be entirely secret and that they should be an unofficial junta. First they would have to find loyal officers who would help them do the spadework of digging out the rank weeds of subversion. All of them set up similar systems doing the same things, and it is with regret that we find ourselves concentrating for the purposes of this narrative solely upon the idealistic efforts of the army.

General Ramírez noticed that one of his ADCs, a handsome and rapidly rising star of the service, was particularly vehement and outspoken about the strategic importance of the republic both in the inevitable war against the Soviet Union and the more immediate struggle against the atheist Marxists. Ramírez summoned the capitan to his office, and the young man found himself faced by all three chiefs of staff.

"Capitan," said the general, "am I right in believing that you would be prepared to fight and die, and even to use means that are against your Christian conscience, to preserve the motherland and the national way of life?"

"Yes, sir," replied the capitan, sensing promotion.

"Good," said the general. "I suppose you are aware of the dangers we face from the Enemy Within?"

"The Communists, sir?"

"Yes, Capitan, and all their fellow travelers who are helping them bleed the country to death. Capitan, I propose that you and all the men you recruit to work with you should be officially posted to our strategic observation posts in the Antarctic."

The young man's heart sank into his boots. This was not a promotion to his liking. "The Antarctic, sir?" he said, and he felt his left leg begin to shake behind the knee.

"But of course, we wouldn't actually send you there. Instead, you will go underground in this country. Capitan, you are to recruit and form independent cadres to root out subversives and subversion. The files of the Army Internal Security Service will be opened to you, and you will arrest, detain, and question these subversives about what they know. You will be arresting people without warrants, without charges, and without legal process." The general raised his hands in a gesture of helplessness and exchanged resigned glances with Admiral Fleta and Air Chief Marshal Sanchis.

"So you can see for yourself, Capitan, how serious the situation has become and to what desperate means we have been driven."

"Yes, sir."

The general continued. "Sometimes, Capitan, we in the military (and this is, Capitan, one of the lessons of history) are driven to adopt uncivilized methods in order to ensure that civilization itself may continue to exist. It is the hardest burden to bear if one is a soldier, a terrible burden, and a terrible responsibility. Do you understand what I am saying, Capitan?"

"Yes, sir."

"What I am telling you, Capitan, is that these enemies of civilization must be taken out of circulation permanently, for the greater good of all."

"Permanently, sir?" echoed the capitan.

"Permanently," repeated the general. "However, we cannot allow under any circumstances the honorable name of the armed services to be besmirched by those who seek to undermine our efforts and, indeed, our very existence." The general paused for effect. "This means that officially your organization does not exist. If it is exposed, we will deny all knowledge of it and will take no responsibility. If you are exposed, Capitan," said the general, leaning forward on his elbows, "and the evidence is irrefutable, we will try you by court-martial for exceeding your duties and acting without orders, and you will be shot by firing squad."

The Capitan said nothing at all and was contemplating hasty withdrawal when the general broke into his thoughts.

"There will be at your disposal a liberal quantity of funds. You will submit accounts and reports to us, which we shall immediately destroy. We will promote you with immediate effect to colonel, and you will be put on special salary with allowances for hazardous work and unsociable hours. You will operate from the Army School of Electrical and Mechanical Engineering. We have emptied the officers' wing, which has many small rooms suitable for temporary accommodation of prisoners and other suitable facilities such as bathrooms. Is this all clear?"

"Yes, General." The capitan felt as though he were being steamrollered.

"Good," said General Ramírez. "We have provided for you a small fleet of Ford Falcon motorcars, some painted in the colors of the State Telephone Corporation and some in the colors of the State Oil Company. They have very spacious trunks, Colonel."

"Yes, sir."

"Very well, Colonel. You will return to this office tomorrow at eleven A.M. precisely, and we will go into practical details. You are dismissed."

The new colonel saluted smartly and marched from the room. Outside the door he removed his cap and went and sat in the lavatory for twenty minutes. Panic rose from his stomach, and he seriously considered fleeing to Ecuador. But then he remembered the "liberal quantity of funds" and the promotion, and he thought, *I'll just see how it goes.*

Inside the room Admiral Fleta asked General Ramírez a question. "Do you think you can rely on him?"

"I think so," replied the general. "To begin with, I am having him tailed by the Army Internal Security Service, and if he does not take his duties seriously, he will be taken off them."

"And posted to Antarctica?" asked Air Chief Marshal Sanchis. The other two laughed.

The colonel found it much easier than he had expected. He consulted the files of the Army Internal Security Service and found that there were two categories: "C" for *"communistas"* and "SV" for *"subversivos varios."* The colonel was stupefied by the number of files. There were hundreds of thousands of them, and he thought, *Everything must be worse than I thought.*

Being a military man, and therefore a lover of order and system, he decided to start at the beginning of *A* and simply work his way through. He decided to ignore for the time being everyone who was living outside the capital, and he photocopied the first fifty files and took them home. On his way he bought a very large office diary and a business pack of postcards. He bought a child's printing set and composed the following standard message:

Dear——

Please attend at the security wing of the Army School of Electrical and Mechanical Engineering on the——day of ——19——at——A.M./P.M. Report to reception and wait. This is for the purpose of routine inquiries. If for any reason you cannot attend at the time stated, please ring 47867132, so that alternative arrangements can be made.

The next day he hired a secretary and delegated to her all the responsibility for arranging interviews, sending off the postcards, and acting as receptionist. He spent the first week putting his office in order and practicing his interview technique with the aid of a mirror and a tape recorder.

In the second week the *subversivos varios* began to arrive and wait nervously in the waiting room, wondering what they had done wrong and what the interview was for.

The colonel interviewed four people in the morning and four in the afternoon, except Friday afternoon, when he wrote his report to General Ramírez. He felt at the end of two weeks that he was getting nowhere, and he was already bored and frustrated.

The interviewee would sit fidgeting nervously, and the colonel would look up from the file at the student, or the housewife, or the social worker, or whoever it was and say, "It says here that during the playing of the national anthem it was observed that you failed to stand up/ continued talking/laughed disrespectfully," or he would find himself saying, "It was observed during a trade union meeting that you laughed derisively at a joke about the navy."

The frightened student/housewife/social worker would make lame/frightened excuses ("I'd hurt my leg," "The other person asked me a question," "My boyfriend was tickling me"). The colonel would frown very severely and sigh disapprovingly. The interviewee would become even more nervous, and the colonel would stand up and walk around the room and demand to know about subversion and subversives.

The interviewee would look confused and say, "I do not know anything," and the colonel would give a stern lecture on patriotic duty. Cowed and unhappy, the victims of his speeches would hurry away, and he would sigh and shake his head and think, *What was the point of all that?*

He grew excessively irritable and began to lose his temper more and more quickly as his interviewees failed to provide him with anything interesting or exciting, but he managed to control himself until one day he interviewed a radical lawyer.

The man wore round John Lennon glasses, he had greasy long hair, he had spots among his stubble, and the colonel thought he probably had no muscles at all. The colonel felt that irrational fear and hatred that most military men have of people who they suspect are homosexuals. The man put the colonel's back up before he even spoke, with his bohemian necktie, his vest from a charity shop, and his sandals.

The lawyer came in and sat down without being asked, looked at the colonel with a kind of contemptuous and expectant impertinence, and started to roll a cigarette.

"You may not smoke in here," said the colonel brusquely. "I detest it." Slowly and casually the radical lawyer put the cigarette to his mouth and lit it. The colonel snatched it from between his lips and crushed it beneath his boot.

"I hope you realize that I only came out of curiosity," said the radical lawyer. "There is no law at all which says I had to come."

"I want to ask you some questions," said the colonel. "This is nothing to do with the law. It's a question of cooperation."

"And what happens if I don't 'co-operate'?" asked the lawyer, lounging back in his chair.

The colonel did not answer. He picked up the file; it said, "The suspect makes a policy of defending in court antisocial elements and subversives."

"You defend left-wingers?" asked the colonel.

"I have the right not to answer questions if my own lawyer is not present. In fact, if I have not been arrested or charged, I don't have to answer any questions anyway—I want to know your name, Colonel."

"You want to know my name?" asked the colonel incredulously. "You?"

"My organization finds the names of militarist pigs, and we report their activities to the Human Rights Movement and the UN, of course."

The colonel was stunned. "You called me *cochino?*"

"Cochino," repeated the lawyer. "It is a word that applies to the type of Latino-Nazi of which you are a specimen. 'Nazi' is spelled N–A–Z–I and 'cochino' is spelled C–O–C–H–I–N–O if you want to write the words in your illegal report. I assume you'd like to learn to spell."

The rage and frustration of two weeks' futile effort boiled over in the colonel. He strode up to the lawyer and grasped him by the unbuttoned lapels of his vest. He hauled him out of the chair and flung him against the wall, so that his head hit it with a crack.

The lawyer groaned, recollected himself, and then sneered, "So force is the only language a pig understands?"

The colonel drew back his fist and crushed the man's nose so that blood streamed down his chin. He wiped it with the back of his hand and said, "You prove my point."

"You have made no points," shouted the colonel. "You are a disgusting little queer who thinks he's important. You have called me a pig and a Nazi! What else would you call me?"

"¡Fascista!" replied the lawyer.

The colonel punched the man hard in the stomach, and he collapsed on the floor, groaning and doubling up. The colonel, raging with contempt and disgust, kicked the man hard in the kidneys twice and then dragged him across the floor and out into the corridor. He opened the door of one of the little rooms that used to be for visiting officers and threw the lawyer inside. As the man groaned and moaned on the floor, the colonel said, "When you can talk to me with some respect in a civilized manner, then I will let you go."

The colonel was shaking with rage and indignation when he sat down at his table and tried to prepare himself for the next interview. In spite of himself, he shouted at the young woman and made her cry.

Two hours later the man was banging on his door, shouting, "I need to go to the toilet!"

The colonel listened from his office, and the rage rose in him again. He strode to the door of the man's room and said in a voice full of disgust, "You can damn well piss yourself."

When the colonel drove angrily home that night in his State Telephone Company Ford Falcon, the radical lawyer was still in his cell, unfed, pissing in the corner of the room.

24
Gloria and Doña Constanza Hatch a Plot

Everything in Uruguay had traditionally been exceedingly staid and tedious. The country had been run for years by two parties of the center, the Colorados and the Blancos, which commanded hereditary loyalties rather like the Whigs and the Tories in eighteenth-century Britain. However, any differences in their policies were only vaguely discernible. The situation was analogous to that in Colombia, with its Liberals and Conservatives.

However, things had begun to change when dozens of enthusiastic splinter parties began to proliferate in the universities, where the more or less idle children of the upper and middle classes had ample time and money to become disillusioned with everything and talk endlessly through the night of how it all had to be changed. Gloria de Escobal, whose father was an ambassador, oscillated between joining the Frente Amplio and the Party For The Victory Of The People, and finally opted for the latter, even though it was very much smaller.

Gloria was twenty-five years old, had been educated at Roedean in Brighton, England, and had married a man with so much money that she had had nothing to do except fly to Buenos Aires to go shopping or go to Punta del Este and lie in the sun. In the winter she usually went to Italy.

She bore her husband a son and then announced that she wanted to go to the university. Her husband and family protested; but she went anyway, and her husband did not finally divorce her until her left-wing associations became too embarrassing and dangerous. With the permission of Gloria's parents he abducted the child and then won legal custody in the courts, so Gloria decided to have another child on her own, whose father was an irrelevance.

Gloria was not a member of the Tupamaros guerrillas, but because of their activities, it very soon became uncomfortable to be left-wing at all. The placid government of the center found itself, as did the entire country, whirling on its heels in confusion and indecision wondering where the next grenade was going to come from and who was going to be assassinated next. The Tupamaros thought that throwing cobblestones like the students of Paris was effeminate and ineffective but were as surprised as anyone else when the exasperated military seized power and repressed the whole country barbarously for eleven years.

Gloria de Escobal's little party was still technically legal, but she began to notice that familiar faces were going missing, and she began to hear stories of torture and murder. She packed up her possessions, gathered her baby in her arms, and moved to Argentina. She settled in a very expensive flat in Belgrano, Buenos Aires, and lived comfortably enough on money sent by her father and on what she earned as a secretary.

She tried to persuade the armed men who abducted her to let her keep her baby with her, but they told her it would be taken care of, and she had to leave it in the flat alone, even though it was only one year old. Gloria's father was told that the baby was with Gloria in prison. Gloria was told that the baby was with her father. The baby was taken to Santiago de Chile and dumped in a public toilet. The men also took her possessions and sold them for their own profit.

Gloria was taken blindfolded to the Ondetti Engineering Works, recently gone into liquidation, and its buildings empty except for prisoners. Gloria heard the metal doors close behind her and was pushed down the metal steps into the basement. She was blindfolded for two weeks and was not allowed to speak, but she was astonished when she realized from the whisperings of the guards that they, and all the prisoners, were also Uruguayans.

Gloria was fed three times over the fortnight and did not sleep at all because of the screaming and because the torturers used to put on record players very loudly to try to drown the cries of agony. Sometimes they tortured the prisoners in groups, and sometimes Gloria was taken out alone.

Compared with the Argentinean torturers, the Uruguayans were very civilized. All that they did to Gloria was to bind her wrists behind her back with a piano wire and then string her up by them from a beam, with her feet in a tank of salted water. Then they gave her electric shocks all over her body, but mostly, of course, on her breasts and genitals. They were supposed to ask her about other Uruguayans in exile in Argentina and about left-wing activists she knew of in Uruguay, but usually they forgot.

Gloria was lucky that she only lost the use of her arms for a few weeks and was taken to a military airfield to be flown to Montevideo, where she was imprisoned without being tortured or murdered. This was because the Argentineans, in a further exemplary case of international interintelligence service cooperation, had told them of a wonderful idea of legitimizing her captivity.

The group that had been brought back from Buenos Aires was bundled into a truck and taken to the Villa Maravillosa, where they were herded into a room and remained there, handcuffed, while the army filled it with rifles and ammunition.

When the television cameras arrived, the prisoners' blindfolds were taken off, and they were led out of the Villa Maravillosa in single file and in handcuffs. Then the TV crews were brought to the villa and shown the terrorists' enormous cache of arms.

Since Gloria was now a prisoner officially, her father, the ambassador, was able to pull strings to get her out. The prison psychiatrist in return for certain inducements diagnosed her as having been temporarily insane and under the influence of brainwashing, and she was released on the understanding that she would leave Uruguay and that her father was to be held personally responsible for her future conduct.

Childless and homeless, Gloria wandered those parts of Latin America that would still allow her in, until she met Remedios in Mexico City, where the latter was trying to recruit exiled Montoneros for her guerrilla group at home in her own country. Gloria stopped being a theoretical Communist who sympathized with the terrorists from a distance and went back with Remedios to become a practicing Communist who actually was a terrorist.

Gloria dropped her upper-middle-class airs and attitudes in the mountains, but her aura of culture and conviction gave her a kind of concentrated self-confidence that the other *guerrilleros* respected. It was tacitly understood that if anything ever happened to Remedios, Gloria would probably become the leader. She took Tomás as her lover but never bore him a child because of the effects of the torture.

Gloria and Doña Constanza became close friends; this was surprising in some ways and unsurprising in others. It was unsurprising because their backgrounds were similar, but it was surprising because whereas Gloria was intensely serious and intellectual and had the air of one who would never again know happiness, Doña Constanza was intensely frivolous, could not be bothered to talk about politics, and was deliriously happy all the time. Perhaps they became so close because they were both excellent warriors, because Gonzago and Tomás were brothers, and because each saw in the other's qualities something to be envied.

One day Constanza had returned in disarray and covered with the droppings of swifts from a particularly exhilarating and virtuoso performance with Gonzago on a ledge behind a waterfall and was sitting with Gloria at the edge of the camp, watching the long procession of leaf-cutting ants bearing their supplies home. They were like a band of little *guerrilleros*.

"Do you ever think of your husband?" asked Gloria suddenly.

"Not really," replied Constanza. "That all seems a long time ago."

"It was only a few months," observed Gloria.

"I know, but all the same. I wonder what he is doing. I expect he is making purple earthquakes with some mulatta girl."

"I expect he has bitten his fingernails back to the armpits with worrying about you," replied Gloria. There was a silence. "I often think of my husband. Don't get me wrong, I'm very fond of Tomás, and I could not go back to all that; but I did love him, especially to begin with. One has so many romantic dreams."

"What was he like?" asked Constanza.

"Oh, tall, good-looking, very rich."

"Sounds lovely," remarked Constanza.

"Well, it was, but he never really knew me. He never even wanted to or tried to. I was just his pretty wife, whom he kissed on the forehead when he got home."

"Hugh did not even do that," said Constanza. "He only talked about rugby and polo. He never fucked me into orange fragments like Gonzago."

"Then he is probably not making purple earthquakes with some mulatta girl, now is he?"

"Oh"—laughed Constanza—"I think he was always doing that, and that is why he was not interested in me."

"I wonder whether your husband ever got the money together to leave under the bridge. Do you think he did?"

"Oh, I expect so," said Constanza. "He always did the right thing and always on time. He was like a German."

"Why don't we go and get the money off him then? I expect he has still got it, if he is as punctilious as you say."

"I expect he has been waiting for us to get in touch," said Constanza.

"All we have to do is give him a new ransom note. Then we swap you for the money."

"And then," continued Doña Constanza, "I run away again."

"It is a bit mean, though, isn't it, to do something like that to someone? I mean it is completely unprincipled."

"We will give him the money back after the victory," said Constanza cynically. "Let us go and see what Remedios says."

Remedios was very dubious indeed. "For one thing, it appears that the army is active in the area. I do not want to end up losing men and equipment for nothing. Secondly, how do I know that you, Constanza, have not dreamed this up as a means of escape and that afterward you will not betray us?"

Constanza was very offended, and an indignant expression crossed her face. "That is ridiculous!" she said. "For a start, even if I do not come back, you have still got half a million dollars in return. And I could not possibly bring soldiers and things back here because I do not know where we are!"

"We could blindfold her on the way there," said Gloria, "if you really think it is necessary."

"I will agree to that," said Constanza, still angry with Remedios. "But I am coming back anyway, because of Gonzago and because I want to be here."

Remedios sighed, still looking doubtful. "I will think about it," she said, "and I will tell you my final decision tomorrow."

As Gloria and Constanza walked away from the hut, Gloria said, "By the way, why have you never become pregnant by Tomás? Isn't it about time?"

"Oh," replied Constanza, "I thought two children were enough. I got myself sterilized in New York."

Gloria was surprised. "I thought you were a Catholic!"

"Oh, yes, but religion has nothing to do with the practicalities of life. Why have you not got pregnant by Gonzago?"

Gloria smiled very sadly. "I, too, was sterilized, in Buenos Aires."

In the morning Remedios changed her mind. She sent Federico to fetch the two women, and they proceeded to her hut in a mood of eager anticipation. "I wonder what she is going to say," said Constanza.

What Remedios said was that she had seen Aurelio, "that funny-looking *cholo*" and that he had told her that when he had gone to Chiriguaná to sell his corn, the army had just left. "But he did say," added Remedios, "that there are still Jungle Rangers patrolling. He says they are a long way to the east and the local Indians are giving them a hard time, so we should be all right. We do not know exactly what the Mountain Rangers are doing, but that is not going to be your problem down on the savanna."

"Does that mean we can go?" asked Gloria.

"Yes, it means you can go. Aurelio is coming here tomorrow morning to guide you through the jungle so that you do not fall into his traps, and he will guide you back again. As for precisely when he does that, you will have to arrange with him yourselves. As for you, Constanza"— Remedios looked hard into her eyes—"I have decided to trust you, but if you should double-cross us, I promise you you will be tracked down and shot. Do you understand?"

"Of course," said Constanza. "But as I am not going to betray you, you will not have to shoot me."

"Good," said Remedios. "Gloria, you are in command of this expedition. I want you to take Federico because he comes from that village himself and knows his way around. I also think you should take two others with you."

Remedios smiled to herself. She knew perfectly well that they would choose Gonzago and Tomás, and she understood that Constanza was much less likely to escape with Gonzago jealously waiting near Don Hugh's hacienda. "And by the way, Constanza . . ."

"Remedios?"

"If your husband has any guns or ammunition or explosives in his hacienda, we would be very grateful for them."

Aurelio was waiting for them at dawn and led them away without a word. He took them through the jungle unerringly even though at times it seemed that there was no path. There is no need here to describe the journey, but let it be said it was long, made insufferable by carnivorous insects, it was humid and sweaty, and also let it be said that Aurelio could see Parlanchina accompanying them all the way, just a couple of steps behind Federico. Her long hair was flowing about her hips, and she was chatting all the time as her ocelot trotted beside her.

Aurelio left the *guerrilleros* at the edge of the jungle, where it becomes savanna, and pointed out to Federico exactly how they were to get to the village, even though Federico already knew. They were to meet again at that spot in precisely one week. "If you are not here," said Aurelio, "I will wait two more days."

After they had gone, Aurelio spoke to Parlanchina. "Gwubba, is it well that you should love a man who is not a spirit?"

"Papacito," she said, "I know things that you do not."

All of them were surprised when they surveyed the village through Gloria's binoculars, the very binoculars that had once been General Fuerte's. All of the fields around the village had been razed, and a rampart topped with barbed wire had been constructed at each end of the street.

"Has the army taken it?" asked Constanza.

"Let us go find out," replied Gloria.

When they were closer, Gloria handed the binoculars to Federico. "See if anyone looks familiar." Federico scanned the village with growing excitement.

"I have seen my father!" he cried. "He has a new gun! I have seen

Misael and Josef, both with guns, and I see Dolores the whore smoking a *puro* on the rampart. Ay! They are all armed!"

"I think that they have organized a defense against the army," said Constanza. "They had double reason to."

Cautiously the party approached the village. When they came out onto the razed field, Federico waved his rifle and shouted, "Don't shoot! Don't shoot! It is I, Federico! It is I!"

A figure detached itself from the small group of people that came to see what the shouting was about and began to walk toward them. It stopped, as though to make sure what it was seeing, and then began to run. Federico ran forward, too.

Father and son stood facing each other in the middle of the field. Neither spoke, but both smiled. Federico saw that his father looked the same but smaller, and Sergio saw that his son had grown into a man. Then Sergio's eyes fell on to the Lee-Enfield. "My son," he said, "you stole my rifle. With it you killed an innocent man. I have been ashamed."

Federico held the rifle before him in both hands. "Father, it has since killed some men who were not innocent. Here it is, I return it."

Sergio took the rifle and weighed it fondly in his hands. "It is a fine gun." He unslung the M-16 carbine from his shoulder and presented it to Federico. "I think you will need a gun, Federico, so take this one. Pedro stole it from the soldiers. I do not need two rifles."

Father and son embraced, both of them weeping, while the little band of *guerrilleros* stood waiting discreetly on one side.

Then they walked together into the village, creating a sensation that has been seen there neither before nor since. It was not the return of Federico that caused it; everyone had always known that, as sons do, he would one day return.

What caused the stir was the sight of their former mistress dressed in khaki combat fatigues, slim and sunburned, with her hair loose and flowing down her back, with two grenades swinging from her belt, and a semiautomatic rifle slung across her back. They did not know what to say or think, but as each one recognized her, their jaws dropped in amazement.

Doña Constanza put one hand on her hip and said, "What the blue fuck are you staring at?" That caused further amazement, and to one old man who followed her, gaping and pointing, she said, "If you do not close your mouth, I am going to fill it with horseshit and kick your black ass until it bleeds!"

She put her nose in the air, as in days of old, and followed Federico and the others to consult with Pedro, Hectoro, Josef, and Misael. They listened gravely to the history of the village since Federico had left it and then informed the four men of their plans. It was agreed that the *guerrilleros* should enjoy the hospitality of the village.

"It seems to me also," said Pedro, "that as we are both fighting the same army, there would be good reasons to fight together."

"When do you expect the soldiers back?" asked Gloria.

"We do not know. Perhaps we could send you a message when they come, and we will attack them before they attack us."

Gloria had a thought. "Do you know Aurelio, the *cholo?*"

"I know him," said Pedro. "He is a fine hunter. I give him tools, and he gives me medicines from the jungle."

"Do you know how to find him without stepping into his traps?"

"Of course," said Pedro. "He showed me so that our trade might continue."

"Excellent, then," replied Gloria. "You must tell him when the soldiers come, and he will tell us."

The following morning Doña Constanza left her weapons in Sergio's hut, and Gloria bound her hands together. The party trudged the two miles up the track to Don Hugh's hacienda. Gloria surveyed the house with her binoculars and said, "We are very lucky. He is here." She sent Federico and Tomás around the house to reconnoiter, and when they returned, the party stepped out of the shadows and marched boldly down the drive. Gonzago whipped out a knife and held it at Constanza's throat, for a more theatrical effect.

When Don Hugh answered the frantic banging on the door, his heart leaped and sank simultaneously. He beheld three warriors, Gonzago, Tomás, and Gloria, armed to the teeth, and with them someone bound up who looked exactly like his wife when she had been young. He looked again and realized that it really was his wife. "Constanza?" he said.

"Hello, Hugh," she answered, genuinely glad to see him, as though he were a cousin she had not seen for a long time.

"Let us save time," said Gloria briskly. "We are the People's Vanguard. As you see, your wife is alive and unharmed, and we are prepared to release her to you under the terms originally proposed. Half a million United States dollars. We also require you to hand over any weapons, ammunition, or explosives that you may have in the house."

"I have nothing of that sort," replied Don Hugh.

"Do not lie," said Constanza sharply, and then realizing her mistake, added, "They will search the house anyway. They told me."

"Search the house," said Gloria to the two brothers. They came out with two rifles, a Browning automatic, and several boxes of shells.

"We very kindly left you the shotgun," said Gonzago, smiling his charming and sparkling smile, "so that you may continue to shoot pigeons."

"Half a million dollars!" demanded Gloria.

Don Hugh sighed heavily and with resignation reentered the hacienda. He came out shortly with an old brown suitcase.

"Take it," said Gloria, "to the middle paddock, and empty it. Then refill it and bring it back." Don Hugh did as he was told, and Gloria was satisfied that the case was not booby-trapped. Don Hugh came back, and Gloria inspected the case minutely for tracking devices. She pushed Doña Constanza toward Don Hugh, and she and the two men retreated up the drive, with Tomás carrying the case.

"Did they say where they were going?" asked Don Hugh, getting out the keys of his Jeep from his pocket.

"They are going to Valledupar," lied Doña Constanza, according to plan.

"I'll give them an hour," said Don Hugh decisively, "and then I am driving to Don Pedro's. We'll take the airplane to Valledupar, and when those scruffy bastards turn up, we will be waiting for them with half the army."

"I hope you do not expect me to come with you," said Doña Constanza. "I am so tired I could sleep for a week."

Don Hugh suddenly remembered that his wife was back, a fact that had escaped his attention owing to the chagrin of his having handed over half a million dollars. He put his arm around her shoulders and kissed her on the forehead. "You poor darling," he said. "It must have been a terrible, terrible experience. You cannot possibly imagine how worried I was! I have been running around in circles, tearing my hair out!"

"Do not exaggerate," said Constanza cruelly. "I do not suppose you did any such thing."

Don Hugh looked very surprised; his wife, who had once played every game by the rules, was spoiling his play.

Silently Doña Constanza took her husband by the hand and led him to the bedroom. She made love to him slowly and tenderly, for the last time, for old times' sake, to say good-bye and to say she was sorry.

Don Hugh was both suspicious of and astonished by her new voluptuousness, her new figure, her new sensuality. "When I come back . . . I think it will take about a week to pay off the police and the judges . . . let's go on a second honeymoon! We can go to Rio or Paris!"

Constanza nodded.

Don Hugh roared off in his Jeep, and Constanza watched with just a little regret, just a little pang, as she saw his big rugby player's shoulders swing the wheel and disappear in a cloud of dust. *Sometimes,* she thought, *things happen too late.*

Doña Constanza sat down and wrote a note:

My Dear Hugh,

I have been away a long time from you, and in that time everything with me has changed. I do not think it possible for us to pick up and start again. So I am saying good-bye. It was sweet of you to pay out all that money for me, and I shall always remember it with gratitude. However, I know that you could have paid a lot more without even noticing the difference, and I do not think you have ever been happy with me. I do not have anyone else (how could I if I was a prisoner?), but I feel I have to start my life again. I am going to Costa Rica and then to Europe. Give my love to the children. One day I will be in touch, when I am sorted out.

I am sorry,

Constanza

She went upstairs and found her checkbook. There was a lot of money in her account, and one day it might come in useful. She also took a photograph of Hugh and the children.

Back in the village it was impressed on everyone that Don Hugh should not be told that Constanza had gone back to the mountains and that he should not under any circumstances be told that she was *guerrillera*.

They stayed in the village for five days. Federico was amazed to find that his little sister, Francesca, had grown into a beautiful young woman, and she laughed at him when he warned her about men.

"You are in more danger of guns than I of men," she said. "It is you who should be careful!"

The party met Aurelio at the appointed time and went back to the camp. Constanza decided never to tell Gonzago about her last tender hour with Don Hugh. Sometimes when it would be a good thing to lie, it is even better simply not to tell the truth.

Aurelio had seen Parlanchina walking behind Federico, as before. "Gwubba," he said, "did you not marry a god?" But Parlanchina only tossed back her hair and smiled her secretive smile. Federico began to have aching dreams about a beautiful wild girl who lived in the jungle.

25
The Two Virgins

Federico was not entirely satisfied with his new gun. It was more modern than the Lee-Enfield, and it was shorter. The bullets were smaller, it was also self-loading, but then that was a temptation to waste ammunition, which it was very important to conserve. But then again, it was far easier to get hold of the bullets; the old .303 had been a problem in that respect.

What did not satisfy him was that first, the M-16 was not as accurate over long ranges and secondly, that the self-loading mechanism on his weapon could very easily jam and was fiddly to clear. The first fault was annoying because he had come to specialize in sniping and was one of the *guerrillero* band's chief hunters of meat. The second fault was downright dangerous in a skirmish.

He tried repeatedly to swap it for a Kalashnikov or a hunting rifle, but none of the others wanted to change. They had all grown used to their weapons and considered it unlucky to part with them. Federico particularly wanted a Kalashnikov because it was extremely simple and even seemed to work when full of mud, but those were exactly the reasons that everybody wanted to keep theirs, so he was obliged to resign himself to having to keep his M-16 scrupulously clean and well oiled. Remedios promised him a Kalashnikov should the group at some time acquire one.

Federico used to try to keep track of the activities of the Mountain Rangers. These men were very highly trained mountaineering soldiers whose original function had been to protect the Indians against the rapacious intrusions of brigands, *bandidos,* and other representatives of modern civilization. But nowadays they were mostly men with binoculars and high-definition telescopes, infrared night sights, and a brief to locate the guerrilla bands and report their whereabouts. They were under orders not to fire unless there was no choice and to be as inconspicuous as possible. Remedios and the *guerrilleros* were justifiably anxious about their activities, and it was part of Federico's job, since he was very fit and agile, to scour the area for them and shoot them on sight.

It was, however, fortunate for everyone that the Sierra Nevada de Santa Margarita was vast, unmapped, and in most places inaccessible because otherwise the bloodshed upon both sides would have increased dramatically. The authorities usually assumed that any Mountain Rangers who did not return had died in a fall and did nothing about it, while Federico took their weapons and hid the bodies as decently as he could.

Generally the Mountain Rangers were dropped in pairs by helicopter in convenient places, from which they would again be picked up five days later. In the interim they were supposed to scale nearby peaks and observe any activity within range of their apparatus. The method they employed was to survey adjacent areas systematically, so that in the course of a year the whole cordillera was covered.

But it was an extremely tough and difficult job, and if the truth were known, actually impossible. It was not just that they were expected to climb several peaks in five days, loaded down with their provisions, their rifles, their climbing equipment, and their surveillance apparatus, but also that the mountains themselves were against them. In the peaks it was bitterly cold at above about fourteen thousand feet, and the weather kept changing all the time. It was quite possible to climb a mountain all morning in beautiful sunshine, reach the top, take out your binoculars, and five minutes later be completely enshrouded in cloud and freezing rain mixed with driving snow and stinging dust. Additionally, the frost at night split the rocks in the mountainsides into shale, and it was quite possible, especially in wet conditions, to find yourself sliding backward and downward rapidly at the same time as trying to climb forward and upward.

The guerrilla groups quickly got wise to the Mountain Rangers. They moved farther down the slopes into the dense jungle that sheltered the mountain slopes to quite a considerable height, and when they heard the sound of helicopters, they moved promptly into the valleys that the Rangers had surveyed the week before. In this way they only had to move once a year, for just a week. They also found that the Rangers were quite easy to kill off.

There were two reasons for this. First, the Rangers never seemed to expect to see anyone who was not an Indian. This was because usually Indians were the only people they did see, as the guerrillas always stayed out of sight when the helicopters arrived. This lack of close encounters made them incautious and slapdash and the easiest possible victims of ambush. Secondly, the Rangers would have had such an exhausting and miserable life if they had worked as expected that quite often they did not work at all. It was just a question of arriving, camping for five days in the same spot, and then being picked up again. They did not appreciate that just because they had got away with this for two years, it did not mean that their throats would not be cut as they slept in the first week of the third.

Nevertheless, the activities of the Rangers still worried the guerrillas. It was always possible that at some time the Army Air Fleet Command might decide to randomize the searches, and it was also possible that a helicopter might arrive without being heard, as the acoustics in mountain ranges can be very idiosyncratic.

Federico, therefore, was on permanent solitary patrol to look out for Rangers. He was allowed to treat this job as casually as he liked, and if he had wanted to, he could have taken others with him, but he was very like Pedro the hunter, whom he had always admired and tried to emulate when he was a boy. He was serious about what he did, he liked to stalk alone, and he devoted much time to honing his skill.

Federico had actually killed two pairs of Mountain Rangers. The first two he had shot while they were roped together, scaling a face high above him. They had fallen an immense distance, and he had had trouble finding their bodies, which he buried under heaps of shale so that the condors would not desecrate them (he had developed a strong sense of decency in this respect ever since he had failed to protect from the vultures the body of the first man he had shot). Federico had borne their equipment in triumph back to the camp, having to make two journeys to do it, and Remedios had praised him before the whole group.

The second pair Federico shot when he came around a corner on the side of a mountain and saw below him in the valley two Rangers trying to violate an Indian woman who was fighting back frenziedly. One of the Rangers was trying to beat her into submission with his rifle, and the other was on the ground with his arms around her legs, attempting to topple her over. Federico shot the first man through the head while he was on the backswing, and he fell flat on his back.

The other man stood up, froze for a second, and then ran. The Indian woman picked up a rock in her hand and actually give chase. Federico was not used to rapidly running targets, and it took him four shots to bring the man down with a bullet in the leg. He fell down and sat clutching his thigh, rocking in pain, and the Indian woman caught up with him and beat his skull with the rock. Then she stood up, straightened her garments, wiped her brow with her shawl, went back to retrieve her hat, and walked proudly and firmly off down the valley. She did not even look back to see who had saved her, no doubt assuming that it was another Indian who was only doing what he ought to do. Federico took their equipment back to Remedios and received more praise.

When Federico saw no Rangers, as he very seldom did, he usually returned with some meat for the camp. It was so easy to shoot the stupid and docile vicuña that after a while he began to feel guilty about it and instead shot the feral goats that roamed at high altitudes. Lower down he would shoot wild pig and any dog that had rabies. These dogs were not eaten, of course, but destroying them was a civic duty that even outlaws observed.

But one night Federico dreamed for the hundredth time of the beautiful wild girl with the huge brown eyes and the black hair down to her waist, who lived in the jungle. He awoke thinking, *This means that I must go into the jungle and shoot the Jungle Rangers*, but it is certain that what he was hoping was that if he went into the jungle, he would find the girl who had given him so many restless and delirious nights.

He went to ask Remedios for her permission, and she refused it outright. "I will not give you permission. You cannot go down there. For one thing, Aurelio watches the jungle for us, and we do not need you to go, as the Mountain Rangers are much more of a worry for us. Also, Aurelio has left traps everywhere, and you do not know where they are. Also, you know the mountains and the savanna, but you do not know the jungle in between, and you would get lost almost immediately, and you would never come back. Also, there are no Jungle Rangers in this area at the moment, and I will not give you my permission to waste everyone's time, including your own."

Federico went off on his usual route toward the peaks, and when he was out of sight of the encampment, he skirted around the sides of the valley and began his descent into the jungle. He calculated that he could tell his direction from the sun in the jungle just as easily as he could in the mountains.

Gradually the vegetation became noticeably more lush and impenetrable, and the humidity grew apace, so that Federico had to stop more and more often to slake his thirst in the streams and splash himself. Over his head the canopy became inexorably thicker and there was less light. He began to find himself swatting insects at every step.

Suddenly he stopped. It was as though someone were saying to him inside his head, "I will not give you permission. You cannot go down there." They were Remedios's words, but it was not Remedios's voice. He stood and shook his head. "You do not know the jungle," said the voice, using Remedios's words. Federico shook his head again, as though he were shaking a fly out of his ear. He took a step forward, but his legs seemed very heavy, as though he were carrying a great weight or someone were bearing down on his shoulders. He sat by the path to think about whether he should go on with his plan. Everybody had always warned him about going into the jungle. It was a place of swamps, of hostile Indians with blowpipes and poisoned darts, of snakes, of darkness, of sudden cliffs and holes concealed by creepers. It was a place of forgotten death, where people go insane from being lost. Federico sat there a long time with his common sense doing battle with his obstinacy. He was at that age when a man has that fierce self-confidence and fixed male pride which reveals that he is still not sure if he is yet a man. As he sat, his fear fed his obstinacy. He stood up and walked, resisting the force that pushed him back, like someone leaning with both hands against his chest. He conquered that force and strode on into the perpetual dusk of the jungle.

Parlanchina appeared at the edge of the clearing and beckoned to her father. He laid down the corn-planting stick he was whittling and followed her as she wended in and out of the trees. Every few paces she stopped and looked at him, beckoning with sorrowful urgency. Aurelio hurried in her wake.

In Latin America they call it the *tigre*, but it is not a tiger, except in fierceness and courage. The largest jaguars are nearly seven feet long, not including the splendid striped tail. It is like a leopard but is far more solidly built, with a massive head and powerful legs, and usually its coat is golden brown in color, with black spots on the legs and black rosettes on the flanks. Sometimes they are pure white cats, and very rarely there are beautiful godlike cats of velvet black. These latter confer chieftainship upon warriors of some Indian tribes when they are slain by that warrior in single combat and their pelts are taken from them and worn with dignity. The black jaguar is sacred and mighty, and the Indians consider it the bravest.

The jaguar hunts according to the natural advantages of its habitat. In Argentina, on the pampas, it kills sheep and cattle. By rivers it catches fish and turtles. In forests it shreds the flesh of the tapir. In the jungle it lies motionless upon the branches and leaps upon monkeys and birds. Often it lies upon a branch above a path, because animals, like men, prefer to travel by the easiest ways. But jaguars do not often attack man; they have acquired the wisdom to pass him by, for he is the most dangerous animal on earth.

Federico walked on, glimpsing the sparkling birds in audacious colors shrieking in the trees, watching the monkeys crashing away from him through the branches. Sweat poured down his brow and stung his eyes just as mosquitoes stung his arms and his neck. He was beginning to think of going back. He paused on the path, and above him a *tigre* growled its coughing growl.

Federico started back, startled, and slipped onto his back, twisting his ankle. He half rose to his feet and scrabbled desperately to unsling his rifle. The great black *tigre* arched its back and opened its mouth; it hissed and snarled from the depth of its chest and looked around for a chance to escape, thinking quickly where to leap. In wild panic Federico raised the M-16 to his shoulder, aimed it clumsily at the cat's head, and pulled the trigger. Federico's already racing heart accelerated yet further as nothing happened. He had forgotten to release the safety catch; he had to look at the unfamiliar weapon to find it. His eyes, in his desperation, passed over it twice before he identified it and released it with his sweating and shaking fingers. He remembered to cock it. The cat looked at him again, hissing, as though telling him to leave, but Federico raised the gun once more to his shoulder and fired at the cat's head. But the gun was neither supported nor aimed as it should have been, and the bullet sped harmlessly from the wavering barrel to strike chips from the branch above the cat's head. As the bullet ricocheted away, the cat flinched flat on its stomach against the branch and then rose furiously to its feet and crouched to spring.

Federico wildly tried to fire again. But this time the self-loading mechanism jammed, and Federico was still struggling with his unfamiliar rifle and its unfamiliar slide when the *tigre*, its eyes blazing with hatred and magnificent furious courage, leaped from the branch. Its huge paws landed squarely against Federico's shoulders and bowled him over backward. The *tigre* sank in its claws and with one cut of its teeth ripped out Federico's throat.

Federico died as if in a dream. A great silence rose in his soul, and he felt nothing of the pain in his body. He thought for a second of Francesca and how beautiful she had become. He thought of Sergio and of how he had been forgiven for stealing from his own father. He thought with pity of the man he had killed whom he had not saved from the vultures. He thought of the vulture he had killed for Profesor Luis. He thought of his mother making *arepas*.

"I tried to prevent you," said the voice that was not Remedios's voice. Whether Federico opened his eyes and saw Parlanchina, or whether he saw her only in the dream of his death, it is not possible to say. But she stood over him, her brown eyes filled with tears, her long hair falling about her face.

"You are the girl of my dream," he said. "You are the wild, beautiful girl of the forest."

She smiled. "Like me, you have died a virgin. I tried to prevent you. But you pushed me aside. I have come to lead you."

Federico saw how beautiful she was; he saw that her skin was soft and perfect, how her breasts were budding, how long and straight were her legs. She held out her hand to help him up, and he went with her, without seeing how the *tigre* was tearing his body which had been as exquisite and as perfect as Parlanchina's. He did not see or hear Aurelio speak sharply to the cat so that it slunk away. He saw only Parlanchina by his side, leading him by the hand, looking at him sideways, and smiling the smile of one who knows mischievous secrets.

Aurelio dug out the extremities of Parlanchina's grave. He saw that her bones were white and clean as they lay in the tunnel of the bed of brush. He saw also that the bones of her beloved cat were clean and had fallen among the bones of his mistress. The termites had performed their task well. Aurelio laid Federico's body with Parlanchina's, and he looked one last time at the slim, long limbs and the adolescent face tanned dark with the mountain sun. He pushed the body nearer the others' so that their bones would fall together and intermingle.

He closed the grave and thought about how he had first seen Federico when he was a boy and had killed an innocent man by accident, and he thought about how Parlanchina had followed him in the jungle.

"Gwubba,"—he accused her—"did you lead him to death because you love him?"

"No, Papacito," she said. "I tried to prevent him. But some things one cannot prevent. He came to his death because he loved me."

Aurelio looked into her dark, glowing eyes to be certain that she told the truth. She smiled at him with both sadness and happiness.

"Then you did not marry a god?"

"No, Papacito."

26

The Blossoming of Colonel Asado

When the colonel returned to work the next morning, he opened the door of the radical lawyer's cell and was appalled by the stench of stale urine that assaulted his nostrils. The lawyer was sitting on the edge of the mattress, a picture of abjection, with blood still caked on his lips and chin.

"Get out!" said the colonel. "And remember who are the right people to respect in future."

"Respect?" said the lawyer, looking up. "How is it possible to respect men of violence?"

"You are the first man I have ever struck," replied the colonel, "and I did it not as a soldier but as a man."

The radical lawyer laughed bitterly. "You want information out of me about people who are struggling for a better world, so that you can keep it as it is. You are prepared to beat people up to achieve that. You are a *fascista*!"

The colonel said nothing. He went out and locked the door. He returned a few minutes later with a bucket and a mop. "Before you go," he said, "clean up this mess."

"I refuse," said the lawyer. "It was not my fault that I was locked up in here with no toilet."

The colonel roughly shoved the mop in the man's hands and said,

"You clean it up or you don't go." Then he left, locking the door behind him, and went to his first interview.

Today he found it much easier to bully and browbeat the frightened people who arrived. One woman, a teacher, he slapped across the face, and that evening there were three people locked up for not giving information, including the lawyer, who had mopped up his room but had threatened the colonel with litigation for false imprisonment. The colonel did not know what to do with him, fearing that the man would sue and that he would end up in front of the firing squad.

As he drove home, he was thinking, *The man's a worm, an insect, the very kind of dregs who ferment anarchy and destroy the motherland.* He remembered what General Ramírez had said about removing subversives from circulation "permanently," and he thought, *Well, this creep is a genuine subversive, all right.* He decided to do his patriotic duty, but it caused him to sleep not at all that night.

In the morning he shot the man in the chest, even though his hands were shaking and the act revolted him. When it was dark, he carried the limp corpse out and dumped it in the capacious trunk of his Ford Falcoln. He drove out of town and left it on the municipal rubbish dump, where he covered it over with rubbish. During the night the scavenging strays that lived off the dump uncovered the body, and when the disposal workers found it in the morning, it was already half eaten by dogs. It got only a column inch in the local paper, and the body was unidentified. It was buried with a small wooden cross at its head which said *"Non Nombre."*

The colonel was relieved on his own behalf, and he also had a brain wave. He consulted the deceased's file and confirmed that he had been registered as living alone. He decided to go through the man's flat to see if he could find any information there about those subversive clients.

He had to force the door with a jimmy when no one was looking, but he got in without any trouble and found that the flat was a dump. There were ashtrays full of cigarette ends, dirty clothes scattered about the floor, an unmade bed, whose sheets had obviously not been changed for weeks. The colonel went to the man's desk, and in another brain wave, he stuck a piece of paper in the typewriter and tapped, "I can't stand it anymore. I'm leaving."

The colonel went through the desk and took any papers that looked as though they might be useful. Then he found himself looking at the books on the man's shelves; he saw books like *Das Kapital*, Freud's *Psychopathology of Everyday Life* and Reich's *The Mass Psychology of Fascism*. He thought, *I was right to kill that slime*.

The colonel searched the rest of the man's apartment, and in a drawer by the bedside table he found a gold ring with a tiger's eye set in it. He took it out. *That must be worth something*, he thought, and then put it back. A minute later he opened the drawer and took it out again. "Why not?" he said out loud. "The bastard won't need it now." He put it in his pocket and instantly felt very guilty. He took it out again and looked at it with the intention of putting it back in the drawer, but instead he put it on his little finger and left it there.

As he left, he noticed that he had badly damaged the door with the jimmy and thought, *Since this looks like a burglary, I'll have to make the whole place look like a burglary*. He went back in and carefully strewed the contents of the flat about the floor; somehow it still did not seem right, so he gave up trying to arrange it as an artist's impression of burglary and threw everything around as violently as he could. That looked a lot better.

Later that day the colonel decided that it was time to recruit more interrogators because it was going to take an eternity to get through all the files on his own. He recruited three comrades from his own regiment, with the permission of the general, who promoted all of them. The general then summoned the colonel.

"Colonel," he said, "I am concerned, having read your reports, that things are not being done as thoroughly as I would like. It seems that you are bringing people in by sending them postcards. I appreciate that this is economical, but I also think that anyone who turns up having received a postcard could not possibly be a real subversive."

"No, General," replied the colonel, "but I wished to be thorough, and it occurred to me that the perfect way to disguise the fact that one is a subversive is to behave as though one is not. I think it is better to be sure, Sir."

"I see," said the general.

"Also, I have," continued the colonel, "already detected one such subversive, and his case is, ah . . . terminated, sir."

"Very good," said the general. "But I think perhaps you should concentrate more on those who fail to turn up at all. And another thing . . ."

"Yes, sir?"

"If cases are to be 'terminated,' as you put it, I don't like the idea of people receiving your postcards, which can be found later by relatives. Do you catch my meaning?"

"Yes, sir," said the colonel.

"I think it better if you were to arrive at their residence in plain clothes and escort them to the School of Electrical and Mechanical Engineering. I suggest they should be blindfolded so that they do not know where they are taken." The general put on a wise and confiding tone of voice. "Between you and me, Colonel, I should tell you that psychologically this is an efficient way to proceed, because if your interviewees are a little frightened, they will be more likely to give you information. In the line of duty, Colonel, one sometimes has to frighten people, however distasteful it may be."

"Yes, sir," said the colonel.

"And another thing. You really must expand the operation somewhat. I want you to form proper task forces. And don't worry about the cost." General Ramírez waggled a finger. "Just send all the invoices to me, and I will deal with them through the Army Benevolent Fund and the Army Widows' Pension Investment Scheme."

The colonel instructed each of his three comrades to recruit four more ideologically reliable people, and soon his interview center was full of activity. The twelve men recruited by his comrades went to bring in the subversives in teams of four, usually after dark, and the colonel and his three comrades interviewed them. The colonel began to notice that the suspects often arrived in a badly beaten and shocked state, but the men told him they had put up violent resistance to being escorted and that they had had no choice. "Very good," said the colonel, who was picking up some of General Ramírez's mannerisms and turns of phrase.

The trouble was that you could not return badly beaten people to their homes to complain that they had been arrested and abused by the secret police. The colonel simply kept them at the center, and soon it was severely overcrowded. The whole situation was beginning to get on his nerves, with having to organize meal rotations, bathing rotations, lavatory-visiting rotations, invoicing and interviewing and getting nowhere, and, worst of all, having to listen all day to people banging on their doors, shouting about their rights, and weeping. Sometimes when he could not stand it anymore, he went into the cells and kicked them about until they shut up.

One day the men brought in a young woman, very smartly dressed, beautifully made up, and very self-confident. She smiled at him confidingly and sat down. "Now what can I do for you?" she said.

For some reason she made the colonel nervous just by the way she looked at him. He began to question her about subversion, but she just gazed back at him and continued to smile that confiding smile.

"What do I have to do to get out of here?" she asked. "I think I'd do practically anything." She had put on a sexy drawl and said "anything" in a manner so enticing that the colonel shivered.

"Anything?" he said.

"Oh, yes, anything," she replied.

They looked at each other for a moment, and then she stood up, walked to the door, and turned the key. She returned to the colonel and came very close to him. She put her lips to his ear and whispered hotly, "Just tell me what I can do for you, and then let me go." She leaned back and smiled brightly, looking at him. She began to toy with the buttons of his shirt, and he began to feel aroused. She was wearing something musky and sultry. She turned away and glanced at him over her shoulder. Then she kicked off her high heels and began to undress very slowly just to tease him. He watched fascinated, horrified, and confused. His heart began to beat faster, and he felt a little weak. When she was naked, she turned around and displayed herself to him, raising her arms and doing a little pirouette. "Do you like it?" she said.

"Madame, I must ask you to put your clothes on," he said stiffly.

"Oh, don't be such a spoilsport," she said, and she drew very close to him and started to undo his shirt buttons. She pouted.

"Madame," he said, "I must warn you . . ."

"Oh, sh," she went, and sealed his lips with a forefinger. She began to undo the buttons of his fly and slipped in a cool, elegant hand. Against his will he felt himself harden and swell, and he began to breathe in gasps. She draped herself across the desk and held out her arms to him.

"Madame . . ."

"Oh, come on"—she pouted again—"be a bad boy for once."

He clambered on top of her but felt so awkward and ridiculous that his erection failed him. He struggled with himself but soon climbed off, feeling disgusted and humiliated. "Just get out of here," he said angrily.

"Oh, don't be angry," she said, adopting the voice of a mother soothing a child over a hurt. "I was only trying to give you a good time."

She began to dress efficiently, and the colonel's erection came back again at the thought of what he was about to miss. He went up behind her and spun her around, ripped off her panties, and lifted her onto the edge of the desk. He drove himself into her and came in a few short jerks as she clung to him with her arms around his neck and her legs locked around his back.

When she had left, he looked at her file; it said "Call girl; known to associate with trade union officials in a business capacity."

So he had just had a free one from a hooker. He was deeply enraged and humiliated. It had all been completely sordid.

But it changed the way that he looked at his women prisoners. As he questioned them and felt his power over them, his penis would harden and the hairs on his legs would tingle. He began to feel like a god, and he began to feel that the women were disposable and usable, to be squashed like flies. But no more women offered themselves to him, and he began to grow impatient. One day he gave in to himself.

She was a pretty, bright-eyed sociology student of nineteen with blue eyes and brown curls. She said she did not know anything, and he lost his temper, as nowadays he always did. He struck her across the side of the head and sent her crashing to the floor. He looked at her sobbing there, helpless and whimpering, and he drew his belt out of the loops of his trousers and lashed at her as she writhed and screamed on the carpet. "Tell me, damn you!" he shouted. "Tell me!"

"But," she said, in between sobs, "I don't know anything!"

He knelt and turned her over. Her mascara had run down her face with her tears. He tore open her shirt and pulled her brassiere above her breasts. "You had better tell me," he said as he kneaded them with his hands.

"Oh, God," she moaned in despair, and she lay there sobbing

helplessly as he unzipped her jeans and pulled them off, and then her underwear. She lay motionless and continued to weep as he raped her.

From then on the colonel raped nearly all the women who came through his office, especially the young and pretty ones, and then he locked them up. Sometimes he raped the prettiest ones several times before leaving them to his work force, which had developed the same habits as himself. The colonel did not care anymore. He had complete power. He knew he could do anything at all.

The colonel got into the routine of beating up all his prisoners. They told him lies first for the sake of having something to tell him, but he did not care anymore about that either. He just arrested those implicated and beat them up, too. He discovered that people, especially girls, have a particular horror of having their faces disfigured, and he began to keep a poker permanently stuck into the gas fire. He learned that the prisoners referred to him as *Asado*—it means "angry," and it also means "barbecue." The name gave him grim satisfaction, and he did not mind when his colleagues addressed him by it. On the lips of the prisoners it bespoke his power, and on the lips of his colleagues it bespoke ease and familiarity. His three comrades were already known as El Electricista, who like to question people with the aid of a cattle prod, El Verdugo (the hangman), who employed the strappado, and El Baño, who liked to drown people.

It was impossible to send all the people home after their treatment, and so the ones who did not die under torture were usually shot through the vertebrae of the neck, as it was not too messy. Eventually the sports field of the Army School of Electrical and Mechanical Engineering would not contain any more bodies, so the colonel began to explore alternatives. He had a crematorium built, and he had some bodies dumped at cemeteries, where they were buried as *"Non Nombre."* He commandeered an army transport plane and dumped bodies over the jungle, where their deaths were blamed on terrorists—these were known as free falls. Some he had dumped out at sea, but he stopped this when the tide brought them into holiday resorts in embarrassing numbers.

Very soon the newspapers were full of stories about people being abducted by armed thugs in Ford Falcons, people who disappeared and were never seen again. Relatives began to deliver habeas corpus writs to the police, who were confused by the whole thing. "We cannot honor your writs," they would say, "as we have no records of ever having arrested them." Colonel Asado put a stop to all this by arresting any journalist who reported the disappearances and any relatives who kicked up a fuss. They soon got the message, especially when the navy and the air force got in on the game as well. A silent terror descended upon the capital city of the nation.

Colonel Asado opened four more centers and had sixty people working for him. He grew very rich by selling the possessions of those who vanished, by discovering that General Ramírez never bothered to check through the invoices that he sent him, and by accepting money, before he killed them, from those who attempted to buy their freedom.

27

Of Cures, Cats, and Laughter

La Estancia

MA CHÈRE MAMAN,

I have so much news, Maman, since I last wrote, that I scarcely know where to begin! I do hope that my last letter did not depress you too much; I was myself formidably depressed at the time, but things have much improved since then, mostly because I now have some hope for Françoise.

Do you remember that I mentioned a *brujo* (a sort of sorcerer) called Pedro? Some people call him El Legatero because he knows how to catch alligators alive. You may remember that he told Françoise to eat raw coral snakes for her cancer; but she refused to eat more than one, and her remission went into reverse.

Well, he came back a few days ago and told me that he and an Indian were holding a special healing session in the village where he comes from, and he invited us to come along. He said, "You should both come because the señora's illness is half because of you." I was very puzzled and did not know whether to be insulted or whether to find this ridiculous. However, I did not dare to say anything because the man was very serious and has a kind of mystique about him that is positively awesome. He is very tall and lean, with muscles on his arms like a Foreign Legion physical training instructor, and he dresses in clothes he makes himself from the animals he catches. He once caught a rogue jaguar for Don Pedro (the man with the airplane) and shot it through the eye to stop the skin from being damaged. How anyone could shoot so well with an old musket, I cannot understand. Anyway, he is very grizzled and dignified, and I confess that his invitation seemed more like an order.

Françoise was very weak and tired, and I nearly did not take her on the night concerned. But in the end we drove fifteen miles to the village over the most appalling dirt tracks, and when we arrived, I found it in a state of siege, except without any besiegers. There were ramparts across the street, draped with barbed wire, and everyone, even the women and children, was armed to the teeth. I asked a woman what was going on and she said, "We are waiting for the soldiers." I asked her if they were Communist revolutionaries or something, and she looked at me as if I were mad and burst out laughing. But at least she showed me the way to the healing session.

It was in an awful dingy little *choza* (the kind of hut you see in the Andes), and when we went in, I could not see anything at first except the fire burning in the middle. A voice said, "Sit down," and I realized it was Pedro, the sorcerer. He was naked except for a loincloth, and he looked very sinister with his face half in shadows and the flames glowing red on his body. He said, "Have you eaten no meat, no sugar, and no salt?" and I said, "No, we have not."

He told us to tell him about our illnesses, and the woman next to me said that she was a prostitute (forgive me for mentioning such a thing) and that in plying her trade, she had developed a bad back. She said her name was Dolores. Then there was a man called Misael, who looked a bit like Pedro, tall and muscly and about the same age. He said he was there instead of his baby son who had terrible burn scars. I thought this was a little strange, but everyone seemed to take it as normal that you could be healed on someone else's behalf. There was an Indian who said his name was Aurelio, a very strange-looking character, with a Mongoloid face, a long braid of hair, and very short and stocky. He said he was there to help Pedro with the spirits. He kept having bits of conversation with someone completely invisible to the rest of us, whom he addressed as Gwubba. I thought he was probably half mad, if not completely so.

Pedro and the Indian both lit huge cigars and then filled a gourd with stuff they call ayahuasca; I think it is a Quechua word, but I do not know what it means. They made each one of us drink a whole gourdful while Pedro chanted and the Indian rattled a rattlesnake's rattle. The tea tasted very foul, and I nearly choked; it was greasy and bitter and bit at the back of the throat.

We sat there for about an hour while they chanted and rattled, and suddenly Aurelio said, "The spirits are here." At exactly that moment I began to feel very nauseated, and so did Françoise. My heart was racing, and I was suddenly completely disorientated. I could not sit upright anymore because I could not tell which was the floor or the roof or the walls. I could not see anything either, because stripes and blobs of bright colors, especially blue, kept floating across my eyes and big balls of fluffy purple light were shooting toward me and then shooting away. At one second the walls of the hut were so close that I could not breathe, and the next they were miles away so that I felt as small as an ant. I was pouring with perspiration, and my lungs would not cooperate.

Then I found myself back at home sitting under the bougainvillaeas, admiring the moon, then I was back in France as a child, trying to pick a fig that was too high up for me to reach, and then I was back in the hut, but I could not see the others. I tried to crawl around to find them, but the floor kept tilting so that I just slid around, and at one point everything turned upside down so that I was crawling on the ceiling. But I felt so heavy that I could barely move at all, and when I cried, *"Au secours,"* I emitted only a strangled yelp.

Eventually everything calmed down, and there they were, still chanting and rattling. I was just thinking, *Thank God it is over*, when they began to turn into animals. They were oxes, llamas, vizcachas, jaguars, ocelots, toucans, and caimans, and they swapped from one to the other with such rapidity and suddenness that I forgot my alarm and watched with a kind of hypnotized fascination. At one point I saw a beautiful young girl with hair down to her waist, standing behind the Indian with her hands on his shoulders.

When that was all over, Pedro moved over to Françoise, who was flat on her back. He opened her shirt and exposed her breasts, a sight so gruesome that I cannot bear to think of it. Pedro took the flesh of one breast into his mouth and sucked very hard on it. Then he came away and started to salivate into the fire. Believe me, Maman, his saliva turned into a scorpion that landed in the embers, scuttled about, and then shriveled into ashes. He repeated this procedure on the other breast, and spit, of all things, a snake a yard long into the fire, where it writhed as it burned away. Then he came to me and sucked cactus spines out of my belly!

At that point I passed out, and when I woke up, Aurelio and Pedro were starting the whole thing again, and we had to drink more ayahuasca. I was reeling from the effects when I realized that I could see everything out of the back of my head. I actually turned away from them in order to watch. Then Aurelio said something to me with a voice so deep and macabre that I fainted from terror and did not wake up again until morning, with my mouth feeling like an old boot filled up with Parmesan cheese.

Everyone else was already awake, and Pedro said, "Will you take a *copa?*" and he gave me a little cup of *chacta*, which is very powerful. It burned a hole in my stomach, but I instantly felt better.

I said to Pedro, "So was my wife's cancer natural, or are you going to tell me it was caused by evil spirits?"

He replied very gravely, "If you think for a minute, everything is natural, and everything is spirits."

Maman! I can just see you crossing and recrossing yourself as you read these words! But I have to tell you the wonderful news that in the week since then Françoise's cancer has gone into a very rapid remission and that she is bright-eyed and happy for the first time in months! She tells me that she saw the same things as myself, but that when I was unconscious she saw an angel, an hermaphrodite angel! She says it had a spear and a pair of scales and that it kissed her on the mouth so she tingled all over. She is convinced it was the archangel Raphael, but does not know why. Both Françoise and I are utterly ecstatic that she is getting better, as you may imagine. I was anticipating her death within a few weeks, and my heart was very heavy, and which is now as light as a wren!

If that were not strange enough, we were afflicted immediately afterward in this area with the most extraordinary plague, though I hasten to add that it is a benign one. You may have noticed (how could you help it?) that there are muddy paw marks on the paper and that my handwriting is unusually erratic. This is because there has been a large black cat trying to sit on the paper as I write and also taking swipes at my pen as it moves. "What is so strange about that?" I hear you say. "My son loves cats." What is so strange, Maman, is that we are absolutely inundated with a flood of cats of biblical proportions. I cannot describe to you the sheer quantity of these animals that have appeared out of nowhere! They are sitting on fence posts, on gates. They are draped voluptuously across roofs and branches; they are in my Jeep, in the house, in the stable, in the fields. I cannot sit out at night, as is my wont, because three or four cats instantly leap on my lap and onto my shoulders, and they also occupy Françoise's hammock on the porch. I have to turn them out of my sink before I can wash my hands and also out of the shower last thing at night. In the morning Françoise and I wake up stifled and sweating from the weight of cats on our bed, and sometimes they wake me by sticking their coarse little tongues in my ears and purring. I cannot tell you how tickly that is!

The odd thing is that I go around the house constantly shutting all the doors and windows, but they still appear and wrap themselves around my legs, as though they could walk through walls.

Another funny thing is that as yet they have not, despite their omnipresence, annoyed me at all. They are not the usual mangy, fleabitten, and half-starved thieving little cats one normally sees around here but are big and sleek, with fetching faces and charming demeanors. They do not steal food or dig up the garden or leave mouse entrails all over the floor. Mostly they spend their time sitting on their haunches as though expecting something to happen, for which they are prepared to wait patiently. They are very affectionate and purr unfailingly if you tickle their ears and cheeks. They are quite fearless and contented, and at night the sound of crickets has now been entirely replaced by the sound of purring, which strikes the ears as a kind of muffled roar, like hearing the sea from a distance. It is a much more calming noise than that of the crickets, and I, for one, am quite happy about it. Françoise was at first anxious about getting hay fever, because she is allergic to cats, but so far, God be praised, she has not been affected, apart from tripping over a cat in the corridor when she went to the bathroom in the dark. Both she and the cat were fortunately unhurt.

These cats are not just here on the *estancia*; they have apparently invaded the whole district. Within a radius of twenty miles everyone is overrun by them, and the dogs, it seems, are too scared to come out. I have seen small black-and-white ones with happy expressions, ginger ones, white ones with one blue and one green eye, immensely fluffy ones in smoky blue, and short-haired tabbies, but the most remarkable ones are the big black ones. I have become very fond of the one that sits on my blotter and tries to stop me from writing.

I have to say that yet more odd things have been happening. The bridge at Chiriguaná recently exploded quite spectacularly, killing four soldiers. The dust of the explosion traveled as far as here, so that everything was turned white. The army camped there for a month and then left, and afterward there was what I can only describe as a plague of laughing. I have not been able to get any sense out of most of the locals for quite some time because they have only to look at you to burst out into guffaws. My washerwoman inadvertently sprayed me with *chicha* beer because she was drinking it when I came in to speak with her on account of her distracting chuckling. Instead of apologizing, she went off into further howls of hysterical mirth until I, too, was infected with it and began to laugh. Françoise came in to find out what the joke was, and very soon all three of us were screaming with laughter, our faces dripping with tears, and clutching our stomachs with the pain of the muscular contractions. The only way I could stop was by crawling out of the door and sticking my head into the rain barrel. My throat hurt terribly afterward, and so did that of Françoise, but we still cannot help laughing when we remember it.

Everyone here is now paralyzed with ferocious hilarity, and all work has completely ceased. I fear very much that soon someone will die as a consequence. Around here no one seems to think such extraordinary events as plagues of cats and plagues of laughter have any significance. I have been told that before I came, there were in various places a plague of falling leaves, a plague of sleeplessness, one of invisible hailstones, a plague of amnesia, and another time there was a rainstorm for several years that reduced everything to rust and mold.

I am pleased to say that since I last wrote, the People's Liberation Force has apparently forgotten about me, and I am bringing back the children. Also, I have heard the Doña Constanza Evans was recently ransomed by her husband for half a million dollars and then absconded immediately to Costa Rica. I thought she was a terribly haughty and stiff woman, and so I think her husband is lucky to be rid of her even for so large a sum.

Do you think you could investigate the possibility of sending over a new Land Rover engine? Mine is now thirty years old and has been restored so many times that there are no more spares of oversize pistons or rings that one can obtain. The exchange rate is so appallingly adverse nowadays that I think it would be cheaper to send one from France, and I will pay you with what is left in my account with the Crédit Lyonnais.

I hope you find this letter more cheering than my last. It is strange how one can be in the depths one minute and on the heights the next (and, of course, vice versa).

In conclusion, Maman, let me illustrate how much better life is by saying that outside there is a little black-and-white cat with yellow eyes that has been teaching itself to walk the tightrope on the clothesline—it has fallen off three times—and in the kitchen I hear Françoise and Farides, the cook, roaring with laughter.

I kiss you many times.

Your loving son,

ANTOINE

28

The Battle of Chiriguaná

After a protracted, discreet, and gentle courtship, including two years of fervent engagement, Profesor Luis, native of Medellín and dedicated educator of peasants, was to be married to Farides, native of Chiriguaná and cook to the French couple recently cured by Pedro and Aurelio. They were to be married in the little adobe church at Chiriguaná by the itinerant priest with whom Profesor Luis used to discuss the ideas of Camilo Torres and Oscar Romero.

Josef was overjoyed to see the priest again because he could now, having paid the priest for a proper burial, afford to pay him for three masses to be said for the repose of his soul and its rapid passage through purgatory. Once safely in heaven, Josef believed, he would be able to fornicate an infinite amount of times with inexhaustible pleasure, and this was his secret reason for having spent so much money so conscientiously on his death and resurrection. The priest had already told him that there was no sex in heaven, but Josef replied that this was self-contradictory, and therefore, "even God himself could not believe such a thing." The priest sighed and left him to his simple peasant logic.

The *cura,* Don Ramón, was forty-five years old. He had served the same vast parish ever since he had left the seminary at the age of twenty-three, riding through it in the same pattern and at the same sober pace on his mule. He sometimes had to go without shelter because down

on the savanna there were no *tambos* as there were in the mountains, and
often he fell asleep under the stars wrapped in his *gara*—his leather
saddle blanket—unfed and unwashed. He would arrive in a village, his
black garb covered in white dust, and bless unions, perform baptisms,
and conduct funerals and masses for those dead since his last visit. He
accepted gratefully the hospitality of his parishioners and was not above
sleeping with the animals to save his hosts any trouble. He was small,
graying, a little stout, and he bore the air of one infinitely oppressed,
weary, and resigned; when he made the sign of the cross, one felt that
he truly understood its significance, for his own life was one of suffering
and sacrifice. Now that his eyes were failing him, he relied on his own
memory for the services and on his mule's memory for traveling his
established route.

Don Ramón was a *cura* of conscience, but many of his fellow priests
accepted unscrupulously the offerings that their parishioners left in the
church for the consumption of the Virgin and of the dead and used them
for themselves. It was customary for the *cura*, in return for absolution,
to have the pick of the pretty women and father numerous little bastards, known curiously enough as *anti-Cristos*, and to do deals with the
dying in which he smoothed their way to paradise in return for their
patrimony. Many priests became very wealthy landowners. The church
hierarchy in the big cities were two thirds plutocrats and oligarchs who
yearned for military government, rich vestments, and the extermination
of radicals and who utterly despised and distrusted priests such as Don
Ramón, who believed that loving one's neighbors included looking after
their interests. Don Ramón had once been threatened with defrocking
for being "political," and since then he had found his vocation a cause
of grief.

The little adobe church at Chiriguaná had a corrugated iron roof,
bulging and distorted walls, painted pink, and no seats of any descrip-
tion upon its floor of packed earth. The pious among the locals had filled
it with tinsel, dirty mirrors, and gaudy homemade statues of the Virgin.
Above the painted box that served as the altar there hung a grotesque
Corpus Christi, its ghastly countenance contorted in death, its body
twisted and lacerated and of a pallid yellow hue, a crown of thorns made
of lemon spikes upon its head, and all over it were huge clots of crimson
and scarlet blood carefully molded for realistic effect. Above the door

facing it was a similar Christ in Agony, and many times upon visiting the place, the priest had been depressed by its tawdriness and wished that upon the crosses there had hung radiant crowned Christs in eucharistic vestments, the Christus Rex that he adored as his personal image of the Savior. The *cura,* however, was accustomed to tolerate and understand the flexible piety of his flock and even attended without misgivings second baptisms, the Yacucheo, where the *brujos* exorcised all evil spirits amid clouds of cigar smoke and pagan chanting. He attended the Lanta Tipina, the rite of the first haircut, but he would not attend La Ispa, because he objected to having to drink baby's urine.

Farides was dark-eyed, black-haired, and always smiling. She had the appearance of an Haitian and would have looked perfectly in place in one of Gauguin's paintings. She would one day be plump; but as yet she was soft and curvaceous, and she had about her an air of archness accentuated by her habit of wearing a white flower above her left ear. For the wedding she had borrowed every bit of the brightest and most colorful clothes that she had been able to find in the whole district, including Felicidad's scarlet stockings and gold-sequined skirt. She regretted being so heavily decked out as the sun climbed toward the hour of siesta, when her perspiration beneath her makeup began to make her feel like a stewed chicken.

Profesor Luis was dressed in his only suit, left over from his adolescence in Medellín, when he had still lived with his respectable family. He had grown a few inches since then, and the suit was now too tight and too short in the sleeves and legs. To disguise the short sleeves, he made himself a pair of handsome white cuffs out of cardboard, and to disguise the short legs, he wore well-polished black ankle boots with prodigious silver rowels that made him look as macho and as dashing as Pancho Villa himself. About his neck he wore a black western-style tie, and on his head he wore a black guarapon sombrero that he had bought from an Indian once in Cochabamba.

The couple were well loved in the whole district, and their youth, their comeliness, and their tender devotion to each other had touched a sympathetic chord even in the heart of Hectoro, who said only one remark in the whole day. Normally he only said one remark per day because of his hyperbolical pride, but today it was because he was afraid that the sentimental sob lurking in the back of his throat might catch him unawares. He said, "The Campa Indians consummate their marriages in the center of a cheering circle of the tribe. Why don't we do that?"

The bride and groom set off from the village on two of Don Emmanuel's finest horses, with flowers and tinsel entwined in the halters and tailpieces. They rode side by side and were obliged by the party to kiss at every crossroads, amid cheers of encouragement. Behind the couple rode the rest of the village on horses, donkeys, and mules amid much mayhem caused by Don Emmanuel's gray stallion. Misael could scarcely prevent it from trying to mount the female animals and bite the backsides of anyone who insulted it by overtaking. The accompanying cats got between the animals' feet, and others watched from the roadside, twitching their tails and purring.

Behind the villagers came Don Emmanuel on his tractor, his great belly bursting out between his buttons and his red beard glistening in the sun. He was pouring forth as usual a torrent of ribald comments and imprecations to the women in the group, who were replying in kind, and behind him he towed his largest trailer crammed to the brim with the village children and cats, with two of the cats even sitting on the mudguards, clinging on with stoical aplomb.

The party raised a happy cloud of white dust as it processed to Chiriguaná, and this caused not only a change in their appearance but the genesis of a considerable thirst, which was assuaged on arrival with *chicha, chacta, pisco, aguardiente, ron cana, guarapo,* Aguila beer, and liberal amounts of fruit juices, while the abstemious cats lined up to lap at the waters of the Mula. After this the civil wedding was to take place in the plaza because there was not yet a town hall.

The mayor was also the local policeman, which engendered a desirable reduction in local bureaucracy and meant that only one man needed to be bribed rather than two; for this reason the locals were also trying to get him appointed as magistrate and *gobernador*. Today he was dressed, unusually, in his uniform and wore his sash of office in the national colors across his chest: red for the blood of national martyrs, yellow for the sand and the sun, blue for the sea and the sky, and green for the jungle. He had brushed his hair and shaved and was for once unaccompanied by his goat. He puffed his chest out and drew his stomach in, and the community was proud that he was their mayor and their policeman even though he was cross-eyed, had a scar across his nose, and had sold his twelve-year-old niece from Valledupar to Pedro the grocer for 122 words.

The mayor had not been able to find the screed for the civil marriage service, so he was obliged to extemporize his own, which was short and to the point, and then he announced, "I now declare and affirm that you are married lawfully according to the statutes and processes of the republic. Long live the republic!" The policeman cut short the cheers and vivas of the throng by firing his pistol in the air, causing many cats to bolt for cover. He put his gun back in its holster and said, "I have not yet finished. As your mayor I am entitled to make a speech, and that is what I intend to do."

The policeman looked to the sky for inspiration, coughed to clear his throat.

"A good woman," he said, "is like a good she goat. She is beautiful, graceful, forgiving, abundant, and fertile. She is a good companion and abolishes solitude. Farides is beautiful, graceful, forgiving, and she has already abolished the solitude of Profesor Luis. Only time and activity will tell if she is fertile." He winked slyly, and the people cheered bawdily. The policeman held up his hand for silence. "And a good man," he continued, "is like a good he goat. He is handsome, noble, protective, and fertile. He also is a good companion and abolishes solitude. Profesor Luis is all these things, but only time will tell if he, too, is fertile! May I take this opportunity to wish you both all the energy you will need to find out if this is so!" The people cheered again, and once more the policeman raised his hand.

"A good couple is like good music. To be good, it must be female and full of grace and tenderness, but it must also be male and full of strength and will. Then you will have true *duende* and true *saudade*. In Profesor Luis I see indeed machismo, and in Farides I see *gracia*. May they always make sweet music together!"

On cue, the little band summoned from Valledupar by the mayor broke into a sentimental air from Vilcanota and began a *retreta* that lasted for the rest of the day. There was in the band a tiple player who played astonishing tremolos, a fat man with an ancient sousaphone almost unrecognizable for verdigris, an assortment of drummers, a trumpeter from Mexico, and a small Indian playing a *quena* and panpipes. They played at first in the center of the plaza, and then played perambulatory style among the crowd of cats and celebrants until finally they had to retire owing to the efforts of alcohol and the impossibility of trying to play and not trip over the cats.

It was impossible to cram everyone into the church for the religious ceremony, and Don Ramón and the couple themselves had difficulty in finding their way to the front. Don Ramón removed the cats from the altar and from their perches on the crucifix and then conducted the service with simple dignity without the aid of a missal. He gave a short address in which he reminded the congregation that Don Luis was a true son of Christ because he gave his life and efforts for others and that Farides was a true child of the Virgin because she, too, had spent her life in service. He commanded the congregation to care for the couple as they deserved and to strive always to make them happy and appreciated. He finished with the blessing, and then Aurelio stood up and picked his way to the front.

"I too have a blessing," he said, and looked at Don Ramón for his permission. Don Ramón nodded, and Aurelio placed his hands on Farides's shoulders. She smiled at him as he said first in Aymara and then in Quechua, "I consecrate this virgin to the moon." He moved over to Luis and placed his hands on his shoulders. He said first in Aymara and then in Quechua, "This virgin I consecrate to the sun." He stepped back and joined their hands, and over them he made signs to signify the sun, the moon, the fish, and the serpent. Aurelio was now personally satisfied that the couple were really married properly.

"Thank you," said Luis, who had, like everyone else, not understood any of it, and Aurelio nodded and returned to his place, moving the large black cat that had occupied it.

The policeman announced from the back, "I now declare a carnival! You men had better take care: The girls are well armed, and not one of them is to be trusted!"

Everybody left the church in a buzz of excitement and trooped off to the plaza in gaggles. There they elected Farides *regidora*. Hoisted high on people's shoulders, she waved and smiled and smacked any hands that found their way up her legs, squealing with mock outrage. She demanded to be processed along the narrow street, and halfway along she raised her hands and clasped them together above her head.

At the signal the girls, whom no one had noticed slipping away, appeared at first-floor windows and balconies and roofs and released an avalanche of flour, eggs, and water onto the men and cats below, who with one mind scattered to take evasive action under the balconies. The avalanche ceased, and Misael poked his head out and looked upward. A bag of flour on the end of a cord descended sharply upon his crown, and Felicidad giggled with delight as she hauled it back up again. "Ay! Ay!" the girls applauded from their fortresses, and then Misael stuck his head out again, and a balloon full of water caught him full in the face. He danced out to the center of the street and was buried in a cascade so dense that he looked like a man sculpted roughly out of lime. He raised his arms and shouted, "*¿Es yo solo que tiene cojones?*" and the men responded to his challenge to their virility by bravely pouring into the center of the street to join battle.

The men threw eggs, *arepas,* guavas, mangoes, papayas, *canchas,* and the women responded with their flour and their *globos* of water and their eggs until there was a vast, frantic, laughing, screaming, perspiring, soaking wet, befloured melee occupying the whole town and transforming it into a genial slippery snow-white mess of mayhem and stampeding felines. After half an hour of this furious engagement Felicidad blew the policeman's whistle that she had borrowed for the occasion, and at the shrill blast everybody stood still and looked up. The policeman, who had preserved his dignity and his uniform under Felicidad's balcony, stepped out and declared, "The battle is over, and the girls are the winners!"

The laughing pretty girls above the streets clapped their hands and cheered, and the men booed, "*¡Abajo las muchachas!*"

Felicidad called to the policeman, "*¡Senor Jefe!* We want to discuss the truce!" He looked up at her, and she emptied a bucket of water over him. He bellowed with outrage, and she emptied a bag of flour over him, followed by a *globo* for good measure. "Never trust a woman at carnival!" yelled Felicidad, and once more the unprepared men were pelted from above.

The battle continued unabated until some intrepid souls barged open the doors and entered the houses to engage in battle at close quarters. Furniture flew and people fell over the cats and rooms were laid to waste as the struggling and squealing girls were carried out bodily to be dumped in all their finery into the river. Many men were unchivalrously pulled in when they held out gallant hands to help the bedraggled maidens clamber out again, and many deep friendships were formed that deepened even further as the day progressed into evening with the aid of alcohol and dancing. Soon there would be more weddings and more carnivals, and then more weddings and more carnivals, and thus the population would happily increase both in quantity and merriment.

The next morning Farides very archly put a red flower above her left ear and promenaded along the street with a smug and knowing expression while the revelry continued tirelessly, pausing in three days only for siesta, when the town reverberated with purring and snoring. The cats, still looking dignified and serene, padded among the revelers, eating the broken eggs with raffish streaks of pastry congealing in their fur. Like everyone else, they would have a lot of serious cleaning up to do later.

Dolores the whore gave Farides a little can filled with white cream. "If Luis ever strays or his manhood fails," she whispered, "you rub this on your *chucha*, and without fail he will wriggle and rattle with lust for you. I bought it from a *canoera* when I was in Iquitos, and it is made from the genitals of the *bufeo*." Dolores winked and took a puff on her *puro*. "It is powerful cream. Keep it carefully."

Farides blushed and smiled. "Thank you, Dolores. I shall keep it and hope I never need it."

29

Colonel Asado Makes a Little Mistake

Olaf Olsen, from Norway, was a very powerful industrialist and was in charge of the local operations of an American company that produced rough-terrain vehicles both for civilian and military purposes. It never concerned him that there were stories of people vanishing because he was an upright conservative man, he did not know of anyone who had vanished, and like many others, he thought that the only people who vanished were people who deserved to.

Mr. Olsen had a pretty blond daughter called Regina, who was taking a year off between school and university, and who was living at home with her father. Mr. Olsen believed that Regina should know what it is to work, and so he gave her very little pocket money and was pleased when his daughter advertised her services as a baby-sitter. One of the women for whom she baby-sat, and with whom she became quite close friends, was another blond, a woman of about twenty-six, whose name was Esmeralda.

Esmeralda was a single parent, and when she was younger, she had been the kind of urban terrorist that throws bricks through police station windows and sets fire to the clubhouses of elite golf courses. Naturally she had grown out of it and was now working as a bank teller, but she still had some friends from her radical days. She was on Colonel Asado's list, but Colonel Asado did not know her address. He arrested one of Esmeralda's friends and for some reason did not torture or rape her; in an unwonted access of generosity he spared her life and her body in return for Esmeralda's address. Esmeralda's friend listened to the screams generated by El Electricista and told Asado Esmeralda's address.

She hurried home to telephone her friend, but she was not there, so she decided to phone first thing in the morning.

First thing in the morning Regina turned up to baby-sit, not knowing that both Esmeralda and her baby had stayed overnight at her boyfriend's house.

Regina opened the gate and started to walk up the path. She looked up and saw that four men were coming for her, having slipped out of the shadows in the porch. Regina had heard all the stories about abduction, rape, torture, and murder, and unlike her distinguished father, she believed them. Instead of waiting to be asked for her identity card, she fled through the gate and started to sprint up the street. Colonel Asado sprinted after her, dropped on one knee, aimed his pistol at her, and fired. Regina fell to the pavement; she was pitched into the capacious trunk of the State Telephone Company Ford Falcon and driven away for interrogation.

El Electricista had a big metal grille, well earthed. When it was not in use for interrogation the officers used to put a tabletop on it and use it for eating their meals. El Electricista was very fond of his metal grille, and he called it Susana. In fact, all the torturers not only became very fond of their implements but also got very fond of their jobs, which they performed with exemplary zeal and efficiency.

Hardly any of them ever went home anymore for fear of missing something. They left their shifts late and resumed them early, sometimes not sleeping for twenty-four hours at a time. They ate at the school, bolting their meals, and they slept on the premises, oblivious of the screams and hysterical weeping and the loud music they played twenty-four hours a day to try to drown it. They had become obsessives, compulsives, addicts.

El Electricista was to get the first opportunity to do his patriotic duty with Regina. He tore the clothes off her body and thought that something was wrong; he turned her over and found the bullet wound at the base of her spine. Asado came in and said, "So what? Pretty, isn't she?" and he searched through her belongings so that he could pin her identity card to the "Case Terminated" form. Regina returned fully to consciousness while he was looking and found that she could not move her legs. She looked about her, wondering where she was, realizing she was naked and that two men were looking at her identity card.

"It isn't her," said Asado, a feeling of panic rising in his stomach.

"So?" replied El Electricista. "We can have some fun with her anyway."

"No, we can't," said Asado. "She's foreign. Look at that address. She's got a rich daddy. He might be important, too. He might be an ambassador. I'm afraid this means trouble." He turned to Regina. "Who is your father, and what does he do?"

"Please can I have my clothes?" she said.

"Oh, I am sorry," said Asado, becoming gentlemanly. "It was necessary for us to remove them in order to examine you. You have been wounded."

"I can't move my legs," she said.

"Don't worry, we'll take care of you," said Asado, and he went to fetch a blanket for her.

El Electricista went with him. "For God's sake," he said, "let's just get rid of her. How will anyone know? We'll give her a free fall."

"Wait, and we'll see," said Asado. They returned with the blanket. "Now tell us about who you are and about your family. For the medical record."

When he had been told, Asado telephoned the Army Internal Security Service and gave his code name. He found out that Olsen and his daughter were definitely classified as "untouchable." Asado thought he had better do as El Electricista had suggested, but something, perhaps his instinct for self-preservation, suggested he should do what any sensible military man would have done in the same circumstances. He passed the problem on to the commanding officer of the intelligence service. He arrived very rapidly and took Regina away to the confidential wing of the military hospital. They removed the bullet and her life was saved; but she would always be paralyzed in the legs. She was passed back to Asado, and he was told to look after her while the hierarchy decided what to do. The trouble was that it could not decide; it was caught between the embarrassment of letting her go, to the public

outcry about brutality and the demands for explanations from the Norwegian ambassador, and getting rid of her, which could have been
even more embarrassing if anyone had witnessed her abduction. Which
they had.

Esmeralda's neighbor told Esmeralda, and Esmeralda telephoned
Mr. Olsen. He acted with extraordinary speed and decisiveness. He
telephoned a friend of his, a very correct and honorable general in the
national army, Esteban Correra, who commanded the armored brigades.

Together they went to the police headquarters and demanded to see
the chief of the city police. A surly, overweight policeman knocked on
the police chief's door and entered. He came back out and said, "He's
busy, he can't see you now."

General Correra got out his identity card and handed it to the
policeman. "Show this," he said, "to the chief, and tell him that if he
is not out here in twenty-five seconds, I will have him arrested and
shot."

The police chief was out of his room in five seconds, beaming with
concern and helpfulness. What he told General Correra was something
that shook him to the core and enraged him.

"General," he said, spreading his hands helplessly, "we have forty
or fifty new people in here perhaps every day, not including the ones
who have been coming for months. They wave writs of habeas corpus
at us, but we can't help them because we don't have these missing people
and we don't know where they are. There are just too many cases for us
to investigate them, and so we have to ignore them. I'm surprised,
General, that you have come to us anyway."

"Why?" said the general. "Obviously one goes to the police in cases
of kidnapping."

"I'm surprised you have come to us," said the chief of the city
police, "because it seems that everyone except you knows that it is the
armed forces that are doing the kidnapping."

General Correra was stunned. "Impossible!" he said.

The chief of the city police took him by the arm and told him
confidentially, out of Olsen's hearing, "I know personally, and in my
professional capacity, all the heads of the security services in this country, and I can assure you that it is undoubtedly the armed forces. This
information is top secret and is strictly for you alone. Between you and

me, you should go and see General Ramírez to get this sorted out."

General Correra turned to Olsen. "Go home and leave this with me. I have someone to see."

General Correra was a fine, brave man who never hesitated to do the right thing. He was very tall and fit, very dignified, and very intolerant of evildoing. He was known to be politically a "moderate," which in military terms meant a potential subversive and to the general public means a conservative.

He went to see General Ramírez, demanding a full internal military investigation of the abductions. He even said that as long as he, Correra, was in charge of the tank brigades, there would still be someone left to uphold the honor of the army. General Ramírez told him that he was already aware of the situation and was inaugurating steps to deal with it. He told Correra that he was already aware of the Olsen case, that the girl was being released immediately, and that the officers who had illegally abducted her would be court-martialed. He congratulated Correra on his prompt actions and his integrity, and said, "The army needs more men like you, General."

After Correra had left, General Ramírez made a telephone call, and General Correra was not seen again for a week, when his tortured and bullet-ridden body turned up on the same municipal garbage dump as had the radical lawyer's.

General Ramírez wept openly at Correra's funeral as he delivered the eulogy and made a telling speech against the terrorism that had now claimed another spotless victim. The speech was reported in full by the national press, which had developed better instincts for survival than had the decent and ingenuous General Correra.

But Olsen refused to give in to despair. He had heard the city police chief's first remark that it was the armed forces that were doing the kidnapping, and he went to the Norwegian ambassador. The ambassador already knew about the abductions; like the Mexican Embassy, the Swedish Embassy, and the United States Embassy, he had been inundated with requests for help and asylum from people desperate for help, none of them until now Norwegian citizens. The supplicants told him that only two major embassies were never helpful, the British and the Soviet, for opaque reasons of their own, possibly not unconnected with import deals which they did not wish to imperil.

The Norwegian ambassador went to see the president, having previously made unanswered representations through his own Foreign Office, as well as his embassy.

When he entered the president's office, he saw that the president's wife was sitting on his knee. The president had found her, during one of his exiles, in a strip club in Panama, where she had worked as an "actress." She was forty years younger than he and was very pretty in a rather distasteful way. The ex-manager of the strip club, one day to be president himself, was now the foreign secretary and had published numerous books on the occult at the expense of his own ministry. In his own opinion, this was justified because the books were dictated to him by none other than the archangel Gabriel. The two bouncers, or, rather, doormen, of the club were now respectively the minister for agriculture and the minister for public health.

The president's wife was feeding him with Turkish delight, his particular favorite. "Come on now, Daddykins," she was saying, "I won't give you any more until you've signed this eeny-weeny bit of paper for your 'ickle playgirl."

"I can't, sweetiekins," he said. "It costs too much."

She pouted and wiggled on his lap. "No more Turky-Wurky delight!" she said, placing a piece against his lips and withdrawing it as he opened his mouth to receive it.

"Oh, all right then," he said, patting her richly sequined backside. "Just for you, my little pussycat." He leaned over the paper and appended his signature in his shaky hand. Cooing, his wife leaped off his lap and kissed him on the forehead, leaving thereon in bright scarlet the imprint of her lips. She took the paper and minced out of the room, glancing seductively at the ambassador as she left.

The president looked at the ambassador helplessly and said, "My wife," as though it were some sort of explanation. "Now, what can I do for you?"

The ambassador put his case to the president, who listened impassively as he chewed his way through the box of Turkish delight. When the ambassador had finished, the president said, "My dear Ambassador, I have heard exactly the same things from you as I have heard from six other ambassadors in the last month, and I have to say that I know nothing about it, nothing at all. I have interviewed General Ramírez, Admiral Fleta, Air Chief Marshal Sanchis, and the heads of our security services, and they are all as mystified by these occurrences as I am. We are all of the opinion that it is part of a Zionist plot to destabilize the country in preparation for an Israeli invasion of our southern states."

The Norwegian ambassador was incredulous. "I beg you to be serious, Your Excellency," he said.

"Oh," said the president, "I can assure you that I am serious. We have definite evidence from the Naval Internal Intelligence Agency and the Air Force Internal Security Agency; I have their reports in my desk."

The ambassador was tempted to indulge in ridicule. Instead, he said, "Your Excellency, I cannot believe that a man of your political experience and intelligence could possibly take such reports seriously. They are just too absurd and too impossible. In your position I would have the men who submitted those reports committed to an asylum for the insane."

The president smiled and shook his head. "Ambassador, I must tell you that I am party to information on this subject that you are not, and I have taken it so seriously that I have already authorized the detention of certain Jews and Zionists whom the security services know are certainly involved."

The ambassador became angry. "Your Excellency, this proves only that you have Nazis in your security services!"

It was the president's turn to become angry. "Ambassador, may I remind you that it is possible to abuse diplomatic privilege?"

The ambassador stood up and said very firmly, "Your Excellency, if there are pogroms in this country, no civilized nation on earth will have anything to do with you! May I remind you, just for an example, that it is Norway which is constructing your entire hydroelectric program? I have to say to you also, Your Excellency, that my government expects instant results in the search for Regina Olsen! The army has her, Mr. President, as is obvious from recent events. I suggest you start with them."

The president closed his eyes and sighed wearily. "Ambassador, I will do all I can, but I must tell you that a man in my position has to tread carefully with the army. I think you are fully aware of that."

"Yes, Your Excellency, I am aware of that, but as Norwegian

ambassador I am charged with the care of Norwegian citizens. You will be aware of that."

The president opened a drawer of his desk and took out a revolver. He held it in the palm of his hand and pondered its weight. He showed it to the ambassador. "I have only one of these," he said. "The army has thousands."

When he left, angry and frustrated, the Norwegian ambassador decided not to tell the uxurious old president that he still had lipstick on his forehead.

30

The Return of María and the Return of the Soldiers

Work in the governor's office almost came to a halt as General Fuerte's absence became more prolonged. Without his guiding hand the staff lost all sense of purpose and direction, and the secretaries filed their nails, did embroidery under their desks, discussed their romances, and played charades. Capitan Rojas, Fuerte's ADC, found to his chagrin and humiliation that none of the staff would do as he said or take his tirades seriously; they would pat him on the head, make soothing noises as though to a child, and offer him lemon juice sweetened with *choncaca*. He became at first infuriated and bitter and then lapsed into depression and apathy, which was broken only by his desperate pleas to the brigadier to locate the general.

"The trouble is," said the brigadier, "that he granted leave to himself and did not fill in the forms. No one knows where he went or what he was doing or for how long he intended to stay. I have no positive proof he has disappeared!"

The brigadier was nervous all the same because he had heard on the military grapevine about all the senior officers who had disappeared and had also heard some hints on why it had been happening. He was understandably anxious not to cause his own disappearance by starting an investigation and was tempted to list the case as a desertion, since he had heard from Capitan Rojas that the general had gone off with his donkey and was disguised as a peon. He decided to do nothing, apart from taking over the civilian administration himself pending the general's return.

One morning Capitan Rojas, flushed and breathless from running up the stairs, burst through the door of the brigadier's office, saluted, and said, "Sir, María has returned but without the general!"

"María?" asked the brigadier. "And who is she?"

"General Fuerte's *burra*," said the capitan. "She came down the Chiriguaná road before my very eyes and went into her quarters."

"The general's donkey," mused the brigadier. "How strange. Is she well and unharmed?"

"Yes," replied Rojas. "Except that she is covered with the dust of travel and is plainly pregnant."

The brigadier opened a drawer and drew out a report form, which he filled in carefully, questioning the capitan for details. "Chiriguaná," he said, "is a hotbed of revolution. I think we can safely assume that General Fuerte is dead at the hands of the terrorists. I shall advise General Ramírez of my opinion and await his instructions. In the interim, kindly breathe not a word of this to anyone."

"No, sir, and what shall I do with María?"

The brigadier looked up at him and raised his eyebrows quizzically. "Look after her yourself, Capitan."

The capitan saluted and left. He returned to the stable and found María lying on her side; on the straw were afterbirths of four little black bundles of fur. María heaved herself to her feet and began to lick her progeny clean. The capitan watched, his military mind unable to believe the evidence of his senses, as the unusually large black kittens began to mew piteously for milk. Then he realized that here was an emergency, because the kittens could not reach María's teats, since kittens suckle lying down and donkeys give suck standing up. Relieved to find himself at last with a problem that could be easily solved by quick decision and firm action, he strode off to the shops and returned with a baby's bottle. Kneeling carefully so as not to soil the knees of his uniform, he tentatively began to milk María. She snorted and pushed him sideways. He made comforting noises and imitated the clicking noises that the general used to make, and María let down her milk. With scrupulous fairmindedness he fed the kittens an equal amount and was charmed by their closed eyes, their helplessness, their stubby little tails, their pathetic mewing, and their big, silky ears. He felt that he could not in all conscience leave them to María to care for on her own, and he moved his camp bed into the stable so that he could feed them every two hours day and night. He became so besotted with his little charges that the girls in the office began to refer to him as Capitan Papagato and had to go down to the stable to deliver him his lemon juice sweetened with *choncaca* and any documents which he had to sign. His previous apathy and depression gave way to a seraphic contentment, and when later the black cats grew to the size of pumas, he went everywhere with them padding at his side like dogs. They demolished his quarters with their frolics and wrestling matches, and Capitan Rojas had a quadruple bed made so that there was room for all of them to sleep. He applied to change his name by deed poll to Papagato and thereafter went proudly by the name originally imputed to him in ridicule. His authority over the girls became absolute because of their irrational terror of the huge yellow-eyed cats, and the other girls in Valledupar became fascinated by his mysterious rapport with them. Capitan Papagato ordered an extra portion to be attached to his enormous bed and believed that no man had ever been so blessed by fortune.

Figueras was less blessed; after the three months of his cure from common gonorrhea and Barranquilla syphilis he and his brigade were ordered back into the field and told that specific and spectacular results were expected. Nervously and more slowly than proper military caution merited, the column of trucks headed back toward the scene of their previous defeats and camped as inconspicuously as possible on the savanna three miles from Chiriguaná. The patrols that Figueras felt obliged to send out returned with no information except that the local population seemed to be convulsed with unabatable laughter and that the whole area was swarming with cats. "I know that already," said Figueras. "They are constantly under my feet, and their damnable purring prevents sleep."

Pedro told Aurelio of the soldiers' return, and he in turn informed Remedios. He guided her and her *guerrilleros* through the jungle by safe routes, and they arrived in the pueblo two days before Figueras's planned advance. Remedios returned Federico's meager possessions to Sergio and embraced him. "You had a fine son," she said. "We all miss him." Sergio sighed. "I too miss him; but he talks with me in my dreams, and Aurelio says he is very happy and is married."

Remedios, proudly atheist, Marxist, and materialist, sighed inwardly with pity for his superstition and said, "I am very happy to hear it."

General Fuerte was brought down by the band on the end of a rope tied around his waist. He had become so dejected that he had neither spoken nor moved unnecessarily for two months. He slept fitfully in an upright position, and Father García, convinced that the general had in fact already died, recited over him a mass for the dead even though his body was plainly still working. He had become like a dumb mascot or an old painting that no one examines closely anymore. When Franco became irritated by having to drag the general along with the rope, he merely coiled it around the latter's waist and put the end of it in his hand. The general walked behind Franco like an automaton, leading himself by the rope. When the guerrilla band arrived at the pueblo, Franco drove a heavy stake into the ground and attached the general's rope to it. The general walked slowly around the stake until he was completely wound up, and he sat catatonically against it through all the events that followed with two cats in his lap and one draped around his shoulders, purring.

That evening everyone noticed that the cats were becoming febrile; they paced restlessly, clawed at tree trunks, and climbed up on the roofs of the huts. The dogs slunk under tables, and the horses, donkeys, and mules were whinnying in the fields and galloping pointlessly from one end to the other.

"Something is going to happen," said Pedro to Remedios.

"Yes," she said, "we are going to fight a battle that will never be forgotten. The animals can feel death in the air."

Remedios, Pedro, Misael, Hectoro, and Josef met for a council on strategy and tactics. Remedios wanted to harry the army with short surprise attacks in the usual guerrilla fashion. Misael wanted to fight a defensive battle from the ramparts and fortifications of the pueblo, and Hectoro was in favor of a cavalry charge at dawn into the enemy camp, armed mainly with machetes. Misael said that since they now had two machine guns, it would be child's play to mow the soldiers down as they crossed the open spaces. Remedios maintained that with her plan they could keep the enemy continually confused and disorganized and just wear away at their resistance without incurring any casualties of their own. Hectoro maintained that they could simply cut the enemy to pieces while they were still sleepy and unprepared. None of them was prepared to change their minds, and a serious argument followed that threatened to destroy the new alliance before it had even passed its infancy. Josef then appealed for the right to be heard.

"Listen," he said. "They are all good plans. We should use all of them."

"How?" demanded Remedios and Hectoro at once.

"Like this," said Josef, and he beckoned to the others to follow him into the street. He took a stick and began to draw in the dust, a difficult operation because of the lightning assaults of the cats upon its flicking tip.

"Here," said Josef, "is the pueblo, and here is the rampart. On the rampart are our two machine guns, and the two machine gunners and their loaders are the only people in the whole village." He drew another line, and Remedios bent down and removed the cat that leaped onto the end of the stick. "Here," continued Josef, "right out at the side are Remedios's guerrillas, who will provide crossfire across the open space and make little attacks from the side when the new magazines have to be loaded into the machine guns. You," he said, turning to Hectoro, "should take every single horse, mule, and donkey, even if there are not enough to ride them, and go with your cavalry right around the back of the soldiers, following them at a distance so they do not see you. When we have massacred the soldiers and the ones that are left are lying low or retreating, the machine guns will cease fire, and so will Remedios, and you will charge through from the back and cut the soldiers to pieces!"

"Bravo!" exclaimed Hectoro.

"¡Excelentísimo!" said Remedios, patting Josef on the shoulder. "But why do you think they will attack in a simple frontal assault? They may do something more complicated."

"No, they will not," replied Josef. "They are still commanded by that fat officer who was here before. He is a coward and a fool who will always do the simplest thing. Also, he does not know that we have the *guerrilleros* here and he does not know that we have machine guns. He is expecting to overrun a small pueblo of people armed only with rifles and machetes, and I am sure that he does not expect us to know that he is coming. It is obvious they will just attack us in the quickest and easiest way."

"If this works," said Remedios admiringly, "you should change your name to Bolívar."

"It will work," said Josef. "And furthermore, I have a little trick with the machine guns that I heard of in Bolivia from the Chaco War with Paraguay."

On the next day Hectoro departed with his cavalry and skirted wide around the savanna to bring himself into position behind the army. He forbade campfires or lights of any kind and went himself to watch the camp. In the morning he saw Figueras addressing his officers and saw the officers go off to brief their men. He stayed long enough to see that the brigade was advancing in arrow formation and fanning out. He ran back to his cavalry and sent one of the children galloping off across the savanna to warn the pueblo of the imminent attack.

After their nerve-racking but uneventful advance the soldiers were choked with dust, perspiring in waterfalls beneath their helmets, and kicking out irritatedly at the cats that tripped them by playing with their bootlaces.

They halted at the edge of the razed fields, and Colonel Figueras came forward to examine the village through his binoculars. He noted with fear that there were ramparts and fortifications but then saw with relief that the village was completely deserted except by cats. He calculated that with two thousand men and no defenders he was fairly likely to survive the engagement. He retreated to the back of his brigade just to be sure and gave the order to advance with bayonets fixed. The whole brigade was nonchalantly advancing across the burned fields when Josef popped above the rampart and let fly with one machine gun. He cut a swath through the line of infantry and watched the men throw themselves to the ground. He stopped firing and shouted at the top of his voice, "Quick, someone! The machine gun has jammed."

The soldiers sprang to their feet and charged, and simultaneously the second machine gun opened fire, Josef opened fire, and the *guerrilleros* fired at will from the side. In the incomprehensible hurricane of bullets the soldiers whirled and fell for half an hour. Those not dead pretended to be, including Figueras, who flung himself into an irrigation canal and lay still before he crawled desperately away.

The machine guns ceased, the *guerrilleros* ceased, and two hundred soldiers threw aside their arms and ran back to cover as a stampede of mules and donkeys rushed through them, hurling them to the ground and trampling them. The two hundred rose to their feet, and Hectoro and the men and women of the village burst upon them, firing revolvers into their chests from point-blank range and hacking their limbs and heads with their machetes. Coldly Hectoro dismounted and walked among the carnage, slicing the throats of all who still lived. Over each one he spit and muttered, *"Hijo de puta."*

Over fifty men of the brigade, including Figueras, escaped back to the camp and, leaving all their equipment behind, sped back to Valledupar in the trucks. Figueras noted with relief that he was the only surviving officer and that Major Kandinski was also missing. He began mentally rehearsing the history of his heroic exploits against overwhelming odds that he would include in his report.

Back on the field of slaughter the victors were both jubilant and appalled. Shaken, pale, and trembling, they embraced one another and then wandered dumbly among the fallen.

"They were innocents," said Misael. "Look at them, they were all boys."

"Yes," said Pedro. "Little boys with mad leaders and fear in their hearts."

"Most of them have pissed themselves," said Josef. "Look at their trousers."

The bodies lay strewn like broken scarecrows, twisted, bloody, and unreal. They lay with their last expressions still on their faces: terror, agony, and incomprehension. The victorious warriors, not a single one of them even scratched, were stricken dumb with a horrified shame and were too consumed with remorse and pity to declare a fiesta or jubilation of any kind. They sat among the dead, idly stroking the cats and murmuring prayers.

"We cannot bury all of these," said Remedios.

"We cannot burn them," replied Josef. "It would be a sacrilege."

"We can bury them with Don Emmanuel's tractor," suggested Pedro.

"And I will conduct a funeral," said García. "They should have a proper funeral."

"Go and get the tractor, Pedro," said Josef. "We will gather the bodies before the vultures get them."

The victorious rebels worked in pairs, removing rings and identity disks and private papers and then carrying the bodies by their ankles and armpits to the side of the field. "I think," said Doña Constanza, "it would be best to bury them in the canal that I had dug before I left. It would be simple to cover them over with the excavated earth, and then we could lay them side by side instead of in a heap. It would show more respect."

Remedios was working with Tomás. She turned over her twentieth body in order to carry it away, but she gasped with dismay when she saw its face. Hurriedly, she bent down and rifled in the man's shirt for his identity disk. She stared at it and turned it over, as if it should say something more on the back. Then she sat by the body and buried her head in her knees. She began to sob, and Tomás put his hand on her shoulder. "What is it, Medio? Did you know him?"

Remedios looked up at him pitifully, the tears rolling down her cheeks. "It is my little brother Alfredo. I have not seen him since he was twelve years old. It might have been my bullet that killed him. I did not know he was conscripted."

Tomás sat down beside her with his arm about her shoulder and wept with her. "Medio," he said, "we have all killed our brothers today."

She pulled herself together and stood up. "I hardly knew him."

Remedios would not let Alfredo be buried separately. The bodies were transported in the trailer to Doña Constanza's canal, the operation taking most of the night and the following morning. As the spade of the tractor buried them beneath the spoil of the canal, Father García recited the burial service and the names of the dead and then said a mass for their souls. Only Hectoro refused to attend, and Aurelio hesitated long, before he blessed them in Aymara and in Quechua. The cats gathered on the far bank of the canal and watched the whole proceeding.

Remedios filled several *mochilas* with identity disks and draped them around General Fuerte's neck. "Go to Valledupar," she told him, "and be with your own kind."

Without a word General Fuerte walked out of the pueblo, his bags jingling and clanking. The *guerrilleros* took *despedida* with him as far as Chiriguaná, where they wished him good luck, took *copas* to drink his health, and flagged down a truck to take him. He went without comment or expression, but he bent down and picked up a cat to take with him.

The plague of laughter was now over.

31

The Continuing Efforts of Olaf Olsen, Colonel Asado, and His Excellency the President

Olaf Olsen was precisely what one would expect a successful Norwegian businessman to be. He was forty-five years old, blond, much younger-looking than his years would warrant, and very clearheaded. He retained his Norwegian passion for skiing and being very fit, and he had divorced at exactly the time when it became a craze in Scandinavia. He came originally from Oslo and still had a house there, roughly halfway between the Munch Museum and Vigeland's park. He had joined his company in Scandinavia when he was a young man and had risen in it meteorically, entirely upon his own merit.

As an important foreign industrialist he knew almost everyone who mattered. He systematically exerted his influence on all of them, and he began to notice that he was always accompanied at a distance by four men with anomalous trilby hats pulled low over their eyes. He ignored them, apart from wishing them good-day when he doubled back and passed them. Their confusion and embarrassment when he did this used to give him a little satisfaction to compensate for his growing despair and indignation.

The first thing that Olsen did was go back to the police, who confirmed that they had been notified by the army of an official operation at the place and time that Regina had been abducted. The police had an unofficial agreement with the armed forces that they should be notified of all operations, because in the past the police had often been called by witnesses to the kidnappings and there had been several gun battles between the police and the military. The policeman who was in charge of logging radio messages was at first too terrified to tell Olsen what he wanted to know, but his fear was overcome by a handful of American dollars and Olsen's assertion that he knew someone who could have him shot. The policeman furtively ran through the log and told Olsen that his daughter had been taken by a task force from the Army School of Electrical and Mechanical Engineering.

After leaving police headquarters, Olsen visited every hospital in the capital and for a hundred miles around. There were not many of them, but at each one he had to "give a donation to the hospital" in order to be shown the admission lists. It turned out to be quite futile, as all cases brought in by the military were entered under the wrong sexes, the wrong nationalities, and the wrong names. He even found one entry which said "Pato Donald" and another which said "Ratón Miguel."

Olsen wrote to the president through the Norwegian ambassador and told him that if his daughter were not released within ten days, he would inform the national press, the Norwegian press, and the press in the United States. The president's office replied immediately that the heads of all the security forces had been instructed to find her, giving her case top priority. Olsen could not understand this, as he had already told the president's office exactly where Regina was and who had taken her. In the following ten days he received these letters:

From: Army School of Electrical and Mechanical Engineering

DEAR MR. OLSEN,

We are sorry to hear of the disappearance of your daughter but are surprised that you informed the president that she is with us. As you know, we are a military college and therefore take no prisoners, even in wartime. Good luck in your search.

From: Army Internal Security Service

DEAR MR. OLSEN,

We are sorry to have to tell you that our investigations have revealed that your daughter, Regina, has eloped to Thailand with her lover. She felt that you would have opposed their marriage, as the gentleman in question was a black man, forty years her senior, who was involved in anarchist politics, having spent twenty years in prison for child molestation.

We are very sorry to have to give you this bad news.

From: Chief of the city police

DEAR MR. OLSEN,

I refer to the letter recently received from the president's office and also to the visit you paid to us in the company of the late General Correra. If you want to find your daughter, I must remind you of what I told you on that occasion.

There is in this country a very dirty war going on between elements of the extreme right wing and elements of the left. All the evidence points to the fact that Regina was caught in the crossfire of this dirty war in a case of mistaken identity and is now in the hands of *right-wing extremists,* whose identity at this time I am unable to reveal for various reasons you will understand.

I sincerely wish you the best of luck in your search and advise you to exercise as much caution and discretion as paternal love will permit, in dealing with these very dangerous people.

From: Service of State Information

DEAR MR. OLSEN,

We have made extensive enquiries into the whereabouts of Regina Olsen, your daughter. Our information reveals that your daughter was a secret member of the extreme left, and was involved in terrorism. We believe that she has gone into hiding.

From: Foreign Ministry Intelligence Division

DEAR MR. OLSEN,

Our inquiries in the case of the disappearance of your daughter, Regina, reveal that she was a secret member of an extreme right-wing terrorist organization, the Double C, and was killed in a gun battle between them and a left-wing gang in Colombia. We are sorry to have to be the purveyors of this sad news.

From: Interior Ministry Internal Security Office

DEAR MR. OLSEN:

We were very distressed to hear of the sudden disappearance of your daughter, Regina, and have made every effort to find her, sparing no expense.

We are informed that she was last seen hill walking in the Sierra Nevada de Santa Margarita, and reports suggest that she fell to her death down a disused mine shaft whose location we have as yet been unable to ascertain. We are desolated to have to give you this bad news.

Olsen left the country without telling anyone and went to the United States, where he received a lot of help and good advice from senators and congressmen of the Democratic party, and then flew on to Norway. A few days later a large gang of armed men wearing anomalous-looking trilbies burst into his flat in its plush suburb and, not finding Olsen, shot his cleaning maid instead.

Back in Europe, Olsen campaigned tirelessly. His Holiness the Pope wrote three times asking Regina's whereabouts; the American secretary of state demanded the same information when he arrived on an official visit; the International Free Church Committee in Switzerland wrote, demanding to know; the Labor and the Democrat parties in Great Britain wrote, demanding to know, as did the Socialists in France. To all these, the president wrote to say that he was still looking.

Meanwhile, death went on as normal in the Army School of Electrical and Mechanical Engineering. Colonel Asado had had a brilliant idea to save himself paper work, and he and his men cruised around the

city in their Ford Falcons, looking for people who looked like subversives, drove the kinds of cars that subversives drove, lived in the kinds
of areas where subversives lived, and if they were good-looking women,
so much the better, unless you were El Verdugo, who liked to sodomize
young men as well.

One day Colonel Asado said to El Baño, "I bet you I can bring in
a prettier woman than you!"

"How much?" replied El Baño, irked by the challenge.

"One thousand pesos!" exclaimed Asado.

"I accept the bet!" cried El Baño.

When El Baño returned with his catch, Asado was already raping
in turn two little sixteen-year-olds with their arms tied behind their
backs and their faces streaming with tears. El Baño watched them
sobbing and said to Asado, "OK, you win."

In the meantime, the embassies of foreign nations were becoming
ever more skeptical about the president's stock reply to their inquiries
about missing persons; the president always said that they were the
victims of the internal feuding of the left wing. Then someone in the
American Embassy began to keep statistics and realized that people
vanished in batches: 14 Liberal Christians, 4 progressive Catholics, 7
nuns of the third world movement, 20 prostitutes, 41 Rosicrucians, 53
trade unionists, 25 homosexuals, 19 hippies, 5 artists, 11 journalists, 4
film producers, 4 magazine editors, 7 authors, 8 evangelists, 3 Angli-
cans, 3 Mormons, 35 Jehovah's Witnesses, 8 Hare Krishna devotees,
2 from the Divine Light Mission, 85 Socialists, 60 Democrats, 40
from the Vanguard party, 33 from the National party, 20 from the
Liberal Democratic party, 41 from the Radical Party, 18 from the
Christian Democrats, 43 from the Social Democrats, 2,114 from the
Communist party, 66 from the Human Rights Movement, 1,563 from
the women's rights organizations, 100 pacifists, 100 from the Antinu-
clear League, 22 Rotarians, 903 from the Marxist Front, 20 scoutmas-
ters, and nearly 2,000 Jews and Zionists. The remaining category,
which disappeared regularly and not in batches, was "young women."

The United States Embassy sent copies of this list to the other major
embassies, which sent copies home to their respective foreign offices,
and the president one morning found himself deluged with official
formal protests from other countries about "organized totalitarian re-

pression." Even the Soviet Union protested, now that it had imported all the food it had been angling for, and only Great Britain lodged no protest, as usual.

But the president had bigger worries of his own. In a country which fights no wars, where the life of the people is an offense to the obsessively ordered mind of the military, and where government is so chaotic and corrupt that most civilians would prefer a military government, it is a top priority to find something for the military to do, in order to prevent it from concocting a coup. The president was occupying himself with trying to find an external enemy, and to this end he was reading his way through piles of history books and keeping the state archivist busy by ordering him to check through all the old treaties that had not been destroyed by mold or termites, been burned by being used to light the gasfire, or been sold to American universities. He found that in 1611 his country had owned a rock in the middle of the Pacific Ocean, which had been captured by English privateers and claimed for King James, and which, since then, had remained the property of the British. The president consulted the collection of the *National Geographic* magazine in the State University Library and discovered that the island was uninhabited except by turtles, lizards, wild pigs, seals, wild goats, seabird colonies, finches, and a ship-wrecked sailor from New Zealand who now lived there as a hermit.

The president consulted his astrologer, his tarot card reader, and the chiefs of staff, who were all unanimous in approving the plan, and accordingly the president released to the press his "Carta Historica," which is still printed in full and with pride in the nation's history books.

Compatriots!

There is an infamy and a shame that have hung over the national conscience for so long that they leave there a scar which tarnishes perpetually the otherwise brightly shining star of our honor! It is my duty, as it is yours, my countrymen and fellow patriots, to remove this scar, to heal finally this suppurating wound!

As you will all realize, I am referring to La Isla de los Puercos, in the Pacific, which, though originally ours, was stolen from us and colonized by an infamous colonial power, whose name I cannot bring to pass my lips, so foully does it taste upon them! You all know to which colonial empire I refer, and I know that you hate it with all your hearts!

Accordingly I have ordered our noble armed forces to retake the island, regardless of sacrifice, to salvage our honor and for the greater glory of our blessed and beloved motherland! *¡Los Puercos Son los Nuestros! Patria o muerte!*

The British had no idea that Endeavor Island was known in Spanish as Pigs Island and failed to realize that it was crown property that was about to be invaded. But the armed forces and the nation were united in war fever. Everywhere graffiti and posters sprang up proclaiming *"¡Los Puercos Son los Nuestros!"* and crowds gathered in the square outside the Presidential Palace, shouting and chanting, flushed with patriotic fervor. It did not matter that no one knew where the island was; what mattered was becoming euphoric and drunk and even embracing policemen and soldiers. Never had a nation been so united, and even Asado gave his victims a day off from being tortured and raped.

The president informed the chiefs of staff that the island would be heavily defended and that a very large force would be needed to stage a successful attack. Accordingly, the navy, which had only two battle cruisers (American, survivors of World War II) and four frigates (coal-fired, British, built in the 1920s), commandeered five merchantmen to transport the soldiers and the coal needed for the frigates. The air force realized that the island was out of range of its aircraft and accordingly had huge fuel tanks mounted beneath either wing of its aircraft, which could be jettisoned when empty. The army realized that its huge provisions warehouses were empty because of black marketeering and hoped there would be enough food on the island when they arrived with five thousand conscripts (General Ramírez did not want to risk losing his regulars).

In the glorious battle that ensued, the air force lost ten planes. Two were lost on takeoff because the pilots were not used to handling aircraft with a full load of bombs plus extra fuel tanks. Three were lost because the small explosive charges placed to jettison the extra tanks were in fact too large, and the wings were blown off. Three were lost because the pilots were unused to long-distance flying over the open sea, and they got lost, ran out of fuel, and crashed ignominiously into the waves. The final two were lost because they failed to identify themselves when flying low across the path of the USS *New California*. They were brought down by guided missiles. The ten aircraft that reached La Isla de los Puercos dropped their payloads with immaculate precision and killed a large number of turtles.

The navy arrived and shelled the island while the soldiers, seasick, starving, and covered from head to foot in coal dust, disembarked. They landed on both sides of the island with the intention of enclosing the defenders in an inescapable ring of attackers. They advanced boldly with the navy's shells crashing ahead of them, and sometimes among them, until the soldiers of the eastern side saw the soldiers of the western side coming over the crest toward them. At last the enemy! A ferocious battle ensued that raged for four hours until the commanders' radio operators managed to speak to each other during a lull. A cease-fire was ordered, a victory declared, and the soldiers embraced each other, weeping and cheering. At the top of the hill the national flag was raised as the many verses of the national anthem were sung with unusual enthusiasm, and the army made camp.

Exactly 940 men were killed, and roughly 2,000 were injured. The soldiers stayed on the island until all the animals were eaten, and then the navy took them home. They arrived, seasick, starving, and covered once more from head to foot in coal dust, to a hero's welcome. They were fed for nothing in restaurants, entertained for nothing by prostitutes, and feted unsparingly by rapturous crowds during a weeklong national holiday. The press printed banner headlines—¡AHORA LOS PU-ERCOS SON VERDADERAMENTE LOS NUESTROS! ("Now the Pigs Are Truly Ours!")—and 940 soldiers' names were read out at the State Service of Remembrance, plus 10 names of the air force, and the name of a navy man who had died in a boiler explosion on one of the frigates. Also, 950 families were promised generous state pensions, which for some reason that they could never understand they were unable to extract from the bureaucracy.

When the British finally realized what had happened, and a task force of Royal Marines arrived, they found only a lot of animal skeletons and an old hermit from New Zealand who was using an unfamiliar Latin American flag as a cloak.

The president calculated somewhat arbitrarily that he had reduced the chances of a coup by 10 percent. He called a snap election, which he would have won on the "Los Puercos Victory Vote" even if he had not taken the precaution of filling the ballot boxes in advance. The country's few demographers noted wearily and cynically that the population had yet again appeared to double in the five years between elections.

32
Exodus

On October 28, 1746, the citizens of Lima had just celebrated the feast of St. Simon and St. Jude. It was a beautiful night of the full moon, and the earthquake totally destroyed the city in three minutes, killing six thousand. The ocean retreated for two miles, and the ensuing tidal wave rushed in and destroyed Callao. In 1647, on May 13, two thousand were killed by an earthquake in Santiago. On March 31, 1650, an earthquake lasting a quarter of an hour obliterated the city of Cuzco, and a priest hung for five days over a precipice, suspended by his ecclesiastical robes. An image of the Virgin torn apart in the Church of San Francisco miraculously repaired itself, and once in Lima a statue of St. Peter turned face-about on its pedestal. In the village of Chapi-Chapi the image of the Virgin processed from its niche in the wall to the door of the chapel. When the priest tried to remove it to the village for safety, he was prevented by a hailstorm, which ceased when he restored the Virgin to her niche.

The mountains along the western side of the Americas daily give birth to themselves with heroic pangs, convulsions, and contractions. As the continents drift westward, the great plates of the planet grind, slide, and slip, squashing the Pacific coast and compressing its mountains higher by the year. They rise faster even than they split and flake in the frosts and are ground down by the ice of glaciers, the scouring of the dusty wind, and the buffeting of the hail. The great chain of mountains, of which the travailing Andes form five thousand miles, are like a leviathan in the throes of tormented constipation and agonizing gripes of wind. The titanic pressure upon the bowels and sphincters of the earth produces the most gargantuan hemorrhoids, the most prodigious fistulas, and the most formidable colonic prolapses imaginable by God or man. Valleys disappear beneath torrents of mud, crevasses open and close, rivers change course, and the mountains are thrown ever higher. The passes are so high that once upon a time the only sensible way to get from Lima to Iquitos was to take several months by steamer, via Liverpool, for the price of sixty pounds sterling.

If the Andes are the bilious excrement of a planet's indigestion, what a palace of pure beauty they are also! They beckon with promises of solitude and peace, with whispers of gold, silver, lead, copper, and clean waters, aphrodisiac air, lost civilizations, and hidden prelapsarian gardens of innocence.

After the massacre of Chiriguaná, Remedios and the entire population knew that they would never again know peace and isolation. They knew that sooner or later whole armies would descend upon them to pillage, sack, and rape and render their victory hollow with their vengeance. They knew that next time there would be tanks and gunships, howling jets, and not demoralized conscripts but the elite regulars who guarded the *portachuelos* on the borders. Everyone knew that it was time to leave and start a new life elsewhere. Many left to join relations in other areas, but two thousand people joined the small army of those who were to go into exile in the mountains, cross the border, and start anew in some forgotten valley of safety. Remedios and her *guerrilleros*, having seen, dealt, heard and smelled total war at first hand, gave up their dream of armed victory and joined the dream for the start of a new creation, a new world, and a better way of life. But they took their own and the soldiers' weapons with them, in case of external threat and from force of habit. Don Emmanuel went to see Don Hugh, Don Pedro, and the French couple and advised them to leave before the invasion broke upon them with the force of a holocaust. Don Hugh and Don Pedro flew to the capital; Antoine and Françoise with their children, but without ever knowing why, joined the refugees for the sake of their vision of elysium and because of Don Emmanuel's enthusiasm. If it did not work out, they could still return to France.

The preparations for departure took two weeks. Every possible item of food, tool, utensil, household good, and object of sentimental value was packed up in bundles ready to load onto the animals. Don Emmanuel, with Hectoro's help, organized parties of vaqueros to round up all his herds and those of the people who were also leaving. Unashamedly he rustled all of Don Hugh's and Don Pedro's horses and cattle, knowing that they would rebuild their herds on insurance money and government reparations.

The whole area became a scene of chaotic last-minute packings, unpackings, discardings, and retrievals, hampered by the antics of the cats, which took it as a matter of course that all this was a game for their amusement. Hectoro became so maddened by their incursions into his luggage that he shot one at close range; the animal blinked at him and patted at the tassels of his machete scabbard and the leather drawstrings of his *bombachos*. Realizing that the animals were indestructible, Hectoro put away his revolver and resigned himself to their quirky attentions.

Don Emmanuel and his men roped the horses together from the halter in hierarchical order, with his gray stallion at the front. He did the same with the mules and donkeys. At the front of each string of cattle he placed a bull, and at the front of the foremost string of cattle he put Cacho Mocho, the bull with the broken horn, who was the undisputed king of all the local bulls, a veritable giant, which was the only bull that had been allowed into Don Emmanuel's garden to eat the flowers and was as gentle as a virgin's touch. The chickens were to be carried in boxes on the pack animals, and the goats were to be driven in flocks, being too willful and excitable to rope together. The dogs, they knew, would follow anyway.

At dawn on the day of departure the thousands of animals were loaded with the impediments of exile, and by midday the work was completed. Each person was assigned responsibility for an equal section of the train, and then, when the heat and humidity grew too oppressive and people became tetchy and irritated, everyone retired for siesta, except for Doña Constanza and Gonzago, who went to make love furiously by the Mula, and Profesor Luis and Farides, who went to make love more gently and decorously on the table in the schoolhouse.

When everybody reemerged in the early evening, the cats were once more febrile and jumpy, and the animals were plainly close to panic. It was difficult to get them all moving, and they were almost impossible to control. Dust rose in asphyxiating fogs, loads fell off and were replaced amid oaths and expletives, people's feet were trodden on by hooves, mules lay down and refused to move, and cats darted among their feet or hitched rides on the other animals, digging in their claws to stay seated and making the animals snort and rear and roll their eyes with anxiety at the pricking in their necks.

That evening the pilgrims made camp on the edge of the savanna, and the trucks, armored cars, and tanks began to roll out, column after column, from Valledupar. In one of the trucks sat Figueras with his platoon of twenty men. He had been demoted to lieutenant and stripped of his decorations despite having personally arrested a demented ter- rorist with bagfuls of identity disks who had wandered through the gates of the headquarters with a cat in his arms.

Early in the morning the animals were close to panic again as Aurelio led the column through the jungle. Up in the trees the monkeys whooped, crashing from branch to branch, and the toucans and their gaudy cousins shrieked and flew in circles. "Something is very wrong," said Aurelio. "The animals are unhappy with this path. With your permission we will go up this hill and walk along the ridges."

"It is all one to me," replied Pedro, and the column moved leftward to climb the long, gentle slope through the extravagant lush vegetation.

Don Emmanuel had an idea. He came up to the front and said, "I think we should cut a couple of trees across the path so that they have difficulty following us. Like this one." He pointed to a tall, bushy tree by the pathside.

"You start cutting it then," said Aurelio, and he and Pedro nudged and winked and watched with eager amusement as Don Emmanuel drew his machete and swung it. The blade clanged against the bark and leaped back, ringing and quivering, and Don Emmanuel let it fall to the ground so that he could clutch his jarred wrist and fingers and dance up and down, grimacing. He bent forward to see that there was no mark on the tree and looked up to see Aurelio and Pedro grinning.

"That tree is a quebracho," said Aurelio. "The wood is so hard that it can be used for paving roads. Try another one."

"Quebracho?" said Don Emmanuel. "An ax breaker?"

"And a machete breaker, too," said Pedro, handing Don Emman- uel his machete and pointing to the section that had chipped off at the edge.

"You are both sons of whores," said Don Emmanuel bitterly. "This was my favorite machete."

Don Emmanuel refused to be defeated. He walked beside Aurelio, pointing out suitable trees to fell, and Aurelio was saying, "No, that is a rubber tree; it would be a waste. No, that is a brazil nut tree; it would be a waste. No, that is a sacred tree; it would offend Pachacamac."

"I give up," said Don Emmanuel. "Even though the animals are leaving piles of dung that even a blind man could follow."

"Try this one," said Pedro. "But do not even start cutting it until everyone is past."

Don Emmanuel felled the balsa tree in a couple of minutes and returned to the column with his honor satisfied.

Steadily they mounted the slopes of the escarpment, a long hump of land that protruded at a height of ten thousand feet far out into the jungle. At the top the people and the cats and the other animals sat in the sunshine, drawing breath and reveling in the cool wind and fresher air. Below them they saw the thin strip of jungle between the mountains and the savanna, and to the north the vast jungle, waving and green, that spread over the horizon. To their left arose the mountains, inviting but awesome, and to their right were discernible through binoculars the abandoned pueblo, abandoned Chiriguaná, and the thin strip of the glistening Mula. The people looked back with nostalgia and regret upon the land of their birth, their labor, and their fiestas, and everyone was thinking, *One day we will return.*

The party was just picking itself up from the grass of the escarpment when the reason for the recent febrility of the cats and the whimsical obstreperousness of the pack animals suddenly became very clear. There was a distant rumble, and the earth began to shake beneath their feet, quivering from side to side like some vast lump of guava jelly. The people and the animals were thrown to their knees or onto their backs, and the cats leaped into their arms and clung on for salvation. The two thousand knelt, rocking with the tremors and with the terror, all reciting the litany of their sins at once, so that Father García had to hear all of them simultaneously and grant mass absolution amid the rumbling and the babbling. García calculated that the earthquake lasted for the exact duration of two Ave Marias and a Tota Pulchra Est.

The earthquake ended with gentle belches and gurgles in the entrails of the earth, and the people, still crossing themselves, invoking angels and spirits, rose unsteadily to their feet. They looked out across the landscape and saw that their former homes were immersed in a shimmering and swirling sea of brilliant silver, for the sunshine was sparkling off the pale white dust raised by the vibrations of the earthquake. They did not know it, but their homes beneath the dust remained perfectly intact. "Ay! Ay! Ay!" exclaimed the pilgrims, overcome with awe and transfixed with the beauty of the sparkling sea on the plain. They had stood there a long time, watching the ocean of dust gently settling, when they heard a new sound of roaring and rushing. A mile away, above the valley in which they had formerly been traveling, a stupendous wall of water four hundred feet high suddenly burst between the cleft of two mountains and traveled in a vast arc before crashing onto the jungle below and tearing it to matchsticks as it hurled apocalyptically down the Mula Basin in an advance of majestic and godlike inexorability, throwing a mist of spray high into the air and roaring like herds of Herculean bulls engaged in inconceivable prehistoric struggles.

Dumbstruck, the crowd stood and bore witness as the mighty spout of foaming and glistening water continued to dive unendingly from between the mountains. They watched the plain turn into a featureless muddy sea, glistening brightly and ever-spreading on to the horizons. Very gradually the colossal spout began to diminish, until two hours later it was a waterfall cascading into a lake.

Without many words the people made camp on the escarpment. As evening fell, they walked around each other's encampments, holding cats in their arms for comfort, and those who had wronged each other in the past and bore grudges apologized and embraced. Old friends shook hands, and people who had never talked in the past exchanged confidences. Such things are caused not by fear but by the revelation that there is nothing stable in the whole universe and that everything is finally a matter of chance, which can so suddenly throw the lives of people into chaos. People find their protection withdrawn, and this cuts wounds in the hearts of those who never before have felt helpless and small and shows them how precious is everything temporary and mundane. In the presence of such momentous force, such indifferent callousness, such mindless and irresistible cataclysm, one knows with absolute knowledge what it is to be an ant inside an anthill when it is trodden on by the foot of a thoughtless man.

The vehicles at the front of the column of invaders found themselves driving into a rapidly rising flood. The whole column was halted and the major general of the Portachuelo Guards came forward and surveyed the scene from the top of one of the trucks. "I have seen this sort of thing before," said the major general. "That tremor shook something loose in the mountains, and this is the result. We will have to turn about."

With great difficulty the vehicles maneuvered back and forth in the encroaching mud until it was finally possible to return to Valledupar in advance of the water, which came to within fifty miles of the town and then gently receded.

The government declared no national emergency, and no rescue operations were attempted. As far as they were concerned, the revolution was justly buried and forgotten.

On the top of the escarpment Pedro turned to Aurelio, "Is Carmen under that?"

"No," said Aurelio. "We live on that high ground over there on the other side. It is untouched. She will believe that I am dead, but when I return, she will find that I am not."

Pedro gazed out over the enormous lake that was now placid beneath the moonlight and tickled the ears of the cat that was rubbing his cheek with its own.

"We were lucky to escape from that."

"You were lucky I was here to listen to the animals," replied Aurelio impatiently.

Josef came up behind them and stood with them a moment, "Think of all the money I have wasted," he said, "paying Don Ramón for a proper burial and the three masses."

"Do not concern yourself," replied Pedro. "I think Father García would do it for nothing, so you would still get a burial and three masses having paid out for exactly a burial and three masses."

Josef nodded and absorbed the logic of Pedro's words.

"All the same," added Pedro, "you would do more good in the world by being fed to my dogs, eh, *cabrón?*"

33

The Economic Miracle and the Incarama Park

It sometimes happens that in relatively powerless and impoverished countries there arise men of enormous vision who are frustrated and offended by the limitations of their lives and seek to reach out for the stars on behalf of themselves and their nations. It is as if they wished to cry out from the mountaintops, "Behold! How mighty are our dreams! Look on at the birth of Greatness!" It also may happen that two such men arise at the same time, and when this happens, the world must look on in awe. In our case the two men were the economics minister, Dr. Jorge Badajoz, and the mayor of the capital, Raoul Buenanoce, whose activities, although not directly connected, ran curiously parallel.

It was just beginning to be possible for the president to feel a little more optimistic about the economy; the urban guerrillas had seemingly miraculously disappeared. He had heard the rumors about their secret extermination by the armed forces but was relieved that now every bridge he opened was not blown up the day after the opening and that power cuts were caused nowadays not by bombs but by good old-fashioned incompetence. He was also pleased that so many trade union leaders had vanished inexplicably during the recent general strike because their successors were more moderate in their demands for higher wages to offset the 200 percent rate of inflation. He had inaugurated campaigns of hundreds of arrests against strikers for breach of the peace and obstruction, and General Ramírez had very kindly sent a large number of plainclothes soldiers among any groups of strikers to incite them to violence. As soon as this happened, the police arrived with their batons and water cannons and released clouds of vomit gas, which caused the strikers to spew violently at the same time as being drenched and beaten over the head. The workers, having experienced the hell of flailing around on the ground in a rank lake of vomit, became understandably more content with their steadily falling standard of living, and industrial harmony was largely restored.

The rural guerrillas in the mountains and jungle were not a problem as far as the president was concerned. He never went into the interior himself, did not want to, and did not care what all those dirty and illiterate peasants got up to as long as they stayed out of the capital. The ones who did arrive and set up home in shantytowns and *favelas* he discouraged by ordering the city police to burn down their cardboard shacks, load the peasants into trucks, and off-load them as far away as possible in the countryside.

Now that economic progress was possible, the president appointed Dr. Badajoz to perform the miracle. He was the chairman of the State Oil Company and was also in the chair of the Free Trade Council. He had extensive contacts in the world of international banking and, having been educated at Eton, was a snob and an Anglophile. He had taken his degree in economics at Harvard and had been completely converted to Friedmanite monetarism, in the belief that market forces can cause prices and inflation to stabilize in an atmosphere of competition.

Dr. Badajoz came to office and inspected the state of the economy on his first day: There was an external debt of fifteen billion dollars, a balance of payments deficit of five billion dollars, almost no reserves of foreign currency, and the growth rate was actually in negative figures and was being called the shrink rate. He found that the government for fifteen years had had a policy of nationalizing all failing industries, and now the state employed nearly half of all urban workers. He also found that in the past the state had passed formidably protectionist measures against imports, thus helping keep in business a great many inefficient companies. Dr. Badajoz decided to sell off the state industries and to remove the prohibitive import tariffs but was forbidden to create unemployment by the president, who believed that all the unemployed would become terrorists. Dr. Badajoz realized very quickly that it was not going to be as simple as he had thought; the only way out was to gamble on being able to squeeze living standards and increase productivity at the same time, so as to keep everybody employed on increasingly worthless wages.

Dr. Badajoz boldly allowed prices to rise to their natural level on the free market, so that tobacco doubled in price instantly, and gasoline rose by 40 percent. Soon prices on everything were rising by half each month, and he found that he was creating the inflation he had come into office to defeat, so he froze all wages and effectively reduced the buying power of all wage packages to less than half of what it had been before he assumed office.

Dr. Badajoz found he could not raise the country's income through taxation; no one except state employees had ever paid any taxes, and now that he was denationalizing, there was even less tax coming in than before. Everyone other than state employees used to bribe the tax officials not to tax him or her, and in any case nearly all business was transacted in illegal U.S. dollars, whose black-market value was even quoted daily in the newspapers.

Some years previously the government had introduced index-linked stocks and bonds, and people used to use their wages to buy them in order to offset the effects of inflation; they would only cash them in order to go shopping when they could not resort to barter. No one used checks anymore because in the three days they took to clear they lost a lot of their value.

Dr. Badajoz decided to place his faith in oil, coffee, and tropical fruit, the traditional basis of the economy, and began to campaign to give big incentives to agricultural concerns while the decontrol of imports forced manufacturing industry to become more competitive. In this way the country was completely deindustrialized as cheap foreign goods replaced local ones and foreign capital moved in to asset-strip the abandoned industrial base.

Having observed all these unanticipated effects, Dr. Badajoz decided to stabilize the currency by attracting foreign investment, so he freed interest rates and set the official value of the peso at two hundred to the dollar (when it was really four hundred) to reduce inflation, but he turned a blind eye to those who were trading at the real rate. When he realized that his father, one of the richest men in Latin America, was about to die, he carried his noninterventionist credo to its logical conclusion and abolished death duties.

The great economist's best asset was his credibility among the major figures of world banking. It may have been his lean, cadaverous seriousness, his precise English, his Savile Row suits, and his air of aristocratic savoir faire, but whatever it was, he got everything he wanted out of the foreign banks. He raised six hundred million dollars from a group of American banks, he raised three hundred million from European banks, and three hundred million from the IMF on easy repayment terms. He even opened a branch of the National Bank in Paris.

It was so easy for him because the dramatic drop in the standard of living and the flood of cheap imports had halved inflation to 100 percent, and the increased internal competition had raised the rate of growth to 5 percent. A good coffee harvest put both the balance of payments and the foreign reserves healthily into the black.

Had he been as wise as his reputation suggested, he should have retired at that point so that someone else could reap the whirlwind, but believing that all was under control, he foolishly carried on. The president still forbade him to create unemployment by his denationalization program, but the foreign corporations that bought the industries were not interested in running them; they merely took away all the machinery to their own countries, leaving armies of unemployed. Badajoz had to reemploy them, even though he had nothing for them to do, so that the number of state employees remained the same as before and the state's share in the nation's spending began rapidly to rise.

The doctor also found that there was a major sector of the economy that he could not control, and the president even refused to tell him how large it was. "It would only upset you," he had said, "and I cannot bear to think about it myself." Badajoz realized he would never get inflation defeated as long as the armed forces spent whatever they wanted. They had their own chemical, shipbuilding, textiles, steel, and aircraft factories, and they spent vast sums abroad on German tanks, American fighters, British radar, French helicopters, and missiles from wherever they could be had. Additionally, they would not let the economics minister veto the purchase of six airliners by the national airline, on the ground that they would be useful in the event of war. They were supposed to be used on new routes to Japan and Singapore; but no one ever went there, and the aircraft remained idle. Badajoz also discovered that it was customary among businesses to pay the military up to 5 percent of any deal as "goodwill" money, and he could not stop the navy from investing heavily in nuclear research and hydroelectric plants. In short, as the economic situation in the country improved, the military saw its chance of demanding ever greater sums of money.

It seemed as though everything happened at once. The tractor and car industry, which consisted of five large companies, collapsed in the space of one month because of cheaper imports and the overvalued peso. The new agricultural revolution, which had been meant to save the economy, had to proceed on foreign machinery. Dr. Badajoz had freed interest rates to prevent dollar speculation, and suddenly they went higher than the rate of inflation so that all the farmers went bankrupt and nobody would invest in anything anymore. People sold all their assets and speculated instead on the financial markets. Foreign capital poured into the economy to take advantage of the new interest rates, and one month later poured out again, taking the government's money with it in the form of interest payments. Three banks collapsed and went into liquidation because they could not call in debts; if they had, the ownership of the indebted factories and farms would have come into their hands, with no chance of ever making a profit from them.

Successful speculators on the wildly fluctuating financial markets went abroad on lavish holidays and spent forty-one billion dollars over two years, mostly in the United States, because the peso was still officially overvalued against the dollar, thus making dollars cheap. For the same reason imports increased 55 percent in one year.

After three years of the economic miracle, Dr. Jorge Badajoz took stock of the following information in his ministry's annual report: Since he had come to office, 90 percent of credit and currency was in the hands of the state, living standards had dropped by 50 percent, and so had manufacturing output. The foreign debt was sixty million dollars, and inflation had doubled to 400 percent. The treasury had printed the first-ever million-peso note. Dr. Badajoz sold everything he had and, bitter, disillusioned, and sad, disappeared suddenly with trunkfuls of dollars and was next heard of living in Uruguay.

Raoul Buenanoce was a cultured man who foresaw a great future for the capital under his paternal guidance. Here is his speech upon acceding to office in the same year as Dr. Badajoz:

"We have indeed a proud city, with its splendid colonial edifices, its four high-rise blocks, its parks and boulevards! We have here a branch of Selfridges where one can buy leather and jewelry! We have men and women who are as elegantly dressed as those of Paris. We have four theaters that show the best productions of Buenos Aires and Madrid! In 1944 Segovia performed here, and again in 1963!

"But we cannot rest on our laurels! It is my intention that by the end of my term of office our beloved capital will not only be the capital of our proud nation, but the cultural capital of the civilized world! I shall utterly remove the *favelas,* those *villas miserias* that ring our suburbs, and in their place I shall build a park such as the world has never seen! It will be a park where our grateful citizens may go for rest and recreation after they have wiped the sweat of the toil of the day from their brows!"

This noble oration, followed by loud applause, preceded the most extraordinarily ambitious building program in the history of the world.

His first project was to build a giant highway to the airport that would cut right through the middle of the city. He raised one billion dollars on the international markets and cut a swath through the most ancient and historical part of the city, since the highway was to be fifteen lanes wide. It was absolutely straight except for where it had to go around the Norwegian Embassy, which had refused to move until Regina Olsen was released. Buenanoce made three thousand people homeless, and the project was never completed because he was impatient to get on with the park. The last part of the highway ended halfway across a bridge, and everyone still drove to the airport along the old route.

Buenanoce destroyed the shantytowns and moved three hundred thousand people out by force. When they moved back in again, he formed his own private secret service, whose first task was to intimidate the shanty dwellers into absenting themselves permanently. After that he kept the secret service on to keep an eye on his own employees and to root out dissent in the capital.

In building his highway, Buenanoce had used two hundred thousand tons of asphalt, four thousand steel supports, and seven hundred thousand cubic meters of concrete, but this was nothing in comparison with the cost of re-creating the great wonders of the world in the recreation park. "I know exactly what is to be done," he said, smiling through his many chins. "I have enough experience to know that it is necessary to have a very great many plans and, once you start, not to stop."

The immense project was intended to cost the public purse nothing at all, since all investment was to be raised on the private sector by competitive tender, and any losses in running profit were to be borne by those investors. The successful company would be lent fifty million dollars from public funds, which it would have to repay from profits. If work was not completed on time, the company would have to pay twenty thousand dollars per day in penalties.

Thus it was all very businesslike, except that the company that won the contract was run by an air force general, an army brigadier, and a naval rear admiral. Buenanoce raised an extra twenty million dollars for them as a goodwill gesture, and in order to build everything on time, they started all the projects simultaneously.

This is what they began to build: a zoological garden, an aquarium, a giant amusement park, a cinema, a six-hundred-foot tower that revolved at its base, multicolored fountains, a dance hall for fifteen thousand people, and an ecological park. In addition, there were exact reproductions of: all the Maya ruins at Chichén Itzá, the Hanging Gardens of Babylon, the Tower of Babel, the Pyramids, the Leaning Tower of Pisa, the Statue of Liberty, St. Paul's Cathedral, St. Basil's Cathedral, St. Peter's, the Sphinx, the Castle of Cartagena in Colombia, Michelangelo's "David" (twice the original size), Machu Picchu, the Golden Temple of Amritsar, the Fortress of Cuzco, the Taj Mahal, the Empire State Building, the Observatory at Intihuatana, the city of Petra, the Eiffel Tower, the abandoned opera house at Manaus, Notre-Dame, the standing stones of Karnak and Stonehenge, the Temple of the Sun at Teotihuacán, the Temple of Conde at Palenque, the Forbidden City in Beijing, El Escorial, the "Copenhagen Mermaid" (twice life size), the Temple of Viracocha, the Tower of London, the Palace of the sultan of Brunei, Huanaco Viejo, a scale model of the Ural Mountains, the Palace of Huayna Capac, and a scaled-down version of the Panama Canal, spanned by a quarter-size model of the Golden Gate Bridge.

The project was known as Incarama, and soon there began to be rumors that all was not going well. Part of the trouble was that the customs had agreed, in return for certain considerations, not to check the vast containers coming in through the seaports. Instead of Ferris wheels and meal carts, these containers were rumored to be full of tanks, armored cars, aircraft spares, missiles, contraceptives, flannels, national flags, electric cattle prods, toothpaste, toilet paper, calculators, and foreign works of art. Additionally, the invoices seemed curiously inflated, and most of the money inexplicably found its way into fixed-interest deposit accounts in Switzerland, Luxembourg, and Jersey, where it was credited to the shareholders of Incarama.

The construction deadline came and went, and no penalties were exacted. The consortium was given an extra six months for completion and a further bridging loan from city funds of twenty million dollars. Then Incarama collapsed and went into liquidation, leaving none of the individual projects completed. So enormous were the debts that its chief creditor bank also collapsed and had to be taken over by the National Bank, which destroyed Dr. Badajoz's financial projections for that year.

The capital was bankrupt, and Raoul Buenanoce closed down the hospitals and the social services before fleeing to Uruguay with trunkfuls of hundred-dollar bills. The city is now famous throughout Latin America for having its *favelas* situated among the most picturesque classical ruins and for having its water supply delivered by a replica of the Panama Canal.

34

General Fuerte Enjoys the Hospitality of the Army Internal Security Service

The brigadier had read Colonel Figueras's report with wide-eyed incredulity, especially disbelieving the only bits that were actually true, which were those detailing the plague of cats and the plague of laughter. He read of Figueras's heroic attacks and counterattacks against incredible odds and read of a valiant rearguard action in which Figueras held a bridge for twenty minutes single-handedly so that his men could escape. He called in all the survivors and interviewed every one of them. Then he summoned Figueras.

Figueras's ears were still burning from the brigadier's tirade, and his heart was still leaden from his demotion to lieutenant, when General Fuerte, walking like the living dead, crossed his path on the parade ground. Figueras stopped and looked at the shabby, shuffling creature with his stubble, his vacant eyes, his clanking *mochilas,* and his cat folded in his arms. "Who are you?" demanded Figueras.

The general thought for a minute, and replied distantly, "I am very sorry to have taken so long. I was with the *guerrilleros.*"

"With the *guerrilleros!*" exclaimed Figueras. He put his hand into one of the *mochilas,* hoping they were full of coins, and drew out several identity disks. He examined them carefully. "You came from Chiriguaná with these?"

The general thought again. "Someone brought me and the cat in a truck. I am sorry to have taken so long."

"Come with me," said Figueras, drawing his pistol. He stuck it in the small of the general's back and escorted him to the guardroom, where he pushed him in and locked the door. He went back to the brigadier.

"Not you again," was the comment that greeted him.

"Yes, sir," said Figueras. "I have some important news. I have just arrested at great personal risk an armed *guerrillero* who was carrying on his person all the identity disks of those killed at Chiriguaná."

The brigadier sighed wearily. "Lieutenant," he drawled, emphasizing the word, "you forget that my window overlooks the parade ground. You have just arrested an old tramp with a cat and a lot of bags."

"The bags contain the disks, sir, and he told me he had been with the *guerrilleros*. That is the truth," he added.

"Very well, Lieutenant, notify the Army Internal Security Service and have them come to take him away for questioning. Kindly do not let me see your face again for a very long time. You are dismissed."

Figueras saluted and left and went straight to the radio operator with a message for him to transmit. "Do not put it in writing," said the operator, who was familiar with Figueras's illegibility and illiteracy. "Just dictate it."

The general sat in his cell for two days with his cat and did not notice that no one fed him. He had long since developed a method of being completely asleep while remaining awake, and he entertained himself with lucid dreams and childhood memories. He took no notice when no one fed him for three days during the bumpy ride to the capital in the trunk of the Ford Falcoln, but he missed the cat, which had been wrenched from his arms and sent dashing away across the parade ground. "That was my cat," he said sadly.

When he arrived at the Army School of Electrical and Mechanical Engineering, the two pyragues handed the general over to El Verdugo, who read the report that was thrust into his hands.

"Name unknown . . . subject demented . . . believed to be guer-

rilla, Chiriguaná People's Vanguard . . . to be questioned closely . . .
usual questions."

Roughly El Verdugo pushed his victim through the corridors, past
the cells full of weeping prisoners and the stench of excrement. The
general did not see the notice on the wall which said, "We will keep on
killing until people understand." He did not see the bare light bulbs or
the hysterical naked girl covered with bruises and burns who was pulled
past him by the hair. He did not see the dried pools of blood on the floor
or the streaks of it on the walls, and he did not smell the putrefying and
burning flesh. He was seeing an emperor butterfly on a bloom of acacia
and a hummingbird in a blue lupinus.

El Verdugo pushed the general into the hanging room and tied his
wrists behind his back. He attached a *carabina* on a rope to the bonds
and took up the strain on the rope, which ran through a pulley bolted
to the ceiling. El Verdugo, with scientific detachment and expertise,
jerked suddenly on the rope and noted with surprise that despite the
cracking of the shoulder joints, the general did not cry out. "Who are
you?" he demanded, jerking the rope again.

"Emperor," said the general, still dreaming.

"Emperor of what?" said El Verdugo, jerking the rope again.

"Acacia," said the general.

El Verdugo went to his desk and wrote, "Subject says he is emperor
of Asia."

"If you are trying to be amusing," said El Verdugo through gritted
teeth, "let's see how this amuses you." He hauled the general up to the
ceiling and let him drop, suddenly clamping the friction brake mounted
on the floor beneath his foot. The general's shoulders cracked with a
noise like a snapping bough. "Who are you now, Emperor?"

"They've taken my cat," whispered the general, his eyes filling with
tears. "Where is my cat?"

El Verdugo returned to his desk. "Subject is plainly a lunatic," he
wrote, "and insensible to pain."

He let the general down and cut his bonds, so that his arms hung
uselessly at his side like those of a jointed wooden doll. El Verdugo was
reluctant to give up, but he had more responsive and satisfying victims
to torture, so he crucified the general upside down on the grille against
the wall. He hung there all night, dreaming of cats, seeing and hearing

nothing of the twenty people whose bodies and whose sanity El Verdugo broke while the capital slept.

The next morning El Verdugo handed the general over to El Baño. El Baño looked expertly into the empty eyes of his victim. "I'll make him talk," he said, and led the general to his special baths. He threw the general into a tank and held him under. The general dreamed of being in the womb and stopped breathing. His bodily functions had slowed so near to a complete halt that El Baño could have held him under for an hour with no result. When El Baño withdrew his hands, the general did not rise, gasping and choking, as the others always did. He lay smiling beneath the water with a string of tiny bubbles emerging from his mouth. El Baño dragged him out and immersed him in a bath of urine and feces, holding him under for four minutes. He gave up and had the general taken away so that he could instead torture people who groveled and pleaded and acknowledged his total domination.

It was El Electricista who restored the general to sanity and to the reality of pain. He strapped the general to Susana, his metal grille, and slipped rings over his fingers, earthed by wires to the grille. He threw a bucket of water over the motionless body for better conductivity and switched on his *picaña*. He ran it down the general's leg, and the body shook and convulsed. The general felt a bolt of lightning tear his muscles to pieces, and he awoke instantaneously from his long reverie. He jerked his head up and found he could not move. "Who the hell are you?" he demanded.

"El Electricista," replied the torturer, "at your service." Delighted with his success, he applied the cattle prod to the other leg. The general jolted and screamed. "That's better," said El Electricista. "Now who are you?"

"General Carlo María Fuerte," said the general. "Military governor of César. I am going to have you shot when I get out of here."

"But you won't," replied El Electricista. "So you are the emperor of Asia and a general, eh?" He touched the *picaña* on his victim's navel for several seconds.

Once more the general convulsed uncontrollably and howled. Breathless and racked, he repeated, "I am General Fuerte."

"You are a guerrilla from Chiriguaná," said El Electricista, touching the *picaña* to the general's mouth.

When the screaming died away, the general spit the blood from his gums and said, "I am General Fuerte. I was kidnapped by the *guerrilleros* months ago, and then they released me."

"Liar!" exclaimed El Electricista, and he pressed the *picaña* into the general's left nipple, smiling and relishing the shrieks and the smell of burning flesh and the spasms. His erection began to grow.

"You know which bits I am working up to, don't you?" he taunted. "Tell me about the guerrillas and the other scum you associate with."

The general was about to tell him when he pressed the point of the prod into his right nipple. He was about to tell him when he touched it to the base of his penis on the right-hand side. When the general had finished urinating uncontrollably and sobbing and retching, El Electricista said, "I think you were about to tell me something?"

The general started to tell him about being captive and about how this was all a mistake when the prod was applied to the base of his penis on the left-hand side. When he resumed consciousness, El Electricista poured more water over him and said, "We haven't tried the best bit yet, have we?" and he ran the prod against the general's testicles and up his penis to the tip. The general felt his body tear a thousand times into tiny shreds, as though ripped by pincers, and he did not wake until the next morning, when he found he could not use his arms, and he recollected the previous day's torture.

El Electricista came in for him and kicked him to the ground. "I have a treat for you," he said, and pulled the general by his hair to the electrical room. On the grille was a young girl of about sixteen, naked and bruised, her body covered with burns and blotches. El Electricista took a revolver in one hand and a whip in the other. He put the *picaña* in the general's hand and switched it on. "Torture her," he commanded.

The general was stunned. "I will not," he said.

The whip wrapped around his body, and the metal shards embedded in its plaits tore strips of flesh as it cut across him. "Torture her," screamed El Electricista, "or she will torture you!"

"I don't have the use of my arms," replied the general. "And if I had, I would break your neck or die in the attempt."

"Brave words, *comunista!* You have made your choice."

The tortured and terrified girl looked up at him with horror and pleading in her eyes as he pretended to be about to touch the prod to her breasts and her genitals.

"No, no, no!" she was repeating. "Please, no."

"You know all about this, don't you, *flaca?* Now shall I play with you, or will you play with this nice gentleman?"

"I can't," she said desperately.

"I can," said El Electricista, leering at her and lowering the *picaña* very slowly toward her breast.

"I'll do it," she said. "Please, I'll do it."

The girl was sobbing, blinded with tears, as she obeyed the torturer's instructions. "I'm so sorry, I'm sorry," she kept saying as she touched the *picaña* to the general and he shook and screamed.

El Electricista was saying, "On the balls, you bitch. No! Longer than that! Harder! More water!" and he was slashing her with the whip if she stopped or hesitated. In the end the thrill became more than he could bear any longer, and he raped the girl frenziedly across the general's unconscious body and then shot her through the throat. He left the general on Susana for the night and savagely kicked the body of the dead girl, shouting, "Bitch! Bitch! Whore!" Then, pulling himself together, he went off for his date with his girl friend, to see *O Lucky Man* with subtitles in Spanish.

"My poor *querido,*" she said. "You look so tired. You shouldn't let them work you so hard."

He laughed suavely. "One has to do one's duty."

When Asado returned from the special liquidation assignment two days later, he strolled into El Electricista's room and said, "How's it going? Anything new?"

"Not much. Just got one lunatic in. I've thought of a novelty, though."

"A novelty?"

"Yes," said El Electricista. "You make them swallow a string of little electrodes, and then you ram the *picaña* up their backsides."

Asado laughed. "Very nice one! Have you tried it yet?"

"I have," replied El Electricista. "I tried it on the lunatic. It works exquisitely."

"Who is the lunatic?" asked Asado. "Is it worth toasting him a little?"

"He came in saying he was emperor of Asia, but he is really a *guerrillero* from Chiriguaná. Now he says he is General Fuerte. He is mad but tough."

Asado was taken aback. "General Fuerte was comandante of officer training school when I was a cadet. General Ramírez ordered me three weeks ago to investigate his disappearance from Valledupar. Which cell is he in, the lunatic?"

"Third on the left. I've kept him standing for two days in the cramp cupboard. I would not bother if I were you; he is no general, just a Communist tramp."

General Fuerte, on the verge of death, was transferred hurriedly to the Hospital for Sick Soldiers and, having stayed there for four months, was transferred again to the Villa Maravillosa Military Convalescent Home, where gradually his arms returned to life with the help of expert physiotherapy. He shared a ward with a young Norwegian girl in a wheelchair who said she was Regina Olsen and that she had been shot and abducted by the army to a torture center. In the ward there was a young airborne capitan who had gone insane and kept repeating, "They were *cholos*. It was me who did it. I am the guilty one. It was me." Regina told Fuerte that the young man had accidentally massacred a tribe of Indians, and the army was too embarrassed to let him out. "They won't let me out either," she added. "I shall probably be here forever. I don't know what happened to you, but I expect you'll never leave either. No one does. You are lucky," she added. "The last mistake in here had his teeth broken with hammers."

Over the next week both Regina Olsen and the mad capitan were gone overnight. The general was glad for them if they were safe but worried in case a cynical solution had been found. One morning he put on his uniform, went for a stroll in the high-walled gardens, and noticed that there was a climbable tree with a branch that overhung the wall.

He jarred his ankle on landing and limped to the roadside. He flagged down an already overloaded bus and showed his identity card to the driver, who was too scared and impressed to charge him for the ride and even made a detour to the army airfield. He threatened three officers with court-martial if they continued to resist his orders to assign him a pilot and a light aircraft to take him to Valledupar and very quickly got his way.

When he walked into the office of the brigadier, he did not even say hello or return the other's salute.

"No questions!" said the general. "I have been on a top secret mission, and I have no time to talk. Who are the best soldiers we have here? Come on, answer me!"

The astonished brigadier said, "We still have a company of the Portachuelo Guards, sir."

"Good," said the general decisively. "They are to be ready for combat, provisioned for three days, and transport is to be arranged plus two empty trucks within one hour exactly. I also want three medical orderlies. See to it. I have an emergency to deal with."

"Yes, sir," replied the brigadier, saluting, "and may I say, sir, it is good to have you back. I am much relieved. I feared for your life."

"Thank you," said the general. "I did as well." And he left to visit his own office but changed his mind and returned to the brigadier, finding him on the telephone to the quartermaster. He signaled to the brigadier that he could wait until the call was over. When the orders had been transmitted, the general told the brigadier, "Under no circumstances whatsoever tell anyone, even General Ramírez himself, that I have been here or that I left with the troops. I am still officially missing and acting under higher authority. Is that clear?"

"Higher than General Ramírez?" asked the brigadier. "Surely there is no higher authority?"

"You are showing your ignorance," said the general. "There is much higher authority. Please send someone to fetch the spare key to my quarters, and have them bring it here. At sixteen hundred hours the men must be in the trucks on the parade ground. I shall stop en route to brief them."

When the general entered his quarters, he found them as they had been left, except that they were dusty and smelled dank. He heard a noise at the door and saw it swing open a little so that a chink of light appeared. His hand went to the holster on his belt, but then he stepped forward and bent down. He stroked its back as it arched and twined itself around his legs. "Little gato," he said, "I missed you. And how on earth did you know where I live? And how did you live?"

The cat mewed beseechingly, and the general opened a small can of corned beef for it and put it in a saucer. He went to change into combat gear and spent the forty minutes before his departure making in the door a crude but functional cat flap. He left a note in the brigadier's in tray: "See to it that my cat is fed daily at 1800 hours."

35

The President Discovers the Aphrodisiac Properties of Reducing the Military

At the same time as Asado was concluding his first illicit deal to sell the orphans of his activities to childless couples in Europe and the United States, the three chiefs of staff were deep in discussion at the Senior Officers' Lodge.

"I tell you it's exactly the right time!" exclaimed Admiral Fleta. "The public adore us because of Los Puercos!"

"They also adore the president," rejoined General Ramírez. "It was all his idea, and he has received most of the credit, plus a huge majority in the election."

"He would have got that anyway," reflected Air Chief Marshal Sanchis. "Everyone knows it was rigged."

"He would have won without rigging it, though," said Ramírez. "That's obvious."

"All the same," said Fleta, "the capital is bankrupt, the social services are finished, inflation is over four hundred percent, and wages are frozen. The public is seriously discontented. I think they would support us."

"But they are blaming that on Buenanoce and Badajoz, not the president!" retorted Ramírez. "His position is invulnerable."

"But why does the opinion of the people matter?" asked Fleta. "They are prejudiced, irrational, and idle. Surely we can rule without them?"

"I suppose so," said Sanchis, "but we've got to be able to rely on the tacit support of the middle classes, who admire discipline and order and hate politics. We can safely ignore the workers because we have already crushed the unions, and the left wing is splintered into about forty warring factions. They are a joke. Did you know that there are five Communist parties all claiming to be the real and original one?"

"There are six now," said Fleta.

"How so?" asked Ramírez.

"One of the parties expelled an activist for being homosexual, and he took some of the party with him. They're known as the Mario-comunistas by the party that expelled them, and *they* call the others the Machocomunistas. It's all very droll."

"Indeed," said Sanchis. "And I hear that the Trotskyists, the Marxists, and the Anarchists are in open warfare. We don't need to fear the left at all; when they order a firing squad, they form a circle."

"Why have we been exterminating them then?" asked Fleta, genuinely puzzled.

"Because they still create a lot of havoc," replied Ramírez, "and they're the dung of the devil."

"This is a diversion, though," interjected Sanchis. "Are we going to assume power or not?"

"On the whole, I'm in favor," said Fleta.

"Right," said Ramírez. "I suppose, all things considered, I will agree, but only because it's for the good of the country. Power doesn't interest me as such."

Fleta raised a cynical eyebrow. "Does that mean you have no intention of taking the presidency?"

"Oh, no," exclaimed General Ramírez. "I don't mean that at all. After all, the army is the senior service, and the largest, so it's only natural that I should be president."

"May I remind you that in the last fifteen coups before *La Violencia* it was always the army chief who was president?" said Fleta icily. "I think it's only fair that the navy be given a chance for once."

Air Chief Marshal Sanchis broke in. "I must remind you both that the army is deeply unpopular with the people and that the navy is extremely small. The air force is by far the most popular service owing to its romantic image. I should also remind you two that you are both sixty-three years old and due to retire from active service in two years. I am only fifty-seven years old."

"Look at Stroessner in Paraguay!" exclaimed Ramírez. "And at Pinochet in Chile! Gómez in Venezuela! They carried on into old age!"

"Maybe so," replied Sanchis. "But in this country military presidents have always observed the tradition of retiring at sixty-five. If you break traditions like that, people very soon begin to call you a megalomaniac." Sanchis looked from one to the other meaningfully.

"I don't care what people call me," replied Ramírez huffily, "especially representatives of junior services."

"Old military presidents always suffer lapses of judgment," replied Sanchis. "Look at Pinochet. He was crazy enough to call an election. Look at Galtieri; he went to war with Britain."

"But so did we!" exclaimed Fleta.

"Yes, of course, but we didn't tell them, and they never found out for months, by which time the war was already over."

"I resent your implying that I am senile," said Ramírez. "If you were in my service I would have you shot."

"I, too," said Fleta. "As a man of honor I should challenge you to a duel, but as a civilized man of manners I cannot."

"I was only trying to say that it would be a bad precedent to break with an honorable tradition," said Sanchis patiently. "I know that neither of you is senile."

"What about a fourth man?"

"You mean a puppet president?" asked Ramírez. "But we already have one!"

"We're talking about the well-being of our country," countered Sanchis. "Surely a puppet president would not be adequate."

The conversation carried on in this vein into the early hours in the withdrawing room of the lodge, and nothing was formally decided, except that they should have another discussion along the same lines on the following Monday. A tape of the conversation was delivered to the president by the Service of State Information, and in the following days he became very thoughtful and preoccupied. For their part, the chiefs of staff left the meeting each convinced that something had to be done to reduce the power of the other two. A tangible mist of plotting began to fill the corridors of power.

One of the things that one can say without fear of contradiction is that long-serving military men tend to think alike; the only exception that springs immediately to mind is the radical military government of Peru, which instituted land reforms amid a welter of bureaucracy worthy of the most egregious civilian government. Let us consider them to have been honorary civilians, and return to our own country, where General Ramírez, Admiral Fleta, and Air Chief Marshal Sanchis began identical campaigns of mutual destabilization.

An armed force has three main areas of vulnerability: personnel, equipment, and command structure. One can diminish the effectiveness of all three by attacking just one of them.

It all started innocently enough with four army helicopters mysteriously crashing in the mountains in the same week. Ramírez, without any real evidence, assumed that this was too much of a coincidence and judged that it was a case of collusive sabotage by the navy and the air force. He arranged for a limpet mine to be attached to a naval frigate and for an air force missile cache to explode. Sanchis and Fleta immediately assumed that the other two forces were in collusion against them, and in the next two weeks the army lost two tanks to ground-to-ground missile attacks, the navy lost a reconnaissance helicopter and an offshore patrol boat, and the air force lost a brand-new jet fighter from France.

All the commanders were furious and summoned their respective chiefs of clandestine elimination operations, exhorting them to do their patriotic duty for large sums and informing them of precisely which "traitors" were to be terminated with extreme prejudice.

The bomb under General Ramírez's platform at the officers' passing-out parade went off after the ceremony and killed no one. The assassin's bullet intended for Admiral Fleta passed harmlessly through his hat, and the grenade in Air Chief Marshal Sanchis's briefcase failed to detonate. They all became deeply nervous men but continued to plot together as though they had no suspicions of treachery. The president continued to examine the transcripts of their conversations and wondered if he dared risk the fury of the military by having them arrested for high treason and then shot. He decided to bide his time and see how far he could encourage the three commanders to destroy one another and their respective forces. He summoned each one in turn to the Presidential Palace and warned them rather vaguely of plots he had had intimations of from the Service of State Information. These plots, he told them, were being hatched by "certain members" of the other two services; naturally the information was highly confidential and should be divulged to no one at all under any circumstances.

The chiefs of staff began to put into motion plans for infiltrating each other's security services. This was almost impossible. You cannot, for example, infiltrate an army man into a naval organization because membership applications would be carefully scrutinized by the naval vetting office. Instead, it was found necessary to offer huge bribes to known members of other services, and no one knew anymore who was a single, double, or triple agent. The subsequent atmosphere of suspicion and paranoia caused the operations against civilian subversives to cease almost completely because it took up so much time and energy to find, torture, and dispose of the operatives of the secret services of the other arms of the military. One of the ironies of all this was that although all the assassinations, abductions, disappearances, and explosions were automatically blamed by all of them on left-wing terrorism, the left suddenly found that it was no longer being persecuted, and it crept warily back out of the woodwork.

The Communists were once more free to distribute newssheets condemning each other's organizations and calling for unity, and anarchists once more were free to paint slogans on bridges and police stations; the Trotskyists were once more free to accuse the Communists of Stalinism; the Maoists once more came out to preach perpetual revolution and collect centavos in aid of the Shining Path guerillas in Peru. All of them talked enthusiastically as if the revolution were already achieved, argued with one another about ideological purity, and secretly missed the days when they had been forced to operate in elaborate secrecy, use passwords and secret drops and secret meeting places in rat-infested cellars. The relenting pace of persecution made them feel less important, and insulted their pride. The Maoists and the anarchists therefore began to leave bombs by military targets, not knowing that unofficially they would never receive any credit for it. If they had known this, it is doubtful that they would have bothered to leave any more of them, for nothing irks a revolutionary more than being dismissed as an irrelevance and as not deserving of notoriety.

The campaign between the military gained in momentum and viciousness. Regular officers began to disappear from their homes in the trunks of Ford Falcons, and their bodies appeared at graveyards and were buried as "*Non Nombre*." Bodies were hurled from airplanes into the jungle until the Anuesha, Jibaros, and Bracamoros Indians began to accept into their mythology the idea that the wings of angels can actually fall off, causing them to crash to the ground. The navy found a current that did not wash bodies onto the beaches of holiday resorts, and the sharks became used to the sound of the engines of the launches that brought them their dinner and were milling around awaiting their arrival. The surface of the sea briefly turned bright red and foamed and heaved with the furious thrashing of the sharks as they fought for morsels. Those unfortunates still conscious attempted to swim away and were dragged down suddenly like fishing floats, only to bob to the surface again, to be dragged down once more. The army attempted a similar method of disposal in a large tank of piranhas and discovered that they did not quite live up to their voracious reputation, leaving the soldiers the unpleasant task of having to fish out the partly stripped bodies. That particular experiment was discontinued, and someone had the idea of trying to dump the pirhanas in Admiral Fleta's swimming pool. The latter only had the pool for the purpose of status, and no one ever swam in it, so that the first he knew of it was when he was walking around his very large estate and saw the starved fish floating dead on the surface. He took it as a practical joke in poor taste and never realized that it had been a particularly fatuous attempt on his life; just as hopeless, in fact, as the famous CIA plot to stage a Second Coming of Christ in Cuba so as to topple the atheist Castro.

Nobody can be quite sure of how many lives were lost in this clandestine internecine struggle because all records were destroyed before the scandal could be investigated. A scandal was what it became because the officers were the progeny of those kinds of families that are in a position to make a fuss when their sons disappear. Some of the protesting families began to disappear as well, and the scandal grew rapidly to epic proportions until even the newspapers began to print little snippets about it. The armed forces themselves, and the president also, blamed it all on the terrorists, but it was already common knowledge that only the military, the State Telephone Company, and the State Oil Company had sufficient Ford Falcons to abduct people on such a scale. When terrorists abducted people, it was usually in battered old cars from the 1950s, which were all they could afford.

The president ordered the chiefs of staff to put an end to the terror, without actually stating that he knew they were responsible for it, but he was secretly relieved when it abated not a jot. The military grant was particularly calculated on a per capita basis, and the reduction in personnel was good for his anti-inflationary policies. He was also pleased at the reduction in potential coup participators.

The dirty war began to extend down through noncommissioned officers, and then to ordinary regulars, and finally to conscripts. The Ministry of Defense began to receive requests from people wishing to buy themselves out, and the president heard that they were all being refused. He happened to mention during a TV interview that according to common law, all military personnel were entitled to appeal directly to the head of state in matters of military justice, and he signed the subsequent flood of buy-out applications without even reading them.

Those who could not afford to buy themselves out began to desert back to their towns and villages, and much energy was wasted in trying to track them down. The depletion in the Force de Frappe over the period of one year was extremely dramatic, both in terms of equipment and personnel, and the president was highly pleased. The only blot on the horizon was that Sanchis, Ramírez, and Fleta were still intact and plotting, as the tapes continued to reveal, and moreover, they seemed to be hinting that the terror was to be wound down. He saw that on the transcript Ramírez was recorded as having said, "I think it's high time we crushed this terrorism. Don't you agree that we should all take definite steps?" And the other two were recorded as having made "affirmatory grunts." He read that there was still no definite date for the coup and still no clear leader.

With a light heart the president called in on his wife's gaudy little chamber. She pouted as he came in and reached out her arms.

"Daddykins has called to play with his naughty little schoolgirl," announced His Excellency.

36

¡De Tu Casa a la Agena, Sal con la Barrigada Llena!

There was once a painter who traveled into the cordillera in order to paint an invisible picture of Christ. When he finished, the local Indians scrambled up the rocks to examine it and found that it was, in fact, a picture of Viracocha. A Chinaman passing by went up to see what it was that was causing such excitement and found to his surprise that on the rock was a picture of the Buddha. The painter stuck to his assertion that it was Christ who was invisibly portrayed, and a loud and rancorous argument developed. In the midst of the altercation one of the Indians noticed that the portrait had erased itself.

The truth is that the mountains are a place where you can find whatever you want just by looking, as long as you remember that they do not suffer fools gladly and particularly dislike those with preconceived ideas.

"I always meant to ask you," said Pedro, "why you did not stay in the mountains, where you know how to live, but moved to the jungle where you had to learn everything from the beginning."

"It was because," replied Aurelio, "living in the mountains which were not my home would have made me homesick. In the jungle I am more free of memories."

"Even so," said Pedro, "would you guide us and teach us how to live before you return home?"

"I have to do as you ask; I had already decided it, or you all would be dead in a few days. But I must tell Carmen. There is a tunday up here, and I will send her a message."

The convoy of people and animals was climbing up the end of the escarpment whence they had witnessed the flood and was ascending toward a short plateau, a puna, which divided at the end into two valleys. Aurelio went ahead and found the huge hollow log set on cairns, with holes bored in it by fire. He took the club that was left inside it and began to beat the log so that it resounded and boomed. At one end he could make high notes, and in the middle, deep ones. By varying the rhythm and pitch, he was able to add emphasis and connotation to the simple code and tell Carmen that he would be gone a long time, doing something very important. He waited until he saw the smoke from the damp leaves that Carmen burned to tell him that she had heard, and then he put the club back into the body of the tunday and rejoined the multitude.

"Have you noticed," said Gloria, "that these cats keep getting bigger?"

"I cannot pick them up anymore," replied Constanza, "but they still play like kittens."

Father García, who was walking with them, made no observations on the subject because he was just beginning to elaborate in his head a new theology that was becoming more and more interesting and convincing with every foot of altitude and also more heretical.

The *guerrilleros* were walking with the ease and economy of practice, but the villagers were already breathless and aching in the calves and thighs. The animals were merely plodding in a herbivorous dream, snatching mouthfuls of vegetation as they passed it and looking as though they had grown mobile lopsided whiskers of grass and flowers.

When they arrived at the lower slopes of the mountains, it was realized that no one had a very clear idea of where they were going or what they were going to do when they got there. Under the circumstances one choice seemed as good as another, and so when Sergio told Pedro and Hectoro that in a dream Federico had told him that they should find the source of the flood, they shrugged their shoulders and agreed, except that Aurelio said there would be no food along the flood valleys because it would all have been swept away.

"We will walk every day," said Sergio, "and with luck Federico will tell me every night where we are to go on the next day."

"With respect," said Aurelio, "Federico is not an Indian. In the mountains Indians travel only in straight lines, no matter what is in the way. In this manner we never get lost. Tell Federico to take us in straight lines and to admit when he is lost."

"He is a spirit," rejoined Sergio indignantly. "Spirits do not get lost."

"You do not know spirits then," said Aurelio. "They know little more than they did in life and have the same faults, including the ability to get lost."

Once on the puna the people stopped to gather alfalfa and ichu for the animals and loaded it in bundles on the backs of the already burdened beasts, because there is one golden rule of the mountains: "From your house to that of another, always go with your belly full!" The Indians themselves could ignore this rule because they could keep going for days on coca, which miraculously reduces hunger and thirst and gives energy but which frequently kills them at an early age as their bodies consume themselves.

While the others gathered fodder, Pedro and Misael went off together up the slopes to stalk a small flock of vicuñas that was browsing above. Circling, the two men climbed above the animals and then crept down out of sight and downwind. At close range they managed to shoot four of them as they ran, and the flock took off at high speed across the rocks. As the men descended to call for helpers to bring the bodies down, Misael said, "How are we to feed two thousand on four vicuñas?"

"We cannot," replied Pedro. "But we have plenty of food in the packs. Those who cannot hunt can live on plants for the time being."

Down on the puna the animals were skinned and dismembered, and Pedro and Misael gave away what they could not carry themselves. Aurelio took the skins because he knew how to make the warmest garments and boas out of them, which would be needed before long if they were to take a *portachuelo* above the snow line.

At the end of the plateau the travelers took the right-hand *quebrada* and had to scramble over the alluvial llochlia that always seems to accumulate at the bottom entrance of any valley or ravine and that consists of scattered piles of rocks and animal bones.

All about them they saw the remains of the past life that had once made these mountains a veritable ants' nest of activity. On the slopes were the *andenes*, the terraces built up on walls of stones that once fed the old civilization. On the valley floor were the fallen remnants of small houses built of *tapiales*, a mud version of Don Emmanuel's bricks, made in a lattice of planks. The people could see by the outlines of walls that these were places where farmers once lived on their *chácaras* and herded llamas and alpacas for wool and meat, and where now there were only one or two *tambos*, travelers' huts roughly constructed of bundles of maguey fiber bound together.

As their pathway rose ever upward, the plants changed. Already there was nothing growing here that would have been recognized in the emerald lushness of the jungle or on the expanse of the Mula Basin. Up here there were long grasses, acacia, guinual and quishua trees, and delicate twisted shrubs with white flowers and silver-downed leaves that gave off a delicious aroma when burned. Here and there, in places sheltered from the wind but not from the sun, stood fire brushes, some of them forty feet high, their scarlet flowers flaming brilliantly in exuberant drapes of blossom, and at five thousand feet there were fragrant strands of cedar, constituting the little woods that the Indians call *jaguey*. High above there wheeled black vultures that the people thought were condors (until they saw a real one), and there were white alcamarini birds among the rocks on the sides of the slopes.

To the people these unaccustomed sights, these strange plants, and the little vizcacha squirrels that ran chittering away from them, seemed to be miracles from another creation. And how cold was the water of the streams, so that when you drank it, you developed a headache instantaneously and rubbed your temples, saying "Ay, ay, ay!" with the pain and making up your mind not to use it for washing your intimate parts until it was warmed a little.

They wondered at the small wild cattle that roamed free in the valley, so different from the huge *ceibus* that they had experienced hitherto and that were raising a constant lowing as though passing messages to one another. Sometimes one of them slipped on the rocky paths or when crossing a river, and then the people would have to reset its scattered or sodden load and bully it into rejoining the *recua* so that it could be tied back into the train. All day there were shouts of "*Ay, mula!*" "*Vamos, bribón!*" and the long, drawn-out "*Tscha-a-a-ah!*" to keep the beasts moving. For a little while a small wild bull followed the train, and those at the back nicknamed it Nicolito and tried to persuade it to approach nearer; but it was wary and turned away, standing on the top of a knoll to watch them go, so that afterward they missed it with the same feeling that you feel when you say farewell to someone who under better circumstances could have been a friend.

The cats, which were still growing bigger all the time, gamboled among the rocks, ambushing one another and rolling down inclines as they wrestled. Some of them were padding seriously beside the people they had adopted, and others were trying to creep up on the wild goats and birds that were too wily to be caught. The cats hated to wet their feet in the streams and rivers and were especially afraid of the *pongos,* the white-water rapids; they would sit growling at the water while everyone passed over and then pace anxiously along the bank as they receded into the distance. When at last the anxiety of losing their people grew too much, they would gingerly cross, raising their paws to shake off the freezing water at every step and growling in their throats.

The biblical procession passed through a small settlement of *chozas,* where the people hid from behind their doorways and peeped out, confused and alarmed. *"Shami,"* said Aurelio to one of them, in Quechua, "come here." Hearing his own tongue, the man cautiously came out, and Aurelio exchanged greetings with him and asked where one might camp the night. The man, whose throat was hideously bloated from *coto*—a deficiency of iodine—seemed to be retarded, and Aurelio obtained little sense from him; but he waved vaguely up the valley and said, "Beyond the *campiña."*

They passed through the *campiña,* where the *cholos* were growing potatoes, barley, and alfalfa in small plots and where sheep were grazing on the slopes above, and found themselves in a lunar world of volcanic tufa and ash, which swirled and choked them every time there was a gust of wind, ever stronger and colder as they ascended.

Already the snowcaps topped the mountains around them, and riding the updrafts, the condor vultures spread their enormous wings and circled at mighty altitudes in the hope of carrion below. Somewhere from the heights above a shepherd was playing music; it was the haunting, wistful music of the Inca people, who make the *quena* flute from the great hollow thigh bones of the condor and play yavari by blowing it inside the olla, the earthenware pot that causes the notes to echo and linger with pain, with longing, and with unbounded nostalgia.

Dolores's little girl, Raimunda, was suddenly stung painfully by a mountain scorpion, the ubiquitous *alacrán,* and her foot swelled up while she screamed and howled with both surprise and anguish. Dolores made the child hold her foot in the icy stream, and then Sergio took her on his back, where she clung, still crying, with her arms around his neck, and her foot throbbing and pulsing as though it contained an exploding sun.

They journeyed past some of the old mining works that had been producing gold, silver, quicksilver, and lead long before the conquistadores ever arrived with their rapacious souls of broken glass and chipped flint to enslave the miners after learning from them all their secrets, paying for it with the miners' bones. Those who looked and knew what to see could still find the beautiful Inca pots that used to be buried with the dead and are consequently known as *huacas.* They were made of a pair joined together, carefully ornamented with intricate, grotesque, and skillful moldings. They could be made in the form of animals, or ducks, and given acoustic properties so that when you poured water from one to another, the sound would imitate the animals, and if there were two ducks, they would make the sound of ducks fighting, so that other ducks would become alarmed and join in the clamor. The art of making these whimsical and enchanting pots is lost, and now they are found only in graves and as shards among the ruins of that arcane civilization.

One might also find by the streams long-discarded *porongos,* the gold pans over which people would squat, tirelessly sifting the silt until only the bright specks of gold remained. Where there were lodes, *farallones,* one could still see the narrow entrances to mines, or the places where giant vertical seams had been ripped from the mountain sides, and perhaps there would be the ruins of the great kimbaletes, huge dinosaurial machines of granite where a rocking stone would crush the ore with water and quicksilver. Everywhere there lay great piles of discarded ore awaiting the greedy hands of some new conquistador.

In the streams one might still find the ingenious runoffs and channels of the gold farmers, who knew how to extract by the force of their own motion the flakes of gold from the sediment, and perhaps nearby there would be the pieces of the clay *guayra* ovens for refining, which worked without bellows because their shape caught the wind.

But it was long since that the adventurers had gone, now that rich men made money by speculating with money and not having to do real work. It was long since that one had heard the eager question in Quechua "*¿Ori cancha?*" or risked the *desconfianza* of the suspicious Indians and the fatal onslaughts of armed *ladrones* who lived by parasitism on those who worked and slunk away to kill each other over their gains. Nowadays nobody arrived with a mule and a pick axe to stake his *pertenencia* and work his body to ruin either to die of exhaustion or to go home rich. Nowadays people desecrated ancient graves and left herbs under their heads at night so that they would dream where the gold was buried, and there were no more mad adventurers whose greed was jeweled with hardship and heroism.

When that evening the multitude made their encampment, Aurelio showed people how to catch freshwater prawns by damming the stream with stakes driven into the bed, through which willow twigs were wound. A hole was left in the middle and a basket held up against it so that the water flowed through, leaving the crustaceans in the bottom, to be patiently shelled and avariciously eaten.

The animals were hobbled and given the fodder that they had carried on their backs, and the people heated food over little fires, wishing that they had tents and ponchos. Some of them amused themselves by burning patterns in their gourds with heated knives, and others told stories or sang. Many were already beginning to shake and sweat and shiver with *terciana*, the mountain fever as inevitable as it is inexplicable; it can lay a man out such that he feels he is about to die, but then an hour later he feels better than ever before and walks with a new sprightliness, only to find himself cast down again so that he never felt so *raquítico* in all his life.

As the fires were lit and the lowering sun blazed crimson and scarlet off the snows of the peaks, the skies turned turquoise before they darkened. The cats, inveterately nocturnal, left to hunt, and when the stars were scintillating like diamonds in the cobalt and indigo cushion of the night they returned, bringing cui and ducks, vizcachas, and wild goats for the people to eat.

"They are quite something, these gatos," people said, and ate with one arm around the animals, caressing their soft ears and cheeks. In the morning the cats would be the size of pumas, but that night they huddled together for warmth, cat and human alike, and the valley echoed gently with the sibilant reverberations of purring.

37
Nemesis:
General Fuerte Calls In On the Escuadrón de la Muerte

General Ramírez had recently resumed his adolescent habit of biting his nails. He had just torn a thumbnail off with his teeth and had caused the root of the nail to bleed on one side. He was enjoying chewing the nail at the same time as comforting the wound by tucking his thumb under his fingers.

He was a worried man. He had lost a staggering amount of men and equipment in the internecine dirty war and had begun to feel a steady diminution in his power and influence. He felt that even the president did not take him seriously anymore, and now there was this business with General Fuerte to worry about, as well as there being still no decision on who would be president after the coup.

If Asado had consulted him, Ramírez would have told him to "disappear" General Fuerte, but Asado, acting without orders, had taken the general straight to the hospital. Every day that the general remained alive would make it harder to get rid of him; but something had to be done all the same, because he was well known to be inflexibly fair and principled, and if he were ever let out, he would undoubtedly become more than an embarrassment. Ramírez knew very well that Fuerte commanded a huge loyalty in his own forces, which would, if push came to shove, obey him rather than the high command. Ramírez had arranged for General Fuerte to be released in a week and then obliterated in a car crash, but now there was the news that Fuerte had somehow escaped from the Villa Maravillosa, and no one knew where he had gone. He had telegraphed Valledupar, but it had said that no, the general had not returned from leave yet, and yes, it would let him know when he returned.

General Fuerte took only two days to reach the capital from Valledupar and on the first evening's encampment had briefed the officers in these words:

"Gentlemen, we have before us an important mission for which speed and efficiency are of the essence and where surprise will be the key element. It has come to the attention of the highest authorities that certain renegade officers acting without orders have set up a concentration, torture, and extermination camp in the old officers' wing of the Army School of Electrical and Mechanical Engineering. The establishment contains both civilian and military of all services who are being tortured to death in a manner which you will unfortunately see for yourselves. Our orders are simply to arrest the renegade officers and bring out the prisoners. Fortunately we can expect little or no armed resistance, but no one should hesitate to shoot to kill if that occurs.

"No special tactics will be required; we will simply walk into the place and overwhelm them with numbers. I shall lead the men in, and your job will be to ascertain as rapidly as possible the layout of the place, neutralize all opposition with the minimum of bloodshed, and commence evacuation.

"Gentlemen, you have been chosen for this mission because you are considered the best, most reliable, and most honorable troops in the country. The importance of this mission should be underlined for you by the fact that it is being led by a general and not by a comandante or a lieutenant colonel.

"Gentlemen, I apologize for lack of details in the plan. Unfortunately the plan of the building has not been obtainable, but I want Number One Platoon to be responsible for guarding the renegades under close arrest. Number Two Platoon should concern itself with bringing out those prisoners who are unable to move on their own and laying them as carefully as possible in the empty trucks. Number Three Platoon should gather together those who can still walk and prepare them for the journey back to Valledupar, by which I mean that they should be washed, clothed, and fed, using what can be found on the premises. The prisoners will be terrified and disoriented, and you must ensure that they are treated gently, courteously, and calmly. Number Four Platoon will take responsibility for preventing the entry at the gate of anyone who is not driving a Ford Falcon. These latter should be allowed in and then arrested, with force if necessary. Needless to say, the platoon should also ensure that nobody leaves.

"Gentlemen, you may dismiss to brief your platoons. Tell your men that the honor of the national army is at stake and that I have every confidence in the Portachuelo Guards."

The following evening the convoy halted in the wilderness of the Incarama Park and encamped in the gloomy ruins of El Escorial, next to the Temple of Viracocha. The general imparted to the officers revisions and improvements to his plans and then went out to smoke a *puro* under the stars. Smoking *puros* was a habit he had picked up among the *guerrilleros,* and he began to cast his mind back over the months he had spent with them. He remembered with half a smile his fervent arguments with Father García and thought of something he should have said to him. He pictured himself saying, "There is nothing at all wrong with our laws and institutions and our constitution, which are all democratic and enlightened. What is wrong is that they are enforced by people who do not consider themselves bound by them." The general kicked a stone into a shrub and watched bats the size of hawks wheeling and veering among the ruins. He laughed to himself. *I have become a kind of guerrilla myself. I have soldiers who are not strictly under my command. I am acting without the permission of General Ramírez.* He pictured his commander-in-chief in his imagination and thought, *I never esteemed that man anyway. He is not a soldier; he is a politician. I wonder if Remedios would have praised what I am doing. Or would she resent me for stealing her thunder?* He returned to his bedroll and lay turning over his plans in his head until he fell asleep to dream of heliconius butterflies.

At eleven o'clock the following morning the convoy of trucks stopped outside the gates of the ex-officers' wing of the Army School of Electrical and Mechanical Engineering. Number Four Platoon poured out of the first vehicle and overpowered the two astonished guards at the sentry box. The gates were opened, and the convoy rolled into the courtyard and halted. As the Portachuelo Guards ran into the building, the trucks, one by one, did three-point turns, until all of them were facing the gates, ready to go.

As predicted, there was no resistance. The torturers were working in shirtsleeves when the platoon commanders burst in on them with their men, disarmed them, and made them lie face down on the floor. Asado, terrified and sweating, was made to hand over all the keys and made to accompany a sergeant to unlock every door and cupboard in the wing.

The guards were shocked and nauseated by what they found. The stench of burned flesh, of feces, of sweat, urine, and fear made it almost insupportable to be in there at all, and everywhere three were fetid pools of putrefying blood and excrement. Some of the soldiers put their rifle butts through the bars of the cell windows and smashed the glass to let in some fresh air, and none of them knew what to do with the prisoners, who, naked and skeletal, huddled apathetically against the walls and watched them vacantly with the eyes of those already dead. Some of them were indeed already dead; General Fuerte himself was able to identify the bodies of Regina Olsen and the mad capitan in a room full of entangled corpses awaiting disposal. "We cannot do much for them," said the general. "Leave them."

The prisoners were pitifully wounded; most of the men had been crudely castrated, so that their scrota hung in rotting tatters. All of them were covered in a patchwork of bruises, burns, whiplashes. Some of them had broken teeth and missing eyes and ears, and others had missing fingers and toes. The soldiers found them easy to lead, even though they thought they were being led to more torture. "I don't know anything," they said as the orderlies washed them gently in the baths, "I don't know anything."

The corporal from Number Three Platoon found a room with "War Chest" on the door which was filled to the ceiling with clothes, and he and four men brought armfuls of them to the changing rooms of the baths while the others of the platoon dressed the passive prisoners in whatever they could find from the heap that roughly fitted.

At the gate the soldiers of Number Four Platoon arrested El Verdugo, who was returning from the shops, and the soldiers of Number Two Platoon carried out the nonwalking prisoners to the trucks. These prisoners thought they were being carried off for disposal, and those who could still weep or call out did so.

From the electrical wing of the school two instructors watched the scene at a window. "I wonder what is going on now," said one.

"Don't ask," replied the other. "Don't even think about it."

General Fuerte entered the conference room where the torturers were being held. All in all there were fifteen men, and the general recognized Asado, who also recognized him.

"General!" exclaimed Asado, and he sprang to his feet and saluted.

"I remember you," said the general. "You won the Medal of Honor at the Officer Training College."

The general turned to a corporal. "Take two men and ensure that every telephone is disconnected. After that, delegate six men to carry out all the filing cabinets to the trucks." He turned back to Asado. "Sit down, man. I do not return salutes to barbarians."

The general left the company comandante in charge and departed in three trucks loaded with the wounded. He drove to the Hospital for Sick Soldiers, having discovered that all the civilian hospitals were closed, and ordered the medics who were hanging around to get the patients off the trucks. He went to the reception desk and spoke to a young woman of the Army Medical Regiment. She gave him a pile of forms. He picked one up and found that it was three pages long. "You must fill in one for every patient," she told him. The general dropped the pile of paper heavily on to her desk. "No," he said. "You can fill them in or ignore them as you please. I have too many patients for all that."

"I must insist," replied the young woman. "How many do you have?"

"About sixty," he said, and then added, "And you are in no position to insist." He tapped the insignia on the shoulder of his combat jacket. "Do you know what that means?"

The girl looked at it. "It means you are an officer."

"It means I am a general!" he said fiercely. "And it means that if you or your hospital do not set yourselves in motion immediately, I will bring in my guardsmen and have you all arrested. Now, move!"

The intimated girl rang through to the emergency room, and soon the hospital was in a flurry of activity. The girl stood beside the general with an appalled and wondering expression on her face as she surveyed the human wreckage that was going by on the stretchers. "Who were they?" she asked, speaking as if they were already dead.

"Terrorist victims," said the general.

"I am sorry I did not recognize your insignia," said the girl. "I have never seen a general in combat gear before."

The general returned to the Army School of Electrical and Mechanical Engineering, and soon the convoy was heading back to Valledupar, having locked up the gates of the school.

That evening General Ramírez tried to telephone Asado and found the line dead. He sent around a motorcycle courier, who reported that the place was locked up and unguarded. Ramírez sent around a small body of pyragues, who reported that it was as deserted as the *Marie Celeste*, "Except for some dead bodies." Ramírez felt more than ever that his power was slipping away, and he tore the nail off his forefinger and chewed it meditatively while the cuticle bled.

Despite the attentions of the medical orderlies, three of the walking wounded died on the bumpy and prolonged journey, from the effects of internal bleeding. The rest of them Fuerte left at the Valledupar Military Hospital with strict instructions that their admission was to be kept confidential "on the highest authority." He devoted a week to interviewing the torturers and going through the information in the filing cabinets. The girls in the office were delighted to see him, until they realized how much work they now had to do. They were ordered to photostat twice every paper in the cabinets and address one copy to the address of each "next of kin" as entered on the forms. They were to bundle the second copies in alphabetical order and address each parcel to the New York *Herald*. The originals General Fuerte put into a bank vault in Asunción.

He flew to Mérida and mailed his bundles and his copies for relatives and then flew back to Valledupar to organize the secret but legal court-martial of all the torturers, with himself and the brigadier presiding. To save time and energy, he decided to try them all at once, since the evidence was the same for all of them, the witnesses were the same, the excuses were the same, and the sentence was to be the same.

Fuerte and the brigadier brought in one witness after another from those who were in the Valledupar Military Hospital. The general quoted long passages he had copied from the files.

He had to remind the commandante frequently of his obligation to defend the prisoners to the best of his ability, but the latter found the task repulsive, and repeated what the prisoners had already repeated many times, "They were acting under orders." The general found out very quickly what he already knew, that the orders came from General Ramírez.

Asado said, "But it can never be proved. The service was unofficial."

The general tapped his pen on the table. "It is very easily proved," he said. "You did not destroy all his orders as instructed. I have them handwritten by him, as left by you in your filing cabinets."

"Then you know, sir, that it was not our fault. We did our duty according to our orders."

After several days of the hearing, the general and the brigadier decided to call an end to what had become a tedious charade. They called in the fifteen torturers for sentence. It was the brigadier who spoke.

"During the Nuremberg Trials it became established as a principle of international law that 'acting under orders' is not an excuse for the kinds of atrocities you have daily committed under your own admission and according to the sworn testimony of witnesses. This court finds you guilty on all charges: of murder, false imprisonment, illegal abduction, assault, malicious wounding, theft, burglary, breaking and entering, rape, false arrest, obeying illegal orders and so on and so on. General Fuerte will now pass sentence."

General Fuerte put down his pen and looked at the torturers solemnly. "The standard sentence for crimes of this kind is, according to the Military Penal Code, that you should be put to death by firing squad."

The torturers found their knees beginning to shake and their lips to quiver. Asado felt panic arise in his bowels, and he could scarcely restrain himself from defecating.

"However," continued the general, "I am going to use against you methods similar to those that you have used against others."

The general paused again and then continued. "Your methods remind me of medieval times, and therefore, I will pass a medieval sentence to fit your crimes. No doubt you have heard of trial by ordeal; people used to be forced to plunge their hands into boiling water or to walk across burning coals. I sentence you to trial by ordeal."

When the men were led out, the brigadier turned to the general. "What do we do about Ramírez?"

"Nothing yet," said the general. "I have released all the papers to the foreign press. No doubt he will resign and then be arrested and tried legally. If that does not happen, we will have to arrest him ourselves and try him by court-martial."

"An internal coup?"

"Exactly."

The general returned to his quarters and fed his cat, which in an astonishingly small amount of time had grown to the size of a puma. He went to the stable and fed María with cane leaves, and then he took the cat for a walk with Papagato and the other animals.

That evening the torturers were flown several hundred miles over the jungle and thrown out of the airplane. They floated down on their parachutes, to become entangled in the trees of the territory of the Chuncho tribe, a Neolithic people who still practiced six-month trial marriages and cannibalism.

38
Days of Wonders, Days of Debilitation

Dawn found the wanderers shivering with cold and with fevers. They huddled despondently around their little fires, chewing guava jelly and blocks of *panela* to get themselves going and complaining of headaches. The air was so cold and so pure that it hurt to draw breath, but most of the plains folk had never before seen the vapor of their breath condense, so they took deep breaths and puffed their cheeks to watch themselves create fog, exclaiming, "Whooba!' and laughing at the other people enveloped in their own mist. The cattle, too, had never seen it before and jumped nervously at every exhalation, while the cats tried to play with it, sitting back on their haunches and flailing with their paws. There was also a low mist on the ground up to the height of their knees, so that everybody seemed to be walking on a cloud, like the dark shadows of angels or lost spirits awaiting at the gates of life. When the sun rose rapidly below them at the eastern end of the valley, people gaped, for never before had they been so high above the sun; the mist about their feet began to rise up to their thighs and then to their waists, so that the children could not see and the adults were cut in half. When the mist reached their heads, everyone who was standing sat down to be able to see anything at all, and it was as if they had descended into a twilight, for the sky had disappeared and it had grown half dark.

Suddenly the mist vanished, and the day lightened. As the sun began to thaw their bones, the people shivered again, as they had on waking, and had to goad themselves into activity. They brewed coffee, wrapped their possessions into their packs, filled their canteens and their gourds at the stream, and began to tie the animals back into their train. The horses and mules seemed to be perfectly fit, but the great *ceibu* cattle were obviously suffering from their night in the unaccustomed cold; their eyes were rheumy, their chests rattled, and their nostrils were dripping. Don Emmanuel inspected them with concern, for most of them were his, and he was sentimental about them. He resolved that somehow he would have to protect them at night against the frost, or many of them would die, especially since the trek would take away their fat.

Don Emmanuel had been very surprised when he had heard that Doña Constanza was with the guerrillas, and he was even more surprised upon conversing with her to find that she had discarded her oligarchic manners, had become the lover of a campesino, and now found his ribaldry amusing and a pretext for badinage. The first thing she had said upon seeing him was, "*¡Hola, cabrón!* And how are your dingleberries? Do they still adorn your nether parts?"

"Indeed, they do," he replied. "I am seeking volunteers to pluck them off."

"Then," said Constanza, "you will find here many of your old friends from whorehouses to oblige you."

"I see," said Don Emmanuel, "that you have found a fine young man to remove yours."

"Your eyes do not deceive you, Don Emmanuel, though unlike your fine self, I wash often enough to prevent them from accumulating."

In the whole gathering there were only two people who felt at sea with strangers, Antoine and Françoise Le Moing, who really knew only Farides, who had been their cook. In the changed circumstances of the exodus it somehow did not seem appropriate to have servants, and so they stuck with Profesor Luis and Farides, doing their half of the work in order to avoid isolation. Profesor Luis found the French couple well educated and interesting, so he and Farides devoted much conversational time to improving the others' Spanish and knowledge of local history.

They had ascended through two *quebradas* when Pedro spotted a cave up on the right, to the north, and he and Aurelio went up to see it, because Aurelio said he had a notion of what it was. When they entered, it was almost immediately dark, so Pedro left to fetch his lamp.

When it was lit, they penetrated far into the shadows by the glimmering of the yellow light and saw that there were niches cut regularly into the walls and that out of the rock were carved fish, serpents, symbols of the sun and moon, jaguars, and grimacing guardians. Pedro held up the light to a niche and drew back, startled. He held it up to another niche and gestured to Aurelio to look.

They were in a catacomb. In fetal positions the ancient mummies, their skin stretched angularly over their bones, their lips shrunk back from their teeth, their hair still sticking up in ragged tufts from their dusty scalps, sat in a parody of life, their jaws sagging open in eternal, frozen surprise. There were spiders and blind insects living among them, and in one of the niches an eyeless silver-white snake uncoiled from the neck and disappeared in alarm into the belly of its home, where it hissed in the hope of peace.

"We should not tell the others," said Aurelio. "This is a sacred place, and besides, they would think it a bad omen."

"I think it a good omen," said Pedro. "That one can be dead for so long and rest undisturbed. Do you think there is gold here?"

"If there is," said Aurelio reprovingly, "it is not ours, and it is no use to us. Leave them."

"I have never seen so many dead," remarked Pedro as they scrambled down the loose shale.

"Of course you have," said Aurelio. "At the battle in Chiriguaná."

"Maybe one day those boys will be found," said Pedro, "and people will say, 'I have never seen so many dead,' and wonder why they are there."

"There will be bullets among the shattered bones," said Aurelio. "It will be very clear."

"But no one will ever hear the true history of it," said Pedro.

"We must ask Profesor Luis to write it," replied Aurelio, "and then bury the paper in a box with the bodies."

They rejoined the plodding column and rose over a low ridge onto one of the long, high plateaus that are known as *pajonales*, which surprise mountain travelers by their unnatural flatness and the length of their grasses. It was decided that the animals should be allowed to feed so that the people could gather fodder and rest.

They were not quite near to the snow line, at the exact altitude where most people suddenly feel very ill with *soroche*. Only Aurelio and Don Emmanuel out of all the two thousand had been to this height before, and they had already seen the signs of sickness.

"We should stay here at least three days, maybe more," said Don Emmanuel, "or we will have a lot of trouble."

Aurelio agreed, so he and Don Emmanuel went and talked to groups of people to tell them about the *soroche* and that they had to stop in order to minimize it.

Almost everybody already had terrible headaches, and some were suffering from diarrhea and vomiting. It was a superhuman feat to lift one foot and place it in front of another, and it was necessary to stop every fifteen paces to draw deep breaths. An insuperable fatigue, irritability, and apathy had descended on animal and human alike, and even the cats were too disgruntled to stalk one another in the grass.

Don Emmanuel explained to the people. "You will all be ill for a while because there is less air up here to breathe. If you think you are dying, do not be deceived; you will soon feel better. Each of you must find your own way to deal with it. Some people eat a great deal and drink a lot of alcohol, but for others this only makes the *soroche* even worse, so they have to eat and drink very little. Again, some people should get used to it by keeping busy, and others should lie in the dark and do nothing. My advice is to eat a lot of *panela*, chew coca if you have it, and fuck as much as you can. You may have already noticed that the mountains make your loins itch worse than a laundry girl in Iquitos!"

Most people felt too bad even to smile, but Farides looked coyly at Profesor Luis and smiled, and Gonzago and Constanza had already been following this advice and were feeling very good. Felicidad, who had not known chastity since early puberty, had never felt less like making purple earthquakes in her whole life. She lay in a defeated heap, her temples pounding, her breath rasping in her throat, with a *mochila* over her eyes to block out the light, groaning. The animals, beyond reach of advice, lay in the grasses chewing wearily, feeling as bad as the people they accompanied but suffering more stoically, for it is a truth that if you have no words with which to express anguish, your anguish will be proportionately diminished.

Misael felt his ankle begin to hurt and announced that it was going to rain. Those who knew him and the infallibility of his ankle moved far off onto the slopes and rigged up rough shelters between the rocks. The rest looked up at the brilliant clear skies and saw that there was not even a cloud upon the peaks; they laughed skeptically and stayed on the *pajonal*, where in the middle of the night they found themselves drenched suddenly with paralyzingly icy rain and lying in a rapidly mobilizing bog. Cursing and bemoaning their misfortune, they gathered their sodden possessions and squelched their way to the slopes, while the cats, which in the morning would be the size of jaguars, prowled among the mountainsides looking for caves, where they licked the freezing water from their hides and lay together in luxurious tangled heaps for warmth and company.

Morning brought little comfort to the miserable people huddled together, wet through, feverish with *terciana* and *soroche*. For the first time they were demoralized and filled with dismay, regret, and hopelessness; they missed desperately the dusty plain that formerly they had cursed as too hot and humid; they were beginning to feel the terror of their unknown destination and the life of exile that awaited them. Few of them had slept, and not one of them liked the rain to be freezing and numbing when they had remembered it as warm, welcome, friendly, and sensuous.

With the first gray light of the day there was a new miracle, which would have caused much wonder if it had not caused more misery; for a cloud came rolling and churning toward them along the *pajonal*, billowing and swirling, and at the same time a cloud descended rapidly from the sky so that they were enclosed in a conspiracy of wet mist that seemed to be indulging in some gratuitous act of personal malice. It was impossible to see beyond the length of one's own arm, and people fell over boulders as they called to one another or tried to gather together their possessions in order to try futilely to dry them. Moreover, the cats were nowhere to be found, and since the people had become accustomed to their presence as a good omen and a sign of supernatural favor, now that they had vanished it seemed that good fortune had vanished also. It was not until bitter blasts of wind had made the people yet more wretched but had blown away the sea of cloud that the cats were seen emerging from caves and crannies to stretch and yawn in the weak sunlight and set about washing themselves. They had not only grown to the size of jaguars, but now, whereas before there had been huge tabbies, huge blue-and-white fluffy cats, and huge black-and-white cats, and deaf white cats with odd-colored eyes, there were only jaguars, most of them silky black but some with tawny coats and dark rosettes. For the first time some of the people were afraid of them, for the jaguar is the most ferocious of the American cats; but when they played as usual, brought guanaco for the people to eat, it was found that they could still purr when pleased, and so it was as if the supernatural favor had returned.

That day and on the following day the people stayed on the *pajonal* to acclimatize and let the animals feed. At night they joined the cats in their caves and crannies, grew warm in the musky feline heat, and recovered from their sickness lulled by purring, only to be awakened in the morning by the rough tongues of the cats, which had taken to cleaning their human companions when they had finished cleaning themselves.

"I remember when she only used to tickle my ears," said Antoine to Françoise. "Now she abrades my entire face!"

"We are her kittens," replied Françoise, shivering now that the warm cat had gone off about her business. "I just hope that she does not try to carry us around by the collar!"

When the epidemic of *soroche* and depression was over, and there was a fine, bright morning in which to travel, the voyagers packed up their animals with unspoken accord and set off westward once more. At the end of the plateau, where it divided into three *quebradas,* one ascending, one descending, and one level, they came across a ruin.

Not even Aurelio knew exactly what it had once been. All that remained were four massive walls banked into a square mound. Everyone gathered around it, wondering at its presence in this ethereal wilderness, as through its function were merely to state that there is nowhere that no one has ever been. The stones interlocked with such precision that Francesca, drawing a knife, could nowhere insert it between the stones, even though they were all kinds of polygonal and rhomboidal shapes.

"How on earth did they do this, so perfectly?" asked Don Emmanuel. "Without even iron tools to cut with?"

Aurelio smiled. "They did not use tools at all. Every stone already fitted perfectly."

"How?" demanded Pedro. "Nowhere are found stones like this."

"We had herbs to soften the stones so that they could be worked like clay," said Aurelio, "and we had herbs to harden them again into stone. That is why they are perfect and for no other reason."

"I do not believe you," said Don Emmanuel. "That is not possible."

Aurelio stamped his coca leaves in his gourd and sucked the pestle a moment, like an old Frenchman smoking a pipe. "If you believe it is impossible," he said, "then you will never find the secret, and you will always have to toil with iron in order to make it always less perfect than this." He placed his hand on the stone and patted it lovingly. "We knew the secret of the stone," he said proudly, "and you never will."

"We make good houses from *tapiales*," riposted Sergio. "What is the use of making stone like clay when clay is already clay?"

"It lasts longer," said Aurelio, "so long that it outlives those who built it."

"Then why," demanded Hectoro, "Do the *cholos* live in dirty little *chozas*?"

"Because the secret is dead. Our priests and our nobility who knew it were all killed in the name of the god who wanted our gold and silver. We lost everything to civilization. These stones are like a body that decays slowly when the spirit is flown, and those of us who are left are like the hair that still grows on the body when it is dead."

"I do not believe that either," said Don Emmanuel, who clapped the melancholy Indian on the back. "Those of you that are left are like the last seeds of a great tree that is cut down. The seeds will grow to great trees, nourished by the ash in the ground from the old tree that was burned."

"When seeds are widely scattered," replied Aurelio, "they grow up, but they do not make a forest."

"When those trees in turn scatter their seeds, the spaces are filled up," said Don Emmanuel, "and then there is a forest."

Aurelio looked more hopeful. "It is to be wished for. But all the same we will never know the secret of the stones, forest or not."

"You will have to use *tapiales*," said Sergio, and everyone laughed at his easy reasoning.

At the end of the valley the choice of three routes had to be made: to continue level into the middle branch, to descend by the leftward one, or to ascend into the snows by the rightward one.

"Federico says upward," Sergio told those at the front.

"Then he is mistaken," said Don Emmanuel. "That way goes up a glacier and ends nowhere, as one can plainly see."

The argument that followed was resolved by the decision that Don Emmanuel and Aurelio should ascend the glacier to reconnoiter the possibility of a route and to see, if they reached the top, how lay the land ahead.

The two men tied a rope between them, and Don Emmanuel took the leather *gara* from a mule, much the the puzzlement of the other. Both men agreed that the ascent was highly dangerous and quite pointless, for there could be no question of taking the cattle up there, and moreover, it was clear that the glacier led up a long ridge, possibly only very narrow, that connected two peaks and probably had a precipice on the other side.

Convinced that they were about to explore a hazardous cul-de-sac, the two men approached the glacier and clambered over the moraine of boulders that it had been lazily pushing before it over the centuries. At the base the snow was dirty and packed into ice but as they progressed upward, the shell of fresh snow sparkled brilliantly in the sunlight and caused them to narrow their eyes and wince. However, the shell was weak, and Don Emmanuel suddenly disappeared up to his armpits. He floundered forward to regain the surface, and on they struggled, sweating despite the freezing snow and often finding themselves sinking deeply. Aurelio went in front because he was the lighter, and he found this policy vindicated when his weight broke the snow bridge over a narrow crevasse. His fall dragged Don Emmanuel flat on his face, and Aurelio glimpsed bottomless blue walls of ice below him as the other hauled him out. They sidetracked to find a crossing place, but in all Aurelio fell into four crevasses, and Don Emmanuel into two as he broke through in Aurelio's wake.

It took them five exhausting hours to reach the ridge, and they sat at the top in the thin air as a nipping wind whipped up the snow about them. Aurelio had made the ascent in bare feet according to Indian tradition, and he chafed them with snow. The vista beyond the ridge was stupendous; far below them a berivered valley curled downward from the south, green and verdant, and beyond rose peaks higher and ever higher, glistening, white-capped, and awe-inspiring. They could see no passes at all beneath the snow line, and both of them knew that soon the travels of the people would have to end, for most would die in trying to cross the range before them.

They were still gazing across at the jagged roof of the world when a low rumbling sounded behind them. They turned to see that a vast avalanche was sliding, gathering momentum, from the peak on their right. It was as if the side of the mountain were breaking free and slipping with one graceful motion and a stentorian roar down onto the glacier. The two men watched with fascinated reverence as the thousands of tons of ice, snow, and rock thundered down, throwing up a mist of snow that reached even to where they stood.

Far below in the valley the thunderstruck exiles watched the mighty white torrent descend, bowling giant boulders down the glacier and making the earth rumble beneath them. They fell to their knees and crossed themselves, invoking spirits and angels, all of them believing that Aurelio and Don Emmanuel were surely dead and buried deep in the mighty cascade.

As the avalanche finished and the snow mist began to settle, some intrepid souls climbed cautiously to the edge of the glacier to see if they could spot the two men, and saw 502. Frozen solid and as fresh as the day that they had iced to death, lay Conde Pompeyo Xavier de Estremadura, 50 Spanish soldiers in full armor, and 451 Indian slaves who had met their deaths on an expedition dispatched by the conscientious Pizarro to locate the legendary Inca city of Vilcabamba. Released at last by the mountain that had claimed them, they, their mules, and their baggage were washed up by the waves of the rolling sea that had drowned them in the year 1533, on St. Cecilia's Day.

The stunned witnesses to this phenomenon of natural refrigeration were awakened from their wonder by the whoops of Don Emmanuel as he and Aurelio scudded down the slope seated in tandem on the former's leather *gara*. They dug in their heels to bring their makeshift toboggan to a halt and wandered among the ancient bodies in silent amazement. Before the body of the count, in his rich armor, Aurelio said, "He looks exactly like Hectoro."

Aurelio requested that the bodies be left where they lay and covered over with snow in order to preserve their frozen state. "I have plans," he said, and the people did as he asked, marking each grave in the ice with long sticks cut in the valley. Then Aurelio spoke to Sergio. "There is nothing up there but the sky and a long fall. I was right that spirits may get lost."

Sergio denied strenuously that his son had been lost, saying, "He wanted to show us these dead men."

"We will go where I say," said Aurelio, "if my son-in-law cannot find the way."

Aurelio, feeling proud to have been vindicated, led the caravan along the central valley, which ran level until, after a long trudge, they came to the edge of the very same precipice, except lower down. Looking down over the edge, they saw a sea of cloud below, rolling and breaking on rocky promontories like a great ocean in slow motion, sharply outlined, billowing and eddying. It was a great wonder, but Sergio came and stood next to Aurelio. "So," he said, with a wounded air of superiority, "what of the judgment of the living?"

Beneath them the sea of cloud rose swirling upward, and the people followed the curve of the chasm to the left so that the sun fell upon their backs. When the cloud rose level, there was a new wonder, for each person came face-to-face with his or her own shadowy spirit in the mist. Each spirit had about its head a nimbus of glorious lights and rainbow colors, and when the people fell to their knees in awe and terror, crossing themselves, their spirits, too, fell to the earth and crossed themselves. When they sprang to their feet, so did their spirits, which aped their every movement, until at last, their terror diminishing, the people played with their spirits and tried to see if they could catch them out with a sharp movement. Then the cloud billowed and spilled over the edge, engulfing them, and their shadow spirits with their glorious halos disappeared.

The multitude turned their animals about, and they remade their steps back to the foot of the glacier, followed by the cloud, and there they took the last alternative.

The slope curved gently but rapidly down, way below the towering wall of the precipice whose vertical seams they could see were stained red with iron. A wide river with foaming rapids and sparkling falls flowed down next to their descent, thundering from between the twin breasts of a valley up and behind them to the south.

The people could feel the air grow warmer and thicker as they came down, performing a descent in a few hours whose ascent had taken days. The slope curled around the base of the mountain whose peak was at the northern edge of the ridge upon which Aurelio and Don Emmanuel had stood and which was now concealed by the very cloud that had revealed to them their spirits, beautiful in grace and in glory.

Down they went, and around the slope curled, until they beheld below them the greatest wonder of all, and stood in dumbstruck astonishment at what they saw.

39

His Excellency Becomes an Adept and Begets a Magical Child

His Excellency the president surveyed with satisfaction the results of his policy of divide and rule: The armed forces were in a chaos of confusion and fear, and the chiefs of staff had still not managed to reach any decision about the indefinitely postponed coup. In addition, an appetizing scandal was beginning to grow up around the unsavory person of General Ramírez. The president did not know how this had happened, but it appeared from stories published in the foreign press that the general had been involved in nefarious activities in which many people had disappeared, and it seemed highly likely that Ramírez, the most powerful and dangerous of the chiefs of staff, would soon be obliged to tender his resignation.

While General Ramírez chewed his nails and became more and more uncomfortable, His Excellency, by contrast, spent less and less time fretting over the dangers and difficulties of office and consequently found that time was lying heavily on his hands. He became preoccupied with the continuing economic crisis of the country and of the capital— which is to say, the legacy of Raoul Buenanoce and Dr. Jorge Badajoz.

In particular he was concerned by the sixty-million-dollar foreign debt because the country could barely survive the interest on it, let alone begin to pay it off. Consequently, it was becoming almost impossible to secure foreign credit, and the International Monetary Fund would not help at all because it already had problems with Mexico, Brazil, and Argentina, as did the World Bank and all the major lending institutions, particularly Lloyd's. He tried hard to get the debt payments rescheduled but realized that there had to be found a more dramatic answer to the problem.

He thought of attempting to sabotage the coffee production of all the other coffee-producing countries in the world in order to raise prices in time for the next harvest but was told that any disease introduced in, for example, Columbia or Brazil would soon find its way home again and that Kenya was too far away to sabotage easily. He realized that he could do nothing to raise tin prices, for people would merely use plastic instead, and with OPEC in perpetual disarray he could not raise oil prices either.

He searched in vain for alternatives until his ideas soon lost touch with the realms of possibility. He sent off state-sponsored missions to find El Dorado, even though the legends placed it in Peru, Guyana, Ecuador, or Colombia or possibly even Bolivia. He sent for Indian leaders to question them closely about where the Inca gold had come from, only to receive unhelpful answers, such as "It came from here and went to Spain." He instructed his ambassador in London to demand back the contents of the treasure galleons taken by Sir Francis Drake and even thought of declaring war on Chile so that he could take the nitrate fields that the Chileans had stolen from the Peruvians. Over and over in his mind he revolved the famous adage that "This country is a beggar in rags sitting on a pile of gold," and asked himself, "Where is the pile of gold?" His inquiries revealed that all the concessions on gold, silver, lead, mercury, copper sulfates, iron, tin, emeralds, and mercury were in the hands of the foreign corporations that had had the capital to invest in them, so it occurred to him that these industries should all be nationalized. Then he remembered what had happened to Salvador Allende, and how the United States had reacted when Castro threw out the American tycoons, and realized that that would be the same thing as inviting the CIA to depose him.

Then he remembered having read an article about alchemy, in which it had been stated that certain sages had found the secret of transforming base metals into gold and that it had once been done in public by the imperator of the Rosicrucian order. He ordered the state archivist to go to the university library and photocopy every book it had on the subject of alchemy, and he ordered from the United States a complete laboratory to be fitted out in the disused wing of the Presidential Palace.

The president found his new reading matter turgid, incomprehensible, and contradictory. Most of it was in Latin or Greek, and he had to hire a scholar to translate it. What there was of it in Spanish spoke of antimony, philosophic mercury, the white lion, water auripigment, Citrine Seyre, meridian redness, argent vive, dissolution, coagulation, precipitation, white of black, red of white, citrine of red, moist fire, the crow, the vulture, the red lion, the flying volatile, colcothar, the hen's egg, the fugitive ens, albuminous bodies, slat, feces, the dragon, the perscrutinator of the waters, the stone of the philosophers, magnesia, foliated sulfur, virgin's milk, the rational efficient, botri, verdigris, tragacanth, ixir, the physical quintessence, and the intellectual essence.

His brain whirling and reeling with confusion and incomprehension, he puzzled his way through the works of Basil Valentine, Cornelius Agrippa, Paracelsus, Vaughan, Ficino, Roger Bacon, Geber, Kirchringius, Heliodorus, Synesius, Athenagoras, Zozimus, Archelaus, Olympiodorus, Sendivogius, Eirenaeus, Albertus Magnus, Hermes Trismegistus, and most of the other household names of the hermetic art.

Having filled his laboratory with retorts, test tubes, ovens, gas evacuation cupboards, retort stands, burners, crucibles, and row upon row of brightly colored chemicals in jars, he set to work to create gold from lead. Rather than confuse himself with trying to make sense of collating dozens of unintelligible alchemical tracts complete with mystical diagrams, he decided to work through each tract individually, starting with the Golden Tablet of Hermes Trismegistus.

He was already lost by the fifth paragraph: "Take of the Humidity an ounce and a half, and the Meridian Redness that is the Soul of Gold a fourth part, that is to say, half an ounce; of the Auripigment, half—which are eight—that is three ounces; and know ye that the vine of the wise is drawn forth in three, and the wine thereof is perfected in thirty."

It was quite hopeless; it was impossible to know what any of these sages, adepts, and magi actually meant, all of them being equally obscure.

So the president became what was known in Renaissance times as a puffer—an arbitrary and unguided experimenter. After one or two nasty burns, after having choked on chlorine and been repelled by hydrogen sulfide, after having had the toe cap of one shoe dissolved by a splash of nitric acid and having lost his hair, the president had made for himself a rubber suit with a built-in gas mask and a torch for finding his way about in the clouds of smoke and noxious vapors.

In six months of assiduous experiment His Excellency had not transmuted lead into gold. He had caused four serious fires, three explosions, and countless emissions of toxic gases that left the laboratory noisome for days, even for one wearing a gas mask.

He succeeded, nevertheless, in inventing by mistake an explosive that could demolish anything within two yards of its blast, but whose force was abruptly and inexplicably arrested at precisely that distance. He repeated this experiment numerous times with a great deal of paternal pride and wrote down the recipe with the intention of patenting it in the United States.

His attention was diverted, however, by a conversation he had with the foreign secretary, who was well versed in the occult and was, as mentioned before, personally acquainted with the archangel Gabriel. He informed the president that all alchemical writings were elaborate metaphors describing sexual techniques designed to bring about one's wishes and unify the soul with God, simultaneously.

The president hurried back to his books and, starting with Basil Valentine's *Chariot of Antinomy,* began to translate them into coital guides for magicians, with success far exceeding anything he had achieved when treating them as textbooks for esoteric chemistry. Fired with intellectual excitement, the president labored through the nights, further damaging his health (already impaired by his misguided experiments), believing that here at last was a wonderful way of achieving one's desires at the same time as enjoying the most delicious and tantalizing concupiscence.

He complied an alchemical glossary, of which here are given a few terms:

The Mother Eagle = mucuous membranes
Cucurbit = the female genitalia

The White Eagle = the female lubricant fluid
The Menstruum = another word for the above
Alembic retort = mucous membranes during intercourse
The Eagle = the female
The Lion = the male
The Red Lion = semen
Elixir = semen
Quintessence = transmuted semen
Subliminate = physical ecstasy transmuted into spiritual
    beautitude

Having translated all these terms, and the dozens remaining, His Excellency decided to enlist the cooperation of his wife in seeing how well the instructions could be followed as a sexual metaphor and what results would ensue. She, having worked as an "actress" in a strip club, was perfectly happy to put her Panamanian skills to such novel use, and they proceeded as follows.

During the days they practiced magical chastity—that is to say, they tried not to permit themselves any thoughts of an erotic nature. Any mental images of copulation or nakedness they banished sternly from their minds in order to concentrate upon mundane and strictly untitillating matters. They both discovered that this was no easy matter and confirmed the popular myth that most people think about the erotic most of the time, even if they are the president. The object of this difficult and inhuman exercise was to conserve all their sexual energy for the evenings.

In the evening they took a bath together and washed each other with great scrupulousness and application but not without some hilarity. Then they dried off and retired to the presidential bedchamber, where they performed a little ritual of the president's invention, wherein the president would place his hands on his wife's shoulders, look into her eyes, and intone, "You are my queen, you are the living Isis, you are my priestess," whereupon she would put her hands on his shoulders, look into his eyes, and recite, "You are my king, you are the risen Osiris, you are my priest."

Then they would lie together on the bed exchanging caresses until it was possible to proceed to the next phase, in which she would straddle his lap with her arms about his neck, endeavoring to stimulate solely by voluntary contractions of the vagina. She eventually became very adept at this, and they would be able to continue for two or three hours, gazing in complete silence into each other's eyes until they were quite hypnotized, communing with their higher selves, attaining peaks of ecstacy, obtaining knowledge of God, imagining that they were Isis and Osiris, and strongly visualizing a reduction in the national debt.

In this version of the rite they forbade themselves to achieve a climax or even desire one, because this would make it possible to protract the ritual indefinitely, because it was good for building up magical energy, and because like that, one could repeat the rite endlessly without become ennervated.

This procedure produced in them an extraordinary sensation of energy and well-being and was so delicious and exalting that the president found himself neglecting affairs of state altogether and painting pictures of the angels that he had encountered in his hypnogogic visions. He was also very pleased with himself because being obliged not to reach orgasm had cured him of the impotence caused by the old man's terror of never coming at all. Nowadays he had to have a prearranged signal with his wife to prevent her skillful contractions from causing him to be carried away on the wave's crest.

Having perfected this mystical rite, they proceeded to the third degree, which was identical, up to a point, with the second. The difference was that after two or three hours the couple were to allow their massively pent-up desires to explode simultaneously into cataclysmic climax, during the ecstasies of which they were to visualize as powerfully as possible the reductions of the national debt.

However, it was not quite as easy in practice as it was in theory. The first time they did indeed manage to incandesce with divine fire at exactly the same moment, but it was so overwhelming that they both forgot to visualize the "magical child" of reducing the debt.

The second time the president arrived at his destination before his wife and was too annoyed with himself to visualize properly. The third time he could not arrive at all, because he lost his concentration and his state of exalted bliss in trying not to repeat the fiasco of the second attempt.

On the fourth attempt, however, everything proceeded perfectly according to the alchemical purpose, and they sat entwined, quivering, trembling, and thrilling in mystical ecstasy for what felt like hours on the borderline between pleasurable pain and painful pleasure. They saw angels fanning them with their wings, the bed levitated itself into the air and revolved as it hovered, a window broke into shards with a sharp report, the door opened and closed of itself, they felt the kiss of God on their fevered brows, and they visualized with great clarity the vaults of the treasury overflowing with gold.

When it was over, the bed returned gently to its proper position and the exhausted and inspired couple collapsed sideways in each other's arms amid yelps and tormented gasps. "Daddykins!" exclaimed the president's wife. "Oh, Daddykins!" And they both fell into a blissful slumber that preceded many happy months of creating poltergeist effects, states of holy bliss, and vivid pictures of national solvency.

Every day His Excellency called for a treasury report and perused it for signs of the birth of the magical child. He noted with satisfaction that a Caribbean hurricane had raised the price of bananas and tropical fruit, and that the coffee harvest had not been ruined by rains, as in the previous year. He watched the debt gradually reduce itself to fifty million dollars.

All the same he was not convinced that the alchemy was responsible for this limited result, and his faith in it, despite the assurances of the foreign secretary, was beginning to diminish. Then his expedition to find El Dorado returned to give him the happy news that its engineer had discovered a new deposit of emeralds in the sierra while collecting birds' eggs.

Having learned the lessons of history, the president did not sell the commission to the North Americans but set up a State Mining Company with government credit. In order to attempt to obviate the appalling and inevitable corruption and inefficiency that would result from such a project, he decided to appoint a military officer of undoubted integrity and patriotism to run it. He had just sent the telegram to General Fuerte in César when he received a cable from Valledupar that General Fuerte had been assassinated during the night.

Despondent and frustrated, he went to visit his wife, who had been in bed all day with stomach cramps, which he thought must be due to their supernatural alchemical exertions. He was met in the corridor by his wife's lady-in-waiting, who was screaming hysterically and crossing herself with the rapidity of a machine gun and the fervor of St. Catherine. Unable to get any sense out of her even by slapping and shaking her, he entered his wife's chamber to find her cooing over a small furry black bundle that was suckling at her breast while pressing rhythmically against it with its paws.

She looked up as he entered and smiled coyly. "Look, Daddykins," she pouted. "I did not even know I was pregnant, and I've just had a little baby. Isn't it sweet?"

He hands behind his back, he bent over and scrutinized the new arrival. He straightened up and pursed his lips.

"Are you sure that I am the father?" he said. "It appears to be a cat."

40

The Threefold Assassination of General Carlo María Fuerte

General Carlo María Fuerte had taken every precaution: He had immediately dispatched the Portachuelo Guards back to their bases on the remote mountain borders and had ensured that the brigadier was the man who signed all orders and directives emanating from Valledupar. Nonetheless, General Ramírez heard on the military grapevine, as one day he was bound to, that General Fuerte had reappeared in César and had resumed his duties. He sent General Fuerte a telegram congratulating him on his recovery and adding that he had personally dealt with the renegade officers who had imprisoned and mistreated him. Then he arranged for an assassination, to be blamed on the left wing, and wrote a letter to the New York *Herald* denouncing as forgeries the documents that they had been publishing. He drafted a resignation note to the president, reread it many times as he wrenched off his nails with his teeth, and then tore it up.

General Fuerte knew what he should expect and doubled the security around the base. However, he resented the curtailments to his own freedom and still went on his walks with his huge cat (which could now only get one paw through the cat flap) and sometimes with Capitan Papagato and his four cats.

The two men had grown to be good friends despite their great differences in age and in rank. It was not just that both men were besotted with their animals, nor that Fuerte was grateful that Papagato had cared for María and her improbable progeny. It was more that they both shared a kind of weariness and sensitivity.

General Fuerte had reached exactly that time of life when a man wonders whether his life has been worth anything, whether anything has been achieved, and whether he really wants to continue as he is. He had been wondering what he might have missed during his long love affair with and marriage to the army and whether there was not somewhere a fresher and better way of life with which to round off his days on earth.

Capitan Papagato, on the other hand, was twenty-eight years old and was already feeling that youth had slipped away unnoticed, consumed by regulations, form filling, drills, mess days, mess dinners, training periods with the Americans in Panama, and haranguing unwilling and illiterate conscripts. He was feeling unfulfilled and was terrified of a life stretching forward relentlessly into a vacuum of shadows.

"I have been thinking of resigning my commission, General," he said one day when they were out walking on the savanna.

"Indeed?" responded the general. "I, too, have been thinking of doing the same thing. I would like to disappear and start again somewhere."

"You surprise me, General; I thought you would want to stay forever and would try to persuade me to stay as well."

"A few months ago that would have been my reaction, before my mission."

"Pardon me, General, but none of us know what that mission was. Are you able to divulge it?"

"Unfortunately not, Capitan, it is highly confidential."

They walked in silence, hands behind their backs like officers inspecting a parade. "Look!" said the general. "A peccary!"

They watched the little animal saunter away at their approach, and the general said, "I intend to leave next week. I want to go on a long expedition to taxonomize the animals of the sierra, as I have done with the butterflies and to some extent with the hummingbirds."

"An expedition, General? Ah!" The capitan screwed up his courage. "Forgive the impertinence, General, but may I accompany you? I would be most interested."

To the capitan's relief and surprise the general seemed very taken with the idea, "But you know, Capitan, that in the army one must give six months' notice of resignation. To leave before then is desertion. I cannot condone a crime."

"Have you given six months' notice?" asked the capitan.

"No, I have to admit that I have not, but I have persuaded the chief medical officer to pronounce me unfit for service, so I will cede command next Wednesday and receive confirmation of retirement in six months' time. I am effectively a free man."

"General!" exclaimed the capitan. "Why not dismiss me?"

"Dismiss you? What on earth for?"

"Anything!"

"The choice is insanity, homosexuality, dishonorable conduct, unsuitability for the service—"

"Insanity, General, I choose insanity. After all, I have four cats and have changed my name to Papagato!"

"I will speak with the chief medical officer," promised the general, "and he is required to interview you. I advise you to take your cats with you and talk gibberish."

"Oh, thank you, General! Indeed, I thank you!"

"Think nothing of it, Capitan. I would welcome your company on my expedition; I do this for purely nonmilitary and selfish reasons."

The capitan shook the general's hand vigorously, his eyes flashing with good humor and delight. "I shall be quite insane for a week!"

"Not so insane," replied the General, "that you forget to buy a burro and pack together all you need for the journey. Leave everything else with the quartermaster, so that you can claim it later."

On the following Tuesday night, having packed up all he needed into sacks for María to carry, the general left his quarters to take a little paseo in the town, dressed in civilian clothes and sporting a battered straw sombrero. This had been his disguise for eavesdropping on conversations in bars, where he would hear the local populace complaining bitterly about the corruption of officials. He had dismissed many from office as a result of this simple expedient.

This night, however, corruption was far from his mind, and he was scenting in advance the balmy air of liberty. He had left a will bequeathing all his effects to the Patriotic Union of Ex-Soldiers, Sailors, and Airmen and the contents of his strongbox in the bank vault at Asunción to the library of the University of California, Berkeley, where he had once delivered a talk to the Department of Contemporary His-

tory on the subject of *La Violencia*. He was fully intending to leave a
suicide note in his room and had already composed it in his mind: "I
cannot live with myself anymore. I am going to drown myself." But
later that evening he was walking home when at the side of the road he
stumbled over something yielding but heavy and barely saved himself
from falling. He pulled out his flashlight and passed the beam over the
recumbent body. It was El Gandul, a local drunk whose idleness and
scrounging way of life had also earned him the soubriquet of El Cu-
carachero. His real name was unknown, nobody knew where he came
from, and twice before, he had been injured from falling over in the
road and sinking into an alcoholic stupor. This time something heavy
had run over his head, squashing his face into the stones so that it was
an unpleasant, bloody, and unrecognizable mess. The general noted that
the indigent vagabond was just the right height and build and pushed
him into the bushes, hoping that he could return with a Jeep before the
body was found by dogs or vultures.

He carried the body into his quarters and undressed it, trying not
to look at the ghastly disfigurement of the face. He dressed the body in
his army-issue underwear (khaki green, cotton, for the use of officers),
which he never wore himself, and heaved it into his bed. That night he
slept in a camp bed on the porch, preferring rather to be bitten by
mosquitoes than to share the house with the stiffening derelict alcoholic.

In the morning he went to the armory and drew, on his own
authority, a delayed-timing explosive device, filling in in triplicate the
requisite form. Under "intended use" he wrote "counterinsurgency."
The device was equipped with a simple twenty-four-hour clock with a
red arrow to point to "time of detonation" and a white hour hand to be
set in advance to the correct time. He read the instructions carefully:

Read these instructions *before* performing any operations on the
device.

1. Check that button marked "set" is pushed IN.
2. Set white hour hand to correct time.
3. Set red arrow to desired time of detonation.
4. Pull SET Button OUT. The device is now *activated* and
should *not* be readjusted unless SET button is pushed back
IN first.

5. Under no circumstances proceed in any order or manner other than here described.

The general set the device for three o'clock the following morning and left it under his bed.

He set about packing his few possessions into María's baggage sacks. He took two changes of clothing, two pairs of combat boots, his medals, ten packs of army-issue survival rations, water sterilization pills, mosquito repellent, binoculars, compass, revolver, army survey maps, a copy of his book *Picaflores de al Cordillera y de la Sierra Nevada,* several notebooks, washing things, towels, a camp bed, a sleeping bag, a large water bottle, a crucifix given to him by his mother, and a new copy of W. H. Hudson's *Idle Days in Patagonia,* which he had not read last time because he had forgotten to ask Father García to give it back. Thinking that he had forgotten something essential, he turned his room upside down until he had added to his baggage a first-aid kit, a machete, four boxes of ammunition, and a pair of scissors. He stood in the middle of his room wondering whether or not to steal his army rifle and then unlocked the strong box under his bed and took it out. He fetched the slide from the other strong box in the living room, and sat on his bed to assemble it. He oiled it carefully and pushed the slide back and forth to check its action. He took his pull through, a roll of cleaning lint, and a can of gun oil, rolled them into a cloth, and put them in his baggage. He mounted a sling on the rifle and checked that it was comfortably adjusted.

He loaded the packs into the Jeep and drove it the short distance to María's stable near his office and left them with her. Then he drove back to fetch his cat and awaited Capitan Papagato's arrival with his donkey and his four cats.

The capitan arrived shortly in peasant clothing, and the two men and their donkeys walked off in silence together toward Chiriguaná, their sombreros pulled low over their eyes, their cats prowling beside the road in the savanna, sometimes ambushing each other and sometimes chasing their own tails.

"I want to confess something to you," said the general at length.

"Oh, yes?"

"I lied to you, Capitan. I have no medical discharge. I am deserting. I hope you are not shocked, but I have felt guilty ever since I told you that."

The capitan looked into the distance and removed his hat to fan his face. "Pretending to be insane is also a form of desertion," he said.

That evening they brewed *sancocho* under the stars and talked quietly. In the undergrowth around them the animals rustled and the cicadas scraped. The general smoked a *puro* with his coffee, and the capitan said, "Now you really look the part of a campesino!"

"You should try it," said the general. "And you will discover its beauty. There is nothing else on earth that wipes out troubles and clears the thoughts as well as one of these."

"Then perhaps you could spare one."

"Of course," said the general, and dug in his pack for a cigar.

Capitan Papagato lit it, and the delicate smoke drifted off into the night, mingling with the scent of bougainvillaeas.

"I feel drunk," said the capitan after a while. "I hope I am not going to be sick.'

"You will not be," replied the general. "The night is too beautiful for that." He paused. "Did you bring a tent, Capitan?"

"Of course."

"Thank God. I knew I had forgotten something important. Even so, it is not the rainy season, and with good fortune we will not need it."

That night, just after midnight, Commandante Comingo Hugo Galdos of General Ramírez's unofficial section of the Army Internal Security Service was waiting for the guard to pass to the other end of his beat. The guard was obviously bored and tired and had stopped to smoke an illicit cigarette in the cup of his hand, looking around a little anxiously in case the duty officer was to appear unexpectedly on a check.

Commandante Galdos had arrived by train in civilian clothes, carrying a briefcase in order to look like a businessman; but his dark glasses made him look exactly like a secret service agent, as did the ill fit of his suit and the square ends of his shoes. Inside the briefcase was a very precise map of where to find General Fuerte's quarters, a plan of the house, details of the movements of the guards, and a long-barreled handgun with a silencer. He had been here in the bushes squatting in a very uncomfortable position, his feet cutting on the leather of the new shoes, his thighs aching, and being bled dry by mosquitoes for two hours, awaiting the ideal moment.

When the moment came, he darted across the road from the bushes and up the steps of the general's house. To his relief and surprise he found the door open and slipped inside, walking straight into a rack that the general kept for canes. Horrified by the racket he had made, his heart thumping and his stomach churning, Commandante Galdos stood obviously still, listening to the terrifying silence.

Breathing more easily at last, he slipped a penlight from his pocket and flicked it on. He found the door handle to the bedroom and turned it very slowly. The door released with a sharp click, and once more he froze with panic and thought of fleeing. Then, he opened the door and was horrified by its grating hinges. He stood still again. He crept into the room, cursing the creaking of his new leather shoes, and shone his light onto the bed. Very quickly and sweating with fear, he pumped four shots into the back of El Gandul as he lay on his side under the sheet. Desperately wishing to urinate, Comandante Galdos went swiftly back into the corridor and walked once more straight into the canes. He cursed, gathered his wits together, and peeked out of the door. Seeing no sentries, he darted back across to the bushes and ran off, only to fall headlong into an irrigation ditch. His hands bleeding from breaking his fall onto the stones, he lay there, perspiring and shaking, until he regained a little of his composure. He went back to the road and headed straight for a bar, where he drank four *aguardientes* in a row and smoked ten cigarettes. A whore sidled up to him, saw his bleeding hands and wild eyes, and sidled away again.

Teodoro Mena Machicado, most experienced assassin of the Revolutionary Socialists (Turcos Lima Front) and known as El Amolador on account of always wearing knife when on missions, arrived shortly after Comandañte Galdos had left. He had hitched on trucks all the way from Isabel, and it had taken two days. He was tired and dirty but full of intent to do his revolutionary duty with the utmost firmness and self-sacrifice. He had so far executed seven senior officers on behalf of the people and was intending General Fuerte to be his eighth. He was ignorant of the fact that so far he had executed no fewer than three officers with left-wing anti-American nationalist sympathies, three moderates, and only one right-winger. But as far as he was concerned, they were all the same, and he was not a man to hedge with caveats and provisos when it came to disposing of class enemies. Itching with revolutionary justice, which only he could distinguish from blood lust, he waited in the bushes for the sentry to pass.

Finding his opportunity, excitement rising in his breast, he flitted across the road, sprang up the steps of the general's house, and tried the handle. He burst in, crashed straight into the canes, and, not pausing to clutch his bruised shins, ran into the general's bedroom. Drawing the lovingly honed butcher's knife from his belt, he threw himself on the body and frenziedly plunged it four times into its chest, slicing straight through the ribs. Then he withdrew it and wiped the blade on the sheet.

On impulse, he tugged at the shoulder of the corpse to roll it over, and in the bright moonlight pouring through the window, he saw the mutilated, caked, and blood-clotted face of El Gandul, crawling with flies, maggots swarming in the open mouth. A nauseating stench suddenly filled his nostrils and made him cover his nose with his hand.

Stupefied and sickened, El Amolador backed off and ran. In the corridor he crashed once more into the canes and limped to the door, clutching his knee. He watched for the sentry to pass and sprinted across the road to the bushes. He ran doubled up for a few yards and then returned to the road.

Gratefully he entered the nearest bar and sat next to Comandante Galdos, who was already glassy-eyed and incoherent. El Amolador ordered a bottle of *ron cana* and drank it without the meditation of a glass or the addition of Inca-Cola, watching Galdos's cigarette smolder down to a stub until it burned two blisters on the man's fingers.

Comandante Galdos stood up, wringing his hands and shouting, "*¡Mierda! Qué maricón de puta! Jésus!*"

El Amolador put a hand on his arm and pulled him back down onto his stool. "Have another drink, *cabrón.*"

The two assassins of two political extremes drank with the thirst of elephants, swore eternal friendship, embraced, discussed the hyperbolical misery of their experiences of the love of women, related sexual exploits with degrees of poetic exaggeration, and were fast asleep with their heads on the counter when General Fuerte's bomb lit up the night and shattered the peace with a resounding boom.

Neither of them awoke. In his unconscious state Comandante Galdos murmured, "¡O qué churcha!" and El Amolador grunted swinishly and said, "What? Where?"

The zoological general slept blissfully under the stars, his arm over the neck of his purring cat, the only man who has been assassinated in his absence three times in one night, once by himself, and who has lived to desert the army and go on an expedition.

41

The Beginning of the Postdiluvian History of Cochadebajo de los Gatos

Almost since the inception of geological time there had been a long valley there, created by the folding of the sierra and the inexorable abrasions of water. At the eastern end there had always been at either side two towering mountains rising vertically into the cordilleran sky. Then there had been, before humans had ever set foot there, a mighty earthquake that compressed the folds of the suffering earth even further and tilted the southern peak at an angle over the mouth of the valley so that its face overhung it and the river cascaded through it.

For hundreds of years the Incas lived in the valley of the hanging mountain and built a stone city there with temples and ziggurats, courts for playing a pok-a-tok, where sometimes the losing teams were sacrificed, and geometrical paved streets lined with low houses and incised stone columns. At the western end of their city they erected stone effigies of jaguars to line the travelers' ingress, and halfway up the northern slope they built the palace of their lords.

Then one day there was a fierce rumbling, and a woman working in a field pointed east and shouted. People ran into the streets and courtyards to watch wonderingly as at the edge of their world the overhanging face of the mountain split into fragments along its seams and slid crumbling and roaring to build a huge dam across the exit of the river. With a great crack the final section of the mountainside split off and crashed to earth, sending clouds of rock dust high into the air to be dispersed in the bitter winds.

The frantic people could not clear the dam faster than the waters rose. They heaved the rocks over the slope at the end of the valley, but many of them were too heavy to lift even with twenty men. They abandoned the uneven struggle when they began to fear that their route back might be cut off, and they left on a long trek in the direction of Cuzco, only to perish in the implacably hostile waste of the *portachuelos*. They were dead long before their valley had become a mighty lake that submerged their city and bore with relentless pressure against the dam, awaiting the time when the mountains would move again, the dam burst, and the waters break free to hurl joyfully through the *quebradas*, crash through the jungles, and spread out in the Mula Basin, only to evaporate once more into the bosom of the sky of their birth.

Thus is was that the travelers beheld from the heights an intact city half buried in alluvial mud, with glistening sheets of water in the hollows. They saw the ziggurat and the temples, the palace of the lords, the roofs of the little houses, and the jaguar obelisks lining the road of ingress.

Remedios came forward and spoke to Pedro. "What shall we call it? La Libertad?"

"Nueva Chiriguaná," suggested Misael.

"No," said Aurelio. "It is a city of cats beneath a lake. Its name will be Cochadebajo de los Gatos."

He said this with such certainty that the flow of suggestions immediately ceased and the name of their new home was passed around. People rolled the phrase around their tongues and found it good.

"*Vamos,*" said Hectoro. "We have a lot of digging to do."

"I will leave now," announced Aurelio, "but I will be back. I have important things to do."

"Come back laden with shovels," said Don Emmanuel, and Aurelio turned his mule around and led it back up the incline to retrace his steps.

He returned to the jungle to be with Carmen while he gathered sacks of roots and herbs. Then he went into the mountains to fast for two weeks and summon the power of the spirits. When he felt that the veil between this world and the next was so thin that he could reach through it, he returned to the jungle and loaded four mules with the medicines. He took three days to reach the foot of the glacier and stayed there for one week to do his work with the aid of Federico and Parlanchina.

The people of Cochadebajo de los Gatos found themselves faced with a Herculean labor, and many thought it was too vast even to attempt. Don Emmanuel, however, having walked the length of the valley, found that much of the water was retained by the remnant of the dam. It took a week of strenuous labor to lever and shove the great rocks over the slope and send them spinning and bouncing into the valley below, where they crashed to a halt among the splintered stumps of what had been a forest before the flood.

As the water seeped away, the outer edges of the alluvial mud began to dry out, and Sergio had an inspired idea.

"¡Escuchame!" he exclaimed one evening in the courtyard of the palace, where most of the people were encamped. "We have very few spades and shovels, maybe two hundred between us, and we have no places to grow food. Let us cut the mud into bricks as it dries and pass the bricks along the line so that those on the slopes may build *andenes*. When they are built, then we can fill them in, and we will have the richest crops in the world!"

The leaders were very impressed. Hectoro said, "It also solves the problem of where to put all the mud. It is a good idea, Sergio."

"To avoid argument," suggested Remedios, "let us agree that no one may occupy a house until enough are cleared for everyone to live."

"No one would obey," said Josef, "even though it is a good idea. It would be better for those who want a particular house to draw lots for it, like in the lottery."

"We have no lottery tickets," remarked Sergio.

On the next day the new system was inagurated, and no one exempted himself or herself from the task, not even the voluptuous and sybaritic Felicidad, who rolled up her skirts and passed bricks with the rest of them.

Over the weeks the people grew thin and exhausted, living on what little food was left, what was brought in by the cats, and what was foraged in neighboring valleys by Misael and his train of mules. On one of these journeys he came across a small Indian settlement and bartered a mule in return for seed potatoes, yucca, corn seed, and three ewes and a ram. From this humble beginning, and further barterings for goats, bananas, and llamas, grew the vast agricultural enterprise that one day became the root of the flourishing mountain economy of Cochadebajo de los Gatos, which was able to trade its surplus with the town of Ipasueno and with villages over all the highlands.

It took several months to remove the worst of the mud; the people were hampered every time it rained, and as the terraces were built, the bricks had to be carried farther and farther away. In the end it was years before the whole town was dug out because work slackened almost as soon as there were enough houses to live in, and people only dug out houses on the two days a week devoted to community service projects or when they felt like moving to a sunnier position or could not stand their neighbors anymore, or when there was a new addition to a family that necessitated a more spacious residence. The stones always bore the dark stains of the centuries' immersion in mud, and it was many months before the damp was finally driven out. The people developed a submarine mentality, for all about them were the traces of centuries of tranquil inundation. They would say, "Swim over to my place tonight, and we'll take a *copa* together," and they would point to a playing cat, laugh, and say, "Look at that catfish!"

During the early phases of the digging the work force was dramatically increased. Something glinting on the western slope had caught Consuelo's eye, and she had put he hand up to shade her vision. "Ay! Ay! Look!" she shouted, and everyone followed the line of her gesture to see in the distance Aurelio at the head of 451 Indians of both sexes and the troop of 50 Spanish soldiers in full armor, as well as the count.

With one mind the people dropped their bricks and their tools and converged on the historical column of derefrigerated human anachronisms. "*¡Hola!*" shouted Aurelio, and led the column toward the crowd.

Pedro stepped forward and strode up to greet Aurelio. He cast his eyes over the column and said, "You are a great *brujo*."

"No," said Aurelio. "The secret in knowing how to do it gently and as quickly as possible."

The people crowded round the new arrivals and saw that they

walked like the dead, with no life in their eyes and without expression. "Are they still dead?" asked Father García.

"No, they are sleepwalking. They will take many weeks to wake up. When they do—" he pointed to the Spaniards in full armor—"you will probably have a lot of trouble with these. You should imprison them or they will imprison you."

"How will we feed so many extra mouths?" demanded Remedios. "There is scarcely enough for us."

"They will eat little until they wake up. I will stay here to care for the *cholos*. As for them"— he spat—"I nearly did not revive them. They are a problem for you."

During the weeks before they awoke, the unfrozen somnambulatory denizens of an imperial age worked like automatons alongside the people. At night they did not sleep but sat motionless with their hands on their knees and their empty eyes open and unflickering. The people talked to them in childish voices and fed them pureed banana and soup, which dribbled down their chins as with babies. The great cats licked their faces and cleaned them as they would their kittens and at night draped themselves across their laps to sleep.

"Why did you do this?" asked García one day. "Why did you bring them back from death?"

"I wanted to ask the *cholos* the secret of the stones," said Aurelio. "And the Spaniards I brought back for vengeance."

"Vengeance?" repeated García. "You are not going to kill them again, surely?"

"No, García. You will see."

When the Indians woke up, Aurelio was mortified to discover that not only were they completely terrified by the strange people around them, but that they spoke a language that was not Aymara or Quechua, Guarani, or any tongue that he recognized. His attempts to befriend them failed, and the night after they awoke they slipped in a body out of Cochadebajo de los Gatos and disappeared into the mountains, gratefully believing that they had escaped slavery.

The Spanish, however, woke up believing that they were in charge of everything. At first they were completely disoriented and confused, in a city they did not remember, with people they did not recognize. But within half an hour of waking, the imperious Conde Pompeyo Xavier de Estremadura had struck Felicidad for not curtsying when she crossed his path, and one of the common soldiers had sexually assaulted Francesca in public and then lashed out at Josef when he had pulled him away.

After several intolerably antisocial and brazen incidents of this kind Hectoro mounted his horse and roped the count with his lariat as he was attempting to order Remedios to fetch him some food. Cursing loudly in his quaint Castilian, the arrogant conquistador was dragged to the colonnade of the jaguars and tied to one of the obelisks. The remainder of the band of ignoble Iberians were rounded up at gunpoint and herded to the same spot, where they, too, were tied to the obelisks.

"I demand," thundered the count in his strange accent, "to be released forthwith, or you will all taste the edge of His Catholic Majesty's sword! Your city will be razed, and every one of you quartered and fed to the dogs! How dare you perpetuate this blasphemous outrage against the might of Spain!"

"You will be quiet," said Hectoro, through clenched teeth, "or I shall remove your *cojones* and oblige you to swallow them." He took out his knife and brandished it before the aristocrat's face.

Hectoro rode his horse to where all could hear and announced, "You have all been dead for four hundred years, and we have very kindly brought you back to life. There is no king of Spain here! There are no kings whatsoever here, and no counts or marquises or princes! You will show humility and gratitude, you will behave with courtesy, or we will cast you out into the mountains to die all over again." He paused for dramatic effect. "To us you are lower than dogs, you have no rank and no privilege, and you will get no consideration from us until you deserve it! I sentence you to one week of humiliation for your barbarity!"

Hectoro swung off his horse and strolled over to the count, who glared at him disdainfully and said with contempt, "You will die, dog, the moment the king hears of this!"

Hectoro spit on the ground, opened his fly, and pissed copiously on the count's feet. The latter turned puce with rage and struggled against his bonds, shouting out blasphemies and imprecations. The people cheered and clapped, and Hectoro ambled back to his horse and swung up into the saddle. He acknowledged the applause of the crowd and gestured for silence. "Do not harm them," he called. "Shame them."

Aurelio turned to Pedro. "Vengeance," he said, and walked away smiling.

For a week the children amused themselves by imitating Hectoro's feat and throwing mud balls that splattered on the engraved cuirasses and helmets and stained the scarlet breeches. Felicidad tugged the count's beard and squeezed his nose while he glowered at her in speechless indignation. Francesca lowered the breeches of the soldier who had assaulted her, and poured pimiento sauce on his genitalia, and Consuelo filled with horse manure the chappele-de-fer of the man who had pushed her and set it back on his head.

The soldiers were not released until every one of them had vowed never again to give offense, on pain of expulsion, and to work relentlessly at clearing the mud. The offensive decongelated soldiery were in effect treated as abject slaves for several months, roped together and made to work at gunpoint. The objectionable and unrepentant count remained bound to the obelisk for one month before he ungraciously conceded to work like everyone else, but, because he was unused to being treated with amused contempt, his fierce pride gave way at length to sorrowful despondency, and he began to waste away. At length even Hectoro took pity on the disheartened warrior, and Remedios, sensitive to his perpetual suffering, his elaborate deferential courtesy, his profound melancholy, and his quaint turn of phrase, began to fall in love with him and bring him gifts of dainty things to eat.

During and preceding these events Father García had continued to elaborate in his head the details of his new theology. Having pondered the incomprehensible evil of the world, he concluded that God had not created it but had created souls. What had really happened was that God had created the devil through a cosmic oversight, and it had been the devil that was responsible for having made the world and tricked the souls into occupying bodies. The only way to struggle back to God was to deny the devil's creation completely, refuse to eat meat in order not to interfere with the process of metempsychosis, and diminish the devil's kingdom by refusing to procreate.

When he preached the New Gospel in the squares, he found that he made no converts at all, and he was forced to admit that even he himself found its practical requirements unpalatable. After many weeks of se-

rious thought he preached the same Gospel, with the rider that Cochadebajo de los Gatos was the beginning of a new Creation, a new
period of God's active intervention in the universe; therefore, one could
eat meat and had an absolute obligation to procreate as much as possible
in order to increase it in size relative to the kingdom of the devil. Father
García's revised Albigensian heresy grew instantly in popularity, and he
became a serene and contented man who exuded an aura of saintliness
and beautitude. His preaching became more and more inspirational and
unintelligible until one day, rapt with mystical ecstasy, he levitated
spontaneously and was able to reach a purring assembly of cats from the
top of an obelisk.

42

The Obsequies of General Carlo María Fuerte

The assorted fragments of El Gandul were gathered together and placed in a military coffin. This was loaded onto a truck and taken to the barracks, where it was draped with the national flag. Before it departed for the capital, the brigadier held a special parade for it.

It was set up on a gun carriage with the general's sword and cap on it, and the whole garrison paraded past it at the slow march, with guns sloped and in full dress uniform. Practically the whole town turned out to watch the occasion, which was the grandest military display ever seen in César. Many of the soldiers marched with tears streaming down their cheeks, and those who had known General Fuerte, such as his office staff, wept so greviously that soon the whole populace was contagiously convulsed with sobs. General Fuerte had been the only honest and honorable governor they had ever had, and so his coffin was festooned with flowers as it passed, and some people cried out incongruously, "¡*Viva el general!*" for want of a more apt expression.

In the plaza the soldiers wheeled into formation and halted. The four little black horses with nodding plumes drew the gun carriage into the center, and there the brigadier delivered a grandiloquent oration in the customary style. He stood at the foot of the statue of Simón Bolívar and spoke these words, which were reprinted in full in the Valledupar *Prensa* the following day:

Citizens and soldiery of Valledupar! A most dolorous duty causes us to congregate in the plaza before the image of our nation's most exalted hero, Simón Bolívar! In this coffin before us, opened too early, lie the mortal remains of our unfortunate and beloved governor, whose existence, although it has been cut untimely short, passed with meteoric luminosity, leaving an illustrious and translucent afterglow in its wake. Even as the varied and beautiful lines of the spectrum through a converging lens are transformed into a scintillating ray of white light, resplendent, so the details which in his work he compiled, united, and synthesized emerged afterward from his lofty brain in the beautiful productions of public peace and harmony whose merit is sufficient to place his sarcophagus in the temple of immortality!

If the disassociation of the matter which constitutes the shell of the human body carries not with it the destruction of personality, if an immortal spirit survives, transmigrating or ascending in infinite and glorious spirals to the affectionate bosom of the omnipotent creator, then his cruel and gratuitous expiration in the conflagration of a subversive explosion is not death and obliteration but a transformation, a mere change from one existence to another! The chrysalis, it is true, has broken its carapace, and the glorious butterfly—the resplendent psychic entity—has flown to happier regions, to merge itself into the Prime Cause of our Being. His noble and refined spirit, spreading like the undulations of the oceanic waves, hovers like the hummingbirds he loved amid the engrossing and perfumed orisons of the choirs of the hierarchies of the celestial inhabitants of the heavenly regions!

Citizens and soldiery of Valledupar! Let us bid farewell to the excellent General Carlo María Fuerte! Let us pray that we shall carry always before the lachrymose eyes of our saddened and subdued souls the perfect image of his magnificent example! Let our tears not wash away the memory of this immaculate and conscientious public servant! Let us remember him with unstinting gratitude, and let us ensure that his successors in office follow his precepts!"

Wiping the tears from his eyes with the back of his glove, the brigadier drew his sword and raised it. The soldiers presented arms, stepped one foot forward, and raised their rifles to their shoulders. When the brigadier brought his sword down, the soldiers fired three volleys into the air, and in response there boomed from the barracks the salute of the field guns.

The people of Valledupar honored the body with a *despedida* as far as the railway station, where it was carried on the shoulders of six soldiers into a carriage.

In an interview that evening the brigadier stunned the whole nation by stating that in his opinion the assassination of the general was the work of right-wing extremists within the army. Everybody had assumed that the outrage would, regardless of the truth, be blamed on left-wing terrorists. General Ramírez hastily refuted the brigadier's contention in a rather too vehement press release, and in this way unwittingly started a rumor that he himself was responsible. His position became ever more insecure and untenable as the rumors spread and as even the national press regained the temerity to reprint the articles from the New York *Herald*. Seizing his opportunity, His Excellency President Enciso Veracruz appointed the brigadier military governor of César and promoted him to general without consulting General Ramírez. When the Revolutionary Socialists (Turcos Lima Front) tried to claim responsibility for the atrocity, no one believed them, and General Ramírez made himself publicly ridiculous by pretending that he did. The brigadier, now general, further stunned the nation by calling a plebiscite in César to confirm him in office. He won easily without rigging the vote, as only Communists tried to organize an opposition. They feuded bitterly over the selection of a candidate, with the result that the left-wing vote was split among nine hopeful representatives, who devoted their election addresses to denouncing each other as capitalist lackeys, revisionists, revanchists, Trotskyists, and bourgeois stooges. The general population, not being familiar with the technical vocabulary of the left, voted for the only candidate whose speeches they could understand, the main reason why Brigadier, now General, Hernando Montes Sosa won the election so easily.

El Gandul's assembled fragments were transported under military guard to the Presidential Palace, and the coffin was placed on a podium in the entrance so that people could call in to pay their respects. His Excellency announced that there would be four days' lying in state, that there would be a state funeral in the ornate Cathedral of Our Lady of the Immaculate Conception, and that he would personally stand watch over the coffin on the first night.

The events that ensued, tragic, duplicitous, and vicious as they were, assumed the proportions of a heroic farce that stretch credence to the limit and bear witness to the manner in which wickedness is invariably repaid in its own coin.

President Veracruz stood his watch over the coffin by having a bed brought down into the hall. At three o'clock in the morning he turned off his alarm clock and let in the four men at the entrance of the kitchens who were carrying a substitute coffin filled to the correct weight with bags of nails. The men from the Service of State Information packed some of the president's new alchemical explosive into the coffin and rigged up a powerful remote pistol-grip detonation device which they handed to the president. Carefully he locked it into the safe in his office, and the four men left by the kitchen entrance, carrying the remains of El Gandul in the original coffin. They drove the truck to the paupers' cemetery and left the coffin at the end of the line of those awaiting in the open air to be buried. In the morning the sexton counted the coffins twice, realized that he had one too many, and, to save delays and complications, buried the last one under "*Non Nombre*," which for once was the truth.

That evening it was the turn of Admiral Fleta to stand watch over the coffin. He dozed in an armchair until half past two, when he went and unbolted the door of the tradesmen's entrance to let in the five men who were carrying a substitute coffin containing bags of ball bearings and two timed limpet mines. The men of the Naval Internal Intelligence Agency left with the other coffin and delivered it to the back entrance of Admiral Fleta's mansion in the suburbs; getting rid of such a hot property was not something he intended to entrust to anyone else.

The following evening was the turn of Air Chief Marshal Sanchis. He slept in snatches on a folded-out-double divan until one o'clock in the morning, when he went and unbolted the doors of the service entrance and let in two giggling call girls of indeterminate vintage who helped him to pass the time until half past three, when he sent them away and let in the five men carrying a substitute coffin packed with bags of nuts and bolts and containing two time-fused fléchette anti-personnel bombs. The men of the Air Force Internal Security Agency then left with the other coffin and delivered it to the side entrance of Air Chief Marshal Sanchis's house in the suburbs, where it was left in the cellar for disposal at a more convenient date.

On the last of the nights of the vigil, General Ramírez paced up and down the hall, chain-smoking, chewing his fingernails, and going to the lavatory every ten minutes. At three o'clock in the morning he went to the service doors and unbolted them to let in the four men of the Army Internal Security Service who were bringing a substitute coffin filled with fragmentation grenades and two timed directional claymore mines. The four men heaved the other coffin onto their shoulders and bore it out to the truck, which they drove to General Ramírez's estate and left in his garage.

All this bears witness not so much to the wavelike motion of coincidence or to the inscrutable machinations of synchronicity as to the unified and stereotypical manner in which the military plots when engaged in illicit political maneuvering.

On the morning of the state funeral General Ramírez telephoned the president's office to say that a recurrence of back trouble prevented him from doing his duty as a pallbearer and that he had reluctantly delegated the honorable task to one of his deputies. Admiral Fleta phoned to say that his beloved mother was on her deathbed; therefore, he could not do his duty as a pallbearer and had delegated the task to a commander. He forbore to mention that the commander was a troublesome nationalist left-winger who had once started a mutiny at the Maracay Naval Base but who had been amnestied by President Veracruz. Air Chief Marshal Sanchis telephoned to say that the *paludismo* he had contracted in the *montaña* during his secondment to the Peruvian Air Force had once more laid him low and that he had reluctantly delegated his duties as pallbearer to Flight Lieutenant Rosario Uceda (a man on his staff whom he secretly suspected of being in the pay of General Ramírez).

The president was exasperated by this frustration of his plans to do away with the chiefs of staff, and when it was announced over the radio that none of the chiefs of staff would be present as pallbearer, the latter were equally exasperated at the frustration of their plans to do away with one another.

Nonetheless, each was privately excited about the forthcoming explosion, and President Veracruz suddenly realized that the public was bound to blame the absent chiefs of staff for it. It would be stretching coincidence too far for them to be able to explain their unanimous absence in any other way. For reasons of political expediency he reversed his decision not to blow up the innocent pallbearers. He resolved to do it as the coffin was being borne up the many steps of the cathedral because there would be no one else in close proximity to the explosion.

Fortunately for almost everyone, nothing went according to plan. The organizational chaos of the morning delayed everything considerably. The guard of honor was unable to form up on time because the soldiers from Ecuador and Colombia who were to take part in it were late, owing to fog at the airport, so that just as the service was supposed to take place and Ramírez's bomb was due to explode, the cortege had still not moved off from the Presidential Palace. The Colombian Hussars and Ecuadorian Dragoons turned up at last, and then the axle of the ancient gun carriage broke, so that the coffin was removed to an anteroom while another gun carriage was fetched and hastily smartened up.

In the empty anteroom the claymore mines of General Ramírez exploded with a crash. The weak outer walls of the room descended in slow motion and with dignity amid a swirl of dust and rubble onto the swept gravel of the courtyard. Covered in white dust, the guard of honor ran around in confusion, and Ramírez, who was listening on the radio as he drove, cast his eyes to the heavens.

The president, quite sure that he had not inadvertently pressed the button on his remote detonation device, hastily put his hand in his pocket to check that the safety switch had not moved.

Admiral Fleta was in his living room listening to the excited commentary of the announcer with the radio perched on top of the coffin containing the alchemical explosive. The president fiddled with the controls of his apparently self-willed detonation device, and the disingenuous admiral was obliterated by a blast that consumed him and his armchair but stopped abruptly at a radius of two yards from the epicenter, leaving the rest of the room untouched.

Air Chief Marshal Sanchis was just pushing the coffin containing Fleta's limpet mines out of the ancient Dakota when it exploded, tearing a huge hole in the floor of the fuselage and sending him and the remains of the coffin plummeting eight thousand feet into the jungle below. When the Cusicuaris found the shattered body, they shrank it, set it up on a pole, and venerated it as yet another angel whose wings had inexplicably fallen off. The Dakota managed to fly back to base despite having almost no shell left stretched over its central ribbing. The pilot, faced with the intractable problem of how to report what had happened without implicating himself in Sanchis's nefarious plot, reported that he had been fired on with ground-to-air missiles during a routine flight. He did not mention that Air Chief Marshal Sanchis had been on board, nor did he mention anything about exploding coffins.

General Ramírez was at the same time in the empty ex-officers' wing of the Army School of Electrical and Mechanical Engineering. He had pulled the coffin out of the truck onto a trolley and had wheeled it into the crematorium. He was just pumping the trolley up to the right height to be able to push the coffin containing the fléchette bombs of Air Chief Marshal Sanchis into the oven when they detonated cataclysmically and sent the steel arrows ricocheting and whining about the confined space. General Ramírez was already in shreds and fragments when the huge fuel tanks were pierced. They combusted with a throaty roar that lifted the roof, blew out the walls, and set the entire school afire.

Meanwhile, the huge crowds lining the route of the funeral became bored with waiting and melted away to take advantage of the week of national mourning. The dignitaries of the cathedral waited two hours more, then began to make their excuses to each other and leave. The soldiers were taken by their commanders back to their barracks, and the Ecuadorian Dragoons and the Colombian Hussars were apologetically shown the sights of the city by an embarrassed presidential aide, who finally abandoned them at three o'clock in the morning in a notorious *putería* on the Calle de San Isidro.

The newspapers the following week seemed to consist almost entirely of headlines: BODY OF GENERAL EXPLODES, ARMY SCHOOL INEXPLICABLY BURNED DOWN, FOREIGN SOLDIERS IN VIOLENT INCIDENT IN BROTHEL, ADMIRAL FLETA SPONTANEOUSLY COMBUSTS, PRESIDENT TO ADDRESS NATION.

In the interim, the occasion for all these dramatic events had arrived safely with his friend Papagato and the five cats in the township of Chirguaná, which was half a yard deep in dried mud and populated solely by margays, pumas, and ocelots. They had wandered for two months on the buried Mula Basin, before deciding to follow the cats, which seemed to have definite ideas about where to go. They eventually arrived in Cochadebajo de los Gatos just in time to hear the end of Father García's sermon to the cats and to watch him, in a state of epiphany, levitate down from the obelisk, at the base of which he was later to carve the famous words *Et in Arcadia Ego.*

43
Gifts of Life

Carmen leaped out of her hammock and shook Aurelio awake. "I know my real name, *querido,* I dreamed it! It is Matarau!"

Aurelio opened his eyes. "You should not have told me that. It means I have power over you."

Carmen laughed at him. "Husband, do you think you have no power over me already?" She bent down and kissed his cheek.

He smiled gravely. "Your power over me is as mine over you." He climbed out of the hammock and set about rekindling the fire with dried grass.

Carmen watched him and asked, "*Querido,* what does it mean?"

He looked up. "It is Quechua," he said. "It means forehead of snow."

"That is a paradox," she said. "Here I am, black as night, and not a single gray hair!"

"My name makes no sense either," replied Aurelio. "But it is still my name. You have to understand that some of the gods have no more brains than a monkey and play the same kinds of tricks."

When he had eaten his breakfast of cassava and *cancha,* Aurelio went to cut himself a stick of quebracho. He sharpened it with great labor and difficulty because it was so hard, but to him it was worth it because then the stick would last a very long time. Then he filled his *mochila* with corn and went off to the clearing he had made with his machete. He sifted through his fingers the fine ash of the vegetation he had burned and was satisfied that it was good and that soon it would rain. Methodically he made little holes with the stick and tossed a seed into each hole, covering it again with his foot to give it a chance against the birds and the mice. When Carmen had finished making her *arepas* and feeding the chickens, she came out to join him, and they worked deftly and systematically side by side until the planting was done. Then they went to the little coca plantation and harvested enough leaves to make one *tambo*, the fifty-pound pack of compressed leaves that they would sell to the *cocaleros* when they arrived or that Aurelio would carry to Cochadebajo de los Gatos as a present for the people there. From time to time Aurelio glanced sideways at Carmen, with her copper curls and her *puro* clenched between her teeth, and thought about what it was to be with someone for such a long time and never tire of her and what it was to grow old in the flesh but not in the spirit.

They stopped at midday to drink lemon juice sweetened with *panela* and to eat the *arepas*, sitting side by side in the shade of a balsa tree without saying a word, but squinting at the brilliant light beyond the ring of shade. They both were asleep when they were startled to wakefulness by two explosions and a great commotion over at the mined path. Aurelio and Carmen crept through the trees to see what had happened.

Lieutenant Figueras had not volunteered for the job, but the politicians had decided that they had to give a little in the face of the pressure from the United States to destroy a few cocaine plantations, and the instructions had filtered down via the new commander, who considered it all a waste of time. For him it was natural to think of the one officer to whom he could give the unpleasant task, whose presence he would not miss in the least, and who was incapable of anything more exacting in military terms.

Figueras and his platoon had traveled through the deserted Mula Basin, now reverting to scrub and jungle, and had found a path. With not the smallest idea of where he was going or what he was intending to do, he and his men hacked their way through the encroaching vegetation. They were sweating in rivers, and around their heads and arms hung clouds of stinging insects that tormented them to a point of insanity. In the twilight world of the jungle they were impaled by thorns, sank up to their knees in bog, and were horrified by the yellow whip-snakes draped luxuriously from the branches. Huge spiders dropped from the ferns and clung to their uniforms, and Parlanchina's growls and whoops wholly unnerved them.

Figueras was with the same platoon that he had commanded before his meteoric rise and equally meteoric fall, and the men despised him as much as he despised them. In a customary fit of braggadocio and pointless machismo, Figueras was in point position despite the rule that the officer should always be near the middle of an Indian-file patrol. He was fatter than before because he had swallowed his disgrace with the aid of heavy drinking, and he carried heavy bags beneath his piggy eyes from indulging in his ever less fastidious tastes in cheap whores, whose conquest he no longer marked on his Jeep since the brigadier had fined him for defacing army property without reasonable excuse.

Figueras did not step on the first two mines or the third. Instead, he sprung the trap that Aurelio had laid so many months before. The fire-hardened spikes whipped up in an arc from beneath the leaves of the forest floor and thudded into his chest. Transfixed, his eyes bulging, he grasped the frame in his hands and tried to push it away against the barbs that wrenched in his heart and lungs. Blood gurgled and foamed in his mouth, and he remembered for no reason the beginnings of his days of glory, when he had tossed a grenade spinning into a group of peasants who had prevented him from having a little fun. His last thought, as his legs gave way and he swung forward on the spikes, was "Take the little whore to the schoolhouse and prepare her," and the last picture in his mind was of the two medals that once had hung gloriously on his full-dress uniform, the Silver Andean Condor Medal for Gallantry, and the Gold. He died happily, imagining that he still had them, and that his life had been as he had always yearned for it to be: honorable, heroic, and full of beauty.

The other men had stood horrified while Figueras swayed on the trap. Then they had run forward to succor him and had been shredded by the mines, while one of their number, the corporal, pitched headlong into one of the pits and was pierced cruelly by the poisoned stakes. He died crying and whimpering and thinking of his wife in Tolima, who had left him for another man.

The rest of the soldiers had already run by the time Aurelio and Carmen arrived. Aurelio surveyed the carnage bitterly and blamed himself out loud. "I was so used to having to avoid this section of the path that I had forgotten about it."

"They were soldiers," said Carmen, trying to comfort him. "Their trade was not life, but death. They have eaten the fruit of the tree they grew for others to eat."

"The war was over," said Aurelio sadly.

"People always die from wars that are over."

They left the bodies where they lay, and that night Aurelio's dogs began to feast, until the great black jaguar growled and scared them so that they ran off, whimpering. The velvet cat settled down and growled as it cut the flesh with its teeth, dimly recollecting this same taste somewhere in the past that was the perpetual present of its vision of its life. Then, satiated, it carried a limb off to its cubs, only one of which was black and which would one day also be awesome and majestic.

In the morning Aurelio left Carmen sleeping as he took his tin *tejilinas* and set off along his rubber trail, his own *trocha*. He had an *estrada* of thirty trees that yielded him enough rubber to earn some extra pesos and to use himself if he needed it. But often he wondered why he bothered with the rubber at all; it was not profitable and had not been so in living memory.

There had been a time when the jungle swarmed with *bandeirantes* on the make, who had enslaved and hunted the Indians and brought them the benefits of civilization: shirts to replace their *cuzmas*, and smallpox, influenza, and syphilis to help prevent overpopulation. At that time the rivers were full of little motorized canoes, onomatopoeically called *peke-pekes*, which would be taken on portage at *varaderos*, places where rivers passed each other, separated only by narrow strips of land. Even steamers were sometimes dismantled and transported to another river by the Indians, who were treated as no more than pack animals, and they in turn plied the rivers on balsa rafts that looked Egyptian. In those days one could row out to whores in canoes, who were known as *canoeiras*, and who were paddled up and down by their pimps, the *llevo-llevos*, because the jungle sets one's lust on fire worse than Spanish fly, and everyone, even nuns, experiences the incessant itch of perpetual arousal.

In those days there were still Inge-Inge Indians whose entire language consisted of *inge-inge*, repeated with grimaces, intonations, and gesticulations that expressed with rare precision the exact nuances of meanings inaccessible in more complex tongues. There were still Cascabeles dressed entirely in rattlesnake tails, and there were still people who knew how to shrink heads to four fifths of their original volume by leaving them for a week on poles. When a head was a little decayed, the Indians made a vertical gash in the cranium and removed all the bones. The inside was then carbonized with heated stones, and the head was smoked over a fire of palm roots until it was the right size. Even then one could tell if the head belonged to a white man or to an Indian because a white man's eyebrows were longer. Virtuoso shrinkers of the Cusicuari could reduce a whole human body, but the Putamayos and Yapuras, mere amateurs in the craft, preserved the hands, while the unadventurous Cashibos only collected teeth.

In those days people grew immensely rich on the "black gold," sent their clothes to Paris to be laundered, and brought back entire buildings made of steel to erect in the jungle, which are still there today and which are still too hot to inhabit.

But that was all a long time ago, before someone smuggled rubber tree seeds to Malaysia, and before it was discovered how to synthesize rubber unnaturally, and when that happened, the jungle became quiet once more, and the buildings became entwined with creepers and disappeared.

But Aurelio still gathered rubber, and still smoked it over the fire, to make big black balls of it, and still knew how to make it flow out of the tree to form sheets, and he still knew of one or two useful things you could do with it, such as caulking canoes. Today he was going to tap a little so that the jungle would not forget how it was done and so that the spirits of those long-departed *caucheros* and *shiringueros* would rest happily knowing that their lives had not been wasted or their skills forgotten. Aurelio was doing it because he hated the loss of a way of life, as his own way of life in the sierra had been lost when he was young and as that of the Navantes had been lost.

He had cut the first *bandiera* on the first tree and was watching the latex begin to ooze down into the little tin cup, when Parlanchina crept up playfully behind him and put her hands over his eyes, as she had done when she was a child.

"I knew you were there," said Aurelio. "I saw the cat come through the trees."

Parlanchina took her hands away and hung her arms around his neck. "Papacito," she said, coaxing him, "sit down with me and tell me how the world began."

"Gwubba, I have told you so many times that soon it will be impossible to remember it."

"Once more," she said. "Sit with me."

They sat with their backs against the tree trunk, and Parlanchina enclosed her knees in her arms, ready to listen, looking sideways at her father, waiting for him to begin. He pounded a little coca in his gourd and sucked the end of the pestle.

"I begin," he said. "There fell from heaven a copper egg, from which sprang the Indians. Then there fell a silver egg, from which sprang the nobility. Then, after a very long time a golden egg fell, and out of that egg sprang the Inca himself.'

"And who made the eggs? Tell me, Papacito."

"It was Viracocha, the sun."

"And who made Viracocha?"

"It was Pachacamac."

"And who made Pachacamac?"

"No one, Gwubba. Pachacamac is the one spirit of everything."

Parlanchina thought and rested her head on her knees, so that her hair cascaded down and flowed to the earth. "If Pachacamac is the one spirit, why are there so many gods and so many people and so many plants and so many animals?"

"Because every spirit is a morsel of the one spirit. This spirit may be Pachacamac's fingernail, and this spirit a hair of his head."

"Tell me again, Papacito, why there are different peoples."

"The reason is that when Pachacamac saw the peoples born, he made great bowl in which to wash them. The first people he washed came out cleanest, because the water was cleanest, and they were the white people. Then he washed the next people, but the water was a little dirty, so that when they came out, they were the Indian people. Then he washed the last people, and the water was no longer very clean, so that when they came out the people were the black people."

"Papacito," protested Parlanchina indignantly, "am I to be called dirtier than you?"

"No," said Aurelio. "No, Gwubba. It is only a story of the ignorant. The real reason is that Pachacamac avoids boredom by never making two things the same, so that nowhere in the world are there two things identical. Every people he made different from every other people, and every person he made different from every other person. That is the true reason."

"Now tell me, Papacito, how Manco Capac became the Inca."

"Enough of stories," replied Aurelio, and he sucked again on his pestle. "Tell me why you have not told me that you are to bear a child."

Parlanchina laughed. "Because I knew that you had already seen my belly swell and my breasts grow.'

"It will be a spirit child," said Aurelio. "It will be less of the living and more of the dead."

"It will be your grandchild, Papacito. It will suckle at my breast and grow, and if there is a body for it, it will live in a body. If not, it will live with us and be wild with us in the trees.

"Is Federico with you?" asked Aurelio. "I have not seen him."

Parlanchina smiled with resignation. "He is not your son, Papacito, and he likes to walk in the mountains and watch, as I watch the path."

"I must tell your mother about the grandchild," said Aurelio, standing up and putting the coca gourd into his *mochila*.

"Before you go," said Parlanchina, "here is something for you."

The ancient bitch that had not run with the other dogs was coming through the trees, carrying in her mouth, as a cat carries its kitten, one tiny puppy. Aurelio bent down, took the puppy in his arms, and ruffled its ears. The puppy yawned and tried to suckle at Aurelio's clothing.

"It is a dog that will never bark," said Parlanchina.

"It is not the same," said Aurelio sadly. "It has been bred by a spirit. I wanted to breed it myself."

"You bred it," replied Parlanchina. "It was one of your dogs that was the father."

She smiled indulgently at him as he stood looking at the puppy protectively, giving it his finger to suckle.

"Thank you for the stories," she called, glancing over her shoulder, smiling her mischievous smile, and walking away. The ocelot trotted beside her, and Aurelio watched her go, tall and graceful, chatting incessantly to her cat, leaning down to stroke its head. She was skipping with happiness, and her long hair was flowing like a black river of silk down to her waist. Whenever Aurelio saw her like this, radiant and enchanting, a choke would arise in his throat, and her beauty would make him weep with pity.

When he returned to the clearing, he saw that Carmen's hair had turned completely white, and he knew that at last the whole world had changed and was beginning again.

The years were to prove Aurelio right, even though, as in all periods of improvement and progress there were to be reversals and calamities.

Here the history of the War of Don Emmanuel's Nether Parts comes to a close, and in its place begins the history of the city of Cochadebajo de los Gatos; of the unsurpassable love of Remedios and the Conde Pompeyo Xavier de Estremadura; of Francesca and Capitan Papagato; of Parlanchina's child; of the children of Farides, of Annicca, Dionisio and the Coca Letters; all this being also the History of the New Albigensian Crusade and the terrible crimes of the New Inquisition.

11/21/21   11-19-99
45   2-21-21 — 11-3-19
3   46 (MD)   45

                3   3
         6/